The Shape-Shifter's Wife

The Shape-Shifter's Wife

Carolyn Radmanovich

www.bookstandpublishing.com

Published by
Bookstand Publishing
Morgan Hill, CA 95037
4468_8

Cover Design: Leslie Clark
                  Snowmoon Design

Editor: Sue Clark
                  SJ Clark Literary Specialties

ISBN 978-1-63498-426-3

Library of Congress Control Number: 2016956262

Printed in the United States of America

Review

"The Shape-Shifter's Wife is a story of love lost, love found, and the enduring nature of love. This story takes you on an adventure from present day San Francisco to the Russian River in the 1840s to the mystical mythology of the Native Americans and the brutal clash of cultures. A story to warm your heart and boil your blood."

— Reverend Evelyn Hall,
Leader of Women's Vision Quests
and Sacred Circles

Dedication

I dedicate this book to my husband, Richard, who saved me from drowning, which in turn propelled me to write *The Shape-Shifter's Wife.* He is my best friend, advisor, and guiding light.

I also want to thank God for giving me a few more decades to enjoy living. *The Shape-Shifter's Wife* is an expression of my gratitude for the opportunity to keep breathing, enjoying, and celebrating His/Her gift.

Acknowledgements

Bored from watching endless hours of televised football with my husband, Richard, I was driven to the computer to write this book.

My heartiest acknowledgement goes to Sue Clark, who edited my work, and helped enhance my writing skills through her fiction writing classes. Without her expertise, I could never have completed the necessary revisions and additions. It seems the power of thought and intention led me to find Sue through serendipitous events at a time when I had made the decision to quit my business and dedicate my time to writing.

I want to thank Tony Maniscalco, Evelyn Greiner, and Annette Tull, who took the time to read my first draft and encouraged me to complete the book.

Many thanks to the library staff at the Lane Memorial Library at the Stanford University School of Medicine for their help in my historical medical research, and Sharron Binford for helping me with useful information on childbirth.

Richard was my greatest supporter with his helpful insights for this novel.

Part One

San Francisco — 1989 and 1995

"If you realize that all things change, there is nothing you will try to hold on to. If you are not afraid of dying, there is nothing you cannot achieve."

— Lao Tsu

Chapter One

1989 — The Blackbird's Warning

On Tuesday, October 17, 1989, the Oakland A's and the San Francisco Giants were slated to play the World Series. At 5:00 p.m. I turned my television to the baseball game and then headed for the kitchen to get a beer out of the refrigerator.

During that phase of my life, I lived in a hundred-year old townhouse with my husband and sister. Our place was in the Marina District and I was thrilled that we had a view of the San Francisco Bay from the second floor.

I could hear Larry Gatlin sing the Star-Spangled Banner as I popped the lid off an Anchor Steam beer and took a sip. At that moment, I heard loud banging noises coming from the living room. In my shock, I dropped my beer which splashed my pants and penny loafers.

I ran out of the kitchen to see what was making the commotion and was startled to see a flock of blackbirds flying into the plate glass window. When I entered the living room the blackbirds flew away, and the noise of their battering was replaced by an eerie silence. Even Larry Gatlin's voice no longer filled the room. The television screen had gone black.

I began to wonder if the bird incident could be an omen of something ominous about to happen. A second later, I heard what sounded like an explosion beneath my feet. A booming, deep rumble followed that reminded me of the sound of lions protesting at the San Francisco Zoo just before feeding time. The sudden jolts that followed were so strong, it felt like an enraged giant had picked up our townhouse and was shaking it like a martini.

I staggered from the middle of the living room toward the kitchen doorway. It reminded me of taking a turbulent walk on the shuddering, undulating bridge of the Clown Carnival ride at the Boardwalk in Santa Cruz when I was a kid.

Some anthropology books flew off the bookcase and I stumbled over them. When I reached the doorway to the kitchen my heart pounded as I pushed myself toward the door frame and then held on. I was shoved back and forth.

I could hear dishes break in the kitchen, and the refrigerator crash to the floor. I became aware of people screaming on the street outside. My stomach knotted as I realized we were having an earthquake, a monster of a quake, like an ogre from hell, or a stampeding buffalo herd.

Earlier, Heather had come home from work complaining of a headache, and had gone upstairs to lie down. I called to her.

I heard her answer back. "Alexis, find a safe spot in a doorway and stay there."

The rolling and violent shaking seemed to last an eternity and then stopped. The silence was strange, as if the earth had paused to take a breath.

Books and broken glass were strewn everywhere as I tried to make my way up the stairs to Heather's bedroom. When I reached the third step, I realized the rest of the old wooden stairway had crumbled. I wouldn't be able to get to my sister. I yelled up the stairs. "Stay where you are, Heather. I'm going for help."

Once I got outside, I could see flames everywhere, as if the whole city was on fire. Some of the nearby houses and apartment buildings had collapsed. I thought about the land under my Marina neighborhood and remembered that it had been developed on landfill from the San Francisco Bay. No wonder some of the buildings had sunk. The unstable land hadn't been able to withstand a major quake.

I looked back at our townhouse that was now on fire. I yelled to no one in particular, "My sister's trapped. Help me!"

People were running everywhere, but nobody stopped. A fire truck came down the street, and I ran in front of it waving my arms. I yelled, "Help me! Help me!"

A fireman shouted, "Lady, get out of the way."

I stood in front of the fire truck with my hands on my hips and said, "But, my sister's trapped on the second floor of our burning townhouse."

The driver pulled the fire truck to the curb and four firemen jumped out. As they walked toward me, an aftershock hit and rattled the earth again. This one was strong, but nothing like the earthquake, itself.

A young, mustached fireman, said, "It's okay lady. We're on it."

He and his buddy ran into the building. I tried to follow them, but another of the firemen jumped in front of me and held me back.

"You'll only get hurt. We know what we're doing. Stay here or we'll have to rescue you, too."

With reluctance, I waited on the sidewalk that seemed to be crumbling under our feet. While I stood there I saw a woman running toward me, her arms waving in the air as she screamed. She bumped into me and almost pushed me to the ground. I yelled after her. "Calm down lady or you might hurt yourself."

Mayhem was everywhere. A dog howled when the roof of the building across the street collapsed. A man sprinted by me, hollering, "I can't find my wife." Smoke filled the air and burned my lungs. I heard the sound of sirens from ambulances and fire trucks headed for the Marina.

After a few minutes, the mustached fireman poked his head out of the upstairs window and called to me. "She's okay. Don't worry. We'll get her out."

The fireman with the hose aimed the nozzle at the roof of our building. No water came out.

"Damn old wooden water pipes," he said. "I should have known the earthquake would splinter them."

I watched as another fireman moved a ladder to the window where my sister was trapped. When the fire reached the side of the building, I looked up to see one of the firemen coaxing my sister out of the window to the waiting ladder. She appeared dazed. As she and the two firemen reached the ground, the entire building blew up in flames. Everything we owned was gone.

I ran over and hugged Heather. "I'm so glad you made it out alive. Are you okay?"

"I think so," she said, as she started to shake.

The four firemen returned to their places on the truck, and without saying a word, they drove up the street to another burning building.

I yelled after them, "Thanks so much for saving my sister."

As Heather and I embraced, we cried on each other's shoulders. I held her until her shaking subsided.

My emotions were mixed between grief over losing the townhouse, and feelings of gratitude that we were both alive. I grabbed her hand, and said, "Let's get out of here. We'll walk toward the beach and try to find an area that's safer."

Ambulances and fire trucks were still trying to make their way through the jammed streets. I could see people running into buildings trying to save everything from personal items, to relatives and pets. Some people stood on the sidewalks and cried, holding each other.

All of a sudden, I stopped walking and said, "Oh, my God, Heather. Do you think Lawrence is okay? He was going to leave work in Oakland a little early today and drive home to watch the World Series on television with us."

"Don't worry, Alexis. I'm sure he's okay." Heather took my hand and squeezed it.

When we could see the ocean, we turned right and walked toward North Beach. After striding a couple of blocks, Heather said, "Isn't that our friend, Jackie?"

Holding onto her black, long-haired Chihuaua, Jackie stood leaning against a lamppost. When she saw us, she ran over and gave us hugs.

"Our place is in flames," I said. "Can I use your phone to call my husband's office? I'm worried about him, and I thought they might know what time he left for home."

"Oh, Alexis," Jackie said. "I'm so sorry. You're welcome to use the phone and stay over if you want." She led us up the stairs leading to her dark apartment. We went inside and stepped over broken pottery, newspapers, pillows, overturned lamps, and books.

"The power's out. Let's see if the phones are working," Jackie said as she lifted up the receiver. She hung up and said, "It's dead."

Jackie tossed a throw and pillows off the couch and set her dog down. She then opened the curtains to let in the remaining light of the fading day.

She said, "Make yourselves at home. You're spending the night here. No excuses."

Jackie opened her unlit refrigerator and pulled out some apples and a block of cheddar cheese. "We'll have a makeshift dinner. Since the stove doesn't work, we'll make do with appetizers." She reached for a box of crackers on the counter.

I carried three plates from the kitchen and set them on the coffee table. That's when I noticed Jackie's portable television had fallen over. I set it upright on the stand. When I plugged it in and tried to turn it on, the screen stayed black.

"I should have known," I mumbled.

Heather brought a bowl of fruit and set it on the table along with the napkins. I turned to her and said, "Heather, I didn't tell you that just before the earthquake hit, a flock of blackbirds flew into our living room window. If I hadn't rushed out of the kitchen to see what was causing the noise, I may have been hurt when the refrigerator fell on the floor in front of me. Isn't that weird?"

"Wow, Alexis. That's eerie. Maybe it was a warning or an omen. I'm so glad you weren't injured."

Jackie came into the room with three cans of Anchor Steam, and a bag under her arm. "And, here's dessert, ladies," Jackie said as she opened a bag of Oreo cookies.

I poured my beer, took a long swallow, and put several slices of cheddar cheese on some rye crackers.

Heather said to Jackie, "How did you and my sister meet? Aren't you both professors at the University of San Francisco?"

"Well, yes. We met in the cafeteria there. I'm a psychology teacher, with an emphasis on the neo-transformative process."

"What's transformative whatever? I've never heard of it," Heather said.

"Why, I study reasons humans make profound changes in their lives. Take, for example, this earthquake. Some people will have lost loved ones, or perhaps their homes or property. In a tragedy, people will react in different ways. Some become depressed for an extended period of time. Others will rise above it and make their lives better. Incidents like this can be a spring board to transformation. It forces people to become more aware that life is precarious and unpredictable."

Heather responded, "I'd like to think there's a silver lining to this awful event. I can see where loss begets a revolution in thinking. It's like being pushed off a tall bridge and finding yourself bouncing back up because you're attached to a bungie cord."

"Yes," Jackie said. "That's a good analogy. What I've found in surveying my students is that most of them admit they push their imminent mortality out of their minds and spend most of their lives in denial. If they fall into this mindset, it can promote self-indulgence, laziness, and status quo."

"Ah," Heather said. "I love the idea of transformation of the spirit. It's like the cocoon to a butterfly, or a nymph to a dragonfly, or a tadpole to a frog."

"Say," Alexis said, "since I'm the anthropology professor in the group, let's not forget Native Americans' abilities to shape-shift into different animals and birds. That's always been a fascination of mine."

"Okay, okay," Heather said. "You're beginning to sound like you're coming from left field. Maybe you hit your head running for shelter from the earthquake. Let's talk about something more here and now, like who gets the couch and who gets the floor tonight?"

When we were finished with our make-shift meal, Jackie jumped up from the overstuffed chair, and said, "I'll go look for a flashlight and candles before it gets totally dark. While I'm at it, I'll see if I can find my portable radio."

When Jackie returned, she set up a variety of blue and gold candles throughout the living room.

"Here're some matches," Jackie said, handing me a box of wooden ones. "Why don't you and Heather get busy and light the candles while I go search for the radio?"

Jackie went into her bedroom and a minute later returned with a big smile on her face. She waved a portable radio in her right hand.

By candlelight, we heard the announcer on KGO explain that the earthquake had been at least a six to seven magnitude and warned we would probably have many aftershocks. He said there appeared to be major fatalities at the Oakland end of the Bay Bridge where the Cypress Street Viaduct had collapsed onto Interstate 880. The upper double-deck portion of the freeway crushed all the cars on the deck below.

A bolt of terror tore through my chest and I screamed, "Lawrence."

"Alexis, I'm sure Lawrence is okay. He probably left Oakland way before the earthquake."

No matter what Heather said, I couldn't be consoled. I knew in my gut that Lawrence had been killed on the bridge. No one had to tell me. I knew it as sure as I knew my life would never be the same again.

Chapter Two
September 5, 1995 — Fishing Boots

A man, waving a handwritten sign that read, "Heather Hayes," was standing with a group of van drivers near the baggage terminal at the San Francisco International Airport. He stood out from the others because of his unusual dress. He sported an unbuttoned, black threadbare suit coat, under which he wore a black T-shirt emblazoned with the words, "Poncho Villa Wore Boots."

Heather looked down at the feet of the 280-pound Hispanic, and noted he wore green snakeskin cowboy boots. Despite his unusual appearance, Heather felt relieved to find her ride so soon. She marched over to the man, and said, "I'm Heather Hayes."

"Pepe Ramirez, at your service," he said and shook Heather's hand. He added, "*Mi coche es su coche*," as he pushed her luggage caddy out the terminal door.

As Heather hurried to keep up with Pepe, he said, "Ah, *Señorita* Hayes. I'm glad I've only got the two of you *gringas*. From what I see of your baggage, I doubt if this van could hold any more."

"Why, I only have two bags. Oh, you mean my surfboard. Yes, it might take up a bit of room."

When Pepe and Heather arrived at the van, she could see a gray-haired lady sitting in the back seat. As Heather watched Pepe load the suitcases and surfboard, she contemplated on how great it would be to see her sister and share the adventures they'd had during the past year.

Heather sat next to the older woman, who said, "Aren't you Heather Hayes, Alexis' sister?"

"Well, yes. I am. I'm sorry, do I know you?"

"Why, I remember when you and your family lived down the street from me years ago in San Francisco."

"Oh, Mrs. McNeil. It's so good to see you again. Amazing bumping into each other like this."

"Well, dear, I couldn't help but notice you have a surfboard."

"Yes, that's because I've been on a year's leave exploring Ecuador and its great surf. How's your family doing?"

Mrs. McNeil frowned and tucked a stray piece of gray hair under her small black hat. "Of course you didn't know. My husband died a year ago. Then a couple of months later my son, William, got a good job in Seattle and moved away. I just came from visiting with him. Beautiful city. How are your parents, dearie, and your sister?"

"My parents died about six years ago, Mrs. McNeil. Alexis lives with me when she isn't on vacation."

Mrs. McNeil grabbed Heather's hand and squeezed it. "Oh, my. Your folks were such nice people. I'm so sorry they're gone. Well, tell me. Did Alexis go surfing with you?"

"No, Mrs. McNeil, she didn't." Heather ran her fingers through her long, curly red hair, and tucked it behind her ears. "Alexis and I'd dared each other to take a year off from work. I went surfing in Ecuador and she went canoeing on the Russian River, you know, in Northern California. She also wanted to do research at some Native American anthropological sites around Sonoma and Healdsburg. She was hoping to interview some Native American survivors, and then start working on her new book regarding any new discoveries she made."

Mrs. McNeil looked surprised and then said, "I must say, dearie, that sounds awfully exciting, you surfing and Alexis river canoeing. My goodness, what on earth do the two of you do that you can take so much time off?"

"Well," Heather said, "I'm a nurse, so it's always easy for me to find work. Alexis is an anthropology professor at the University of San Francisco, and she was able to take a sabbatical."

"Don't you girls have hubbies?"

"I never married, Mrs. McNeil. However, Alexis was married to Lawrence for three years but he died in the eighty-nine earthquake. Do you remember when that overpass collapsed on the cars?"

Mrs. McNeil frowned and shook her head.

Heather got quiet for a while. She felt uncomfortable thinking about Lawrence's death. She let out a sigh and then extended her stiff legs.

When Lawrence died, a spark seemed to have gone out of Alexis. Being worried about her sister, Heather suggested she take a year's vacation to get away and relax. She'd told her, since life's so short, let's follow our passions. Let's find an adventure. To Heather's relief, Alexis agreed.

Mrs. McNeil pulled Heather out of her reverie when she said, "You were sure right to have your adventures. While I was in Washington, my son and his family took me camping and fly fishing. I haven't done that for years. It seems to have put me in a new frame of mind. I'm thinking of moving to Seattle to be near my son and his family."

Mrs. McNeil told Heather she'd decided to get back into fly fishing. It was something she and her husband used to do. She said she even enjoyed making the flies.

Her voice became animated as she said, "My husband and I gave it all up when we moved to the City. There's nothing to hold me back now, so why not?"

Heather was taken by surprise that this older woman showed such spunk and adventurous spirit. She took a closer look at Mrs. McNeil and noticed she had on a dated black blazer, and a small black hat, which wasn't unusual for a woman of her age. What amazed Heather was that Mrs. McNeil wore stretch jeans and fishing boots.

"Yes," Heather said. "You're so right. We seem to be thinking along the same lines. What's life if we don't have something that thrills us and makes us want to get out of bed in the morning?"

Mrs. McNeil's face lit up in a broad grin. "You're so right, my dear. By the way, I saw you looking at my boots. I bought these in Seattle for fishing, and it's easier to wear them than pack them."

"Very practical," Heather said. Seeing the boots reminded her of Dr. Randall Olson, an orthopedic surgeon she used to work with at UCSF Medical Center. He was slender, curly haired, and had warm brown eyes that sparked love in her. He always wore fishing boots into the operating room to do arthroscopic surgeries, where water flowed through the scope during an operation, spraying and dripping onto the floor.

Heather worked alongside Randall during his surgeries. They worked well together, like a close team. She fell in love with him the first time she assisted him in surgery, despite the fact that she knew he was married. She had been so enamored, she refused dates with other men. The most she and Randall had ever done was hold hands over a glass of wine. She admired him for this, too. He was loyal.

As long as she worked with Randall, she couldn't stop loving him. That's why she had to break away for a year and go to Ecuador to surf — the only way she could think of letting him fade from her heart. Before she left on her trip, she had given her notice, and knew she'd land a job at another hospital when she returned. Her heart still twinged when she thought of him, but now she was ready to move on.

Pepe brought Heather out of her reverie when he spoke over his shoulder to them in the back of the van. "Speaking of boots," he said. "I have the boots I'm wearing to remind me every day that my brother and I are working to get a dude ranch up and running. A few months ago, we inherited land in Monterey from our grandparents. In about a year, we'll have enough money to build a house and barn. Here are my cards, if you ladies are interested."

Heather took the cards and handed one to Mrs. McNeil, and said, "Why, I'll be sure to take you up on that offer. We were both just saying, it's great to have a real purpose that gets you out of bed every morning."

Heather settled back in her seat and looked at her leather sandals she'd worn on the beaches of Ecuador. Shoes, cowboy boots, fishing boots — they represent the paths people trod, both sacred and profane. They show the choices we've made and the trails we've walked. The type of shoes we wear — moccasins, flats, loafers, pumps, hiking boots, sandals, tennis shoes are a giveaway as to our history, personality, and purpose.

Heather wondered what new paths she was now going to tread since she was free to walk any path she wanted. She was ready to blaze new trails into her future.

Mrs. McNeil interrupted Heather's thoughts and said, "Say, dearie, let's get together and talk about our trips sometime. When I move, I'll send you my new address. Oh, there's my stop. Toodle."

"Good bye, Mrs. McNeil. I'll give you a call."

When the van reached Nob Hill, Heather felt the same thrill she had experienced at the view of San Francisco Bay from their flat where she and her sister had moved to after the 1989 earthquake. Heather motioned to Pepe, and he stopped the van in front, on the corner of Sacramento and Taylor. Pepe helped her take her luggage and surfboard to the elevator. "Good luck with your dude ranch, Pepe," she said as she handed him a tip.

Heather hoped Alexis would have beaten her home, and they could begin to share stories of their trips after dinner. The only phone calls she had received from Alexis were at the beginning of the trip when Alexis would call from her cell phone assuring Heather she was having a great adventure canoeing and having some time alone. Alexis warned Heather that some of the remote places she was going to explore wouldn't get cell service, and not to worry. Heather had responded that much of the wild coastline of Ecuador had no cell service either. Alexis had laughed and said, "We'll be free and untethered."

Heather remembered she had told Alexis to be careful and be sure to return by the beginning of September of the following year or she would worry. Alexis had said, "If I decide I'm having too much fun and not returning, I promise I'll write you a note." Heather remembered the two of them chuckling at this comment.

Heather opened the door to a quiet, stuffy flat. She put her keys on the table and went into her study where she found a handwritten note taped to the computer screen. "My darling sister, Heather. Please turn on the computer and read my letter to you."

Heather, her curiosity peaked, put her purse on the desk, sat down and typed in her password. The screen flashed on with the date, September 1, 1995.

Part Two

Letter from Alexis

"Do not go where the path may lead, go instead where there is no path and leave a trail."

— Ralph Waldo Emerson

Chapter Three
The Letter

Dear Heather:

You were right in telling me to find passion and adventure in my life. I know I've been shutting myself away from social contact because I never really recovered from Lawrence's and our parents' deaths.

I'm writing this letter to explain why I'm not here, nor will I ever be back. At the same time, I have never left and will always be with you.

My dear sister, I will miss you, but I feel someday you may find me if you really want to.

I'll try to explain. As you'll remember, after Lawrence died, I needed a strong tonic for my heart to get out of my depression and despair, so I joined a mountaineering group and we went on a trip to Mt. Shasta. After our hiking party reached base camp, we put up our tents and ate dinner. We were planning on finishing our climb in the early morning hours. The forecast was for more snow, and I was anticipating a cold night. I wanted to warm myself before climbing into my sleeping bag, so I decided to take an invigorating walk.

The sky, dark as expresso coffee, swirled with a touch of latte clouds while I stood watching the ever changing dome. I climbed onto a bluff that had lava rock outcroppings of crimson, orange, and ebony. A faint rainbow blossomed as I watched the moon filter light through the moisture laden clouds.

While finding a comfortable spot, I leaned against the red jaggedy stones in the crystal world of Mt. Shasta. I sat and meditated on all the beauty — so hushed and serene. I was transported into a world I had never known. Thoughts of daily life faded, and I became caught up in that amazing space, as if my mind had become the interior of a vast cave — quiet and tranquil, yet open and free.

I wondered when I would find love again — not only the quiet friendship of love, but the deep passion where I would be willing to commit everything.

My mind quieted as I closed my eyes and I began to make out the vision of a man I felt I was destined to meet, a man muscular and sinewy, wild yet gentle, a man with depth.

As you know, I'd been lonely for such a long time. That yearning had turned into a quiet, hollow aching, which I had hidden from you and everyone. I longed to have a sense of belonging to someone, to feel a thirst for life again.

All of a sudden, I experienced a jolt of energy as if the powerful crystals of the mountain reflected the strength of my desires, magnifying my intentions with force behind them. I stood on the snowy cliff, threw my arms in the air and danced in circles, shouting and yelling for joy. I felt a promise in the air — that I would find meaning in my life again.

Before I left on this vacation to the wine country, a feeling had been building in me. Somehow I knew my life was about to change.

Oh my, Alexis. What have you been up to and why aren't you here? This is so strange finding a typed letter waiting for me instead of my sister.

Chapter Four

Canoeing into the Unknown, September 7, 1994

I rented a cottage alongside the Russian River. After my adventure on Mt. Shasta, I awoke each day with a quiet expectation. Now that I was on vacation in Northern California, I could relax and reflect.

The owner of Randolph's Canoe Company launched my canoe into the river. I took off and explored the river's meandering and straightening ways, with the current always moving on its long course toward the ocean. Thick oaks, tall pines and maples grew near the shore, and lush cottonwoods dipped their roots into the water.

The river flowed through this rich land, giving life to the green hills and valleys filled with rows and rows of grape vines. The swollen green and purple grapes, almost ready for picking and harvesting, would be made into some of the best vino in the world.

I had time to think about my life. Living in the bustling city of San Francisco was great, but I had grown tired of the crowds and noise. I always considered moving to the country, but I could never figure out how to make the break since the death of Lawrence. He left a large void to fill.

I figured a vacation away from the rush of the city and from my stressful job would be ideal at this time in my life. I really needed a break like you had insisted, or perhaps I came in search of my dreams.

I leaned back in my rented canoe. While drifting, I let my arm hang down, feeling the coolness of the deep river of life.

I felt so happy that you had followed up on your promise, Alexis. I knew it would do you so much good.

A Great Blue Heron sat on a tree branch downstream from my canoe. He ruffled his lofty feathers with his beak. As I approached, the large graceful heron flew off, as if warning me of protruding rocks in the river. I realized he was my scout or sentinel.

The heron returned and landed on a cottonwood branch on the other side of the river. He stared at me as if to make sure I was paying attention to his warning.

After a couple of hours of paddling, I decided to land on a gravel bar and have lunch. As I glanced toward the other side of the river, I saw never-ending rows of grapevines, some of which grew up a sloping hill where an ancient castle or perhaps a wealthy vintner's home loomed dark and foreboding on the top. The turrets around the roof sat like a dark crown.

As I stared at the mysterious building, I was filled with a strange curiosity. I wanted to go there and see it for myself. I had a feeling that I'd been there before, maybe in a past life. As I ate my peanut butter and blueberry jelly sandwich, I wondered who lived in that grand home. I even considered walking to the dark house, but I could see a deep ravine which created a barrier.

After I finished eating, I sat and gazed at the river, letting my mind wander. I heard a strange high-pitched sound, like nothing I'd heard before. The vibration was answered by another sing-songy, high-pitched sound. I looked in the direction from where the melody came, and thought I saw long hair floating on the surface of the river. Before I could blink, the brown hair disappeared. I wondered if my eyes and ears were playing tricks on me. Fear pumped through my body.

To comfort myself, I reached for my backpack and pulled out my special Indian rattle with deer hooves that hung from leather straps, which I'd brought along for good luck. I shivered, looking at the rattle. From the moment I saw it, years ago, I knew the rattle held an eerie power.

I recalled a ceremony the Indian elders taught me when I interviewed them for my anthropological work. I began by shaking the rattle in the four directions, a way of honoring the earth. The ritual was calming for me. It made me feel balanced and in tune with nature and the cycles of life.

I said out loud, "Thank you, God, for my life and the beauty of the world. Bring me health and help on my journey."

Next, I positioned my body facing east. After studying the map, I knew the Russian River was positioned in a more or less east/west direction. That made me feel confident of my directions, even without a compass.

When I closed my eyes I began to rattle and I visualized the place where Grandfather Sun begins his journey each day — the place of inspiration, illumination, and new beginnings.

With my eyes now open, I turned on the gravel beach and I rattled to the south — to energy, innocence, and trust. I realized taking a sabbatical from my job to take this trip was already giving me a feeling of aliveness I hadn't felt for years.

I turned again and rattled to the west — the element of water, the direction of the setting sun, and the place of sacred dreamtime. I had already dreamt of a life with a man I could love.

I turned for the last time, rattling toward the north — to wisdom, to the dwelling place of the ancient ones, and to death and rebirth. I began to feel a resiliency coming out of my long struggle with the death of my loved ones, to a possibility of being able to go on with the next phase of my life.

When I completed the ceremony, I sat on the gravel beach, eyes closed, holding the rattle to my chest. I felt a profound gratefulness for being in that moment, surrounded by all the beauty of the river and the abundant trees. Then I had a vivid memory of how my precious rattle had come to me.

Chapter Five

The Power of the Rattle

Remember when I was an anthropology intern, Heather? I was always full of stories about the amazing things my instructor introduced in class. He taught us how to interpret facts and create theories about ancient lives from discovered objects, like tools, musical instruments, and art work.

Well, one day, while I was working at a small museum in the Northern California wine country, two farmers came in. The older man introduced himself as John Duggan and his middle-aged friend as Stu.

Mr. Duggan was about six-feet and a little stooped. He had the bright, cheery countenance of a sixteen-year old boy, his face flushed with excitement.

Mr. Duggan smiled at me and said, "I was wondering if the museum might like some of these things I dug up on my farm, which I have on this here list. I'm ninety-seven years old, and don't know if I've got many years left, so I'd like to give these to the community. I brought some mortars and pestles and Indian arrowheads which I found with my tractor, while working my fields."

"I'm just the intern here," I said. "Let's have Marie, who's the curator's assistant, take a look at your list."

The dark haired, young woman who sat with me at the front desk, peered up at the two men, and said, "Let me take a look."

After Marie read the list, she said, "These items are marvelous. Wait here, and I'll ask the museum curator if she can use any of them in her Indian exhibit."

While we waited for Marie to return, I showed Mr. Duggan and his friend Stu the Pomo and Wappo Indian exhibit. I noticed that only one mortar and pestle sat in the museum's display with nothing written in explanation.

Mr. Duggan showed me three different sized mortars and pestles which he took from his cardboard box. "I think they used this here little-bitty one for cracking open and pounding seeds. Them Indians seemed to need a lot of different sizes. I guess it sorta depended on what they were grindin' at the time. Why, I've also got quite a collection of arrowheads, and some flint for startin' fires and making other arrowhead points. I heard say the Wappo used to run up north to the Lake Country and barter for their fire starter stones. The Indians were in great shape in those days, and they didn't need no horses for great distances, neither."

Marie joined us again. "The curator says we can't take your stuff on loan, but if you want to give it to us, we'll take it if you sign a release. It's hard to promise you'd ever get any of the items back, since it's hard to keep track of so many things."

Mr. Duggan replied, "I'll have to think about it."

Marie said, "It's up to you." Then she turned, went to her desk and started filing papers.

Mr. Duggan asked Stu to go to his pickup truck and get the rest of the treasures. While Stu was gone, Mr. Duggan said to me, "I got one thing I wanna give you for being so kind to me, and listenin' to an old man's yarns. Of all the things I found, this one is the best of all."

I was very hesitant to take anything from him, but excited to see what he'd found.

"I used to plow these little hills on my land, which ended up being Indian burial mounds. The natives used to bury their dead along with their belongings, including baskets and all sorts of ceremonial stuff."

While I rummaged through the items in his box, Stu returned, carrying two grocery boxes. He placed the boxes on the information desk, then sat down in the nearest chair and fanned himself.

Mr. Duggan took my hand and led me to the boxes. He reached inside one of them and pulled out an Indian rattle that had deer hooves hanging down the sides, and a piece of reddish coyote skin on the handle. To look at it gave me the shivers. I could tell the rattle had some special power.

"Here's what I was tellin' you about. I want you to take it 'fore the curator comes in. She didn't even bother looking at my pictures. I can tell you're interested in this stuff, so you should have it."

I looked at Mr. Duggan and said, "I can't. You see the staff aren't allowed to take any of the exhibits."

Mr. Duggan said, "This ain't an exhibit. . .yet. I never planned to give the stuff in these here boxes to the museum. You have to at least take the rattle."

I longed to accept the rattle. I could picture it over my fireplace with my Kachina dolls on each side. I decided to take a chance and said, "I'll take the rattle, but don't say a word to the curator or I'll be in big trouble. By the way, do you know what the rattle was used for?"

Mr. Duggan held it up and swung it back and forth. The rattle made a loud eerie noise. "I heard it was used for a kind of powerful ceremony. You'll figure it out. They say those things can talk to you."

Chapter Six
Death and Rebirth

The pleasant memory of acquiring the enigmatic rattle was interrupted by the screeching of some stellar jays. A hawk had landed in her nesting oak that grew near the river's edge. I watched as the hawk flew off and realized it was time for me to leave, too.

I shoved off from the gravel bar and looked around for the heron who had served as my guide. He seemed to have given up on me.

The farther I paddled, the quieter the river became. All of a sudden the river widened, and with the change came the rush of fast moving water. I realized my limited canoeing abilities might not be enough for deep channels. I hadn't expected this quiet river to turn into a frothing, tumultuous sea of danger.

My canoe headed right for the confluence of two merging channels, which created a great surge of water. Out of nowhere I saw a massive dead tree stuck above the waterline. I tried to avoid the bare arms of the tree by paddling with all my might, but I found myself pulled closer by a strong suction. The water funneled downward and I could see a gushing swirl.

My canoe collided with the dead wood, and in an instant turned over. I held my breath and expected to bob to the surface. Instead, when I dared to open my eyes, the canoe was wedged upside down over my head, held under by a branch of the dead tree.

I could hear the deafening sound of the water rushing by the submerged tree. I saw millions of white bubbles churning in the water around the canoe above me. I raised my arms and attempted to move the canoe off my head, but it wouldn't budge.

I realized I had no air left in my lungs. In a matter of moments I would enter the darkness of death. Fear filled my arteries and grabbed at my chest.

Knowing death was imminent, I prayed a prayer of thanksgiving to God for my good, but short life, and asked that my life be saved. I felt the dread of drowning mixed with the unexpected excitement of facing the adventure of an afterlife.

My chest burned. My body screamed for air. I felt anxiety, as well as a wonderful expectancy that my spirit would become free from my body and I would go to meet God and the angels. I could no longer hold back and my lungs expanded to take in the rush of water. Instead, my body followed its ancient instinct from the sensation of cold water, and my throat closed off in a spasm. Blackness and silence engulfed me.

I dreamed of water nymphs pulling on my arms. One of them grabbed me by the hair and pulled me to her. She kissed me on the lips, blowing something like sweet air into my mouth. I no longer felt the urgency to breath.

The long legged, naked nymphs grabbed my body, and pulled me away from the dead tree, away from the overturned canoe. Their long hair floated sideways, pulled by the current as they swam around my freed body.

Soon I was conscious of a sound, like a melody of the siren, or the song of nymphs and their river. The constant noise of the moving water mesmerized me. Air bubbles went by my eyes and tickled my nose.

The nymphs' hair wrapped around my head and face as the river's force pushed and pulled the water's current. My body felt numb from the coldness of my watery tomb.

One of the water nymphs pushed a crystal into my forehead which felt hot as it pierced my skin. The other nymphs swam in a circle around me as they held onto each other's long hair. Their naked breasts were buoyant in the water and their nipples hard and pink. Their hands reached out to me as they began to rock me back and forth.

My unconscious body bobbed up to the surface, my feet dragging behind. Then I felt gravel beneath my feet. I straightened my legs and opened my eyes as a stranger's two strong arms steadied me in the shoulder-deep water. When I attempted to breath, I gagged and wasn't able to take air into my lungs because my vocal cords were still in spasm.

My savior was a tall, good looking man with a concerned look on his face. He coached me. "Take it slow and easy. Relax. Think of some nice warm tea going down your throat and a cozy fire in front of you. Now, open your throat and let the air in."

He reached over and while massaging my shoulders and smoothing my hair, he whispered, "Angelica, Angelica, you've come to me. My darling. *Ma petit, je t'adore.*"

As I looked up at him in wonder, I tried again, attempting to get air into my closed throat. Three more tries and my throat opened and a wonderful rush of air filled my lungs. I was so thrilled with being able to breathe, I didn't mind being called a new name.

I threw my arms into the air and started yelling, "I'm alive. I'm alive." I'd never felt as happy or relieved in my entire life.

I grabbed that strange, handsome man and hugged him while the two of us stood together in the deep rushing water. I could feel the strength in his enthusiastic hug as I yelled, "Thank you. Thank you."

"I am so happy you're alive, *ma chérie*. Let us get you out of the river." My rescuer guided my hands to the sandy wall on the side of the river. "Hold on to this cliff side while I try to find a way up," he said.

While standing in the turbulent water, I became aware that my halter had been torn away by the river, and all I had on were my shorts. My long, wet hair hung down into my eyes.

As the man started climbing the hillside, I could see he was bare chested and only wore leather pants. A red hawk feather hung from his dark brown ponytail.

He climbed about four feet up the sandy hillside when it gave way. He tumbled back into the river. A quiet low grumble came from his throat.

I was in shock from my brush with death, and clutched onto the side of the cliff. With the water up to my shoulders, the river whirled and eddied as it went by. I became hypnotized by the motion, like a magnet pulling me back into the maelstrom.

I came out of my trance when I heard the man call to me, "Hang on, my angel."

Again, he climbed hand-over-hand. He attempted to get one of his knees wedged onto the loose hillside. When he started to place his other foot, the sandy soil wouldn't hold him and he fell again. I became frightened, thinking I would never get out of the water.

He called out, "Angelica. Don't worry. I'll find a way up."

Feeling heartened by the confidence I heard in his voice, I became distracted, looking at the man's bare, tanned, muscular back. His broad shoulders tapered down to a long slender waist. His biceps bulged as his muscles strained until he found a rock embedded in the cliff and was able to pull himself up.

As he extended his hand to me, I felt his firm grip. At the top of the cliff he lifted me with ease and set me on some lush grass.

With my arms crossed over my bare chest, I laid on my side feeling exhausted, yet exhilarated at being alive.

I couldn't help but wonder, who is this man who'd just saved me?

Chapter Seven

Riding Bareback with Reynard

"*M**a chérie*, you are more beautiful than I had imagined."
The man laid down beside me and began to stroke my hair as he gazed at me.

"I was fishing from the shore when I saw one end of your canoe sticking out of the dead tree. There's a nasty current at this spot."

I wrinkled my forehead as I remembered the wild river.

He said, "I figured someone must be stuck under the overturned canoe. I jumped in the water and worked the canoe back and forth for a while before I could get it free. When I yanked it out, you bobbed up."

Feeling somewhat rejuvenated, I said, "I'm so grateful you saved me. What's your name?"

The man smiled as he reached his hand toward me. He said, "The villagers around here call me Gray Fox, although my given name is Reynard Francoise Rutherford."

I clasped his hand and shook it. He then kissed me on both cheeks. I could feel my face redden as I realized he was very charming as well as handsome in a rugged sort of way.

He frowned and said, "Your forehead is bleeding. It looks like you got a nasty gash."

He took a handkerchief from around his neck and dabbed my forehead. He looked at me with eyes like the vast sky — deep and unfathomable. I became magnetized by his gaze.

"Lie back for a moment while I fetch my horse and we can ride to the rancho."

As I laid down, I wondered if I was really dead and maybe this place was heaven.

Gray Fox made a strange whistling sound and a reddish horse with a black mane came running from the woods. "Ah, here comes Red," he said.

Gray Fox crouched down beside me and said, "Angelica, Angelica." When he stood up he folded his arms across his chest, causing his muscles to bulge. "*Ma petite,* you know you owe me a life. Legends say you must now stay with me until you save mine."

"Thank you, Gray Fox. I do indeed owe you a life." As I said this, I wondered how in the world I could repay him. I really did feel a huge debt of responsibility toward that delightful man.

Gray Fox sighed. "You have come to me as in a dream, the way I had imagined it would happen, the way it was prophesied."

Before I could question him, he picked me up and placed me on his horse with a firm hand to my buttocks. Reaching into his saddle bag, he took out a white cotton shirt and gray vest. Grey fox handed me his shirt to clothe my near naked body and then he put on the vest. When he mounted Red, he sat behind me, encircling my body with his powerful arms. Holding the reins, he led Red away from the river.

I became aware of the allure and charm of that man. The touch of his brawny arms around me awoke the dormant passion I'd suppressed for so long. Was I falling under his spell?

While the horse galloped, I could feel Gray Fox's strong body as we moved in unison. He yelped and howled and encouraged his horse as we rode into the deep forest. He then lowered his head onto mine, our cheeks touching, our hair blowing in the wind, mingling as one. My eyes closed and I lost all awareness.

Chapter Eight
Reynard's Rancho

When I awoke, I was on a large, high bed with four posters. Next to each bed post was a wooden barrel which had been planted in grapevines. The vines climbed up the posts and then to a lattice pergola that extended over the bed from which purple grapes hung.

Floor to ceiling leaded-glass French doors with wood trim filled one wall of the room through which I caught a glimpse of a dark sky and a mass of gleaming stars.

I looked around and saw Reynard prodding burning logs in a fireplace with a large iron poker. He wore gray slacks and over his suntanned chest he had on a gray fox vest. A large black dog lay curled beside him.

Reynard pulled down a drum, which hung over the fireplace, and rubbed the leather for a moment. He began to play a hypnotic rhythm which made me feel sleepy. I didn't want to interrupt his playing so I closed my eyes to enjoy the pulsation in my chest.

My mind drifted to another time and place. I saw a gray fox run through a vineyard and make his way up a mountain with trepidation, as if the fox felt a threat of danger.

When I opened my eyes again, I was alone. The morning sun shone through the opened French doors. The fresh morning breeze ruffled my hair. Feeling a chill, I pulled the fox pelt covers up around my chin until I was warm.

When I climbed out of bed, I discovered fresh clothes draped over a chair. I put on a slip, funny bloomers and then a floor-length dress. Sitting by the bed were a pair of lace-up shoes and long socks, which I put on. I wound my long hair into a bun and fastened it with a wooden clip that I found on a small table.

I looked out the French doors and could see the many turrets on the building. Below me were vineyards that receded down a sloping hill to the Russian River. To the east I saw fruit and nut orchards and field crops. Sheep were grazing in a distant meadow.

I walked through the French doors and onto a wooden deck where I observed people harvesting grapes. Some of the workers sang as they cut and piled fruit onto horse-drawn wagons. I observed that most of the Mexican and Indian workers wore white shirts and pants.

Feeling famished, I looked around and saw a cup of milk which I drank. Not seeing a napkin, I wiped my mouth with the back of my hand. Before I went downstairs, I had a few bites of the bread and cheese someone had left next to the milk. I now felt ready to find Gray Fox.

Where had he gone? Why was he playing his drum while I was sleeping? What was this rancho and was it really Reynard's? I had so many questions.

The thick wooden door to my room was difficult to open because of its shear weight. I managed to open the door wide enough to get my body through. I found my way down some winding stairs. When I reached the foyer, the house appeared to be empty, so I stepped outside to a courtyard which had large tile pavers. I noticed a brick fireplace built in the center of a courtyard. Barrels filled with orange geraniums had been placed here and there.

A stone pathway led toward the vineyards. As I followed the path, I turned and looked back at the house where I had spent the night. I saw a huge, ancient oak growing in front of the house. Its branches reached so high it looked like it was trying to hold up the sky. The base of the trunk was massive, and the bark looked like aged elephant skin.

The three-story house was built of wide wooden slats, dark as dusk on a stormy day. A porch wound around most of the house. A white swing hung by a chain from the ceiling and there were six white wicker chairs in a row. The front door had a stained glass window with a picture of a hawk and a fox. Grape leaves created an arch above them like a frame.

All of a sudden, I remembered the dark house with the turrets I had seen on my canoe trip. Goose bumps ran up and down my arms and I shivered. I got my wish. I had wanted to see the house and now I could experience it close up. How fortuitous, but strange at the same time.

I walked down the dirt road that led toward the river and the immense vineyard where I had seen the workers. Caught up in the enthusiasm of the sound of men and women singing in the distance, I began to hum. I picked up a basket sitting under some vines and carried it with me. My hands longed to pick the purple fruit.

I cut my first stem of grapes with a knife I found at the bottom of the basket. I rubbed the dust off the grapes with my sleeve until the purple was luminescent. I pulled the stem of luscious fruit toward my mouth. Before the grapes touched my lips I could smell their musty, warm ripeness.

A voice behind me said, "Beware of the first bite, my lady."

I turned to see who was speaking to me and looked into the blue-gray eyes of Gray Fox, or Reynard. He winked at me and said, "There's a legend in this enchanted valley which states that if you eat of our grapes, you lose all notion of time. You will stay until the end of your days enjoying the song, the wine, and the company."

"What a wonderful place to be lost in."

I took a bite of several grapes. Purple juice streamed down my chin.

Reynard laughed, took the scarf from his neck and wiped my chin, then put the stained neckerchief back. He smiled and said, "You look none the worse for wear from yesterday's mishap. It must be due to the wonderful fresh air of this valley."

"It's probably due to the kindness and hospitality I've been given," I said. "I wish there was some way to repay you."

Reynard came up behind me and put his arms around my body and held both my hands in his to demonstrate how to cut the stems with a knife. I breathed in his musky scent.

"Ah, *ma chérie, tu es jolie.* You can repay me by allowing me to detain you here so that I can get to know you better. You are so beautiful, my darling. You are so fresh, and wholesome, but there is a touch of the exotic in you."

Oh, Alexis, or should I say Angelica. You lucky thing, you. This man sounds dreamy. No wonder you haven't returned.

Entranced by his smile and good looks, I said, "Thank you for the compliment. I would love to stay a while. I have come to this valley exhausted and had been prepared for a long vacation, anyway. Perhaps I will stay for a while so I can learn more about you and your wonderful rancho. Now that you have taught me how to cut grapes, please let me help you with the harvesting."

After several hours of relaxed labor, we followed the workers back to the yard where the enormous open barrels were filled with grapes. Some of the women climbed into the barrels, and invited me to join them. I lifted my skirt and knotted it in front of me. I smiled as I leaned over and untied the scarf from Reynard's neck. I put it over my hair which had come undone, and tied it at the back of my neck.

Reynard accompanied me to one of the barrels. He cupped his hands and I placed a bare foot in his open palms. Before he hoisted me into the barrel, he rubbed the top of my foot with his thumb. "Pure silk," he murmured. The sound of his voice and the feel of his calloused rough hand sent a tingle through my body.

From the barrel, I caught glimpses of Reynard from time to time as he busied himself directing men in the hauling and repairing empty barrels to be filled with the grape juice when the stomping and sorting of grape skins was done.

The women grape stompers put their hands on their hips. As they swayed in their walk inside the barrel, they seemed to be dancing.

A few Indian men gathered and started to play a very large drum. The grape stompers and I kept pace with the beat.

A woman with long, dark brown hair, came out from the shadows of the barn and held an abalone shell in her hands. I could smell the fragrance of burning sage. She approached the huge barrels where the women and I were standing.

The Mexican women near her grew quiet, and someone said, "It's Carmen. She's going to do the ceremony. *Silencio*."

Everyone quit talking as Carmen proceeded to speak in a language I couldn't understand. She waved the sage smoke toward the East. She turned her body each time she moved in a new direction, waving smoke to the South, West and North. Her face grew solemn as she took a gourd scooper and filled it with the juice of the grapes and raised it to her mouth. She swished the juice around and swallowed, then smiled. "Ah, very good. It will be a wonderful year."

The crowd cheered.

The sound of the drums started again. Sometimes the grape stompers would slip and fall and then laugh. Someone was always available to lend a hand to pull them up.

When the sun started to go down, the women climbed out of the barrels and strode down to the river to wash. I followed them and walked knee deep in the river water to rinse my purple stained clothing and bare feet.

As the cold water hit my legs, I shuddered as I remembered the close call I'd had with death in that same river. I felt so very grateful to be alive. It felt like my past had died and I was reborn.

When the women came out of the water, they dried with towels workers had left on the manzanita bushes. As I waded out of the water, I took a towel and dried my feet and legs. Then, I walked back to the stomping barrels to retrieve my shoes and socks.

I strolled toward the yard and was drawn to the sound of music. In the courtyard, a small band of musicians played violins, guitars, and mandolins. Some of the couples returning from the river danced to the music. Others sat at picnic tables scattered under the great oak tree and drank red wine.

I could smell the lamb and chicken cooking on spits over the coals of a fire set in the open field, and realized I was starving. When I got near the barn, the woman who did the ceremony approached me and handed me a dry skirt and blouse. She said, "I'm Reynard's sister, Carmen. I brought these to you so you can change."

I did as she suggested, and dressed standing behind several thick bushes away from the courtyard, and then I handed her my wet clothes and towel.

I said, "Thanks for your thoughtfulness. It's so nice to have something dry to put on."

"You're so welcome, my dear."

Carmen put the clothes and towel into a nearby basket overflowing with other women's clothes. "I understand my brother pulled you out of the river yesterday. He said you were lucky. Many people drown in our river. It can be very unforgiving. I'm sure you're still a bit unsettled by it." She reached over and gave me a big squeeze. Her embrace felt warm and assuring.

"I was so glad your brother came along when he did," I said. "I would have drowned if he hadn't been there to help me."

"My dear, I want to share something with you. It might sound strange, but you must know that you have come to us, into this beautiful dream world, in response to a need our family has. Reynard was told by his mentor, who is an Indian medicine man, that you're the one who will help us break a family curse."

"That seems crazy. I just met you and Reynard. What could I possibly do?"

"My dear, don't be too hasty. It's because you're new to this land that you bring fresh and new ideas. Do you want to combine your life dreams with ours and help us?"

"I don't know. This is all so sudden."

"Don't feel you must decide now. Live with us a while and let your feelings guide you."

My cheeks burned in response to Carmen, and I said, "I'm very grateful to Reynard for saving me, and to you for your hospitality. But, what do you mean, your family needs my help? I'm a stranger to this land."

She said, "Yes, there's so much more to tell, but you must stay a while so that you can learn to trust us. You can create a whole new dream for your life. You have free will to decide how you want your life to go."

"What you say is very exciting, but I don't really know, yet. I'm going to have to give it some thought."

Chapter Nine
The Two Mysterious Ponds

Reynard sauntered over and motioned for me to follow him. He offered me a stick with lamb and vegetables on it, and a piece of bread. He looked at me and said, "I see you have met my sister. She told me that she sees great warmth and strength in you. I saw her give you a hug. She doesn't do that with many people."

"Carmen is very welcoming. She was talking to me about some family mystery that I'm to help you with, but I don't understand what it is. I'm not sure how long I can stay here, but I'll do what I can. I feel I owe you so much."

"There's no rush. The family problem has been with us for decades and can't be solved overnight. In the meanwhile, you need time to adjust to our Rancho de los Zorros Grises or Ranch of the Gray Foxes. While you are resting and recovering, I am going to take last year's wine to be sold."

I felt panic stricken to be left amongst strangers at this rancho. I yelled, "You're leaving? You can't expect me to stay if you're going away."

Reynard grabbed me and gave me a big hug. As he held me, he said, "I don't blame you for being upset. Try not to worry, my dear. I won't be gone long."

"But how long will it be? I do have a sabbatical from my work as a Native American anthropology professor to do research and work on my book. However, I can't stay for an indefinite period of time."

"What is this you say. . .Native American anthropology? What is that?"

"I teach anthropology which studies people, in the past, the present and as they change over time. It's also about people and the world they experience, the material cultures they create, their beliefs and inner lives. It's a pretty broad topic. I specialize in Native American studies which is the same word as Indian, or some people call them indigenous people."

"You will love it here. We have many Indians living and working on this land. In fact, my brother-in-law, White Owl, is an Indian. You will have a chance to interact and ask questions of the Indians for your studies."

"You're right. I've come to the right place, but how long are you going to be gone?"

"It'll just be a few weeks or so. Please stay and let Carmen look after you. She would love having your company. She gets a bit lonely sometimes. She misses her daughter who is attending school in France. I also have been lonely since my wife died."

"Oh, I'm so sorry. I didn't know. I also lost a spouse sometime ago. I know how it feels to lose a loved one."

"That is so unfortunate, Angelica," Reynard said. "Sorry, my darling."

"My husband and I were good friends since college days, and we just fell into marriage. After only a few years of marriage, he was killed when a bridge collapsed on him during an earthquake. I was distraught. It's taken me a while to feel centered again."

"Angelica, it appears we are both widowed. Life can be hard sometimes, but here we are living life as best we can, not stuck in the past."

"Yes, it has been an effort on my part to feel enthusiasm for life after that, but since coming to your rancho yesterday, I'm beginning to feel a new zest for life. I feel like each day here would be an adventure."

"Angelica, I want to ask you if I can start courting you when I get back."

I was shocked by the sudden question. I'd just met this man. I could feel a blush cover my cheeks, then I took a deep breath, looked him square in the eyes, and said, "Ah-h-h, I guess so. . .well, yes, I think that would be alright."

Angelica, this was such an old fashioned way for Reynard to say he wanted to date you. Knowing you, it must have scared you a bit to think a man was so interested, even if you were becoming attracted to him.

Reynard picked me up and spun me around and around in his exuberance. When he put me down he surprised me with a big kiss on the lips.

"I hate to leave now," Reynard said, "but it can't be helped. I had this trip set up months ago. We have some long-standing clients in Sonoma and Monterey who are waiting to have their wine orders filled. I also have some other important business I must attend to."

Panic rose in me again. "What'll I do with myself while you're gone?"

"Please make yourself at home, my Angel. Carmen told me she wants to make you some dresses, teach you to use the loom and fill you in on a few mysteries of the rancho. Since you are an anthropologist, I'm sure you would enjoy it if she and her husband share stories with you about our local history and mythology."

Curious I said, "Yes. Yes. I think I'll stay. Like you said, maybe I can gather some information for the book I'm planning to write. I hope you won't be gone too long, though. After all, I'm a stranger here."

"I will accomplish my business as quickly as I can. Follow me. I want to show you something. It will help you understand our family better."

Reynard led me to one of the big barns at the side of the yard. As we entered, I could hear men's voices speaking Spanish. We walked closer to where the men stood in a semi-circle around a small pond. At first I could only see darkness. But then I noticed some men were holding torches that reflected off the water, making it come alive.

Reynard took my arm and led me to another small pond. He held a candle above it so I could see better. I noticed a five and a half foot cross at one edge of the pond. Reynard let the warm wax from the candle run onto the top of the cross and held the candle in it for a few moments to harden.

I felt startled when all of a sudden he let out a plaintive cry. "My mama. My mama." Tears ran down his cheeks and into the pond.

Why was Reynard so upset? This was very strange. What was going on?

Reynard dipped a gourd into the pond and brought out some dark red liquid, not at all what I expected. One of the men dipped two of his fingers into the liquid and crossed himself, then each of the men standing near the pond did the same. Reynard touched his thumb to his index and middle fingers and dipped them into the liquid, crossing himself, repeating with reverence, "*Sangre de la Madre. Sangre de la Madre. Sangre de la Madre.*"

Reynard held the gourd out to me, and in a deep voice said, "Mother's blood. Very holy, very sacred." I followed Reynard's example, and dipped my fingers into the liquid and then crossed myself. The whole thing seemed very strange. Goose bumps rose on my skin.

Barrels of aging wine lined the walls surrounding the ponds. After each of the men had made the sign of the cross, one of them opened a barrel of wine and poured a small gourd full of Mother's blood into the barrel. The men then busied themselves filling bottles from the barrels.

Reynard took one of the bottles and poured wine for me into a glass sitting on a table. "Go ahead," he insisted. "You get to taste the world's most glorious *vino*. No one but the people on this rancho know why it is considered such an ambrosial drink. We get the highest money on the market for its marvelous taste and unexpected after effects."

I took a small sip, not sure what to expect from the curious liquid. As the wine slid across my tongue and down my throat, I tasted the mellowness of the aging. The honey flavor caused my chest and belly to warm and tingle. I felt like I was floating.

"Why," I exclaimed, "This mixture of Mother's blood and the Rancho de los Zorros Grises wine is wonderful. I'm sure your wines have a fabulous reputation."

"My darling, I want you to consider these two ponds. Whenever one of the women of this family died, Mother's blood bubbled up and created a pond.

We've come to understand that these ponds represent the women's suffering and sacrifice. Through their eternal love, some kind of underground spring emerged as if they were continuing to sustain and nurture us. You see, the first pond emerged when my mother died right after my birth. The last and largest pond formed after my wife died in childbirth."

Tears welled in my eyes. "I'm so sorry, Reynard. What a tragedy."

"We must see to it that there are no more new ponds, no more suffering."

I wanted to ask whether or not that was related to the family curse, but Reynard put his finger to his lips to indicate silence, and led me out of the barn. As we entered the night air, he looked at me and said, "Much will be revealed to you, but you need time to adjust to our way of life at the rancho."

What, I wondered, are these mysteries and what is Carmen going to be teaching me? I was feeling perturbed having to wait, so I said, "I'm a very curious person and hate to be put off for answers. Can't you tell me before you leave?"

All he said was, "I have to leave at dawn, so we don't have time to discuss it. Believe me, each secret will be divulged to you when you are ready."

I felt frustrated as Reynard took my hand in his and we walked to the courtyard where the guitarists and violinists were playing. I tried to squelch my anxiety as we sat at one of the tables, which had a large bouquet of light blue asters and a wine bottle with a lit candle in it. The red wax from previous candles had dripped down the sides. I dipped my finger into the soft wax and held it up to Reynard who laughed at my antics. He picked up the candle and let the wax run off his nose creating a wax waterfall which froze in place. I knocked the wax off his nose, and we both laughed.

Some women carried baskets of food to our table. Reynard proceeded to eat like he was famished. As we ate, sometimes he would glance at me with his blue-gray eyes, and smile. I felt entranced by those eyes.

All of a sudden, I felt uncomfortable, like a heaviness had filled my chest. When I looked up, a couple walked to the adjacent table and sat down. The woman was gray-haired. The man accompanying her was about Reynard's age and stature. I sensed a darkness about the man.

Chapter Ten
Meeting the Evil Cousin

"That's my Cousin Joseph who has a nearby rancho," Reynard said, "and the older lady with him is my Aunt Lila who lives here at our home."

I nodded and continued eating. I overheard Joseph discussing something in a loud voice with Aunt Lila. What I could overhear was, "Damn scabby settlers. They're saying the land grants are no good any more since Californians are free and independent of Mexico."

What in the world was that man raving about? It didn't make any sense.

Joseph continued. "The settlers are hearing the news and starting to squat on people's lands. If the owners don't have enough guards to shoot the squatters, the owners can lose their land. Besides, with that darn gold rush, it's hard to keep many workers anymore."

My stomach churned as Joseph looked my way. He gave me an insincere smile. I wondered what story this strange man was discussing.

Reynard stood, took my hand, and led me to the couple. "Joseph and Aunt Lila, please let me introduce you to my new friend. You probably already heard I saved her from the river yesterday."

Joseph jumped up and stood too close to me. His dark eyes seemed to pierce my skin. He looked me up and down. "Yes, I heard about the accident. I'm delighted to meet you, my dear. Welcome to our family."

At that moment, the musicians started playing a new song. Couples got up to dance. When I extended my hand to shake Joseph's, he took my arm instead, as if wanting to pull me away to the dance floor. Reynard blocked

Joseph's way and took my other arm. He said, "Angelica is taken for this dance, my cousin, as she is for all dances from this day forward."

As he led me away to the dance floor, I looked back over my shoulder, and said, "Good meeting you Cousin Joseph and Aunt Lila."

Reynard led me to the middle of the dance floor. He twirled me around and then held me in a tight embrace. He said, "I hope you don't mind, but I had to get you away from Joseph. Aunt Lila and my father, George, invite him to our Fall Feast every year. Why, I do not know. He is an evil snake. Beware of him. I warn you."

Other people got up to dance. All of a sudden, the music changed and men and women began to clap to the new rhythm. Reynard motioned for me to grab onto the back of his waist. When I did so, Carmen ran over and grabbed me around the waist, and we became a chain. Soon, a long line of people formed behind us. Even the old men and women joined in. We became like a large caterpillar, moving as one.

The line of people followed Reynard's steps. He led the crowd between the barrels filled with geraniums, around the fountain, and passed the musicians lined up against the wall of the house. When the music stopped, I looked to the east and saw pink around the edges of the sky.

At the first light of dawn, men and women started leaving, some yawning and stretching on their way. One of the workers came up to Reynard and whispered in his ear.

Reynard turned toward me and said, "It is time for me to leave. Remember to listen to the words of Carmen. She is very excited to have another woman around the house to talk to. She can begin to prepare you for your future life here, that is, if you decide you want to stay."

I held back some tears, grabbed Reynard around the neck and pulled him to me. This wonderful man was leaving me here with these strangers. Was he really coming back? Now that I had found him, I didn't want to be parted from him. I had so many questions.

Reynard gazed into my eyes. "Promise you will wait for my return, my Angel. Don't forget, you gave me permission to start courting you when I come back."

I smiled and nodded in return. "Of course I will wait for you, but hurry back. I look forward to our being together again." He gave me a soft and gentle kiss, and then left.

Carmen walked over to me, and put an arm around my shoulder. She said, "Don't worry, Angelica. He won't be gone long. We'll have a grand time, the two of us women. It's been ages since I've had a woman my age at the rancho."

I felt somewhat relieved. This wasn't how I saw my vacation turning out, but I was already experiencing feelings of kinship to this kind lady.

Angelica, I like this lady, Carmen. She'd make a great sister-in-law. . .or should I say friend?

Chapter Eleven
Introduction to the Family

The next morning I felt an ache in my chest and realized I missed Reynard. I started to walk down the stairway from the third floor bedroom when Carmen came to meet me.

I noticed Carmen also had the blue-gray eyes of Reynard, accentuated by thick dark eyebrows and beautiful clean features. She wore her long, dark hair tied back in a ponytail. She exuded a certain air of confidence as she approached me.

"My darling," Carmen said. "I couldn't wait to have you join us, so I came upstairs. Come. Follow me to the breakfast table."

"I'm so glad you're here. I wasn't sure if I could find my way to the kitchen without help."

"I know. This house can feel like a maze unless you're familiar with its passageways. Reynard had this bedroom built onto the top of the house after his wife died."

I put my hand on Carmen's arm and said, "Reynard told me. Her death was so tragic."

Carmen grasped my hand and said, "Yes, it was. Reynard was very distraught afterwards and needed time alone to heal, so his third floor bedroom gave him some isolation and privacy."

"You mean his hideaway was like a man cave?"

"I haven't heard the term man cave, but I guess that's a good description. He loves the fresh air. Says it invigorates him. That's why he leaves the French doors open."

It seemed to me Carmen wasn't in any hurry to get to the kitchen, so I crossed my arms and leaned against the mahogany railing, and said, "I noticed. When I woke up yesterday morning the doors were wide open. I'm really curious. Can you tell me more about the night before last when I was brought here?"

"Why don't you follow me down the stairs," Carmen said, "and I'll tell you. Then I'll give you a tour of the house."

"Sounds great."

Carmen stopped on a landing for a moment and said, "Reynard kept a fire going in the room for you night before last, so you wouldn't get cold. He brought you up this stairway with the assistance of my husband, White Owl. I put some night clothes on you, and tucked you into bed."

I smiled and said, "That was so kind of you, Carmen."

"Angelica, it's my pleasure. I'm happy Reynard is so sweet on you. He told me you agreed to allow him to start courting you when he returns."

"He was so nice to ask me in that way."

As I finished walking down the stairs, I wondered how Reynard and I would get along. I realized that even though he was a wonderful hunk of a man, he was a little on the bossy side. Maybe that was because he was used to the leadership role of running the rancho.

When Carmen and I entered the foyer, I noticed the entry floors had large, rose-tinted terra cotta tiles. As Carmen led me along a wide hallway, she said, "The study to the right of us was put together by my father and Reynard. They're very proud of their book collection that includes many classics Reynard enjoys."

Amazing to think that Reynard was not only a successful rancher, but also a scholar.

"Reynard attended college in France," Carmen continued, "to study ranching and wine growing. You're welcome to look at the books and read whatever you like."

"Okay, I might take a few to my room tonight. Do you know if there are any books on Indians in the study?"

Carmen looked a little puzzled. "I don't know, but if you want to learn about Indians, you've come to the right place. We have some who live on our land who help us with the crops. My husband, White Owl, is an Indian, and I'm sure he'd be happy to talk to you. There's also a Medicine Man who lives nearby. You'll have to ask Reynard to introduce you."

As we continued down the hall, Carmen said, "On the left is the living room that has the original furniture my father brought from the estate the family owned in France. Over here is the formal dining room."

"Do you dress up for dinner?" I said.

"Just wear a nice dress and you'll be fine. I'm going to give you some of mine since we appear to be about the same size. Before you go back upstairs, I'll give you one that you can wear tonight. I'll also have some new ones made up for you."

"You're so thoughtful."

Carmen led me to a large room and said, "Take a look at the crystal chandelier in the dining room, Angelica. Reynard's deceased wife had it brought all the way from France when she inherited some items from her uncle's estate."

"Oh, it's quite beautiful."

At the end of the hallway, we entered the kitchen that had a breakfast area on one side. A large rough-hewn wooden table sat at one end of the area, and a vase filled with orange geraniums sat in the middle.

"I've got some oatmeal warming on the stove top," Carmen said. "Have a seat at the table and I'll bring it to you."

The only one at the breakfast table was a white-haired man who sat hunched over as though he was in great discomfort. When he smiled at me, I noticed beautiful blue-gray eyes similar to Reynard's.

When Carmen introduced us, George and I nodded at each other. I walked over and offered him my hand which he held to his heart for a moment.

"My Angelica, my dear one. I'm glad you're here with us. You seem to make my son happy." George kissed my hand with great gentleness.

What a charming old man he was. "I'm happy to be welcomed into the family," I said, feeling my cheeks get hot. "It's good to meet you, too."

I sat down next to George, and Carmen brought me a steaming mug of coffee along with a bowl of hot oatmeal with honey and raisins. I thanked her. I didn't know how hungry I was until she set the oatmeal in front of me.

"Now you have to shake Jack's hand, too," George said. "He's definitely one of the family."

A large black wolf-like dog, sitting at George's feet, stood up and sniffed me. When I offered my hand, he put his paw up for me to shake.

The morning light blazed through the open window and a breeze fluttered the blue-checkered curtains. A black crow flew into the open kitchen window and then perched on the ledge. He rustled his feathers with his beak, and let out a loud caw. To my surprise, he flew over to George's shoulder and landed.

"Come, my dear," George said. "Don't be afraid of Vasco. He's also part of the family. Go ahead and scratch his head. He likes that."

I reached for some bread crumbs from the table and offered them to Vasco. He flew to my forearm and sat there eating from my palm. When he was done, Vasco flew to George's arm.

George said, "Yes, Vasco likes you, too, Angelica. I believe you have been welcomed royally."

As I ate, Carmen sat down next to me with her coffee mug. I began to gaze around the room. What I was looking for, I was uncertain, but something seemed to be missing. The kitchen had a large wood-burning stove, a water pump at the sink, and several dark wooden cupboards. I noticed a coal oil lamp perched on the kitchen counter and several candle holders with large candles sitting on the shelf — such a rustic kitchen.

I sat up straight and started reciting, "No refrigerator, no dishwasher, no trash compactor, no electric lights, no microwave, no telephone, no electric can opener..."

Carmen looked at me funny, and said, "What're you saying?"

I could feel my face flush. I decided I should stay quiet and not say anything about the fact I'd begun to notice I was no longer in the twentieth century. I didn't want them to think I was crazy. Maybe I was jumping to conclusions. I'd have to test my theory further, and maybe I'd find some explanation.

"I think I need to go outside and get some air," I said. "I'm feeling a bit light-headed." I pushed my chair back, almost knocking it over, and headed for the kitchen door.

I went outside to the large porch. I looked around for power lines or telephone poles, and could see none. Also missing were cars and trucks, but I saw horses grazing on the hillside.

My mind flashed to the river. Since being rescued, I couldn't remember anything that would say I was in my century, the only century I knew.

No, Angelica. You couldn't have time traveled. That's impossible...or is it?

Chapter Twelve
A Rancho Lunch

Carmen came outside to the shell-white porch. She put an arm around me and said, "I hope you're okay. I know it takes time to adjust to big changes. Try to focus on the fact that it's likely you were saved from drowning for a purpose. With us, you now have a new family, and I hope you'll feel comfortable enough to confide in me anytime you feel the need."

When she gave me a big hug, I felt so comforted by the warmth she radiated. I had been feeling homesick.

"Yes, being here is a big adjustment," I said. "I'm from the city and used to the noise and bustle, and I miss my sister. However, I'm very grateful for being alive and for being so welcomed by all of you."

I decided to hide my fears and not say anything more about my observations.

She motioned for me to sit with her at a wicker table. As I leaned back in the chair, I noticed the tall poplars on the perimeter of the property separating the various fields and the rolling hillsides. They looked something like the poplar trees in San Francisco.

"I'd love to have you stay as long as you want," Carmen said. "It's great having your company. All of the children are in France attending school, and I miss their happy laughter."

"What children do you mean, other than your daughter?"

"Reynard's twins are going to school in France. They're ten years old, and my daughter is eighteen."

"I knew Reynard was a widower, but I didn't know he had children."

What a shock that was to me. I couldn't quite picture Reynard with kids.

"Yes, and they're great kids."

A bowl of walnuts sat in the middle of the table, and Carmen moved it closer, then handed me the nut cracker. "We grow walnuts on the rancho. Try some."

"Thank you," I said as I cracked a few nuts and popped the walnut meat into my mouth.

"Reynard's wife died in childbirth right after the second twin was born. Reynard was quite upset for a long time."

"The poor man. It must have been an awful shock," I said. A tear rolled down my cheek, as I thought about the trauma of losing a wife and being left with twin babies.

"Enough about sad times. Perhaps you'd like to see me weave." Carmen pointed to a loom that was at the other end of the porch.

"Sure," I said.

Carmen and I walked over to have a closer look. "The loom's beautiful. It's so large. What do you make on it?"

"I weave wool rugs and blankets, and sometimes shawls. I've been doing it since I was a youngster. It's very tranquilizing for me." She sat at the loom, picked up the shuttle and began to work. Her hands appeared to fly.

I became hypnotized by her movements — in and out — in and out — and soon a pattern started to emerge.

She noticed my interest and said, "If you'd like to learn how to weave, I can show you. It takes a lot of discipline to sit and do this. You must quiet your mind and concentrate on nothing but what you're doing. The pattern you see was handed down from my ancestors."

"The colors are so vibrant and the pattern is beautiful. I would love to be able to do that. I remember my grandmother had a loom, but I was too young to learn, so I only watched. The different colored scraps of yarn were my playthings when I'd visit her."

Carmen looked pleased and said, "Perhaps I should have White Owl buy some wood so Reynard can build a loom for you here on the porch."

"Great. I'll get to see the whole process from beginning to end."

"Now, follow me to the pasture and you can see where the wool for the yarn comes from."

We walked along a path to a large meadow and passed an enclosed fence filled with sheep. Some of the Mexican men were trimming the shaggy wool from the sheep with shearing scissors. The sheep would struggle, but the strong men knew how to hold them in their grip to keep the sheep quiet. After the men finished shearing each one, the sheep would run away.

Carmen said, "Normally, sheep are sheared in the late spring, but we had to wait until autumn this year because the expert shearers are in high demand and couldn't get here until now."

"I can tell by watching them that they're experts. They almost make it look easy."

"You're right. Although, I don't think I'd attempt it."

Carmen put her hands into a nearby basket overflowing with rumpled wool. I followed her example and was surprised at the oily feel of the lanolin in the wool.

"I'll show you how to wash this wool and dye it, and make it ready for the loom. Knowing how to do things from start to finish is a good thing. Later, we'll have Aunt Lila show you how to card the wool and spin it into yarn."

"I'd love that, Carmen. Thank you."

By the way she spoke, it sounded like Carmen was planning on having me stay for quite a while. I thought if Reynard and I develop a relationship, I just might think of staying longer.

When Carmen and I walked back to the porch, she sighed and said, "When I was a girl, I told Aunt Lila I wanted to finish my weaving in a hurry so I'd have a rug on my bedroom floor. Aunt Lila stopped me, and reminded me I should visualize the completed project in my mind and that would create my intention. Then, by the magic of concentration and hard work, I'd finish my rug. I came to realize I could do that with other things in my life as well."

"Aunt Lila is very wise, isn't she? Can you show me the basics of weaving today?"

"Sure, but you'll have to wait until after lunch."

I heard a clanging of a supper bell, and Carmen said, "My stomach always knows when it's time to eat."

When I followed her to the front of the house, I saw an Indian woman hitting a large wrought iron triangle with an iron rod. The triangle hung from an oak tree branch.

Long wooden tables were lined up in front of the house under the shade of the oak tree. A variety of workers emerged from the fields, Mexicans and Indians, men and women. They seemed happy as they headed for the picnic tables.

One table held chopped apples, slabs of cheese, piles of tortillas, and bottles of wine. A pot of beans hung from a chain above a big fire pit, which was attached to iron bars made into a tepee shape. The workers formed a line, plates in hand. They waited their turn to get a ladle of beans. After that, they moved on to the next table to pick up the rest of their food.

Carmen poured me a large mug of wine, and handed me a plate. She said, "Go ahead and get some food before it's gone. There're some mighty hungry people here today. Nothing like working in the fields to stimulate your appetite."

Carmen and I made the rounds for food. The men and women greeted her with affection. I heard several workers say, "*Hola, Señora* Carmen, and *buenas dias, Señorita* Angelica." I was surprised that most of them knew my name.

Carmen said, "Word spreads very fast on the rancho. Most everyone knows about you and are very excited you have come."

I felt embarrassed I was the talk of the rancho.

Several of the Mexican women joined us. When we were seated, Carmen stood and made the sign of the cross. Everyone did the same.

Carmen then folded her hands in front of her and said grace. "Lord, thank you for this food and wine. Thank you for the friendship of these people and their hard work. Thank you for all our great blessings. Amen."

Amen echoed throughout the tables.

As we began to eat, a Mexican with graying hair and a thin moustache, came up to Carmen and said, "*Señora* Carmen, we would like to say our names to *Señorita* Angelica, *por favor.*"

The man introduced himself as Roberto and shook my hand. Carmen explained to me he was their assistant field manager.

Roberto then introduced me to the workers who shook my hand and bowed their heads in respect.

The last person in line was the Mexican cook. Roberto said, "The cook's name is Maria, and she's *mi esposa*. She's a very good cook, don't you think?"

I shook Maria's hand and said, "Your beans are wonderful and the tortillas so light."

Maria mumbled, "*No es nada, Señorita* Angelica. Just plain food. I'm glad you like it."

Roberto turned to me, "Your wine mug is empty. Let me pour you more."

The day was warming up, and I felt thirsty after the spicy beans. "Thanks, Roberto. You're so kind."

Roberto smiled and said, "Everyone. Let's have a toast to our new lady." The crowd held their wine mugs high and said, "*Salud.*"

Holding my mug up, and feeling elated, I said, "*Salud.*"

When everyone finished eating, they began to walk back to the fields to finish their day's work. Some of the women giggled and skipped. Some of the men whistled as they walked toward the fruit orchards or to the barn or the meadow where the sheep were munching grass.

It seemed time for me to do some work, too, although I was feeling a bit light-headed and silly after all the good wine and food.

"Carmen," I said, trying not to slur my words. "You promised you'd teach me to weave."

"Sure," Carmen said. "Let's go back to the porch."

Carmen pulled up two armless chairs, and we sat at the loom next to each other. She showed me the lengthwise threads of warp set in a straight line on the wooden frame. She held the shuttle and wove in the wool yarn which went over the warp, under the next, until soon I could see a pattern forming. She had me sit at the loom and use the shuttle. A thrill filled me. I was actually working at a loom.

Carmen said, "That's good. Later on, I'll show you how to make patterns. In the meantime, you can continue to weave this large section of solid white. Stop when you've made twenty rows, and I'll finish the rest. The next section will be more complicated because it'll have some pattern to it. In the meantime, I'm going into the kitchen to see if Aunt Lila needs help preparing dinner."

Carmen left me alone weaving in the sunshine, forgetting Reynard was gone, forgetting I was an anthropologist.

As I wove, I'd glanced up at the eaves of the porch where a large spider web hung, still damp from the moisture in the air. I could see a rainbow in the web.

"How beautiful your weaving is," I said.

I noticed a large gray spider. When I spoke, it appeared that she'd shaken the web in response.

All of a sudden, a breeze came up, and the web itself became alive, expanding. Then it contracted when the air quieted. As I watched the web and the spider, I had mixed feelings of revulsion and attraction. Most of the time, I felt spiders were disgusting and ugly. The first time I'd run into a web, and the spider danced on my head, I got the creeps. It bothered me that some small eight-legged spiders could be deadly. Yet, at the same time, I admired the symmetry and pattern of their webs, and found beauty in that miracle of the spider's artistry. I realized the web represented my life — the one I'm weaving now, and what I might weave in the future.

The rest of the afternoon, the spider and I focused on our weaving. My mind stopped its chattering, and became quiet. At one point, I stopped weaving and stared at the spider. I thought I heard a very quiet voice say, "Believe in your wisdom." Perhaps it was the wind whistling.

Chapter Thirteen
Dinner with the Family

Carmen returned to the porch and said, "Dinner is ready, my darling girl. You've worked enough. Come in and eat."

I followed Carmen to the formal dining room. "You've already met George and Aunt Lila. This is White Owl, my husband, and that is Gabe, Aunt Lila's husband."

I went over and shook White Owl and Gabe's hand, and said, "Nice meeting you all."

They both smiled and nodded at me.

I sat down at the table next to Carmen. Coal oil lamps hung in the corners of the room, a large candelabra sat on the table, and the chandelier held candles. Noticing there were no electric lights caused my stomach to tingle, but I said nothing.

Aunt Lila filled the crystal glasses with wine and White Owl carved the meat. Carmen handed me a steaming bowl of fresh vegetables.

The food had a home-grown flavor, so uncommon in the city, and the meat tasted gamey. I ate as though I'd had no food for weeks.

Aunt Lila said, "I'm so glad you like venison. We have it often."

"Amazing," I said. "I've never eaten venison. I'm really enjoying it."

After dinner, we went through the long hallway into the front room where there was a blazing fire in a large stone fireplace. The leather couch had a bear skin draped across it. Two coal oil lamps sat on the mantle. Large sword ferns filled the wicker planters situated at both ends of the couch.

George laid on the couch in front of the roaring fire. Carmen placed a red and orange wool blanket over him and straightened his pillow.

Gabe brought out his violin, Carmen sat at the piano, and Lila held a flute. They played Columbia, the Gem of the Ocean, with great enthusiasm. The second song was Old Dan Tucker which Carmen played on the piano while the rest of us clapped.

When the piece was finished, they asked me to sing with them. They taught me a song called, Long Ago. I enjoyed the song so much, I said, "Please. Let's sing it one more time."

We reached a crescendo with the words, "Long, long ago, long ago." When Gabe sang this last verse in falsetto and off key, we all burst out laughing.

I sat down next to George. He took my hand in his, and said, "I'm so glad you enjoyed the music."

"Thanks. I liked joining in. It was great fun."

Then George told me he used to play the violin, but he was no longer able to because of his arthritis.

"Here, let me rub your hands for you. It'll ease your discomfort a bit."

George closed his eyes and smiled while I worked on his gnarled fingers.

I looked across the room and noticed Carmen and White Owl arguing about something. White Owl raised his voice and then left the room. I noticed he didn't return.

As the evening wore on, Carmen asked me if she could accompany me to my room. We walked up the stairway to the third floor. As we climbed the steps, I tripped on my long skirt.

"What a pain these long skirts are," I said.

Carmen said, "I wear pants on the rancho sometimes, and no one minds. Aunt Lila never wears them. . .she's old fashioned. I'll get you a pair of pants from my wardrobe. They're much more comfortable for climbing stairs and working."

Carmen opened the large wooden door leading to Reynard's bedroom. She knelt down, lit the fire in the fireplace and put her hand on my shoulder.

She said, "Reynard has been waiting for you for many years. I must warn you that he is different from other men. The two of you have a destiny you have been prophesied to fulfill. We'll work on preparing you so you'll be ready when the time comes."

"I know Reynard is very different, and charming. How can he have been waiting for me? He never knew I existed before a few days ago. What is this prophesy business I have to get ready for?"

Carmen nodded and said, "I know none of this makes sense right now. Try to be patient, my dear. Reynard will explain everything when he returns."

I decided to let it go for now.

Angelica, you fool. You've got to find out what this prophesy is and how it involves you. It sounds menacing, and I don't want your life in danger.

As if dismissing the mystery with her short explanation, Carmen changed the subject, and said, "Tell me what happened to you today while you were weaving?"

I responded, "I concentrated so much on the weaving, the threads. . .the loom, the in and out. . .it seemed as if the world had disappeared. I also noticed I had company watching me. . .a large gray spider who sat in her web above me. When I commented on how beautiful the web looked, she seemed to vibrate."

Carmen smiled at me with approval, and said, "Excellent start, Angelica. You'll do well. You're a fast learner. A few more days of this weaving will make your mind clear and ready to progress."

Before I could ask her more, she went out the door.

I laid on the gray fox pelt spread, my mind quiet and at peace. My past life, with all its worries and stresses seemed far away to me. I wondered what Carmen was talking about — a destiny to fulfill. I fell into a dreamless sleep.

Chapter Fourteen
Alone with God

After a few days of weaving instructions from Carmen and Aunt Lila, I woke at dawn, dressed and went downstairs. I found Carmen preparing breakfast. I didn't usually rise that early, but because of the lack of modern evening entertainment, such as television or radio, I had no reason to stay up late. Things seemed more in a natural rhythm. I liked that.

Carmen smiled as I entered the kitchen. She wore a blue and white-checkered apron as she bustled about. "Good morning," she said. "We've got nice fresh biscuits, butter, and honey."

Holding a crocheted hot pad, she removed some delicious smelling biscuits from the oven and set them on a wooden trivet in the middle of the table. Carmen poured hot tea into blue flowered China cups, sat down, and pushed the hair out of her eyes with the back of her hand.

I walked over to the side table and picked up a newspaper. The headlines for the *Californian*, read, "Miners Striking It Rich." Carmen looked at the paper and mumbled, "Reynard brought the newspaper from San Francisco last time he was there. Darn riff-raff scums. These so-called miners come from all over the country. Bums are what they are. Downright bums. They want to make a quick buck. Most times they are the gamblers and chiselers who don't want to work for a living. Many of them are youngsters, looking for an adventure, who hope they'll pan a big nugget with some quick work. Settlers, hard workers, families and good citizens they are not."

I glanced at the date before I put the paper down, August 1, 1848.

My knees felt wobbly, and I sat next to Carmen. I took a couple breaths and picked up a biscuit and split it in two.

Before I could speak, Carmen said, "In this place it's often best to experience rather than to ask. Remember life is as you make it. You are your own creator. Let's go for a walk today, and see what we can discover. We'll pack up some of these extra biscuits and red apples for lunch."

I bit my tongue, so anxious to ask questions that didn't seem welcomed right now.

I dabbed honey on my biscuits and ate them while they were still steamy, and wondered where we were going for our hike.

"Carmen, if you don't want me to delve into the mysteries of this place, perhaps you can tell me a little bit about your family."

Carmen, sitting at the table, sipped her tea and said, "My father came from France with his sister, Aunt Lila. George had been a vintner in France. His business was hit hard when different diseases from fungus to nematodes attacked his plants. He read that the vines, when mixed with the hardy native American plants, formed a healthy stock because of the disease resistance of the American roots. He decided America was the place for him.

"When my father and Aunt Lila came to California they brought some of the healthy vines with them. The Alta California governor was impressed someone was interested in growing wine grapes. Of course, with George's offer of good wine and the fact he found a local Spanish sweetheart and had married her, plus they were both Catholic, made it easier for our father to get a land grant. His plan was a success and after some years of hardship, he had the best vines around."

"Amazing," I said. "So your family goes way back to very early California. The governor was wise authorizing them the land grant."

"Father, being very practical, decided he would never be wiped out again with only one crop. He grew several other things, such as wheat, walnuts, and apples. This assured him he would have other produce to rely on if one of the crops failed. This idea worked, as you can see by our rancho today.

"Tell me something about Aunt Lila," I said.

"Aunt Lila, as you know, is married to Gabe, who is a local Mexican."

"Do they have any kids?"

"No, they were unable to have children, although they were tremendous with helping raise Reynard and me, plus my daughter and Reynard's youngsters."

Carmen stopped her narrative and started out the front door carrying a basket of food in the crook of her arm. She said, "Come, let's start walking before the day gets away from us." I hurried to keep up with her.

As she walked she continued her story. "When my parents got around to having children, I was born first and then our mother died giving birth to Reynard. Our father was terribly upset at her death, and left us with Aunt Lila while he wandered the hills desperate to find solace in his beloved mountains and meadows."

"Yes," I said. "Nature does wonderful things for me too, when I'm upset. I can understand his need to do that."

Carmen squeezed my hand. "Here's a good place to have our picnic."

She took a checkered table cloth out of the basket and spread it on the grassy meadow. I removed the biscuits and apples, and we munched on our small feast.

"Please continue your story, Carmen. What happened next?"

She wiped the crumbs from her face. "At the opportune time, father met Mountain Screamer, the Medicine Man who lived on the land nearby. He helped our father cope with his guilt and sadness by teaching him to live in the flow of Mother Nature, to live off the land, to sing, drum, and do ceremony. The Indian ceremonies had been forbidden by the early missionaries years before. Only a few Indian elders knew the old ways. Embracing a white man into the Indian ways was unusual for Mountain Screamer. Perhaps he saw something in father, or knew something of his destiny."

"He was lucky to have Mountain Screamer help him," I said. "I'm glad he came along when he did."

When we finished eating, we packed up our lunch. Then we followed the river for some distance and turned up a small hill dotted with maples.

"Now to prepare you," Carmen said. "I will leave you here until sundown, so you can get to know this land. All places have a history and a distinct spirit that belong to a particular area. Spirit voices are inside the trees, as in this great ancient maple." She pointed and said, "And this rock." Then she moved her arms upward and motioned from side to side. "Or the shifting skies. The voices are not silent. If you become quiet in a place of sublime nature, such as this, you might detect an unseen subtle movement and spirit."

"Okay," I said. "I think I'm ready."

Carmen took my hands in hers and looked deep into my eyes as if to give me strength. She turned around and walked away.

I wasn't sure I wanted to be left alone in that new country where there could be wild Indians, bears, cougars, and who knew what else. As sprinkles of rain hit the ground, I climbed up the giant cottonwood tree's protective branches and felt safer and drier. I leaned my back against one of the branches to rest. From that height, I had a good view of the valley below. I watched as the dark rain clouds were pushed by the wind toward the east, and the sun's rays filtered between cloud breaks.

I'm so glad, sister, you had the good sense to get in a tree. Who knows what was lurking in the nearby woods.

I decided to try some tricks to quiet my mind. I stared at the clouds floating by and decided they represented a change in my life. I looked at the blue sky between the clouds and felt sucked into the cosmos. My world became calm and quiet.

The large shimmering cottonwood leaves, mixtures of green, yellow and orange, sparkled sunlight that bounced into my body, scintillating my soul. The leaves had come alive, as had I. Marveling at the luminosity, I realized I was seeing nature in a new way. Bliss filled my body as I observed the dance of the leaves and tree limbs in the wind.

What was this? My body was disappearing. For me, time had stopped. I was becoming an empty vessel, watching and observing the world around me — the crows soaring on the breeze, the clouds changing shape in the sky, the meadow grass bending and swaying in the gusts of wind.

As my body began to take on substance again, I was curious as to how much time had passed. It seemed like a whole section of the day was missing since the sun had been high in the sky and was now inching toward the horizon.

At that moment, I heard something, or thought perhaps I sensed a presence — almost like breathing. A shiver ran through my body. The manifestation was so real, yet I could see nothing. I thought perhaps it was some kind of nature spirit or maybe the nearness of God. I could feel the essence in my bones, a movement like a subtle breeze on my skin. All the sounds of nature seemed muted. I felt a sudden chill.

As the horizon began to turn pink, the coyotes howled all around me. Were they singing for me, this intruder in their land? I tipped my head back and imitated their yelp. They seemed to become excited because I had joined them in their full chorus.

I heard some twigs break and looked beneath me. Carmen was walking toward my tree. She had her black shawl wrapped about her shoulders. She said, "I see you have made friends with our wild neighbors."

I noticed Carmen had a red shawl draped over her arm which she handed me. "Here, Angelica, put this on. I brought it from the house. You must be chilled."

I jumped down from the tree, hugged her, and turned her around and around. "I heard it, like you said. I not only heard it, I experienced it. There really is a spiritual presence in this land."

Carmen wrapped the shawl around my shoulders and we walked arm-in-arm back to the house, laughing.

Chapter Fifteen
My First Vision

The next day, I heard Reynard's wagons and the clopping of oxen hooves on the drive. The excited barking of a dog came from below Black Mountain, and I thought I heard the cawing of a raven. I ran as fast as I could to the porch and down the steps to where Reynard had begun to unload the wagons.

He had on a gray wool suit with a white shirt, gray vest and tie. His hat matched the suit and he had a feather tucked into the band. His dark brown hair was tied at the back of his neck.

When Reynard turned around and saw me, his eyes lit up. He came to where I stood, threw his arms around me, and hugged me for the longest time. "My darling," was all he said.

"Reynard, I missed you," I said.

A beautiful, dark haired young woman jumped down from one of the wagons. She looked a bit like Reynard.

Reynard introduced me, saying, "Juliette, my little niece, this is Angelica, the mysterious lady I told you I saved from the river."

Reynard turned to me, and said, "Angelica, I would like to introduce you to my niece, Juliette, who has been away at school in France with my two children. She has finished her schooling and has come home to be with the family."

Juliette said, "*Mademoiselle.*" She gave me a warm smile and bowed.

I curtsied, saying, "I'm glad to meet you."

Juliette and Carmen threw their arms around each other and giggled like schoolgirls. White Owl came over and the three of them hugged.

After Reynard embraced Carmen, he handed her five leather pouches, which looked like they had heavy coins in them the way they bulged. Carmen looked with approval at Reynard. "Good year for wine and those who appreciate it," she said.

Aunt Lila kissed Reynard on the cheek. "Welcome home, wanderer."

White Owl and Gabe shook Reynard's hand and unloaded the supplies from the wagons, then led the horses away to the barn.

After dinner, Reynard took me outside for a stroll. We ambled arm-in-arm to the garden on the far side of the house. As we walked through the arch, the moonlight shone on the tall white delphiniums and foxgloves.

Reynard picked a red rose that climbed on the garden trellis and handed it to me. I put it behind my right ear.

"During dinner, Carmen told me you have proceeded very well in your weaving and learning to meditate," Reynard said. "I think you are ready for the initiation."

My heart skipped a beat. An initiation? What in the world did he mean?

"Pack a few clothes and meet me by the bunkhouse at sunrise. We will be going on a camping trip. I'll see you early tomorrow, *ma belle.*"

He leaned over and kissed me on the lips, gave me a tight hug, then turned and walked toward the barn.

I ran upstairs, skipping steps, feeling excited about my next adventure. He's so used to giving orders on the rancho, he didn't ask if I wanted to go. He just assumed I did. Oh, well, I guess I'll see what this initiation is about.

I woke at the first sliver of light, and rushed downstairs with a bag Carmen had given me. Reynard was in front of the barn saddling a beige horse with a dark brown mane. "This will be your horse from now on. Her name is Honey."

After we were all packed up, we rode side-by-side through the acres of vineyards, apple and walnut orchards, and grassy fields where the sheep grazed.

Reynard's dog, Jack, ran behind us. I noticed the large, shiny black crow followed us wherever we went. Reynard explained, "That's Vasco. He is quite smart. So is Jack."

"George already properly introduced me to Jack and Vasco."

As if in response, Jack barked as Vasco flew over our heads. We both looked at each other and laughed.

After an hour's ride, I noticed two small mountain peaks side-by-side on the horizon. Reynard led our horses toward a small cleavage between the peaks covered with trees and thick underbrush. As our horses climbed closer, Reynard said, "This is the private hideaway I wanted to show you."

"It's gorgeous," I said.

Reynard jumped off Red, and helped me down from Honey. He tied our horses to some brush, and I followed him up the hill. He motioned for me to sit down.

Jack ran down the hill chasing a rabbit. Vasco cawed and flew off. Reynard said, "Jack and Vasco like to be out in the open to have their own adventures. They'll be back."

He sat beside me and said, "Two of my Indian friends will be joining us soon for your initiation." He held my hand as we waited.

Wow, people will be watching us? I don't know if I want anyone else but Reynard to be present when he does some strange ceremony. I hope I don't feel self-conscious.

I said, "You know, I'm nervous about this initiation. I don't know if I'm up to it or not."

I squirmed in discomfort while Reynard relaxed and stretched his legs. He leaned against a rock, and said, "Oh, I can tell you are a natural. Anyway, you can stop anytime you want. You only have to say so. There is really nothing to be afraid of as long as you stay centered."

He continued with a big smile on his face. "I want you to know that I only bring my blood brothers here, and people I have saved from death. This is the Mother Mountain. . .and I come to sit between her two breasts, and she nourishes me. Sometimes I meditate here when I need inspiration."

"I can understand your love for this place. Sitting here feels holy, somehow, like this ground is bringing forth a soothing vibration. Even though I'm nervous, the energy seems to be relaxing me. While we wait here, please tell me more about your life."

"After my wife died, I was devastated and took to the mountains. I would sit on the sloping sides to be alone, and yell and cry out for hours."

"Oh," I said. "You must have felt wretched."

"Yes, I did. An old medicine man, Mountain Screamer, came to my rescue and taught me some of the Indian mysteries to help me heal. I'll tell you more about that someday, but for now we'll focus on your learning."

As I listened to Reynard, my body started to tremble. My excitement mounted over being able to hear his story. I kept silent so he would continue speaking.

"Mountain Screamer told me that because I am the nephew of the man who kidnapped his father's people, our family carries a curse. Someday a woman would come to me from water and help me cure this curse. The legend told more, but he said I wasn't ready to hear it."

"Oh, Reynard. A family curse. This is ominous."

"Angelica, there are many mysteries in life few people are aware of, and because my Indian friends live in close touch with Mother Earth, they have learned these secrets and pass them down through generations."

I smiled and nodded my head, knowing I was the woman who came to him from the water. What he was telling me confirmed what Carmen had alluded to.

He continued. "When I pulled you out of the river, I knew you were the woman in Mountain Screamer's vision. You were so different from anyone I had ever met."

"Reynard." I sighed. "Much of the work I did at the university was dedicated to learning about the spiritual life of the Northern California Native

Americans. Despite my attempts to contact them, they were reluctant to teach me their rituals because I was not one of them. In my years of research, I felt frustrated in being excluded."

Reynard put his arm around me and gave my shoulder a squeeze. He said, "From what you tell me, you have been preparing for these lessons your entire life. You are so ready it wouldn't surprise me if you end up having a vision. Today my friends and I will drum for you. While you listen, I want you to quiet your mind and focus on God hidden away in your soul. Tomorrow, when you feel calm and ready, we'll do a ceremony where you will create an intention to visualize an animal who will become your totem or protector."

I couldn't believe what Reynard had just said. Maybe at last my dreams would be fulfilled. I smiled at Reynard and said, "I'm your willing student."

Just like you, Angelica, to go hook, line, and sinker for anything revolving around Indian mythology.

Two Indian men came as Reynard said they would. Instead of breaking up our private talk, they built a fire lower down the mountainside in a small meadow, and sat and drummed.

Reynard brought a wool blanket from my saddle bag and told me to lie down. He said, "I am going to build you a nice fire next to your bedding, and then I will leave you here for the night. I will go down the hill and drum with the other men. Please try to quiet your mind. Listen to the sound of the drums, and see what happens."

"I laid on my back and watched Reynard build the fire. When he was finished, he leaned down, kissed me, and then left. As soon as he was gone, I missed his presence, but at the same time I felt exhilarated at the chance to experience this initiation.

The sun disappeared over the horizon, and a cool breeze blew. I watched the tree branches sway. The coyotes started to yowl in the distant valley, first one, then more until they had a chorus. I noticed the pinkness of the clouds, turning to purple. I closed my eyes and listened to the drumming that no longer sounded outside of me. Was it my own heartbeat? I fell asleep on the mountain feeling safe below the starry canopy.

In the morning, I awoke to a fringe of orange on the horizon. I saw Reynard sitting cross-legged by my fire which he stoked with a stick.

"Good morning, *mon amour*," he said in a gentle voice. He put his hands on my shoulders, and kissed my forehead. "Are you ready for a day of learning?"

I nodded in response. He leaned toward the fire where he'd placed a black pot from which he poured coffee into a blue metal cup for me. "This will get you started. Here, try some of the day-old biscuits my sister baked, and some honey."

I threw off the wool blanket and sat up. Honey oozed down my fingers when I took the biscuit. As I licked my fingers, I noticed the two Indians were gone.

Reynard followed my gaze. "They will be back after they have done a little hunting for dinner tonight. Perhaps we will have some rabbit stew with the potatoes, carrots, and onions Aunt Lila insisted I carry. I wanted you to know, Angelica, that this initiation might get intense, but you can stop anytime you say. Are you sure you want to continue?"

"Yes. Yes, I do. I want to experience this ceremony or whatever it is." My hands felt shaky and my forehead damp from perspiration.

I followed Reynard up a rocky outcropping at the top of a ridge. I sat on the edge and dangled my feet. I started humming a tune.

Reynard said, "For today I will leave you here alone. You are to quiet your mind. It's like focusing and unfocusing your eyes. When you are thinking a thought, let it go. If you have thoughts of your past or worries about the future that you haven't resolved, go ahead and think about them, but you must reach closure on them soon or you won't be able to go on. Remember, there is no reality but this moment. If you spend much time in either the past or future, you will not have the energy for the present."

How can I stop thinking about the past because it's so much a part of me? I do miss my sister and my work, but this is so fascinating. I know I can focus, if I try.

Reynard went on. "Getting closure will be your most important task. You will be able to tell that closure is becoming final when you are able to quiet your mind and have no thoughts. You will be totally aware of your surroundings, and they will become very sharp and clear in your mind. I will leave you here to contemplate the wind and the sunlight playing on the leaves. Before it gets dark, I will return."

"I'm so excited," I said.

Reynard kissed me on each cheek, and said, "I'll miss you."

I reached out my hand to him. He squeezed it, and left.

I spent the morning letting go of my thoughts about my husband, Lawrence, and for once feeling at peace with his death. I released my past, and my job — knowing that I was going to make new discoveries that I never would have made at the university. I began to realize I was becoming liberated from my sister. I could have my own adventures, and no longer needed to rely on her for emotional support. I began to feel empty, but vibrant and whole.

As the afternoon approached, a soft breeze touched my hair. That's when I felt the presence of something. I began to see an image of an amorphous shape being formed. I was curious and looked harder at what I sensed. At that moment, I realized I could make out the breast of a hawk, so close I could feel her warmth and see the rhythm of her heart beating through her feathers. As I concentrated on the outline of the hawk's ribs and sternum, my focus changed to her wings as they spread out against the sky. A light shone on her feathers and the beauty of the pattern held me in awe. My view changed to the soft look of downiness on the hawk's legs and then the contrast of her sharp talons pulled up underneath her body. The last thing I saw was one of the hawk's eyes, which seemed to fill the entire blue sky. That large orb was unblinking and all knowing and all seeing. I was held in the hypnotic stare of her golden iris pulling me deeper into the dark pupil of her eye.

The wind ruffled my hair again and I opened my eyes. I knew I had had my first vision. What it meant, I didn't know, but I was thrilled.

The sun was starting to go down. Still alone, I heard a coyote yelping somewhere in the meadow. I wasn't sure if I should be afraid, but the sound filled me with excitement, nothing like I had ever experienced living in a city.

I walked toward the fire I saw burning at the bottom of the mountain. The two Indian men and Reynard were talking while Reynard stirred a pot that sat on some coals. The contents smelled marvelous.

Reynard turned toward me and said, "Angelica, I can tell something wonderful happened by your expression. Let's not talk about it for a while, so you'll have time to let it be absorbed. Sit down beside me and enjoy this stew we made from fresh rabbit and Aunt Lila's vegetables."

"It smells so good. I'm famished," I said.

"I am glad you have a good appetite. We have plenty of food. By the way, we have company for dinner. These two men are my teachers. This one is my brother-in-law, White Owl, who you already met at the house. And this other one is Mountain Screamer, who is a medicine man and my guide."

The two men nodded at me and grunted.

After dinner, we bunked down in wool blankets and formed a circle around the blazing fire. Jack curled up beside Reynard, and Vasco sat in the branch of a nearby oak tree.

Before I fell asleep, I leaned toward Reynard and told him about the close-up image I had of the hawk, and of the eye.

"The eye was the eye of the Great Spirit and you were caught up in letting go and flying with the spirit. This is a very good sign."

The two Indian men overheard us speaking, and I could see them nod their heads through the flickering firelight. I smiled and nodded back.

Chapter Sixteen
Finding an Animal Totem

The next morning, Reynard handed me some biscuits and dried fruit. He then poured coffee from a black pot which had been warming over the fire. The two men were gone and had taken Jack and Vasco with them. We were alone.

Reynard spoke between bites. "Today we will climb up Jagged Mountain. There is a wonderful view from the top you will appreciate. You can see the whole valley from there and the winding river."

"It sounds breathtaking and strenuous. I just hope I'm in shape to climb today."

"You look strong enough to make it to the top before I do," Reynard said.

After we put dirt on the camp fire embers, we broke camp. Reynard and I rode the horses up the gradual slope of a hill. When it got steep, we dismounted and tied Red and Honey to a tree.

I followed Reynard as he started hiking. I pushed myself beyond what I thought I could do. My heart raced and my breath came fast and heavy. I stopped for a break. As an excuse, I pointed out the purple mountain asters and orange poppies scattered along the way.

When we started again, I seemed to have gotten a second wind. I was happy when Reynard stopped at a meadow fringed with pine trees. He told me to lie down in the grass and then joined me.

There he goes again, bossing me. He's sure good with the orders, but I realized I didn't really mind that much.

Reynard told me his Indian friends often took on an Indian totem, or animal to assist them in their spiritual path. As he pulled out a red gourd rattle from his pack, he told me I was to find my animal spirit through meditation. I was to focus and see if the animal spirit had any messages for me. He then started shaking the rattle.

I wondered what animal would come to me. My mind became quiet and I observed that my heart beat in time with the rattle. I relaxed into the rhythm and forced myself to focus.

After a while, an image of a red-tailed hawk scooped me up with her beak, and tossed me on her back. As we rose into the sky, exhilaration filled my body. I became one with the hawk. The cool mountain air felt soft on my skin and I could smell the fragrance of the pines.

I began sprouting feathers. Only my face was human-like, framed now by downy feathers. I rose high above the two mountains and swooped down at an accelerated rate toward a rattlesnake that was sunning itself on a rock. I seized the rattlesnake in my beak.

A gray fox sat on the ground below and I dropped the snake at his paws. I flew down and together we ate the snake in a communal dinner. My beak tore into the fleshy skin and I shook my head until I had a bloody piece of meat in my beak. I held my head back and let the meat fall down my throat. The trickling blood felt warm and nourishing. I began screeching and flapping my wings. The fox growled. His teeth ripped the soft belly of the snake. Now the she-hawk came to me, opened her wings, and wrapped them around me. I came back to my body, sitting on the mountain top next to Reynard.

When I became centered in my body again, I looked around and saw the rattlers from a snake sitting on the grass in front of me. Reynard picked up the snake rattlers, threaded them through a leather strap, and tied them around my neck. "Very good, my red-tailed hawk," he said.

I felt a mixture of surprise and expectancy. What just happened to me? Was it real?

Oh, my God. You are actually experiencing shape-shifting. You've always been fascinated with the concept. I'll bet you're thrilled.

I looked up and saw Mountain Screamer sitting on a boulder at the edge of the meadow. He jumped down and walked over. He put his hand out and touched the rattler necklace I wore, examining it. Then he touched the top of my head and spoke with great conviction.

"Someday you will be called upon to save not only Reynard, but some of his women relatives, and your own unborn child's life. Feel the strength of the winged ones and remember this day. I have spoken."

After making his pronouncement, Mountain Screamer walked down the mountainside and disappeared into the thick pines.

I was overcome with emotion. I just had a vision, and Mountain Screamer gave me a prophesy. Was he intuitive? How did he know those things? Should I believe him? By God, what did he mean I would save my unborn child's life? I'm not even married.

Early the next morning, I awoke to Mountain Screamer shaking rattles over my body, and then my head. Reynard was gone, and his sleeping blanket was rolled up and placed by a nearby cottonwood tree. I laid still as Mountain Screamer finished rattling above my feet, then put the rattles down in the long grass. I felt shocked that he was here in place of Reynard.

"Good morning, Mountain Screamer," I said as I sat up.

He nodded his head in response.

I wondered why I was being left alone with this medicine man? It's obvious that Reynard trusts him, so I guess I should try to remain calm. This whole situation felt pretty unnerving.

The royal blue sky was starting to brighten as orange colors appeared at the edges of the horizon. Mountain Screamer and I sat in silence and watched nature's majestic show.

When the sun had risen, he sat across from me and spoke. "I have learned from the last of the medicine people. There are few of us left." He seemed lost in thought for a moment, and then continued. "I will share some of this knowledge with you since you are Angelica, the one I saw in my vision, the one who was to come to us through water and a distant time."

Wow. I was definitely the one in Mountain Screamer's vision. I hope he tells me what else he saw. . .or maybe I don't want to know.

Mountain Screamer went on. "Medicine people receive their personal power through prayer, ritual, and vision questing. You'll need to develop your personal power, since you have a strong enemy."

Oh, no. I have an enemy? Why, I don't know that many people here, and the ones I know have been friendly with me. Is he calling me a medicine person? What did I do to deserve all this attention?

All I could say was, "Mountain Screamer, I'm ready to learn."

"First, you must purify yourself to become a fit vessel for the Above Beings to consider worthy. You're to call the power down for your own service and the service of your relatives and friends. You can gain the power to heal, to teach, and to prophesize. When you receive these abilities, you must give the Above Beings all the credit or your power will close up."

I wondered how I'd purify myself? Do I take a hot bath? Okay, I can gain great powers if I listen to this guy and follow his instructions.

With a stick, Mountain Screamer drew a picture in the dust. He pointed to his drawing of a person who was represented by an empty tube. Mountain Screamer made scratches toward the tube. He explained that the cleaned vessel was being filled with power. Then he made marks going out of the tube, which he said was giving power to others.

Mountain Screamer handed me a buckskin package, and when I opened it, I saw it contained a tiny purse with a drawstring. I looked inside and found some dried sage leaves.

"You can purify yourself by burning this sage before beginning a ritual. Move the smoke in the four directions and then over your head. It will help to cleanse your past, and to allow your mind to become quiet. By this emptying of thoughts, you'll become filled with Spirit and Spirit's power. I have spoken."

Mountain Screamer got up. As he walked away, I said, "Thank you. I will remember your words."

Boy, this shaman can really be abrupt sometimes. He didn't even say goodbye. I guess he answered the things I was wondering about.

After Mountain Screamer left, I sat and thought about what I had experienced the past few days. I'd learned to quiet my mind. I'd had my first vision. I discovered my power animal, the hawk, and perhaps had become the hawk herself. I felt excited that Mountain Screamer and Reynard were willing to share their mystical wisdom with me. Somehow I felt I was only beginning to learn.

Toward evening, Reynard walked into camp. He smiled and said, "Do you realize you have become a shape-shifter? You changed from a human form to one of a hawk. I, too, am a shape-shifter, but I often turn into the form of a gray fox, as you now know. If you have any doubts that you changed shapes, look at the rattler tail necklace."

I pulled the necklace from around my neck, and held it in my hand. It was solid — real. Yet, doubts still crept into my mind. Shape-shifting was something I'd heard that shamans and medicine men did. I always thought it was just hocus pocus mythology. Now, I had done this impossible thing. I let go of the necklace and put my hands over my face. What is happening to me?

Reynard put his arm around me. "I know it is hard to take it all in, this amazing thing. You realize very few people ever experience it. It just shows what power you have."

"But," I said, "I'm not a shaman. I guess being initiated by you and Mountain Screamer, and being in this magical place, gave me the ability. I'm in awe."

"We have done enough for this week," Reynard said. "We must get back to the rancho in the morning. I have work to oversee. Just remember, try to incorporate some of your lessons into everyday life. Spirit is no good if you keep it separate."

I sat in the meadow chewing on a piece of sweet grass. I felt mischievous and said, "Perhaps we can conjure up a little spirit here and now, just the two of us."

Reynard gave me an enthusiastic smile, and kissed me. His kiss was sweet and moist, and warmed my soul.

The day had ended as the full moon rose above the clouds sending beams upon us. My spirit soared with happiness to be with this man, and the fulfillment of my life-long dream of learning some shamanic secrets. I was filled with the magic of the moment.

I looked at Reynard, and I caught a glimpse of the sharpness of his nose. Right before me his face changed to that of a gray fox. Maybe this was the moonlight playing tricks on me. I blinked and looked again but Reynard's face had changed back.

Chapter Seventeen
The Village

few days after I had returned from my initiation, Carmen invited me to ride with her into the nearby village to buy supplies. She said White Owl and Juliette would accompany us.

Reynard hitched the wagon to his two largest horses whose thighs were as wide as tree trunks. He said, "*Ma chérie* , I can't go with you today. I've got too much work to catch up on. Go ahead and enjoy yourself."

I stood, patting the horses' noses and feeding them carrots. I said, "I'll go with them, but I'll miss you."

I climbed onto the seat of the wagon. It seemed strange not taking a car or truck. This place was so unhurried, earthy, and timeless, like a dream of years passed.

On the way to town, White Owl offered to let me drive. I took the reins from him and felt myself relax. I felt at peace with the easy trot, and slow-paced life.

We passed meadows filled with tall grass waving in the breeze, and hillsides filled with stately oaks. Sheep grazed along the trail.

When we arrived at the village, a sign read *Ensueño*. I said, "Doesn't that mean daydream or fantasy in Spanish?"

Carmen nodded her head and smiled.

White Owl tied the horses to a hitching post in front of a small adobe hardware store, and went in to buy some supplies. As Carmen, Juliette, and I walked down the board-planked sidewalk, I saw a sign posted on a wall. I stopped to read the advertisement about a traveling priest coming to town.

Carmen read over my shoulder and then said, "Would you like to take mass at the rancho? The traveling priests usually come through this area a couple times a year. So few people live here, there aren't enough of us to start a church. The closest one is south of here in Sonoma which is the old Mission San Francisco Solano. I'll sign our name to this poster, and the priest will be at our place within a week or so. I know our family and rancho hands will want to attend."

I nodded at Carmen, and wondered what a mass would be like in this century, long before the Ecumenical Council met in the 1960s to modernize the church.

Carmen continued. "I'm very curious about Father Jean, this new priest. He comes from France and is college educated and I understand, very idealistic. Reynard tells me they were schoolmates years ago at a university in Paris."

"He does sound interesting. I'd enjoy meeting him," I said.

Juliette responded that she'd like to attend mass, and excused herself saying she was going to look for some of her old friends, so she could tell them about her adventures in France. She then strolled over to a group of young men and women. Some of the women hugged her, and started an animated conversation.

Carmen smiled and told me she was pleased Juliette was so popular with her friends.

I said, "You must be very proud of your daughter. She's quite the lady."

Carmen nodded, took my arm, and guided me to a store. I followed her into the backroom filled with sacks of wool of all types. Occupying the space were looms, spindles, spinning wheels, and spools of various colored threads. Carmen went to a shelf and picked up some white cotton webbing.

"This," she said, "is the warp thread. I'm going to use it to teach you to weave. I feel you're ready for some complex patterns now. White Owl said he'd buy the wood today so Reynard can build you a loom." Carmen told me how important the weaving tradition was for their family. Weaving required dreaming —dreaming of patterns — like patterns I would like in my life.

"Carmen," I said, "what I would love to do is weave a shawl like you do on the triangular loom. I admire your unique patterns and variety of bright colors. Would you teach me how to do that, too?"

"Sure, Angelica. As a matter of fact, I was going to trade some shawls for the supplies we are getting today. The storekeeper told me they are popular with the local women."

Carmen picked out some weaving supplies, such as threading hooks, and reeds. The two of us also picked out some colorful cotton bolts of cloth from which to make shirts and dresses. After Carmen traded the shawls, we went outside and found White Owl waiting for us in the wagon, which was loaded with sacks of flour, coffee, and beans. I saw the wood sticking out from under one of the burlap sacks and felt excited about my new project.

Carmen and I found Juliette in the same spot where we left her. When Carmen signaled for her to come, she waved goodbye to her friends, and came toward us.

"Juliette, come pick out some weaving supplies."

"Mother, please. I'm sick to death of weaving. That might be the way you express yourself artistically, but my way is by oil painting. Let me get some oils, a few canvases and brushes to keep me busy for a while."

Carmen grabbed Juliette by the arm and pulled her away from the wagon, and her waiting father. "I told you. Your father wants you to learn weaving, not useless painting, or reading of poetry and those stylish French novels. If you must get some paints, hurry up, but hide them in your skirts so your father won't see. Here are a few coins."

Juliette took the coins and then grabbed my hand. "Come with me, Auntie Angelica," she insisted as she took off in a rush.

Before I followed her, I overheard Carmen tell White Owl he needed to have the horse's shoes checked at the blacksmith before leaving town.

When I caught up to Juliette, she said to me, "My father thinks art and literature are a waste of time. He grew up barely literate, learning only enough numbers and reading to be able to assist with management of the winery and rancho. He thinks women should stick to cooking and weaving, and I should learn some of the Indian ways. When my Uncle Reynard insisted I go to school in France to watch over his two children, my father relented and allowed me to go. Otherwise, I never would've been permitted such an education."

I looked at Juliette as we walked toward Sam's General Store. I said, "My dear, there are fascinating things about any culture, French, Mexican, Indian. Don't devalue your own. Divergent backgrounds will be highly regarded some day, take my word for it. In the meantime, I'll buy some canvas and paints for myself so I can paint with you. I, too, love literature and poetry, so would appreciate it if you'd loan me some of your books."

Juliette beamed at this comment as we entered the store.

When we had made our purchases and left the store, we passed a tall, dark and robust, middle-aged man, whom I recognized as Cousin Joseph. He had on a fashionable tall hat, and his black beard was well manicured. His thick dark eyebrows, which almost met in the middle, were what set him apart from other men. Below those eyebrows were the wildest dark brown eyes I'd ever seen. He had a square jaw and a wide nose, pronounced cheekbones, and thick lips. Despite his wild appearance, he had a handsome, intelligent face. He walked with an air of confidence, or I might call it arrogance.

The last time I had seen Joseph was at the Fall Festival. He had insisted on dancing with me when Reynard intervened and whisked me away to the dance floor.

Cousin Joseph gave me and Juliette a lecherous stare. His look made me feel like I was naked standing on the public street. He walked over to us and said to Juliette, "Ah, my niece. I barely recognized you all grown up. It's been a long time. Perhaps I will come and pay you a visit."

Carmen, who was standing outside the store waiting for us, overheard him and said, "You aren't welcome, Joseph. Don't you dare come to our home or near Angelica or my Juliette."

Cousin Joseph ignored Carmen and looked at me saying, "How wonderful meeting you again, my dear, and I look forward to getting to know you better. As for my gentle niece, I must not neglect my duties as an uncle." He smiled at Juliette. She seemed to like the attention, and gave him a shy smile in return.

Joseph took my hand, held it to his lips and then bowed. "Ah, Angelica, I remember our meeting at the Fall Festival. Yes, perhaps I shall get that dance someday after all."

He turned, took Juliette's hand, while sizing her up. She turned crimson and giggled. Joseph clicked his heels and walked away.

I felt fearful of that man. He seemed disgusting to me, although somehow charming.

Oh, Angelica. This sounds to me like someone you need to be leery of. He sounds dangerous and could do you and Reynard's family some harm. Beware.

Out of curiosity, I asked Carmen, "Why won't you let Joseph come visit? After all, he is family, isn't he?"

"Yes," Juliette said, "I'd like to get to know my uncle better."

Carmen said, "Just get in the wagon. We must get out of town, now." Carmen seemed angry and fidgety all the way home.

Chapter Eighteen
The Family Curse

The day after our excursion into town, Reynard told me he was going to put the loom together. I walked with him to the barn and peeked in his workshop where he had hammers, saws, awls, and a variety of other tools. Along the wall was a narrow table filled with wood shavings some of which had fallen onto the floor. The aroma of fragrant wood filled the room.

"I'll leave you to your work," I said. "I'll be on the porch reading. I can't wait to see your finished product."

"I'll be as quick as I can, so you don't get all stirred up waiting. I promise I'll bring it to you in a few hours."

True to his word, after three hours, Reynard climbed the porch steps carrying the triangular loom. He was beaming in anticipation of my response. I ran to him and kissed his cheek. "What a marvelous job you did. Thank you so much."

Reynard bowed, and replied, "My pleasure, *ma chérie*. I'd stay and watch you work, but right now I have to oversee the picking of the walnut crop. I'll see you later tonight."

When Reynard left, Juliette and I sat on the wicker chairs waiting for Carmen who was busy getting the weaving materials together. "Tell me about Reynard's children," I said.

"Rebecca and Jason are adjusting quite well to school in France, since they, too, could speak French before they left the rancho. Their father saw to that. They'll be coming back in another year."

"You'll have to teach me some French, Juliette. I studied Spanish in school."

"Sure, I'd enjoy that. I'm so glad you have come to the rancho, Angelica. You make Reynard very happy. I know God has brought you to us."

"Thank you, Juliette. I'm pleased the family has given me such a warm welcome."

Carmen came out on the porch carrying spools of yarn. She told me she wanted to begin her lessons on weaving. "As a treat, I'll lace my discussion with some of the local tales," she said.

Juliette sat in the sunshine reading her book of poetry while Carmen began to talk with me. "I want to tell you about the family legend, so that you can better understand Reynard and Joseph. As you probably know, Joseph is our cousin. Joseph's father, Uncle Maximillian, who is deceased now, had an adjoining rancho."

Juliette put her book down and said to me, "Joseph owns that rancho, now."

Carmen continued. "When our family first arrived, some of the neighboring people took advantage of the Indians, and saw them as free labor. They didn't see them as people, only work horses. Some of the ranchers in this area rounded up many of the Indian people and imprisoned them. They forced the Indians to work on the ranches and farms."

"That's horrible," I said. "Why, that's slavery."

Carmen took my triangular loom and started my weaving for me. The yarn I'd prepared sat in a basket next to Carmen. I'd decided on a solid green for my first project. When the loom was set up, she indicated I should start weaving, and then she continued her story.

"It seemed to be the general consensus of the townspeople, and the people of California, that Indians were less than human and therefore if someone wanted to enslave them, it was nobody's business. Even most clergy didn't say anything about the atrocity. They preached that the Indians were heathens and didn't believe in God, and therefore were of the devil."

"It was so closed-minded of them to think that way," I said.

"Even our Uncle Maximillian kidnapped Indian families and made the native peoples work his land against their will. While the chief was away with a hunting party, Uncle Maximillian killed the Indian chief's wife in the process of taking her children. When the chief, Lone Coyote, came back and found out what had happened, he put a curse on our entire family."

"What was the curse," I asked.

"Lone Coyote swore as long as his people were enslaved by our family members, it would come to pass that each of the wives would bear a daughter and then a son. In the process of birthing a son, the wife would die. When Lone Coyote finished his curse, he disappeared."

"Wow, so that's why George's wife, and Reynard's wife died in childbirth. Now I'm beginning to understand. Is there more to the story?"

"After that, my father, George, went to his brother-in-law, Maximillian, and asked him to give up keeping Indians as slaves. Maximillian called him a fool. My father believed the taking of slaves was a bad thing. He had never done it himself. Instead, he paid his Indian helpers with food and wages, and helped them set up their huts and adobe houses on his property. My father felt helpless to do anything about Maximillian's Indians since he had promised his wife to never use violence on her brother in the process of freeing the Indians."

I said, "Does this mean he never made an attempt to free Maximillian's Indian slaves?"

"George could never come up with a plan that didn't involve a shotgun and a knife. So, no, he never made an attempt. After that, my mother gave birth to me, and my father tried to stay away from her for fear she would become pregnant again. One harvest season, because of the exuberant celebrations, my father forgot to be cautious. My mother became pregnant with Reynard, and this time my father felt very worried. He went to Maximillian and begged him to let the native slaves go, but Maximillian told him to leave. Sure to the curse, my mother died giving birth to Reynard. My father's spirit died that day."

"That's awful Reynard never got to know his mom."

"I barely remember her myself. After that, George was distraught, so he asked Aunt Lila to watch over me and Reynard. Then he went to the woods and tried to heal, and was gone a long time. My Aunt Lila stayed with us and took care of us. She had married one of the Mexican men who'd helped run our rancho. She and her husband were never able to have children, so they were happy to look after us."

"That's great that Aunt Lila was so accommodating," I said.

"She is wonderful that way. She's very nurturing. Well, one day, my father returned, and no one recognized him. He was dressed like an Indian and had his hair in braids, and feathers hung down one side of his head. We were afraid of that wild man."

"Wow, it's hard to imagine George that way," I said.

"I agree." Carmen laughed. "When my father returned, he had several Indians with him. He asked them to work in exchange for horses and supplies."

"That seems fair."

"Yes, it was. My father learned the Indian customs and language and was learning to become a medicine man. He taught us a few things, but my brother, Reynard, was the most taken with the Indian culture. My brother learned to hunt in the Indian way, to track, fish, and ride bareback. He would take sweats with my father and the natives on the property."

"So, that's how Reynard knows so much about Indian customs and mythology."

"He learned a lot from my father and the local medicine man. When Reynard was grown, Father sent him to France to go to college to learn the latest farming techniques on growing various crops, and caring for our vineyards. When my brother returned from France, he brought his sweetheart, Suzette with him."

"What was she like," I asked.

Carmen responded, "She was very sweet and shy, and very smitten with Reynard. Suzette was quite young when she married Reynard, and she became pregnant almost right away. She was always a little frail. I'll never forget when she told Reynard she was pregnant, he turned crimson and ran outside. Our father had convinced Reynard he needed to prepare himself for the worst because of the family curse, and the fact that she was expecting twins."

"Oh, I see. So the curse accelerates when there are twins."

"Yes, and Reynard knew that so he went to our Uncle Maximillian's rancho and met with Cousin Joseph, whose father had poisoned his mind against Reynard. Joseph refused to let him enter the property to talk to Maximillian. Joseph said the curse was just superstition."

"So, that's why you don't like Cousin Joseph. Now I understand. Tell me what happened to Suzette."

"She had a long and difficult birth. The midwife could do nothing to soothe her. A girl and a boy were born. Suzette only lasted through the night, dying in Reynard's arms."

"Oh, it tears my heart out just thinking about it," I said.

"Yes, it really affected Reynard. He ended up doing the same thing his father did. He fled to the mountains for consolation. Before he left, he asked Aunt Lila and me to look after the two babies."

"Thank goodness for Aunt Lila. She became the substitute mom for you and Reynard, and for Reynard's kids, too," I said.

"That's right. Some people think Reynard is crazy, like his father, because he has taken on the Indian ways. I think it has saved him. Both Reynard and my father are attuned to nature and all her ways, and the ways of the Great Spirit. They also know the European ways and the ways of business."

I had become so engrossed by the story Carmen told, my arms hung at my sides, my weaving forgotten, as I stared out at the vast sky.

Carmen broke my reverie. "We must stop weaving for the sun is getting too low in the sky to see well."

Chapter Nineteen
Juliette Has a Secret

After finishing breakfast, White Owl wiped his mouth on his cloth napkin. He said to Juliette who sat across from him, "I'm taking the wagon to the village today. Would you like to come along? You can see your friends or go shopping. Reynard and I have some business with the blacksmith and supplies to buy."

She looked up at White Owl, and said, "No, not this time. I promised Angelica we would go walking alongside the river. I want to show her all the favorite spots where I used to play when I was a child."

White Owl got up fast, pulled his hat off the peg by the door, and snapped a response to Juliette. "Well, have your way then. We men have business to tend to."

Eyeing Reynard, he said, "We've got to be on our way if we intend on getting all our errands done before evening."

"Give me a minute," Reynard said. "I have something important to do before I leave."

Reynard walked toward me and gave me an impassioned kiss. He whispered, "Wait for me tonight, *ma petite*." He winked, turned on his heels, and walked out the door behind White Owl.

Juliette finished her toast and then put her dishes on the kitchen counter. She grabbed my hand, and said, "Come exploring with me. I'll bring some charcoals and an easel for you."

Juliette tied an easel over her shoulder, and clutched a cloth bag holding her supplies. She handed me an easel, and off we went, arm-in-arm, down the path toward the river.

"I enjoy your company so much, Angelica. I feel like you're the only one I can open up to and speak freely about my love of painting and the arts. My family just wants me to do embroidery, weaving, spinning or cooking. . .all the womanly arts. I have only one passion now, and that is to paint my way into the great galleries of the world. Whenever I tell my father this, he gets angry and tells me I have dust in my head. He says a young woman should only aspire to a good marriage."

"There's no reason you can't be married and continue working on your passions," I said.

"I want to be married to my art. I don't want to sit home and be buried in domestic duties. I refuse to be burdened with having to ask my husband's permission every time I want to paint another picture or visit a gallery or read some poetry."

I laughed and said, "What did they fill your young head with in Paris?"

In a hushed tone, Juliette said, "I have been to the heavens and I want to share them with others through my canvases. I have seen the great art of the world in the museums. I have posed in all forms of undress for the greatest master the world has ever seen. I have observed and practiced with the most enchanting and bewitching teacher of the century in all the arts, including lovemaking."

"Juliette, I believe you've matured more than your parents know."

"Yes, I grew up very fast in France. Because of the attention I received, I was made to feel like a beautiful, desirable woman. The most delicate, yet strong hands posed me. I have had the audacity to be able to enjoy all these things to the fullest. My cup runneth over with its sweet wine."

Juliette pulled her blouse up just below her bosoms and then pulled down her skirt, exposing her expanding belly. A faint brown line ran from her belly button to her sternum.

"Juliette, what's going on here?"

"I have the greatest of all creativity, beyond man's workmanship and artistry. I'm not only an artist with my brushes and paints, but with my body. I'm forming a new man within my womb who has the destiny to carry the genes of one of the most gifted artists the world will ever know."

My mouth fell open, and my hand reached out to feel her round protruding belly. "You mean. . ."

"Yes, I'm pregnant and I'm not sure how to tell my family. I doubt they'll understand."

Angelica, your Juliette sounds like quite the rebel for her day and age. You're going to have to find a way to protect her and encourage her in her art. She may be quite the artist.

"Why didn't you marry the artist? Is the father the one you posed for in all states of undress?"

Juliette smiled. "Yes, we did marry, but then he died soon after. I loved my dear sweet man. He had faith in me like no other man I was ever with. He thought I had great potential in my art and taught me everything he could about mixing paints, brush strokes, preparing canvases, and techniques. He was one of the few artists who would go into the countryside and paint from nature. Most of the artists would sit in their stuffy studios and get the garish prostitutes to model for them, or have pictures of dying flowers and rotting fruit."

We set up our easels and began to sketch the sheep grazing in the meadow.

"Juliette, how did your husband interest you in painting?"

"My love and I would go to the cafes in the late afternoon after a day of painting, and sit and drink wine. Other painters would come in to share the camaraderie and talk about their newest work and techniques. Soon, people started talking about Chesan's paintings, and their fresh look. A group of painters began to follow him as he walked the paths of the surrounding mountains or beside the rivers to paint."

"That must have been very exciting to be involved in the society of Parisian artists."

"Yes. Since I'm half American Indian, I was considered very exotic by all his friends. They called me Little Deer. They would ask me to pose leaning against a tree, or gazing off into the mountains. I would oblige them at times, but mostly I wanted to paint, too. Some of the painters were very kind in their remarks about my beginning abilities." Juliette's eyes filled with tears. She placed her hands over her face and sobbed.

"I'm so sorry about your husband's death," I said. "Let me give you a hug."

I took Juliette in my arms so she could cry on my shoulder. I gave her a few moments to compose herself.

Juliette wiped her eyes, then straightened her skirt. She said, "That's all I can discuss right now. Just give me time to adjust to being here and my situation. I'll tell my parents in due time, but I have to ready myself first."

"Agreed," I said. "But remember I'm here to talk whenever you need me."

We packed our easels and supplies, and then walked in silence back to the house.

Chapter Twenty
Alone with Reynard

The following Sunday morning, Reynard invited me on a picnic. As I prepared for our trip, I filled a basket with crusty hard bread, sheep's milk feta cheese, grapes, walnuts, a bottle of Rancho de los Zorros Grises wine, and some glasses wrapped in white linen napkins. I put a red and gray woven blanket under my arm.

Reynard asked if there was a place in particular I would like to go. I said, "I'd been wanting to explore the knoll that I can see from the kitchen window. I really admire the view because of the majestic oaks, and orange and red leafed maple trees."

He nodded his head in agreement as he picked up the basket from the kitchen table.

Since the knoll was only about a mile, we decided to walk the short distance rather than ride horseback. When we got to the knoll, I choose an oak tree with the largest trunk under which to picnic. I placed my blanket next to the oak. We leaned our backs against the rough bark and relaxed as we gazed at the colorful maples down the hill.

I put some crusty bread sprinkled with feta cheese on a red-checkered cotton napkin and handed it to Reynard.

"In order to make this bread, Aunt Lila used the sourdough starter our family brought from San Francisco," Reynard said. "We've been able to keep it going ever since."

"It's magnificent," I said as I tasted it.

I continued emptying the picnic basket. I took out some walnuts which I'd placed in a linen bag tied with a cord, and then laid a bunch of grapes on the blanket. When I was finished, I said to Reynard, "You told me earlier that after your wife died, you left home and traveled to the mountains, and then met Mountain Screamer who taught you some Indian mysteries. Did that provide you with the healing you needed?"

The expression on Reynard's face grew serious. He took a deep breath before speaking. "Yes, eventually. When Suzette died, I was distraught. I didn't even want to continue living, but I knew I had to get myself straightened out. I had my children to raise. I was no good to anybody at the time, so I left them in the capable hands of my Aunt Lila, White Owl, and Carmen."

"Yes, Carmen told me. You're lucky to have such wonderful family support."

"Yes. I am very lucky."

Reynard opened the red wine, poured it into the two glasses he retrieved from the picnic basket and said, "*Santé,*" clicking my glass.

"*Santé,*" I responded.

I sipped my wine. He downed his and poured himself another.

As he swirled the wine around in the glass, he said, "The grief I had was like a huge black stone upon my chest, crushing me. I could barely breathe with the weight of the emotion. I felt as if my love had been surgically removed from me. Because of the children, I took the time and effort to heal."

"My poor, dear man," I said. "Thank goodness you persevered, even though it must have been difficult." I placed my hand over his and squeezed. Reynard moved my hand to his lips and gave it a gentle kiss, then reached over and took some cheese and ate it.

As I munched on the cheese and bread, Reynard continued. "Yes. It was difficult. When I went off to be alone, I hiked to Jagged Mountain. I had to climb hand-over-hand to reach the top, and at times I had great difficulty seeing because of the tears of sorrow that filled my eyes. My darling Suzette was gone from me. Nevermore would I see my love, my sweetness. How could I go on?"

I gulped my wine, and held out my glass for Reynard to refill it. Then I said, "Such agony. How horrible to have to go through that."

After pouring more wine for me, he went on to explain that he felt so much guilt because he had contributed to Suzette's death by making her pregnant with twins and by not eliminating the family curse.

I put more feta cheese on a piece of bread and took a bite. "That must have been quite a shock. Who would have thought that you and Suzette would have twins."

Reynard put his hand to his forehead and rubbed it as he said, "It seems that I, too, had followed in my father's footsteps, to allow the curse to continue. I had tried talking to my Uncle Maximillan, but he turned me away."

"Listen to me. It certainly wasn't your fault. There was nothing you could do," I said as I brushed bread crumbs from my lap.

Jumping up, he started pacing in front of the picnic blanket. "Nevertheless," he said. "I still carried the feeling of guilt. My agony over the loss and my stupidity seemed almost more than I could bear. I probably shouldn't tell you this, but when I was on the mountain, I let loose and started screaming. My screams came from my gut. Once I started, I didn't stop until I was empty. Thus, I was able to release the pain and guilt. I began to feel calm and separated from my body. . .as if I was floating."

I stood and took Reynard in my arms like he was a little boy. I hugged him as hard as I could, letting all my compassion and caring pour through me into his body. Mother Earth's love emanated from the dirt below my feet and up to my arms and hands. Those vibrations of love I directed to Reynard so that his healing would be complete.

His body felt tight at first, and then it began to relax allowing him to sob and quake. I continued holding him. When he stopped crying, I stood on my tiptoes and kissed his salty tears away. Reynard looked down at me, smiled, and gave me a soft kiss.

"You are a wonder, my dear," he said. "You are such a healing person. I could feel your love move through me in waves."

He took my hand and we walked down to the creek, and sat on boulders near the bank. With great gentleness Reynard pulled off my shoes, and then my stockings, rubbing the tops of my feet. I dipped my feet into the cold water. The movement of the current felt soothing. As the ripples ran over my toes, I could feel the magnetic pull of the surging water moving onward, seeking its final destination, the ocean. My mind drifted with the creek, not resisting, letting my life be guided by the fates. My intuition said yes, follow this new path.

Yes, I'm feeling that you were meant to live in that era, Alexis, or Angelica. It suits you well with your anthropology background and fascination with the old west and Indian mythology.

I looked over at Reynard who was oblivious to my dreaminess. He was busy taking off his own shoes and socks. He then rolled up his pant legs, and stood in the creek bed. I watched him wading into the water lifting one foot at a time from the chill.

I said, "I didn't realize you had such a childlike side to you."

"You didn't?" he said as he splashed me.

I squealed, and then splashed him back. He sat on a large rock, grabbed me, and pulled me over his lap, and gave me a couple of small whacks on the bottom.

"Reynard," I yelled. "Don't. No," and started giggling.

Reynard pulled me into his arms, then stood and twirled me around. "I love you," he said. "*Je t'aime,* Angelica."

"You are the dearest man."

Reynard grabbed me and tilted me backwards, kissing me hard. He pulled me back up, and said, "I hope I don't scare you with my passion. You overwhelm me so with your marvelous ways."

"No. No. I enjoy your romantic impulses. Now, please, go on with your story."

Chapter Twenty-One
Reynard's Vision

Reynard leaned back on a boulder and folded his arms. "Let's see. Now, where was I?"

I said, "When you were in the mountains, you were feeling a release and a calmness after letting your grief out."

"Yes. At that point I saw a hawk sailing on the wind currents. He seemed to be watching me. I realized the hawk would be seeing a man who was feeling sorry for himself. I knew if I wanted to be alive again, I had to let go of the past and my life with Suzette. I knew I had to make a change, so I sat down and began to sing to the hawk. When I heard the sound bounce back from the canyon, it sounded powerful and robust. I sang songs to the sun and wind and blue sky. Before long, my songs became joyous. . .songs of thanksgiving for what blessings I had been given. I realized how Mother Nature had always nourished me like my father and Aunt Lila did when I was little. At that point, I knew I was ready to go back and nurture my children."

I leaned over to Reynard and kissed his cheek and said, "Reynard, I'm so glad you were able to experience a healing of your spirit."

"Yes, Angelica. So am I. When I was coming down the mountain to see my family, I noticed a white-haired Indian man sitting cross-legged. He told me he had been waiting for my arrival and requested I sit with him."

"Oh," I said. "That must have been Mountain Screamer, the medicine man who helped you and your father. That's why he came to my initiation."

"That's right. Mountain Screamer told me he was named after the mountain lion. The name also came to him because of his screaming right after his people were taken into slavery. He said he was there to help me heal, and that we had much spirit work to do. He knew I was wondering why this curse was put on me and my father. He was right because I was thinking my uncle and cousin were the only ones responsible."'

Reynard got up, walked over to the grass and sat down. I joined him, putting my arms around him. "I don't think your family should be held accountable for your relative's misdeeds."

"I was feeling the same, Angelica, but Mountain Screamer helped me understand why I was affected, too. He told me that while meditating in the mountains, he became aware of the unity of man. . .that no man is truly an individual but a community. When a single person is ill, or afflicted with an evil heart, he is showing the weakest link in the family. Our lives are interrelated. When the wind blows, a blade of grass and the very foundations of the stars are shaken."

"Wow, this medicine man is amazing."

"He is." Reynard nodded. "Then Mountain Screamer went on to say we are a part of the whole. . .past, present, future, and all of humanity. The lines of existence crisscross. If we want to take it a step further, the universe includes the animals, wind, sky, and earth. We belong to all these, too, only in a different form. We are an ocean of consciousness."

"This all makes sense, doesn't it?"

"It does." Reynard gave me a squeeze. "After Mountain Screamer's talk, he started singing. The song made tears flow from my eyes as I listened to its beauty. He was singing his gratefulness to his spirit maker."

"I've heard Mountain Screamer sing before, and he has a gorgeous voice," I said.

"Come, Angelica. See where this old oak tree splits? There is a big branch on either side. I'm going to climb up, and I want you to follow me."

Reynard picked up the walnut bag and tied the cord to his belt, then lunged up into the tree. He sat on the branch and reached his strong hand down for me. He pulled me up, and I sat on a thick limb. I felt like a child, hiding in a tree with him.

When I was settled on the limb, Reynard continued. "As Mountain Screamer sang, a light emanated from his open mouth. It seemed to be a grayish lavender color and increased the longer he sang. The glow started to fill the area around Mountain Screamer's face, and the light fogged up his features. The more he sang, the more a golden light emanated from him. Wings sprouted from his shoulder blades. His body changed into a hawk, and he flew over the trees toward the blue sky, and glided in circles around the mountaintop."

"So you observed him shape-shifting," I said as I swung my legs back and forth from the tree branch.

"Yes," he said as he took the bag from his belt and took out some walnuts. He put two in his large hands, and with his fingers interlaced, he squeezed. I heard the walnut shells crack. When he opened his hands, the walnut meat was exposed from the shells, and he held it out to me. I munched on the sweet nutty meat.

"Reynard, the walnuts taste so earthy."

Reynard continued his story. He told me he was in awe after observing Mountain Screamer's transformation. He said, "I watched as a man turned into a hawk before my eyes and flew away. This seemed impossible to me. How could it have happened? I knew then that a person can change his shape, as I had been able to change my sorrow into joy and gratefulness. Perhaps this was one and the same. . .this changing shapes."

Reynard said he had pondered those things, when all of a sudden Mountain Screamer put an arm around him, and explained that few people are able to have the power to change their sorrow into joy. Many live a life of bitterness and regret, but he knew Reynard had the ability to overcome that pattern.

"That's a wonderful gift," I said. "I adore you and your spirituality."

Reynard and I jumped down from our perch on the tree limb, and started packing up the picnic basket. As I drained the last of the wine into Reynard's glass, I said, "I'm so happy you have such a powerful resilience."

So am I." Reynard took a sip of wine, and said, "Then Mountain Screamer showed me how to shape-shift with him into a hawk."

I laid on the blanket, my arms behind my head, and said, "So that's when you first learned how to change forms."

Reynard laid on his side next to me, one fist under his chin. "My first flight must have lasted hours, until I finally noticed the hawk circling me. I followed him back to the ledge. I sat with my eyes closed as my body resumed its old heavy form. My muscles filled out. My nose softened. My feet became flat. I was a man again. But this time I was a changed man. . . in spirit as well as in form."

I ruffled Reynard's hair, and said, "I've been given that gift, too. It's magnificent to be able to fly."

"It certainly is. Then Mountain Screamer and I spent many days on the mountain, moving into various forms until I found the one I felt the most comfortable with, which was a gray fox."

"Yes, a gray fox. Somehow that seems to suit you perfectly."

"Angelica, when I was young, my father used to tell me stories about a French fox, named Reynard, who was playful and clever. My father had a dream of me right after I was born. In the dream I learned to turn into a playful fox at will. He later commissioned an artist to put a stained glass window in our front door which had a picture of a red hawk and a gray fox. The red hawk had her wings wrapped around the gray fox. I've always wondered what the red hawk in the picture meant. It's you, isn't it, Angelica? You're the red hawk."

Chapter Twenty-Two
Water Nymphs

S wimming had always been one of my favorite pastimes. As a child I loved to float on my back, and pretend I was a bird soaring in the sky. Therefore, when Reynard suggested we go to his secret swimming hole, I agreed, with enthusiasm.

"This place is so magical," he said. "You must go there on a full moon to get the true effect. And, my dear, tonight just happens to be a full moon. Water spirits live there. Knowing you, I think you'll enjoy them."

"Reynard, I love to swim. It sounds like such a wonderful adventure, swimming during a full moon. But, what's this about water spirits? You're kidding, aren't you?"

"Hush. Just follow me and you will see."

Reynard led me behind his great family home down a meandering pathway to a secluded pond that was so big I couldn't see the other side. I could hear the rhythmic slapping sound of agitated water at the small dock which sat at one end. Water lilies floated like clouds in a dark green sky.

Reynard took off his shirt and I could see the moonlight hitting his bare chest. His skin was like radiant, supple silk, and I desired to touch him.

I started unfastening my blouse. Reynard came over to help me with the buttons. He pulled my arms free from my blouse and laid it on the dock's edge. The moonlight bounced off my white cotton slip as I pulled my panties off.

"*Ma belle*, let me help you take this last impediment off," Reynard said as he held the bottom of the slip and raised it over my head. My arms stretched up to the black sky. I crossed my arms and put them over my breasts in an attempt to hide my nakedness.

Reynard looked at me, and I felt shy from his intenseness. "*Mon tresor, mon amour.* You are more beautiful in the night than in the day, if that is possible."

I got a quick glimpse of Reynard's muscular buttocks glimmering in the moonlight as he dove almost without a sound into the water, disappearing from sight. I waited for what seemed an eternity. He bobbed up, smiling. "We are not alone, my love. Come into the water and you will see your friends. And, please, do not be afraid."

I walked into the water surprised at its warmth. The pussy willows, straight and tall, grew along the edges of the pond. I could see ducks nestled along the sides of the banks with their heads under their wings. The scent of the damp green swamp grass near the shore saturated the air.

An occasional orange or yellow fish swam by under the full moon. I gave a little scream as one of the fish tails fluttered along my bare leg. I pulled back and several fish in a line swam under my left arm. The moonlight filled the pool and the fish became iridescent as they swam near the surface.

I floated on my back looking up at the spectacle of a full moon and bright stars in the sky. I relaxed as though floating in a vat of jello, soft yet with enough substance to give me a wonderful buoyancy. I rolled over and floated on my stomach with my eyes open, looking for more fish. What I saw startled me. Instead of fish, I saw a long line of brown wavy hair moving by me. Startled, I straightened my legs and stood up in the soft mossy sand and took a gulp of air.

Reynard was watching me as he swam on his back. "Don't be afraid of anything you see. Nothing here can hurt you. Try to be open to it."

Curious, I stood on my toes and peered into the water, my nose almost touching the surface of the pond.

All of a sudden, I heard some splashing and saw a quick movement in the shimmering water. I looked at the wooden pier and there sat a lovely creature, a beautiful mysterious woman unencumbered by clothing. My mouth fell open when I saw that, instead of legs, she had a tail that made up her bottom half. Her disarming smile was too innocent for me to feel fear, only surprise.

The water nymph's skin was creamy from her head down to her belly button, at which point her pink dermis disappeared. Below her navel, the light shimmered off the water droplets clinging to the green, gray, and blue iridescent scales covering her graceful tail.

She put her head back and her long dark hair hung down to her buttocks. She combed her hair over and over with a wooden comb fitted with an abalone shell handle. She had a glow about her, almost like a halo.

Another similar female joined her, and took the comb from her friend's hand and began combing her own hair. Their appearances were very similar, as if they were sisters. Then a third, and then a fourth creature bobbed out of the water. The first female began to sing an eerie, high-pitched song. The other females joined in, harmonizing.

My memory sent me back to the day I almost drowned and how I saw what looked like water nymphs surrounding me. I remembered studying water nymphs in my college mythology class. They were fascinating creatures that were considered Grecian minor divinities, possibly immortal or at least long-living mortals who inhabited rivers, streams, lakes, fountains, springs, and ponds. They were said to have magical abilities, which I realized had helped save me from drowning some months before.

"Thank you, my darlings. Thank you for saving my life. Thank you all so much," I said.

The water nymphs gave me shy smiles. They dove into the water, and swam over to me, and began circling, each one holding the hair of the other. The water started to froth around me. I was being pulled into the turbulence. I began to sink.

The nymphs held my hands and guided me step-by-step into the circling maelstrom, deeper and deeper. I felt I could trust them, let my body go limp, and allowed myself to be pulled along. I could see some of the loose vegetation of the pond circle into the swirling element in front of me. At first I was afraid and then amazed I didn't feel the need to take a breath. Perhaps the crystal they had put into my head when I almost drowned had created my ability to breath under water. The crystal began to vibrate. The water got warmer, the deeper we went. I could see two other nymphs leading Reynard ahead of me, and I felt a little safer.

Then I could see a faint light ahead of us and it grew larger as we swam closer. When we approached, there was a narrow dark tube with rock walls, and I began to feel claustrophobic.

Once we got to the end of the tunnel the nymphs started guiding me upwards. At the surface of the water, it appeared we were inside an underground cave which was carved into the rocky wall of the cliff, which I had seen near one end of the pond.

Reynard was already kneeling on the cave's gravel shore. He arranged some sticks in a circle and started a fire. I walked toward it to warm my cold hands. The blackened sticks nearby made it apparent other fires had been there in the past.

As I stood, it seemed that I could hear a roaring above me. It sounded like the rushing of water, but the water leading to the cave was still and quiet. I looked at Reynard with curiosity.

He answered my bewilderment by saying, "The great Russian River is next to this cave. We are under water in a cave made by a lava tube. The tube runs under the pond, and then arches up through the rocky hillside and comes out right next to the Russian River. Through the tube, you can access the pond on one end and the river on the other. It was one of my childhood hideouts and secret places to get away."

"Reynard, this is amazing. . .this place. . .the water nymphs," I said.

The nymphs swam toward the water's edge, and looked with longing at Reynard. They each came up and kissed him long and hard on the lips, then swam back through the tunnel and disappeared.

"Reynard, what kind of relationship do you have with these beautiful creatures?"

In the dim light of the cave, I could see half-burned candles laying in a large abalone shell. Reynard took a candle and lit it, turned to me, and said, "They were my childhood sweethearts, the answers to my sweet fantasies. Once I became grown, they no longer wove their spells on my heart."

"Wow, so you've known these water nymphs since you were a boy."

"Yes, Angelica. And, I, too, wear the crystal, which was pressed into my forehead by these lovely creatures. When I was a youngster, I ventured too near the river and plunged in. Of course the water nymphs were there for me. Later, as I grew, the nymphs taught me to swim with them, going deeper and deeper each time."

"So, they saved you from drowning, too?"

"They did. Angelica, I have never taken anyone here before, but I knew I could trust that you would understand because you had a similar circumstance."

"This place is amazing, Reynard. I'm glad you brought me here. Your explanation makes sense to me."

"When I was a young child, they used to whisper in my ears. Their songs filled my head and heart. They told me, as the medicine man later foretold, I would have two loves. The last would be eternal and time would have no meaning. I always wondered what the message meant, and now I know. *Je t'aime pour toujours, pour l'eternite.* I will love you through time and eternity."

"I love it when you speak French to me. You're such a romantic, Reynard."

"Now that I have charmed you, follow me. We shall traipse along this small stream running through the cave. It will take us to a thermal pond, cradled by Mother Earth, herself. I am sure it will be very soothing to you."

"Oh, it sounds lovely. It would be my pleasure to follow you."

The underground entrance led to a wide tunnel that meandered back and forth. Sometimes we came to an area where Reynard had to choose which chamber to follow. He led the way with confidence as he carried the candle. Only once did he pause, as if trying to decide which way to go.

We reached a very large cavern with a ceiling angled upward almost forty-five degrees, with large boulders covering one side. Reynard held the candle up and said, "Stick your nose near this hole. You can smell fresh air and see a little light."

I could see the candle flicker as he held it up. I was fearful of being in the dark in this place. My heartbeat quickened when I realized if the candle went out, the blackness would be total.

I stood on my toes and moved my face toward the place where he motioned. I took a deep breath and was greeted with a sweet cool breeze. In contrast, the air in the cave seemed thin, and I noticed I had some difficulty breathing. The fresh air was welcome to my lungs.

As my eyes adjusted, I looked at the back of the cave and saw a pond about five times larger than a bathtub. Heat waves rose from the water's surface.

Reynard dripped some wax onto a flat stone and then pushed the candle bottom into it. "This pond is heated by the fiery heart of Mother Earth. I used to come here as a boy whenever I felt lonely. It's hard growing up without a mother."

"I can almost see you here as a young boy."

"While floating in this dark, warm pond, I used to imagine I was in my mother's womb. . .all safe and warm and surrounded by her great and protective love."

"I wish I had been there to give you hugs."

"I do, too, Angelica." Reynard paused for a moment and I thought I saw a tear in his eye, and then he said, "I came to understand that Mother Earth's love surrounds me. I only needed to be aware, to access it. I came to find her love in the earth and trees, in the breeze, in the rain, and in this warm pond. It was all around me, and I no longer felt the loneliness. I realized I could be alone, and not be lonely."

"That's lovely. . .alone but not lonely."

Reynard began to submerge himself into the warm crystalline water. He sank to the top of his chin, and said, "Come in my love."

I stepped into the water, feeling small pebbles beneath my feet. As I immersed my body, I became buoyant. Here in this cave with its velvety night, I floated on my back and closed my eyes. I became a fetus again, listening to the beat of my mother's heart, over and over. A flood of warmth and abiding love filled my heart and inched down to my toes.

In that state, Reynard came to me, gentle as the water. I couldn't see him, nor could I see my hand in front of me. I didn't need eyes to know Reynard was embracing me. We became two spirits of love pulsating and beating with one heart — two intimate shadows — kindred spirits through time.

The only sounds in the cavern were the rhythmical dripping of water from the cave walls, and our sighs as we continued in our lover's embrace.

Reynard said, "Hold your breath," as he grabbed my hair and dipped my head back into the water. When he pulled me up, he said, "You are baptized by Mother Earth."

I spit out some water, and said, "Ah, but now I suppose Father Sky will want to baptize me, too."

Chapter Twenty-Three
Encounter with a Priest

A few days after our cave adventure, I awoke with the urge to bake a sweet bread. After breakfast, I wandered down to the walnut orchard to pick some nuts. As I filled my apron with them, I heard the bell ringing from the house porch, which was used for emergencies or to announce meals. I started running back to the house.

As I got to the top of the hill, I leaned over and panted, not used to running. I looked up and saw a priest pacing back and forth on the porch steps, muttering a prayer to himself, over and over. His dark hair was pulled straight back from his face, and he wore granny glasses. He was a heavy-set man with a barrel chest and large arms. He could have been a workman except for his black clothes and priest's collar. I noticed his face held a look of sincerity and honesty. As I got closer, I saw him fingering rosary beads.

When he saw me approach, he said, "Now we can start. I am Father Jean."

Right away I felt comfortable with that soft spoken man. I noticed his gentle manner and French accent.

"I will give mass right after the midday meal, but first there are those who will want me to hear their confession. . .so you are invited if the spirit calls."

"I am so called. I am ready to do a confession," I said as I tied the treasures up in my apron and set the bundle down.

A covered wagon was situated in the front yard under the shade of the old massive oak. Father Jean climbed a short ladder which leaned against the back of the wagon, and motioned for me to follow. He went behind a cloth partition which separated him from the entrance. My heart raced thinking of all the things I could tell him, and I said, "Sorry, but I need more time to think before I speak with you."

Father Jean said, "Fine. It's best to consider your life before speaking. I'll be here when you're ready."

I climbed down the ladder and noticed that a small group of people had formed a line by the wagon. I sat on a bench under the oak tree, and waited. My face felt flushed. What would I say to him? Where would I start? Do I finally have someone I can truly talk with about my predicament?

I waited until everyone had finished speaking with Father Jean. When the last person left, I climbed back in the wagon and went on my knees, inching my way toward the kneeling rail. I inhaled the scent of candle wax and sweet incense. I took some deep breaths and tried to relax. The atmosphere was hot and stuffy. I could hear the quiet, patient breathing of Father Jean.

"Bless you, my child. May I hear your confession today?"

I crossed myself as I said, "In the name of the Father, and of the Son, and of the Holy Spirit. Bless me Father for I have sinned. My last confession was over six months ago."

"We are blessed to have this sacrament of confession," Father Jean said. "Please proceed."

"Father Jean, I'm the last one in line, so hopefully you aren't in any hurry because I have a lot to tell you after my confession. You may or may not believe what I say, but I guess it doesn't matter. I feel I need to tell someone. I've kept silent far too long."

Chapter Twenty-Four
The Confessional

"You make this all sound so mysterious," Father Jean said. "Just remember, whatever you have to tell me is between you, me, and God. I keep all confessions secret, and your story is safe with me. Please proceed, my child."

"Other than missing church a few times, and being with a man without the benefit of marriage, I can think of no other sins. I'm sorry for these and all the sins of my past life."

Father Jean said, "Say five Hail Mary's and the Lord's Prayer."

"Oh, my God, I am hardly sorry for having offended Thee and I detest all my sins."

"You are absolved, my child. Just remember, don't feel too badly for not attending church. Most people, who live in this remote area, find it difficult to go the great distances to a church. As long as you spend some time in quiet reflection on Sundays, you will make God happy. Also, my advice to you is that you should consider the sacrament of marriage in the future."

I again made the sign of the cross.

"Now, your story," Father Jean said.

"A few short weeks ago, I came here on vacation from San Francisco. The San Francisco I know is different from the one you are familiar with because my city is one hundred and fifty years or so in the future. It sounds strange, but let me tell you how I arrived in this century."

Father Jean cleared his throat, and said, "You can't be serious, my child. You wish me to believe you came from one hundred and fifty years in the future? That's ridiculous. I hope you aren't hallucinating."

"Please listen, Father. I'm not making this up. Some months ago, I was canoeing when I had an accident and Reynard saved me from drowning. I think, when I began to drown, I experienced some kind of time change. It seems I traveled backwards into your century."

"Reynard, who I met with earlier today, told me about your boating accident," Father Jean said. "However, the part you described as time travel sounds a bit crazy, but continue if you must, my dear."

I heard a rustling of Father Jean's robe.

My forehead became damp, and I wiped the cool sweat with the back of my forearm. I took a deep breath of the incense-filled air. Butterflies swirled in my stomach. When I settled down a bit, I continued.

"I'm learning the ways of the people here and have been accepted into Reynard's family as if I were one of them. They've made me feel very special, like I had been expected. I was told by Reynard's medicine man that there's some sort of promise I'm supposed to fulfill. I'm to do something to help the family in some way or other, but I don't know what, yet. I was even told I would save Reynard's life one day as he saved mine. I have grown very fond of him and know I can't leave this place. I feel I belong on this rancho with Reynard and his family."

"Angelica, Reynard is an old friend of mine, and he's told me that the two of you are very close,"

"What I need to tell you, Father Jean, is what life will be like from now until the year two thousand."

I heard Father Jean let out a gasp as the time difference hit him.

I continued on. "As you know, for hundreds of years this land had been in the hands of the Indians who cared for it, never abusing it. As I recall from my history books, the Indians were treated in a shameful way in this century. They were forced onto reservations."

"Yes," Father Jean said. "I agree that it was shameful, but it was supposed to be a way of controlling them better. Go on, my dear."

"Many of them died of the European diseases to which they had no immunity, and many died of starvation because the reservation system was often corrupt. As a result, some of the Indian people turned to alcohol as a consolation and started abusing it."

Father Jean cleared his throat and said, "Yes, many of them are becoming infected by the evils of alcohol."

"Sometimes missionaries were sent to run the reservations and they, as good meaning as they were, thought the Indians were heathens. The white men passed laws making any Indian religious practice illegal."

Father Jean opened the drape between us, and said, "For what you have to tell me, Angelica, we can look eye-to-eye. I do have mixed feelings on the subject of converting the Indians. But do go on."

"In the nineteen sixties and seventies there was a surge of interest in Indian culture. The Indian medicine men were sought as people for the white men to learn from. Some Christian priests even tried to include several of the Indian ceremonies into their mass."

"I understand that idea of melding the religions," Father Jean said. "I have been trying to introduce it into my ceremonies with some success."

"That's great," I said. "Then in the nineteen seventies, the United States changed the laws and made the Indian religion legal. A resurgence of pride in the Indian culture took place. Some members of various tribes went around the country and put on Pow Wows. People by the thousands would go to watch and take their children. Indian art became popular, and many people had it in their homes, so a new industry grew around it."

"I'm happy to hear that about the future," Father Jean said. "Right now is a time of shame on the part of Americans for their dark deeds toward the Indians."

"Father Jean, it isn't too late. I needed to tell you this because I know you can influence many, many people in your ministry. I only hope you can help the people of today have more understanding and respect for the different cultures."

"I would like to try, Angelica. Believe me, I have tried in the past, but it's difficult. People can be very close-minded."

"Father Jean, I would like to talk to you more about creating a plan to free the enslaved Indians of this area, and to break Reynard's family curse. For now, I ask your blessing for my decision to stay here, and whatever destiny lies before me."

Chapter Twenty-Five
Father Jean's Mass

All of a sudden a bell started ringing and I could hear people's voices. Someone yelled, "Lunch, everyone, lunch."

Father Jean exclaimed, "My child, I have so many questions. I knew you seemed different when I saw you. There was something about you. And I almost believe your story, as strange as it sounds to me."

Father Jean made the sign of the cross as he said, "Bless you, in the name of the Father, Son, and Holy Spirit."

I crossed myself as he spoke.

He squeezed my arm and said with great warmth, "Please, let's find some time to talk later."

I climbed out of the dark wagon into the brilliant light. I could see the field workers approach the house. They lined up by a large bucket of water to wash.

I went into the house to help Carmen get the food ready. The two of us carried a basket of cornbread and bottles of wine to the picnic tables set under the shade of the oak tree. A big pot of soup hung over hot coals. One of the worker's wives ladled the soup into bowls.

I felt Reynard's eyes on me before I saw him. His intense look always created feelings of confusion in me. I felt my face flush as I looked into his blue eyes.

"Angelica, *mon petit*," was all he said, as he carried his bowl of soup to one of the tables. When he approached me his shoulder brushed mine with slow deliberation. "Come sit with me," he said.

I took off my apron, picked up a bowl of soup, and walked to Reynard's table.

"I hear you have met Father Jean," Reynard said, as the priest joined us at our table.

Father Jean took my hand and shook it, saying, "*Mademoiselle.*"

Reynard picked a geranium from a small pot sitting on our table and placed it behind my ear. "Now you look complete. The flower matches your finely-colored cheeks." Reynard's face broke into a grin of approval.

Turning to Father Jean, Reynard said, "I'm so glad you are back in this area. It has been too long since I have seen you, my friend."

"Yes, I, too, am happy to see you again. We have much to talk about. Carmen tells me she's made up a room for me, and insists I stay for a bit," Father Jean said.

"Please. Stay as long as you like. You are always welcome here. I have some things I want to discuss with you, also."

Reynard looked at me and said, "I knew Father Jean in France when I attended college. He was going to save the world, and I was going to grow the best wine grapes, and the best walnut meats. We had lots of long talks in the French cafes and sipped many a good wine. This fine man is, indeed, an idealist."

Father Jean nodded, and replied, "I believe from the short conversation Angelica and I had, she is also an idealist. I'm sure we'll have some good chats."

After the three of us finished eating, Father Jean said, "Reynard, I must prepare to give mass to your family and your workers. I see you have even more Indians added to your rancho than the last time I visited. I look forward to making friends with them all."

When the priest left, Reynard held my hand underneath the red and white-checkered tablecloth. "Father Jean knows I'm not a true Catholic, but he doesn't mind. He knows my past, and calls me a shamanic Christian. It appears to be what you are, too. Shall we go to Father Jean's mass?"

We both got up and went to the porch where the mass was being prepared. People sat in a semi-circle under the oak, or on the grassy knoll in front of the house facing the porch.

As I listened to the mass, the monotony of the Latin words put me into a quiet state of mind. I found myself drifting back to when I came to the rancho, my dissatisfaction with my life in San Francisco, my loneliness, and my longing to fit in.

Why was I drawn to this area? Why had I always returned to the Russian River on so many of my vacations? I think it was because I found a sense of belonging there, a sense of peace and serenity in the countryside — in the row after row of vines draped across the wire and wood, of the hillsides above the vineyards filled with trees, and of the bright starry nights unblurred by city lights.

When I visited the Russian River in my other life, I would bike through the countryside, imagining I was going back in time. A sense of ease and calm would fill me. I realized I was more comfortable there than living in the cemented cities with honking cars, and people-filled malls.

And now, I feel at home on the rancho with the vineyards, the fruit-laden trees, the fertile fields. I had come home to Reynard, my sweet, endearing, loving Reynard. I felt tears well up in my eyes and then run down my cheeks.

I noticed Reynard standing in front of me, holding his hands out, smiling, as I came out of my reverie.

He said, "My sweet one."

I realized the time had come to receive the Eucharist at Father Jean's make-shift altar.

I took Reynard's hands and he pulled me up. He placed one hand behind my waist and helped me up the porch steps to where Father Jean was holding the Host. I opened my mouth as Father Jean said, "Body of Christ."

Next, he held up a chalice of wine to me.

"Blood of Christ," he said.

I took a sip and the velvety wine settled in my mouth. When I swallowed, the wine warmed me inside and I felt like a spirit had filled my empty soul.

Chapter Twenty-Six
Saving the Indian Girls

The buggy lunged and bounced, pushing me into Father Jean. "Yikes. What a huge rut in the road," Father Jean exclaimed as he put his hand on his backside rubbing it with vigor. He slowed the horses to a stop and got out of the buggy.

Jumping down from the wagon, he went on his knees to inspect the wheel. "I think we'd better stop at the blacksmiths in town before we head back to the rancho. The wheel isn't long for this world. I doubt it'd make it back home in one piece." With his head still bent down, his large black hat angled off to one side. Before he stood up, he said, "I think I better give it last rites while I'm down here."

I chuckled as I offered my hand to Father Jean, which he took. With his other hand he grabbed the back of the wooden seat and pulled himself into the wagon.

I took the reins and led the horses at a slow trot into town, looking down once in a while to make sure the wheel wasn't tottering. As we pulled up to the closed door of a blacksmith's shop, I noticed a sign in the window that read, "Closed for Refreshments."

Father Jean smiled at me and said, "Samuel is bound to be at Jacob's Well down the street having his daily rounds. He's one who loves his beer or whiskey, and the more the better. However, everyone says it doesn't affect his work. The only problem is finding him and convincing him he's got a job to do."

Jacob's Well was set off at the end of town near a clump of trees. Two Indian girls were sitting on the top steps, shaded by maple trees lining the front of the saloon.

One of the young girls looked to be about eighteen. Her baggy, soiled dress appeared to hide a bulge, which I suspected was due to her being six or seven months pregnant. She was pretty, but had very thin limbs and a sallow face. The other young girl was, at most, fifteen years old, and looked like a younger version of the pregnant woman.

Father Jean turned to me and said, "Stay on the wagon, my dear. I'll only be a minute. In this day and age, ladies don't frequent saloons, especially the likes of this one."

As I sat on the wagon, I turned my attention to the two girls. The youngest one walked over to me with her hand out. "Food, lady? My sista, Sisi, she have baby soon. She need food to feed baby. My name Watu and I hungry, too."

As she finished speaking, one of the men walked out of the saloon and edged up to Sisi. "Come here, my pretty. Come play with me behind the saloon and I'll buy you some food."

The younger girl, her hands on her hips, stood in front of her pregnant sister. "Last time you hurt my sister. Leave her alone. Please to give us money for food. We have mighty hunger."

The man's coat was covered with road dust, and his brown greasy hair hung down in his eyes, hiding his lust. His yellow teeth spit out the words between his dry, scaly lips, "I got a powerful thirst for the older one with the nice swollen breasts. Let me see those things, my darlin' squaw."

The unkempt man grabbed the pregnant girl by the hair, and pulled her down the stairs, and then toward the thick trees behind the saloon. When the younger Indian girl pushed him, he struck out with all his might. His attack threw her across the yard onto the dusty road. She landed on her back, gasping for air over and over, until she caught her breath. She held her bleeding nose and mouth, sobbing into her cupped hands.

The man guffawed and grabbed Sisi by the front of her dress and reached inside her bodice and started fondling her breasts. He pulled at his belt with his free hand.

"Father Jean, help," I screamed as I came out of my shocked state. I didn't wait for him, but jumped from the wagon onto the drunken man's back. I pounded him with my fists, and dust flew off his coat. Pulling his hair I yelled, "You bastard, let go of that poor girl."

The man twirled around and around, trying to get me off his back. I held on tighter the faster he twirled.

Strong hands pried me off the drunken man and laid me on the grass. I looked up and saw Father Jean. His face was transfixed from the kind and gentle soul I had come to know, to one filled with fury and rage. He grabbed the man and squeezed him until the man gasped and coughed.

A small crowd of men left the saloon and gathered to see the spectacle. They cheered and shouted. One man yelled, "That a way, Father. Get the bastard good."

Holding the drunken man by his arms, Father Jean spun him around and around and then hurled him headfirst down the small ravine toward the creek.

Father Jean looked up at me, and yelled, "Let's get the heck out of here before the guy climbs up and decides he's going to try to get even."

I ran over to the two Indian girls and grabbed their hands. We ran as fast as we could toward the wagon. It crossed my mind, as we rounded the corner to the blacksmith's shop, that the wheel on our wagon wouldn't take us far.

Father Jean grabbed Sisi and lifted her like she was a bag of goose down, and ran with her in his arms. I ran pulling Watu when Father Jean passed us, and yelled, "Hurry."

When we got to our wagon, Father Jean lifted Sisi into the back and jumped onto the driver's seat. He grabbed the reins in his big hands. I helped Watu jump in behind her sister, and then got in myself.

"Tell them to hang on for dear life," Father Jean yelled. "I don't know how long the wagon wheel will hold up, but we'll have to make a run for it. At least we'll get a head start. We can ride the horses bareback the rest of the way."

Sisi held her stomach and grimaced whenever the wagon hit a pothole or gnarled root in the road.

I glanced back but didn't see anyone coming. I looked down and could see the wobbly wheel. "Father Jean," I shouted, "Pull over. The wheel's about to come off."

Chapter Twenty-Seven
The Argument

Father Jean unhitched the two horses, and together we pulled the wagon behind some deep brush. He helped Sisi onto the tall, lanky chestnut horse, and jumped on behind her. Watu and I climbed onto the black horse.

Holding the horse's mane, we galloped faster than I was comfortable with. I squeezed my legs to maintain balance. I realized we needed to get away as fast as possible, so pushed away my fears of falling.

Later in the evening, having told my story over and over to Reynard and his family, I excused myself to go to the workers' cabins where Sisi and Watu were resting. Carmen said she'd accompany me so she could help carry extra blankets for the Indian girls. Before dinner, Carmen had helped me clean the girls up and bring them some food, which they accepted with gratitude.

When we entered the cabin, Carmen and I laid the blankets on the Indian girls' beds. I said, "These should keep you warm tonight."

"Thank you, kind lady. We so happy you help us," Sisi said.

Carmen said, "Where is your home, my child?"

Sisi explained. "We live with our families in hills north of village where you find us. Then white men come force our men to work their fields. Our women and children try hunt and gather by themselves. Some children starve first year. Second year some of our men escape and come home. They tell us Joseph steal many Indian people to work fields and tend animals. He use young and pretty Indian girls as wives. If they say no, he whip them. He lock our people up at night so no one escape."

"That's horrible," I said, and fought back my tears.

When Sisi laid down on the bed, Watu continued the story. "When our braves back, they hunt for food. Then Joseph and his men steal our men again plus all women, except us. Sisi and I gone, gathering food in valley. When we come back, we hide behind tree. We see one man try run away, but he shot in back by white man. We run, hide in deep woods many days, scared. We only ones left. We starving, so we go to town for help, but only way we get food is we give ourselves to men at saloon."

Sisi started crying as Watu finished the story. "No one else give us food, but shoo us away, and say we dirty and lazy."

Carmen tucked Sisi into the bed with the remaining blankets, and stood up. "Here, you are safe. Get a good rest tonight. In the morning you'll have more food. There's nothing to worry about at our rancho. You're not a slave here. You're free to come and go. We'll expect you to help us at the rancho to gather some fruit and nuts. We'll have jobs for you when you're better. We need lots of helpers on the rancho, and we pay them for their work."

As soon as we left and started back toward the house, I shrieked, "Those dirty bastards. How can they get away with their abuse of the Indians? Doesn't anyone give a damn?"

Carmen put her arm around my shoulder as we walked. "The laws of present day California are lenient with people taking Indians as slaves. Any Indian under twenty-five, who is wandering about town and has no apparent job, can be taken home by white men and made to work for free. If an Indian says he is mistreated, and goes to a peace officer, by law the Indian isn't allowed to testify in court. I know it isn't just or right, but it's how it is."

I leaned down and picked up a stick and started beating it against a tree until it broke into dozens of pieces. "It's inhuman, that's what it is."

Carmen grabbed my arm. "Honey, it's hard to fight a way of life. When the miners started wandering through this area, some of them brought their own slaves to work the mines. Many of the miners who came from back East brought long years of prejudice against Indians with them, and were ready to shoot an Indian on sight, let alone be civil to him."

I ran to the house and found Reynard sitting on the porch reading a book by a lantern. I stomped over to him, and said, "Reynard, do you know what your Cousin Joseph's been up to? Huh? Do you?" I stood waiting for a response with my hands on my hips and my chin in the air.

Reynard laid his book on the porch rail and looked up at me. "What's got into you, Angelica? First, you bring home a couple of dirty Indian squaws, and then you're all riled up about my cousin who you barely know."

"Listen, darn you," I said. "The Indian girls told me Joseph has been taking Indians against their will and making them work his land. If they try to run away, he murders them. And that's not all. He rapes the poor young Indian girls, too, like sex slaves. Can you imagine? It's intolerable."

Reynard looked at me with a puzzled expression on his face, and said, "Are you telling me you actually believe a couple of squaws? Don't you know they are probably lying to you so they can get a few free meals. They are nothing but saloon scum. I think you are just feeling sorry for them."

"But, Reynard. They were starving," I said.

"How could you believe their lies? You are an intelligent woman. It is only gossip. They want your sympathy so they can live here for free and laze around the rancho like bums."

"Reynard, what they told me was so believable. I feel it's got to be true. How can you stand by and let your cousin kidnap, rape, and murder the Indians? It seems to me you don't want to believe it. You're so much like your father. . .you have no backbone, no courage."

Disgusted with Reynard, I trudged off toward the black pond behind the house.

Chapter Twenty-Eight
Seaman's Chest and the Magic Gown

The muggy night was dark and without a visible moon. Sweat beaded on my forehead after my confrontation with Reynard. I was still feeling angry.

I removed my clothes and put them on the dock. I then waded into the pond, floated on my back, and spread my arms out at my sides trying to calm down.

All of a sudden, the water nymphs popped up. Their sweet water songs filled my ears and soothed me. The one I remembered Reynard called Harmonia swam over and stroked my hair. I flinched at her touch at first, but then relaxed. She motioned for me to sit on the dock. I followed her direction and she sat beside me. Two of the nymphs popped out of the pond carrying a green seaman's trunk bound with leather, which they handed to Harmonia. She set it on the dock, and then gestured for me to open it.

I lifted the metal latch and found a clear, filmy, silk gown with a hood. I put it on over my wet, naked body, and found I could no longer see myself. I was totally invisible. As if the nymphs could communicate with telepathy, the thought filled my head that I could wear this to Joseph's rancho and no one there would notice me. I could observe how the Indians were being treated without being seen.

I allowed the water nymphs to take my hands. They pulled me into the water, and then we swam to the entrance of the main tunnel. They led me past a labyrinth of tunnels, and then showed me how to get to the main river tributary. They left me as I made my way to the river and jumped in and let the current take me to Joseph's rancho. When I saw lights blazing from a two story house, I got out of the water and walked toward it.

I left the water wearing only the robe. I entered the side yard of the rancho, unnoticed by Joseph's men or even his dogs. As I approached, I could see one of his men leading two pretty Indian girls toward the house. The man muttered, "Come my pretty ones. We'll make you warm and welcome in our beds tonight."

I walked, trying not to step on any twigs or dead leaves, so that not even the dogs would suspect I was spying. Behind the house was a long rectangular cabin with iron bars on the windows. A large padlock hung on the door. I peered through the window and could see several Indians lying on the ground sleeping. An older Indian woman was washing a wound on the face of a younger Indian. The woman was crying. She stopped and then said to the man, "I so sorry they hurt you, and sorry about my dear innocent daughters. The bastards steal them from me."

The Indian man said, "I don't care how many times they hit me. I try hard to stop them."

The Indian woman said, "Please don't try anymore. I afraid they hurt you worse next time."

I looked around at the interior of the cabin, and bone-thin Indians of all ages and sizes were sleeping on the bare dirt floor. I had seen enough and started to leave. Then, I stopped. I felt compelled to speak to one of them. I could see the older Indian woman standing near the barred window as if looking out at the night sky. Realizing she couldn't see me because of my gown, I edged up to the iron bars and said, "Don't give up hope. I see how awful you are treated. I'm going to get help. I promise I'll return. Tell the others."

The woman looked around as though trying to see who was speaking to her. Then she said, "Bring help soon."

I turned and walked back to the river realizing the current flowed the opposite way I intended to swim, and I'd never make it home against the current. I walked to the barn to see if I could find a horse. At that moment, a dog let out a bark. Could he see me? Maybe he could smell me. I reached for the barn ladder. The dog barked louder.

I climbed into the loft. A horse was in an open stall below me. I flung myself onto his back. He lurched forward toward the open barn door. I put my arms around the horse's neck and then directed him to get moving by two quick squeezes of my knees. He charged out of the barn with the barking dog chasing us and me holding on for dear life.

I heard the screen door of the house bang closed, as some men ran out yelling when the horse flew by. I knew I was invisible to them when one of the men yelled, "Maybe the dog spooked the horse. I'll see if I can retrieve him. Somebody grab that dog and put him in the house."

I kept the horse at a gallop as long as I could. When we rounded a bend, I stopped the horse and jumped off. I hit his rump and he kept going. I hid behind some dense oak trees and watched as a rider went by in the night air.

Great. I lost them, but now I'd have to walk for an hour to get back to the rancho.

Chapter Twenty-Nine
Proof

Bedraggled and exhausted, I walked the last few feet to the black pond. I retrieved my clothes from the dock and put them on. I walked toward the house and then trudged up the porch steps. I saw Reynard pacing back and forth. When he saw me, he threw his arms around me.

"Angelica, I was so worried. Are you okay?"

"Yes, I'm fine."

"I am sorry I was gruff with you. It is just that I have been stymied by my father from doing anything about Joseph's Indians. I cannot deny it any longer. You were right. By the way, where have you been?"

I told Reynard about the water nymphs giving me the gown which made me invisible, and showing me the way to Joseph's rancho. I explained how I had seen the dreadful treatment of his Indians.

"My, God. Don't ever do anything like that again. You could have been killed by Joseph's men, or torn apart by his dogs. I would never forgive myself if anything happened to you."

"I promise, Reynard, but I'm glad I did it. Now, I'm more determined than ever to formulate a plan."

Father Jean joined us on the porch. After listening to our conversation, he said, "Reynard, speaking of a plan, you will have to excuse me and Angelica. We have some things to discuss."

Father Jean led me over to the side porch. With his hands on the railing, he looked up at the stars. "This is a lonely place for a beautiful young woman to be. Wouldn't you prefer being back in the city with all its activity and excitement?"

"This is now my life. I know there's danger ahead for the family, and I want to help Reynard face it. I owe him my life. His family is mine. His troubles, and curses, mine. I accept them willingly."

"My dear, there must be family and friends back home worried about you. What will happen to them and their lives?"

"All I have is a sister. Our parents died some time ago. My sister and I were close, but she is a very active woman, with lots of friends, and her art and travels occupy her. I know she worries about me, and I wish I had a way to tell her where I am, that I'm happy and fulfilled. Perhaps someday there'll be a way to get word back to her. Right now, I have no idea how."

As I said this, I remembered the backpack, which Reynard had retrieved from the canoe when I had almost drowned. I kept the pack in my room and I remembered I stowed my personal items inside, such as my small thermos, Swiss Army knife, my rattle, and. . . Oh, my God. My cellular phone which was sealed in a plastic pouch.

At this thought, I let out a loud, "Yes," and charged into the house.

I ran up the flight of stairs to my room, pushed open the door, and went over to the closet where I kept my tattered orange backpack. It was the one I had taken on so many hikes and canoe trips. I unhooked the straps and pulled out my cellular phone.

It looked so strange in my hands, so foreign. I flipped it open and saw the numbers and the black plastic surface of the phone. I mumbled, "A telephone hasn't even been invented yet."

Father Jean and Reynard had followed me upstairs and walked in as I held the phone to the light. Their eyes got wide when they saw it.

I turned the cell phone on, and dialed my sister's number. I held it so Father Jean and Reynard could hear the dial tone and the musical notes.

I said, "I'm calling my sister on what we call a cell phone."

Father Jean's eyes got very large as my sister's voice came on the line, and said, "Hello, this is Heather."

"Heather, Heather, it's me, Alexis," I blurted out.

To my disappointment I realized it was a recording and Heather's greeting continued. ". . .and Alexis' house. We aren't home right now, but leave your name and number and we'll call you when we get in."

When I heard the beep, I took a deep breath and said, "Heather, it's me, Alexis. Don't worry about me, I'm fine. Just want you to know I've found a wonderful place and a fabulous man, and I don't think I'll ever be back to see you. But you don't need to worry about me because. . ." Before I could say more, the phone went dead. The batteries must have gone out.

"If I didn't thoroughly believe you before," Father Jean said with conviction, "I do now."

I began to cry in frustration and mumble between sobs, "I'm sorry, Heather. I don't know how to tell you. I can't even write you a letter."

I looked up at Father Jean and Reynard, and said, "Let's go back outside on the porch. I can think more clearly out there."

Chapter Thirty
Father Jean's Story

While we were walking down the stairs, Reynard said, "What was that thing that talked?"

"It's a telephone or a gadget that allows you to communicate through space to anyone you want. It's from the century I lived in before I came here."

Reynard began to laugh and then said, "Angelica, so you are from another century. I knew it when I pulled you from the river. You do fit the prophesies."

"Yes, I lived more than a century and a half ahead of you. And sorry to say, the telephone needs to be charged and chargers haven't been invented in this time period. The telephone has gone dead and I can't use it anymore. I'm surprised it had any juice left in it at all. I guess it made it this long because I had it turned off to conserve the batteries."

"Batteries. What are batteries? I think you are talking crazy," Reynard said.

"No," Father Jean said. "Let her talk, Reynard. She does make sense."

"Batteries are made to store energy. You can plug one into things like an automatic toothbrush, an automobile, a computer, an electric mixer, and make them work. The list is endless. But, of course, you can't understand any of this because your century doesn't have these inventions. Just take my word for it, it's amazing what the next century will bring."

"For now," Reynard said, "I will be content to focus on the present. Mark my words, we will have some interesting talks in the future when you explain these marvels to me."

As we walked, I thought of all the amazing things I could tell Reynard. Without seeing the equipment or having a twentieth century education, it would be hard for him to visualize.

Speaking of technology, I started wondering how the cell phone could work without a cell phone tower. I remember taking Professor Johnson's Eastern Indian Mythology class when he talked about an astral plane where gurus and masters could move into the spirit world while still living in their corporeal bodies. I suppose a similar relationship could exist with water nymphs, who lived in both worlds, astral and physical. Their magical force helped pull the energy of the future century into the present, or the 1840s where my body is now walking, talking, and experiencing this miracle too complex for me to understand. Shape-shifting is convoluted enough to sort out and make sense of, but it seems there's an interconnection between energy traveling through space, and time traveling.

When we got back on the porch, I leaned against the railing, trying to compose myself. Reynard turned to Father Jean and said, "What's this about Angelica living in another century?" Before Father Jean could answer, Reynard looked at me and said, "I know you are different, Angelica. Now, I know why. It is going to take me a while to absorb this information about you."

Father Jean put his hand on Reynard's shoulder, and said, "Yes, after confession yesterday, she told me that she time traveled. It's amazing, but this talking contraption has taken away any doubts I have. She may end up being your family's salvation. . .like a gift from God."

"Angelica, that first day, when I saw you stand up in the river," Reynard said, "your hair hanging down your face, I knew you were the woman I was destined to meet. And you are right, Father Jean. After I saw that contraption, how could I have any doubts that she is from a future century?"

They both turned and watched as I went over to the rocking chair and sat down. Father Jean said, "Angelica, I understand a little of what you're going through. I have a family back in France. My parents died some time ago. My sister is all I have, and she's married and has children. I hope to go back someday to visit, but I don't know when I can arrange it. It's so expensive and travel so difficult. At least I can write to my sister and she to me."

I looked up at Father Jean and I gave him a weak smile. I asked him why he had moved to America.

"To tell you the truth, I am an adventurer and a rebel and this young America is the only place that could soothe my restless spirit."

"Yes," Reynard said, "Jean Jacque, you were always a rebel and a free thinker."

Father Jean seemed encouraged by this and went on. "Angelica, to give you a little background, my parents named me after Jean Jacques Rousseau, a famous French writer and political philosopher, whose ideas inspired the French revolution. Rousseau hated tyranny and loved freedom. He believed man had a natural goodness that was corrupted by political and social institutions."

"While we were students in France, we took political classes together," Reynard said. "I, too, loved reading Rousseau who emphasized the value of feelings as opposed to reason, and of impulse and spontaneity instead of social discipline and civilized restraint. Father Jean was excited to learn that I had grown up with Indians on our land."

"Yes, after talking with Reynard, I longed to go to America to meet his Indians and learn about their spirituality. Becoming a priest was the best way I knew to spread the word of God and an excuse to travel and explore America. However, sometimes being a priest was a contradiction to my beliefs in impulse and spontaneity. That's why I became a traveling priest. I have much more freedom."

"You make a great traveling priest, Father Jean," I said. "Now that I've heard your background, it's no wonder you're so open-minded toward the Indians."

"Upon my arrival to America, I was very disappointed when I discovered most people viewed the Indians as dirty heathens and devil worshipers," Father Jean said. "It seemed no one truly tried to understand their culture. As I traveled the continent I found the Indians I met had a beautiful relationship to the earth and its creatures. They imitated the finer qualities of animals and saw them as their teachers."

Reynard said to me, "Father Jean knows about our shape-shifting abilities, and approves."

"It was amazing to me to learn about your experiences, Angelica," Father Jean said. "Now, that we've talked about our personal stories, let's discuss our future together as friends. I would also love it if the two of you could settle your dispute."

Reynard picked up my hand and squeezed it, and said to me, "I appreciate your strength of conviction. I realize I was wrong about Joseph and his treatment of the Indians. When I resisted your arguments, I was just trying to defend not taking action against Joseph all these years."

"I forgive you, Reynard. I know this is a very emotional subject for you, and it'd be hard for you to admit you were wrong in not initiating a plan."

Getting up from the rocker, I gave Reynard a hug. I said, "My darling, I must tell you that I'm determined to help your family free Joseph's Indian slaves. It is my destiny."

"I'm glad you two have resolved that," said Father Jean. "To add to your determination, I wanted to tell you about my conversation with Dr. Jontu, George's physician, who told me stories about visiting Cousin Joseph's rancho. He went there to attend to some of Joseph's workers. He helped an Indian woman who was having a difficult delivery. He also had to treat several Indians' broken bones and wounds. He was certain those injuries were the result of frequent beatings from Joseph's henchmen."

Reynard hung his head, and said, "I am so sorry I ever doubted you, Angelica. The proof is overwhelming."

Father Jean continued. "The Indian woman he delivered seemed afraid of Joseph, and the physician suspected the baby was Joseph's. Joseph seemed very proud of the baby, and took it into the house to have it cared for by a nurse he had hired."

I said, "These stories disgust me, and make me firm in my resolve to help you, Reynard."

"In a few days," Father Jean said, "I must be on my way. I have many villages to visit. I'll be back here at the end of summer, and perhaps we can put our plan into effect at that time."

Father Jean turned and walked into the house, leaving me at the porch railing with Reynard to ponder our future plan of action.

Chapter Thirty-One
An Impending Death in the Family

One evening after I finished playing Chopin on the piano, I made a low bow to the family as they clapped. During the day I had practiced the classical sheet music that had been sitting on the piano. I was pleased I hadn't made too many obvious mistakes.

When I got up, Father Jean patted the cushions next to him, and asked me to sit down. He looked very serious when he said, "Earlier today, I gave George mass as he lay in bed. He's very ill and in a lot of pain."

"I'm so sorry to hear that. The poor man."

"I think he's afraid to die because he feels he has failed in this life and is responsible for his wife's death. I know you're aware of the family legend and the curse. George told me if he had forced his brother-in-law, Maximillian, to free his Indians, the curse would have been broken. He feels if he had acted, he could have saved his wife, Sarah, and Suzette, Reynard's wife. Instead, there've been many years of heartbreak for the family."

"George shouldn't feel he's to blame," I said. "Even Reynard felt helpless to do anything."

"George told me the reason he never tried to stop Maximillian," Father Jean continued, "was because George had promised Sarah on her death bed he wouldn't hurt Maximillian. You see, Maximillian was Sarah's baby brother, and she thought he could do no wrong. She didn't believe he mistreated the Indians who lived on his land, nor that Maximillian had enslaved them. Sarah wouldn't listen if anyone tried to tell her about how harsh Maximillian was in dealing with the Indian people. George said he told Reynard to confront his cousin, Joseph, or Reynard would die as George was dying, bitter and reluctant."

"Oh, Father Jean, I'm so glad Reynard and his father had this talk. It's been a long time coming. I hope Reynard decides to do something about his cousin."

"I understand," Father Jean said, "as a result of the talk, Reynard is trying to formulate a plan. I'm hoping bloodshed will be averted. Since you have great influence with Reynard, I'm coming to you, Angelica. I'm willing to help free these unfortunate individuals who have been enslaved by Joseph, but only if no one is hurt."

"You know I can't promise such a thing," I said. "On the other hand, perhaps there's a way we can free the Indians without violence. I am hoping that if we all sit down together and discuss it, we can come up with a plan."

"Please come with me to see George," Father Jean said. "He's been asking me about you. He's very curious as to why you seem so different. I told him all the things he has been wondering about you are true."

I took Father Jean's arm as we walked upstairs to the second floor of the house. We entered George's room where Carmen sat beside his bed. A fire burned in the fireplace and lit candles sat on the mantle. I could make out various Indian paintings on the walls. Bows and arrows of various types stood in the corner of the room. A large picture of a young man and a beautiful woman hung over the fireplace. Carmen saw me looking at the picture and said, "That's George and Sarah when they were first married. George and Reynard look so similar, don't you think?"

I nodded my head and then observed George. As he lay in bed, I saw the firelight dancing across his wrinkled face. He looked older than I remembered. Dr. Jontu, his heavy-set physician, was attending him. The doctor had his stethoscope on George's chest. He looked up and smiled at us. I overheard the doctor tell Reynard and Father Jean he wanted to discuss George's condition so he asked them to accompany him outside.

I noticed George's long white hair splayed across the lacey pillow. His dressing gown was still open, and Carmen went to his side to button it.

The old man's cheeks were sunken, and his bright eyes contrasted with his sallow skin. His face was tense and I could see fear in his eyes. He looked up at me and said, "Angelica, darling. Come brush my hair."

Carmen picked up a pearl handled brush from the dressing table and gave it to me. I sat on the bed next to George and started brushing his soft hair. For a moment, he put his hand on top of my free hand, and a look of contentment filled his eyes. I felt love for this old man who had fathered Reynard, and Carmen.

As I brushed his hair, I was able to observe some of the handsomeness I could see in Reynard. George had a strong straight nose and velvety blue eyes. His eyebrows were dark and arched below his broad forehead.

Reynard came back into the room and sat in the rocking chair by the stone fireplace. He rocked and stared into the fire. Carmen sang a French song in a throaty voice which revealed her depth of emotion. When she stopped, Father Jean came in. I walked to the fireplace to warm my hands and saw him place a silk cloth on George's thin chest. Father Jean proceeded to give George his last rites.

When Father Jean was through, George asked for me. I sat on the bed next to him and held his hand.

"Angelica," George said. "You have come to fulfill the family prophecy. For this I'm grateful."

"I feel it's my destiny to help your family. I owe Reynard my life."

"Angelica, your coming here was foretold by my medicine brother many years ago. Reynard knows he must confront his cousin in order to stop this curse. He has the courage I never had. I must die an old man's death. I have been dead since the day my wife died, but never had the courage to truly live and free my brother-in-law's Indians."

Carmen put more logs on the fire, and the flames brightened the room.

We all waited to see if George wanted to continue. He spoke again, and his voice seemed stronger when he said, "My wife also made me promise on her death bed I wouldn't confront her brother."

George raised a fist in the air and shook it saying, "Why, oh why, did you make me promise, Sarah? I wanted to break that promise so many times."

A breeze went down the flue and the logs started popping.

Reynard stopped rocking, stood up and then sat on the side of his father's bed. George raised up on his elbows, and said, "Reynard, I elicit no such promise from you. You're free to do as you please. I wouldn't wish a life such as mine on you. I know I was wrong in asking you to wait and not do anything about Maximillian and Joseph. I know this as sure as I see death's face every night before I go to sleep."

George fell back in exhaustion. His eyes closed and his breathing became softer and deeper.

When everyone started to exit the room, I laid the brush back on the dressing table. Before I left, I looked back and whispered, "I will help, George."

When we were outside George's room, Father Jean told Reynard, "He doesn't have long, I can tell. If there are any things you need to say to him, you must tell him soon."

Reynard and I went downstairs and sat by the fireplace in the living room. Jack nestled beside Reynard. I could tell Jack understood his sorrow and was trying to comfort him.

Chapter Thirty-Two
The Seeds and George

The next day, after Father Jean departed, I decided I needed a project to keep my mind off George's illness. I felt discouraged after I examined my loom, and the small amount of work I'd been able to accomplish. Carmen noticed the look on my face and said to me, "Weaving can teach you many things. One of them is to focus on the vibrancy of being alive and to be in the moment. If you're absorbed in the journey of creation, you can feel good and everything else will pale, even a family illness."

"You're right. I saw how you immersed yourself in your weaving this morning, and you look much calmer this afternoon. At your suggestion, I feel determined to enjoy the process of creation. Weaving helps me see life as one thread joining the next."

Carmen excused herself as she told me she was going inside because she was feeling chilled, and she wanted to check on George.

Before starting to work, I sat on the rocking chair and rocked back and forth as I watched the Russian River meander along its path at the bottom of the hill. Now relaxed, I started weaving with a renewed focus. I became excited as I saw a pattern emerging.

After some time, I took a break. I interlocked my fingers behind my head and looked up at the eaves of the porch. I saw a large spider web, like I'd seen several months before. The spider sat in the center and was weaving an intricate web which had sparkles of the morning dew. The sun shone through the lacey substance and made it seem transparent. I became entranced and realized the spider and I were doing the same work.

When the spider finished her creation, she sat motionless and in total silence, waiting for her dinner. As I peered at the little spider, I thought I heard a small, almost imperceptible whisper. She's talking to me. I laughed at myself for thinking such a thing. Ever curious, I continued sitting in silence, listening. This time I could make out the words — "Believe in yourself, believe in your power."

I realized I could accomplish so much by believing those words.

I thanked the spider, and left my weaving and watching to walk in the family garden on the side of the house. A small white picket fence surrounded the garden to keep out the deer. I opened the latch to the gate and entered. Roses grew up the side of a trellis on one end of the garden, and vines with purple trumpet flowers hung down from the trellis at the other end. The roses were almost spent, as were most of the flowers. I picked up a basket, which lay in the pathway. I placed it on my arm and meandered through the various flowerbeds to pick a bouquet of the last of the Fall flowers.

The days had begun to grow cold, and I could feel autumn begin its slide into winter. I rubbed my hands on the side of my neck to warm them.

I stood on my tiptoes and reached for the bright red roses on the trellis. I snipped two and put them into my basket.

I sauntered over to the lavender and picked several spikes to put amongst the roses. Next, I cut some lacey ferns to add green to my Fall collection.

The garden's latticed walkway held the yellowing leaves of the wisteria. Someone had placed a willow chair under the shade of the green leafy arch. I sat my full basket on the chair, and picked up another one sitting on the small willow table.

Next, I approached several six-foot poles that held climbing string beans. They had been full and lush only three weeks before. The beans had been left on the poles to dry, so the yellowed pods could be picked for planting the following spring. I pulled off some withered pods and put them in my basket.

I sat in one of the willow chairs and shucked out the plump beans, one at a time. As I harvested them, I became one with the spirits of the garden, the rich live soil beneath my feet, the busy bees pollinating the few flowers that were left, the humming birds getting their fill before their flight south.

I cupped some of the shiny white beans in my hand and held them up to the sun. Each one held a promise of new life. Each retained the knowledge of how to form roots, stalks, leaves, and white flowers that would transform into little pods, filled with the plumpness of the bean's life-giving promise.

I opened one of the smaller misshapen pods and found the small beans inside had discolored.

"Bad seed," I said out aloud. "I won't use this one for spring. It's best to throw out a bad seed or it may spoil the rest of the beans with its rot."

I walked back to the house with my two baskets. When I entered the house, I saw Carmen sitting in a chair with a blanket on her legs. She had a book opened in her lap. Her head was sunken down on her chest, and her eyes were closed. She had stayed up late with George the night before and was exhausted. I tiptoed past her, and went up the stairs to George's room.

He lay sleeping on his bed. He seemed to sleep most of the time now. I picked up the pearl handled brush and began to brush his hair. I looked at his face and saw the outline of his bones showing through his thin skin. Over and over I brushed until the tangles were gone and his hair was smooth again.

He opened his eyes, looked at me, and smiled. "Stay with me a bit, my Angel," he said.

"With pleasure, George."

I arranged the cut roses and lavender into the empty vase that sat on his dresser, and held the bouquet to his nose to smell.

"Ah, the fragrance of the work of the rich earth," he said. "I miss the feeling of sun on my face. I yearn for the breeze to blow my hair and to watch my grapevines fill with succulent fruit."

"I know you do," I said, "and that's why I brought you fresh flowers so you could have a bit of nature in your room. I began to think of how you started this rancho with the hard work of your own hands. I can tell by the beauty of the architecture of the laid fields and fertile orchards that you loved your work."

A shadow crossed George's face. "Yes, and I'll never be young again and able to work the fields. I shall die in my bed without my wife by my side."

"George," I whispered, "I brought you some white beans. I was in the garden preparing them to store for spring, and thought you might like to hold some of them."

I put the white beans in George's shaky hands, and put mine around his. He closed his eyes as if savoring the moment.

"George, feel the essence of the beans. They have life in them, and will reincarnate in the spring into a new life form. Someday they will take root in their home of nourishing dirt and moisture. The tiny green shoots will seek the sun, and will grow vines and stalks. These tiny seeds will get to be eight-feet tall. They're like the soul within your body."

I had him hold the withered husks, which had contained the beans. "When our season is done, we shed our bodies, like these husks. I will place these pods into the straw and dirt pile, and rake them back into the soil to supply nutrients for the beans in the spring."

"Yes, I see, my Angel. My body is like the pods of the beans. Dust to dust."

"You do see, George, don't you? Nothing is lost. . .it's only transformed. . .the beans, the flowers, our bodies. We shape-shift out of these bodies, but our spirit is whole and intact, and enduring and endless as the sky."

"You're so reassuring. You make death sound beautiful, somehow."

"George, I love you. You raised and loved and taught Reynard. He's such a beautiful man, not only in body but also in mind and spirit. I thank you for that."

"He was a gentle child and easy to raise. He's always been a good son. Now, he'll have to take over for me."

"I want you to feel at ease about leaving Reynard and the family. I'll stay here and care for them. I have decided that if Reynard will have me, I will marry him."

"That makes me very happy. I feel I can die without worrying about the family. But, I'm concerned about. . ."

"I know, George. We'll have to do something about Joseph. Father Jean and Reynard are working on a plan, and I'll help them, if I can."

"Then I can rest easy knowing that."

George's face grew serious, and a flicker of fear crossed his eyes. I took his hands again, and assured him once more. "I want you to know you don't need to be afraid about dying, either. Remember, you're not your body. You are your spirit. You don't need to be afraid to leave your body since it's only the temple for your spirit. You can leave your tired old vehicle behind, and go on to a new, blissful freedom you've never known. You can go in search of your beloved wife, Sarah. You can go into the cosmos to where God dwells and become one with the Great Spirit and his plan for you."

As I finished saying this, tears flowed down my cheeks. I bent down and kissed George on his forehead.

I could tell by the distant and contented look in his eyes that what I had said filled his heart.

George said in a whisper, "Thank you, Angelica."

As I turned to go, I stopped and looked back and whispered, "I'll meet you next on the spirit plane to where there's endless freedom."

Chapter Thirty-Three
George Shares His Visions

arly the next day, I awoke with a plan to help George. At breakfast, I told Reynard and Carmen, about my intentions. "I must go back to the mountains to do a vision quest for myself and for George. Even though he's ready to die, he's having a hard time letting go of this life because of his fears. I feel I can help him by praying and meditating to connect him with God's spirit. If I can do that, it'll make it easier for him to let death take him."

"Do you want someone to go with you, Angelica?" Reynard said.

"No. You and Carmen are family. You must stay with him to the end and comfort him as much as you can."

After I gathered a few things from my room and told the family I was leaving, Reynard went to the barn to saddle Honey. He took me aside and placed his strong hands on either side of my face and looked deep into my eyes. "Please be careful. I don't want you to go, but I know by your tone of voice, you have made up your mind."

"Yes, Spirit has spoken to me to do this thing."

"I want you to take Jack with you as protection. Vasco may come from time to time to make sure you are okay and report back to me. So, if you see a crow hanging around. . .you'll know it's him."

Carmen came outside with some food, and a drum which she handed me. She said, "I've been making this drum for you in the old sacred medicine way. I was waiting for the right time to give it to you. This drum will help you with your visions."

Carmen and Reynard stood on the porch steps and waved as I passed by. Jack ran alongside Honey as I rode down the dirt trail.

The closer I got to the river, the foggier it got. The dense shroud swirled with the morning breeze. The mist made me feel spacey — as if I was in my spirit and not my body. I began to feel a part of the miasma.

I wore leather gloves, a wool sweater, a heavy coat, a pair of wool britches Carmen had made me, and a broad brimmed hat tied under my chin.

I didn't know where to go, so I let Honey lead me where she would. We rambled up hills and down, into quiet valleys, through streams, and over rocky patches. I saw a lone oak at the top of a dried grassy ridge and headed for it. I dismounted Honey, unsaddled her, and then let her loose, knowing she was trained to come with a whistle.

As Mountain Screamer had instructed me earlier, I took out a package of tobacco from the saddlebag and sprinkled it on the ground around the tree, making a large circle. I placed some corn meal in each of the four directions. This would be the place where my spirit could travel great distances, all within this small space.

I rolled out my wool blankets, and put the leather saddle against the tree to lean on. Jack cuddled next to me and went to sleep, tired from his long walk.

I concentrated on letting go of my thoughts by observing them and seeing them dissolve. I saw the wild brown oat grasses blowing in the breeze and realized, despite the changing of the weather, and the impending winds and heavy rains, the oat grass never bothered about what would happen, or felt concern with the passing autumn days. Its focus was the reality of being supple and malleable as it bent and swayed with the ever-present breeze. Even the wild oat had this wisdom, and it passed it along to me as I sat in silence. Truly, this was the secret of never feeling burdened.

I stared at the velvety, soft blue sky and my spirit released toward its silent vastness. I watched the leaves of the oak dancing in the wind and became one with the leaves, the wind, and the tree.

Looking down the hill, I observed a cloud of dust turn into a whirlwind. It wound around and around, and headed up the hill. All was quiet and calm around me. The leaves were still. The birds were silent. It became warm and humid. Then all of a sudden, the quiet heavy air exploded into a fierce blast of cold wind as the whirlwind funneled through my camp. I stood up and threw my arms around the rough bark of the oak, and held on as tight as I could, while the wind became a fury of movement.

The wind ruffled Jack's fur and he squeezed into the hollow of a thick log which was nestled next to the oak tree. I was relieved to know he was safe.

The wind's current whistled in my ears and tousled my hair. My clothes whipped about me. The leaves and smaller branches flew in all directions. I closed my eyes to keep out the flying dirt and debris. I listened to the harsh howl of the wind as it blew my thoughts and emotions away from me.

When the wind stopped, a soft rain started to fall. With my drum under my arm, I climbed into the oak and found shelter in the branches. I heard the large drops hit the dry grass as the smell of wet dirt filled the air.

From the vantage point of the tree, I saw Jack come out of the fallen log and then seek the shelter of some thick bushes.

I thought of George dying in his bed — waiting for death. I realized how he must be feeling — both longing and fearing — welcoming and yet not hurrying his new friend, death.

While I drummed, I waited for a song to come. I knew the wind would bring me one. I began singing for George to let go of his body, and for me to learn to shift beyond the body while still in this life. As I stood on a strong branch of the large oak and leaned on the trunk, a song filled my heart with a feeling of bliss. My soul began to feel lighter and more buoyant.

I sang until the rain stopped and the grasses dried. I sang while I watched the clouds blowing through the sky. I saw a hawk soaring by, screaming as it passed. I saw a crow sail above me and saw its dark eyes as if they were watching me. Was it Vasco?

I moved to a lower branch and then jumped to the ground. The sun started to go down. The sky went from pink to orange to purple. Wisps of gray, black clouds swirled around and morphed into a dark purple. I gloried in the simple magnificence of the setting sun.

When the clouds on the horizon turned purple, the foxes from every hilltop started a high-pitched yipping, creating a soprano and alto chorus of calls. Each voice seemed to excite the rest of the pack and the number of voices grew.

Dark clouds hid the crescent moon. I called for Jack. When he came, I patted my blanket for him to sit beside me. He licked my face. I scratched his back, and ran my fingers through his velvety, black ears. He shook his head and looked at me for more petting.

"Lie down, Jack. Let's try to get some sleep," I said, as I yawned. Jack let out a bark and laid down beside me, wagging his tail. Right before I lost consciousness I heard the yelp of a lone fox.

I awoke at dawn. I had slept facing east to watch the sky turn colors in the morning. I could see the orange sky between the small oaks framing the edge of the canyon.

Again the foxes yipped their good mornings and goodbyes to each other. Jack sat up, barked and looked at me for approval. "Good boy, Jack," I said, as I patted him. I fell back to sleep for a couple more hours. When I woke up, I felt like drumming again. I held the drum against my chest, so it would reverberate in my body.

While I drummed, I realized I hadn't experienced the slightest fear of the foxes, or other night creatures, only some alarm at the fierceness of the wind. I knew this century was where I felt the most comfortable. I also realized how much I loved Reynard. My shoulders got goose-bumps and I shook, thinking of the curse — that God-awful curse.

I thought of Carmen and all she had taught me, and of the Indian people I was getting to know, and their culture. I thought of the lessons I had learned through my meditations.

Reynard was teaching me to shape-shift and it felt natural to me — as if I was already attuned to those lessons. I realized, in order to be able to shape-shift, I had to let go of my ego and all its desires, and not fear the cosmic flow of energy through me. I had come to know that if I could shape-shift into the spirit of an animal, I could shape-shift into the past or future since they are the same or a continuum on a yardstick.

My desire today was to astral travel out of my body. I had read about gurus meditating and allowing the spirit to separate from the physical body to travel outside it. I figured if I could accomplish this, it would be my way of showing George that he could leave his body to go on to meet his maker and the joys of heaven.

The day passed with my watching nature and meditating. The foxes started yipping as the sky began to pinken around the fringes. A panorama of orangey-red, lacey clouds filled the horizon. As the sky darkened, I searched the sky for the North Star. When I found it, I made a wish about my future relationship with Reynard living our lives together.

Before going to sleep, I played the drum to soothe me. Jack returned from hunting and snuggled up beside me. I petted him, and then we both fell asleep.

I woke to the howling of some foxes. They started again around six and kept it up for a few minutes. Energized by their voices, I sat up, drank some water and meditated. I realized it had been three days since I had eaten anything. I was feeling very light and spacey, and decided it was now or never.

I sat cross-legged and went into a meditative state. I saw my spirit as a line of pale, gray lights rising around my vertebrae. I felt a little dizzy. I had a pleasant tingling sensation move up my arms, shoulders, and my head. I had the sensation that whatever occupied my inner body was rising above me. My body began to feel numb.

My spirit left my body and sat on a tree branch above me. My astral body could look down from this perch at my heavy physical body sitting on the earth. With my eyes closed, my corporal body sat limp. I seemed separate and apart from that form, which carried me around from place to place. My spirit felt light and airy sitting on the branch. I felt blissful and oh, so free — total freedom — freedom from the past, from the future, from my holding onto my century from whence I came, from worries and fears and concerns. I became immersed in this lightness, this freedom.

After some time, I drifted downward to my heavy, waiting body. When I opened my eyes, everything seemed different — so bright and clear. The birds singing seemed louder, the clouds brighter. Peacefulness filled me, and something else — a pleasant tingling vibration in my body, especially my head.

After three days of my vision quest, I felt complete, and ready to leave my circle. I walked down to the natural hot springs I had seen days earlier on the way to my secluded spot. That area had some underground volcanic activity, and the hot lava underneath the earth's crust warmed the spring. I took off my clothes and put my foot in the warm water. The temperature felt wonderful on my toes. The crisp air, however, cut into my body and I shook.

I hurried to the pond. When I lowered my body into the warm water, I saw a deer grazing on some brush, and a snowy egret wading. As I floated on my back, I realized some green and brown-faced mallards had formed a semicircle near my feet. When I gazed up, I saw an eagle soaring in the fast-moving sky. Then I looked out toward the brown grassy hills, the tall oaks, and the soft lacey willows at the edge of the pond. As I absorbed all this, I was overcome with a profound feeling of cosmic oneness with the water, the earth, the flying ones, the animals, and the sky. I was feeling total bliss.

I wanted to yell out to Reynard and George about my experience.

All of a sudden, a bolt of lightning went through my body, and I saw George's spirit standing by the edge of the pond. I realized George had brought this gift to me. He was sharing the vision of oneness he had experienced at the time of his passing.

Chapter Thirty-Four
Welcome Home

The next day, when Jack and I got back to the rancho, I saw a beautiful golden glow from the house, which made me feel all warm inside, despite the cold wind and rain at my back.

When I stepped onto the porch, I saw the wreath on the front door. The confirmation of my vision — George had let go. He had his freedom.

Reynard came running outside and threw his arms around me. He hugged me for the longest time, tears streaming down his face. Sobs shook his body, and I held him tight.

Reynard said with a husky voice, "George is at peace now. Yesterday he seemed to accept letting go of his body. He mumbled something about thanking Angelica. He whispered to me that I must break the curse or it would continue ruining the family. I promised him I would take care of it."

"I'll miss George, but I know he was ready to go."

"We buried George this morning on the hill overlooking the river he so loved."

"That was a perfect spot for him."

I followed Reynard as he strolled to the kitchen with Jack close behind. "Are you hungry, boy," asked Reynard as he filled Jack's bowl with the evening's left overs. Jack chowed down with enthusiasm.

"As for you, Angelica, here's some left-over stew from dinner. I figured you'd be starved, too."

Reynard handed me a bowl, and I ate with relish.

"By the way, Angelica, I have something on my mind I want to tell you. As you know, Father Jean asked me to wait for him to return, and he would help me with our plan to free the Indians. I don't think I can wait now, after my promise to my father. I must take care of this long-awaited fight with Joseph. I am going to confront him. I want you to stay here at the house with Carmen. Do not follow me. It will be too dangerous."

"Oh, my God, Reynard," I said, setting the stew aside. I no longer felt hungry. "What're you going to do?"

"Let us not talk of that right now. I have more important things to discuss with you. Promise me you will be patient and I will tell you later, *mon amour*."

"Okay. I will try to be patient."

Together, arm-in-arm, we walked through the quiet house and climbed the stairs to the third floor. The French doors were closed to keep the rain out. The vines in the barrels had turned a bright yellow with the season's change to autumn. A fire was burning in Reynard's rooftop room. After having ridden in the rain, that room was the essence of cozy. My clothes and hair were soaked through, and I felt as vulnerable as a kitten.

"Up here," Reynard said, "I could see you coming from a long distance. You were riding with Jack close behind you. I knew you were all right because Vasco came back and reported to me. I missed you so much."

I told Reynard about my visions and of working to free George's spirit as well as mine. I realized the place from where I came was now a part of my past. "I feel more at home here than I did in my land. I feel a commitment to being part of your family and have a deep love for you."

Reynard reached over and hugged me. He gave me a long, wet, passionate kiss and then brushed my cheek with the back of his hand as he looked into my eyes. "I cherish you, *mon amour*.

He handed me a crystal glass into which he poured his Rancho de los Zorros Grises sweet port. I held the glass up to the fire and looked at the dark purple color. I watched Reynard swirl his, and smell the fragrance.

"Put the wine in your mouth and notice all the marvelous tastes of the vine," he said.

Sitting on the gray fox pelts next to the fireplace, I drank the wine, savoring each nuance of flavor. My insides began to warm from the wine's effect. I leaned on Reynard, and stared at the fire as it flickered and popped.

Reynard fed me bites of bread he had brought from the kitchen. I laughed at such attention, and blushed.

Gazing at my face, he said, "Ah, my Angelica, your cheeks have turned to peaches and cream. Such a fine color."

I shivered and then wrung out my wet hair onto the fireplace hearth. Looking concerned, Reynard moved to the bed and pulled the fox pelt bedspread back. "Take off your wet clothes and climb under these covers. I'll be your blanket."

I draped my clothes over the chair by the fire. I pushed my wet hair back and rung it out on the fireplace hearth. Reynard took a towel off the dresser and dried my dripping hair and wet body. Then I climbed into the bed.

He removed the leather band from his pony tail and let his thick shiny hair fall, which went half-way down his back. He took off his clothes, staring at me with desire in his eyes.

For a moment he stood by the fireplace warming his body. The firelight danced on his skin. I gasped at his gorgeous brawny build — his firm biceps, his muscular chest, his silky tanned skin. When he got into bed, he smelled of sweet musk and wood smoke. He climbed on top of me, pulled the fox pelts over us, and hugged me. My shivering turned into the fine trembling of passion.

Reynard kissed my neck. Goose bumps ran down my arms. With the softness of a butterfly he touched his lips to my eyelids, forehead, and cheeks. As he sat up, he held one of my hands, took a deep breath, and in a gentle voice, he said, "Angelica, *ma chéri*. Will you become my wife?"

My heart raced and I whispered, "*Oui*, my darling. *Oui*."

He gazed into my eyes with his fire and longing. We stared soul to soul for an eternity. He whispered in my ear, "You are my love for now and forever."

"As you are mine," I said.

He blew across my breasts, his warm breath setting me on fire. His quivering tongue caressed my lips.

My spirit seemed to leave me and move into my love. It felt like two stars colliding in the cosmos, exploding into fine dust and merging. I no longer existed. My past and who I had been were gone. Now, I was only a fragrance, the scent of a sweet smelling rose. There was no more me.

We stayed in the lovers' embrace for the rest of the evening. Time seemed like it didn't exist for us. Our two bodies merged into one.

Chapter Thirty-Five
Anger

Upon awakening at dawn, Reynard announced, "I am going to see my cousin today. I cannot wait until the end of summer for Father Jean to return. If I cannot do this one thing, I do not deserve you, and I do not deserve to live. I must take care of it before we are married. I want you to stay here. You will only distract me. If I don't come back before nightfall, I may not return at all."

A pang of fear tore through my chest. I said, "What do you mean, my dear?"

"I am going to challenge Cousin Joseph to a fight over the ravine. This has been a custom for settling arguments in this area for centuries, since before the white man came. When the Indians had a dispute, they used this as a way to a resolution without others being involved."

"If I don't go with you, how will I know how you are," I asked.

"I will take Vasco with me, and if I have a problem he will come back here and let you know. If I fall into the ravine, it will be my grave. At least I will have died an honorable death, and some of my oppressive guilt will be relieved."

"No. You can't go. I won't let you."

"I have to clear this debt of these many years. It falls in my hands, these willing hands, to vindicate that past wrong. Otherwise, it will fall on my children, and my grandchildren, ad infinitum."

I grabbed Reynard's hands and said, "Are you sure? Are you really sure this is the right thing to do?"

"I know with this on my mind, I can't marry you, Angelica. I am afraid I may bring the curse to you, too. This is my judgment day. I must pay for the lives that have been lost, and I must save those who have yet to be born. If I die, so be it."

I sat with my hands over my eyes and cried. The sobs tore through my body and I shook in terror for Reynard's safety.

I looked up, and wiped my eyes with the inside of my arm. I said, "You're right, as much as I hate for you to go. I want for us to live long, loving lives together, but I can see they won't be happy years unless you do this thing. After what happened to Suzette and your mother, I can see you'll never be at peace unless you go against your cousin."

"I knew you would understand, my Angelica."

"Let me give you one last kiss before you leave, Reynard. I want to fill you with the strength of my love. If we never kiss again, this kiss will have to last me however long I live."

Reynard had a look of longing in his eyes as he pulled my arms behind my back, his fingers entwined with mine, and he kissed me long and hard. I felt dizzy with the almost unbearable bliss of being loved by him.

Reynard let me go and marched through the opened French doors. I ran to the balcony and watched as he then grabbed a rope, which hung from the railing, and rappelled to the ground. I could see him as he moved with determination across the yard to retrieve his horse.

In a few moments he emerged from the barn riding Red. I watched until he disappeared from sight. I then ran to the bed and fell headlong onto the fox pelts and cried. I felt the deep spasm of loneliness. Fear grabbed my heart. His life could, indeed, be taken this day. If that were to happen, I knew it would be like my own life being taken. I was one with his spirit, and he with mine.

I paced the room from one end to the other, and waited for the sun to make its tour of the sky. Jack kept me company. He lay curled up in a ball, and when I pet him, he sat up and wagged his tail. Once in a while he would whine, look about and sniff the air. When the sun was getting low in the sky, Jack sat up and let out a loud howl. It jolted me. I jumped to my feet and knew I couldn't wait one minute more. Something was wrong. I felt it in my very bones.

Running to the edge of the turret, I looked out at the stormy skies. Vasco came flying back and circled twice, making a loud cawing sound. He flew in through the French doors, settled on my shoulder, and continued cawing.

"Oh, my God." I screamed, "He's been hurt."

Vasco flew out the window. I ran down the stairs as fast as I could, Jack running behind me, barking.

I ran into the barn and grabbed Honey. I threw a rope over her neck and without bothering with a saddle, I jumped on. Vasco flew in circles and then in a straight line as if telling us which way to go. Jack ran behind me, still barking. I held the horse's mane in my hands and guided the horse with my legs and knees.

The late afternoon sky filled with dark clouds, and the wind blew Honey's mane back. I shivered as I watched a streak of lightening flash across the hillside.

As I got to the edge of the ravine, the sun had just gone down. I could make out two men standing on a log extending over the chasm to the other side. They were holding long poles made from oak tree limbs.

As I approached, I could hear the loud banging of the poles. I tied Honey to a tree and edged my way to a rock so I could watch, not wanting to distract Reynard. They were fighting with their shirts off. Reynard's hair was tied back. Joseph had a heavy beard. A full moon peeked through the dark rain clouds. As they fought, the thunder in the skies mimicked the noise of the banging sticks. The sound of their battle reverberated off the canyon walls. The lightning responded and paralleled the fight.

Joseph yelled insults to Reynard as they fought, and Reynard answered him. I crawled closer to hear. Reynard yelled out that Joseph was nothing but an Indian slaver and a rapist. Joseph responded with, "Suzette's death was your fault." At this insult, Reynard faltered, and Joseph hit him on the forehead with his pole.

Reynard fell into the ravine.

I dropped to my knees and wept into the thick clover that grew next to the ravine. I felt certain Reynard had just been killed.

Joseph laughed, as he walked off the log onto the ground. Still laughing, he climbed on his horse, and rode away.

The clouds parted, and the bright moon shone into the ravine where Reynard had fallen. I crawled on my hands and knees to the edge and looked down. I could see Reynard lying on a shelf of rock, his body unmoving.

I can't lose another man I love. I have to find a way to get to him. There must be a chance he's still alive.

I put my hands on my chest to hold my aching heart and felt the rattler necklace, the one I received after my first shape-shifting episode where I became a hawk. I pulled the necklace off and held it to my forehead where the crystal had been embedded by the mermaids. I quieted my mind and became very still, concentrating on my breath going in and out, and my chest rising and falling.

Between the moments of the inhalation of air and the exhalation, I saw a vision of something that looked like a wing. The moon shone through it, illuminating all the stripes and patterns, and strong feathers entwined together. As I watched I saw the tiny, downy white feathers around one of the claw feet. They looked so soft and almost furry. I saw the feathers around the heart, the strong muscled chest, and then the wings folded to its sides. As I looked at the bird's eye, it became larger until it expanded into the sky. The eye looked inside me. Silence descended.

How long this vision took I don't know, but when I opened my eyes, I could make out pink in the clouds and knew the sun would be coming up soon. I felt exhausted and rolled over and found Reynard curled up in a fetal position next to me, blood dried on his forehead. I cried out with excitement. I took off my cape and put it over Reynard. Small, downy hawk feathers flew off the cape when I laid it around him.

I shuddered at the realization that I had shape-shifted into a hawk during the night and somehow had been able to retrieve Reynard. No one would ever be able to explain to me how I had done it, but there lay Reynard beside me.

I whooped and ran for Honey, jumped on and galloped as fast as I could to Mountain Screamer's lodge. He was sitting cross-legged, arms folded, his eyes closed.

"Hello Red Hawk Woman," he said without opening his eyes. "You have great medicine. Yes, I will go with you to help Reynard."

Mountain Screamer flung his rawhide medicine bag over his shoulder and accompanied me on his horse.

Chapter Thirty-Six
Crazy Woman

Some weeks later, Carmen approached me at lunch. "You know, Sisi is nearing her time of confinement, and this will probably be a difficult birth since she's not well. I think it's time we found a midwife for her, or we'll have a difficult time trying to assist her ourselves. I know the look of these sick ones. There's not much chance she'll survive, but the baby may."

"What do you think we should do," I asked.

"There's a woman in the nearby hills on the way to town who everyone calls Crazy Woman. She's known to be a good midwife and healer. If you're interested, we can ride out to her house when we get these dishes put away."

By mid-morning, we saddled up our horses and rode to find Crazy Woman. Carmen said, "Please try to stop worrying about Reynard. The doctor said he needs complete bed rest for the next month so that his concussion can heal. There's nothing you can do now. This is a good excuse to get you away from him, so he can get his proper rest. When you're around, he wants to stay awake and talk."

"Yes, I know you're right. It's just that I worry so much about him. He's taking so long to heal."

"The doctor assured us he'll recover. It'll just take time. Right now, you need to focus and have your energy about you when you approach Crazy Woman. Her powers are hectic and it's said she can pull you into her dizzying spiral. Be on guard. I want you to put this crystal in your pocket. If you feel dizzy at all, put your hand inside your pocket and rub the stone."

As Carmen and I approached a run-down cabin, a middle-aged, big-boned woman with tangled graying hair came running out. She was yelling and waving her arms in the air. "Huggle, buggle, double bubble. Relations come and relations go. They now come to have me tell them so."

We dismounted, and tied our horses to the nearby tree. We walked toward the house, keeping our eyes on that strange woman. She stood on the porch with her arms outstretched in welcome, which gave me a slight feeling of safety.

When we stepped near the porch, Crazy Woman jumped down from the top step to the ground where we stood, and started hugging us. "Ah, all my relations. All my two-legged relations have come."

As we hugged Crazy Woman, I could feel a joy fill my heart. Without knowing or needing to know why, I rejoiced at such a warm welcome by this strange woman.

"Holly, golly, golly me. Come, come, and sit my loves. My tea is what you need. Warms the tummy. Fills you up."

Crazy Woman led us into her cabin, and motioned for us to sit on some chairs placed around a table. A teapot sat on the table along with cups, saucers, cloth napkins, and silver spoons. In the middle of the table was a vase filled with purple catnip and white angelica flowers. Crazy Woman pulled off a couple of pieces of the angelica and put it in the tea pot to let it seep.

"Angelica," she said. "I'm making your tea from these white flowers which also bear your name. According to a French legend, an angel revealed to a peasant woman that angelica would cure the plague and be good against evil spirits. Wickedness lurks in our future. Drinking this tea will help us fend it off."

Carmen and I looked at each other. Carmen's eyebrows went up and her shoulders shrugged.

Before either of us could speak, Crazy Woman went on with her chatter. "An imminent birth. Ah, yes." She put her hands to her brow and closed her eyes, lowered her head, and mumbled, "An evil illness brought on by lustful men. This is bad, very bad. A baby of mixed breed to be born. But to survive? That's a problem as well as the mother, yes. But what shall we do?"

Carmen looked into Crazy Woman's eyes, and said "How did you know all this before we'd even spoken? Has someone told you we required your services?"

"Jumble and jump. Scatter and bump. I know all, if I just go into my center. My center is where it all is. You both have a good center. You can learn to access, and then you'll have success," Crazy Woman said, shaking her head.

I looked at her, and said, "You're psychic, aren't you? You know the future by certain powers you were born with or developed at a young age. I've heard of people like you. It's quite a wonderful gift, but sometimes a difficult one to bare. It must bring great responsibilities with it."

Crazy Woman sat up straight, her eyes brightened and then she spoke to me. "Yes, but you, too, have great gifts that bring many responsibilities and burdens along with great joys."

Crazy Woman looked normal when she spoke to me in this way. I thought perhaps she had come out of her trance, and was speaking to us in a more conscious state of mind.

I responded to her. "You're correct. I've only recently begun to realize my gifts. I hope I can live up to the expectations of those around me."

"No problems. No problems," Crazy Woman sputtered.

"As you seem to already know, I'm Angelica, and this is my fiancé's sister, Carmen. We come from Rancho de los Zorros Grises, where George Rutherford, the owner, recently died."

"So sorry to hear, but he lived a good and long life. Good man he was."

"Yes, he had a beautiful spirit," I said. "By the way, is there a name we should call you?

"A name, a name you ask me?" Crazy Woman said. She seemed a little taken aback, as if no one had ever asked her this question before.

"My birth name was Geraldine. Most people call me Crazy Woman." As she spoke, I could tell she was no longer Crazy Woman.

"My brother's name is Joseph. I was born of Maximillian. My mother was Mary, but Joseph's mother was our Indian servant, Little Crow. This is a dark, dark secret. No one knows this but me, now that father is dead. Even Uncle George didn't know of Joseph's true mother."

I saw Carmen's mouth drop open at this new information.

Geraldine went on. "Father was married to a lovely young woman, Mary. Father couldn't be with only one woman, so he frequented the saloons in town, and the whore houses. He gave mother syphilis, and it made her sterile. . .you know, barren. After me, she couldn't have any babies. Mother had terrible pains in her stomach, and took to the opium and stayed in bed a lot."

"So," Carmen said, "you're my cousin, Geraldine?"

"Yes. I'm your cousin."

"Everyone said you'd disappeared many years ago or had died."

"Well, here I am," Geraldine said, "fat and sassy."

"Please," Carmen said, "tell us more about your family."

"Well, my father's servant, Little Crow, was a beautiful young Indian woman, who had a bit of the medicine background from her father. Little Crow gave birth to Joseph, but she wasn't allowed to tell anyone for fear of death. She'd had a little reading and writing from being around us and from our book learning. She kept a little diary under her pillow, and one day I found it. That's how I knew she was Joseph's true mother."

"Oh, my God. Aunt Mary wasn't Joseph's mother," Carmen said.

"No, she wasn't. It was Little Crow, but Joseph always treated her like a nasty primitive animal. He had no respect for her because father said she was Indian and inferior to us. Both Father and Joseph mistreated her, and often swore at her when she didn't wait on them fast enough."

"I always thought Aunt Mary died giving birth to Cousin Joseph," Carmen said.

"She died from the ravages of syphilis about the time Little Crow birthed Joseph, so that gave our father a perfect way to cover up who Joseph's real mother was. He decided he'd just say Mary died giving birth."

"That's terrible. What happened to Little Crow?"

"Sometimes Joseph would throw rocks at her. She'd call up her power animals, the crows, the blackbirds, and the ravens. . .her totem family. The birds would flock by the hundreds into the great oak in front of our house. When Joseph went outside, they'd fly down and peck him. He was so afraid of the birds, that he'd run into the house crying."

"Thank goodness," Carmen said, "Little Crow had some form of protection."

"I'd feel sorry for Little Josito," Geraldine said. "That was my nick name for him. I'd wash his wounds, and cradle him as he shook and cried. When he got older, he'd get his shotgun and shoot at the birds if they came at him. He always understood they were Little Crow's medicine birds."

"How did you handle being around that kind of negative energy?" I said, hoping I wasn't intruding in their conversation.

"Well, Angelica, when I turned fifteen, I spent a lot of time in my room because my father was so crazy. I hated it when my father enslaved hundreds of the local Indians, and made Joseph into his cohort. My head did funny things, and I needed to leave before I ended up in an asylum."

"I can understand that," I said, "but how did you ever get away?"

"When father and Joseph were busy overseeing the Indian slaves harvesting some crops, I snuck off and rode into town."

"Since you didn't have any family support when you left, who helped you?"

"I married a miner, Johnny, who was the first man to ask me to be his bride. He took me away to this cabin to live. He put up with my crazy ways that seemed to bring him no end of entertainment."

"I'm so happy you had someone to love you," Carmen said. "Where is Johnny, now?"

"He died about five years back, and here I am all by myself. I do get town folk nosing around up here. They come to ask for my cures. After they get well, they don't want nothin' to do with me."

All of a sudden, Carmen jumped up and ran over to Geraldine, and grabbed her hand. "My cousin, Geraldine. Gerry, Gerry, Gerry. I'd wondered where you were all these years. We played together when we were little. . .I remember. You were such a cute little girl, and so full of life. It must have been horrid living with your father and Joseph. Can I hug you like I did when we were little?"

Geraldine didn't wait to be asked again. She sprang up and hugged Carmen. They began to cry as they rocked each other back and forth, and then laughed. Geraldine jumped and leaped around the table. Then she grabbed Carmen and twirled her around.

I hopped out of my chair and it fell onto the wooden floor with a loud thud. They both looked up, startled at first. Then they grabbed my hands and we danced together.

"Relations, relations. . .we're relations. Follow me and we shall see."

Geraldine grabbed a black-knit shawl off the coat rack, and put it around her shoulders. She took our hands, pulled us out the door and steered us behind the cabin and up the hill. Geraldine walked faster and faster on the crooked dirt path. It became harder to keep up. She seemed to be driven to get to the top of the hill as fast as possible. Carmen and I started panting and sweating, but Geraldine seemed unfazed by the steepness of the trail.

A breeze began to blow and the pine trees along the pathway swayed, and the bushes quivered. As a drizzle of rain began, I raised my head toward the cool drops.

When we got near the top of the hill, I realized Geraldine's hurry was to beat the sun before it went down. My lungs felt like they were about to burst as I tried to keep up.

"Sparrowy, Sparrowy," Crazy Woman shouted at the top of her lungs. "Sparrowy, show yourself. It is only sisters of the breast. We come in peace and with good tidings."

Chapter Thirty-Seven
The Ceremony

Awoman jumped from a tree branch and landed in front of Crazy Woman, no longer Geraldine. Carmen and I gasped at the suddenness of her appearance. "I'm Sparrowy. I'm one with the sisters and here to assist."

Sparrowy was a short, plump Indian woman who appeared to be about fifty-years old. She wore her long black hair tied back by leather thongs. Her eyes sparkled, and her long sharp nose filled her face.

Crazy Woman grabbed her friend, and gave her a bear hug. "I knew you'd make it. I knew. I knew. Sisters, meet Sparrowy, the Medicine Woman of Black Mountain country. The last of her kind, and my helper."

Sparrowy said, "And sometimes mine, mine, mine."

Crazy Woman pushed us inside a cave hidden by some pine branches at the end of the trail. Walking into the dark recesses, Sparrowy lit some kindling that sat on the ground. Next, she added wood from the stack alongside the wall.

The light of the dying sunset peeked in, filling the room with orange and pink light. The last of the sun's rays touched the clear crystal Sparrowy held. She spit on the crystal and rubbed it on her own forehead, and then on Crazy Woman's brow, who was sitting beside the fire. She came over to me and Carmen, and also rubbed the stone over our foreheads.

Sparrowy put the crystal in her pocket and then replaced the pine boughs across the entrance to the cave. She sat cross-legged before the fire. Carmen and I sat down in imitation of the two medicine women.

As I sat in the circle, I felt the warmth of the fire and the hand of Crazy Woman on my right, and Sparrowy on my left. Was I out of place with these women of power?

Crazy Woman shouted as if in reply to my question. "We're all sisters here. We're all two-leggeds. Spirit sisters are we."

As Sparrowy started pounding a hoop drum she'd removed from the wall of the cave, Crazy Woman stood up and gyrated to the rhythmic sounds. Her movements were infectious. Carmen and I couldn't resist joining Crazy Woman in her primal motions.

The firelight danced on the walls of the cave. Souls joining. Souls dancing. Spirits uniting.

Outside, I could hear the gentle rain fall and then increase with the wind. Far away, I heard the first thunder. The wind shrieked and howled outside, pushing the thunder clouds so close the roar and rumble filled the cave.

Lightning lit up the room, then the brightness faded and fire embers were the only light present.

I had no idea how long we danced. Time seemed a distant concept in that cave. Ancestors, Native Americans, ranchers, modern day yuppies all danced in unison that night, no limitations of time and space.

We joined hands, and the beat of Sparrowy's drum continued as a heartbeat. We leaned back, our long hair hanging near the dirt floor, our chins arching toward the rock ceiling. We spun like the Earth around the stars and moon, like galaxies spinning in and out, like comets and meteors out of control. Sparks from the fire jumped up as did our spirits — right out of our bodies and into the ether.

When I awoke, the four of us were lying on the cave floor sleeping. The fire had long since gone out, and the smell of acrid smoke was in the air.

I saw Crazy Woman rise on her elbows and look around at the rest of us. She held her finger to her lips for me to be silent. She then motioned me to follow her outside.

I blinked in the sunlight. Crazy Woman handed me a gourd of water to drink. I took a couple of large sips and wiped my mouth with the back of my hand. Crazy Woman took the gourd and drank and then opened her arms to the light. "Ah, day has come to greet us," she said as we heard a lone coyote howl.

She leaned her head back and also let out a long howl. She waited as if listening for a response. A coyote, poised at the top of the hill, didn't disappoint her, and howled back, making two quick barks. When Crazy Woman heard him, she laughed. "Yes, he says it's going to be a good day." Crazy Woman and I watched as the coyote turned from the path, ran down the hill, and vanished into the brush.

All of a sudden, I watched Crazy Woman transform and before me stood Geraldine, again. As she took both my hands in hers, and looked into my eyes, she said, "Angelica. Angelica. How do I tell you, my modern one, that you're on the path to awareness. You have practiced the ways and have the gift. Only a little more work and you can be there. Don't be afraid. You can let go. The heavens will take care of your gentle spirit."

"Yes, I'm learning that lesson," I said.

"Above all, speak your truth as it comes to you from your heart. You'll know the answers you need if you allow yourself a time of silence. All knowing comes from that place."

Carmen emerged from the cave and stretched. "Good morning my sisters," she said, smiling. Looking at Geraldine, Carmen said, "I'm so happy to have found you, Cousin Gerry. I want you to stay in our lives from now on."

Geraldine took our hands, and bid us sit down on the large boulder next to her.

"I'll come to your rancho for the births, but the births will not be who and what you think. Much sadness, much gladness, many surprises."

Chapter Thirty-Eight
Juliette Argues with Her Parents

As I approached the house carrying some eggs and fresh chives in my apron for the morning omelet, I heard loud, angry voices coming from the porch. As I got closer, I heard White Owl say, "You can't know how you have shamed us. You, who we trusted to watch over your young cousins. You are older and should have been responsible instead of becoming a harlot."

I could see White Owl, who had his hands on his hips, standing next to Juliette. She sat on the handrail of the porch, and reacted to her father's insult by jumping down and yelling.

"You can't possibly understand how much I can ache for the one I love. He was a wonderful, talented man, and I wanted to keep a piece of him wherever I went. I'm happy that I'm pregnant. I don't care what you think."

With that exclamation, Juliette turned and ran down the steps toward the wooded knoll at the east end of the vineyard. As she fled, I overheard White Owl mumbling, "Yes, I do know how one can ache for the one he loves."

I stayed at the garden gate until I saw White Owl walk back into the house. I climbed the steps to the porch and went through the kitchen door, so I wouldn't run into White Owl's darkened face.

Carmen was grinding the coffee when I entered, a dour look upon her face.

I said, "Kid problems, Carmen?"

"Yes, something like that."

"I couldn't help but notice Juliette has gained a bit of weight, lately. Could it have something to do with that?"

Carmen broke into tears. I walked over and put my arms around her and let her sob on my shoulder.

"I can't understand kids these days. You'd think you could trust them, but now this. . ."

"Tell me what happened, Carmen."

"I couldn't understand why Juliette wasn't happy to see her old Frankie when she got back. They were best friends when she left for France. I noticed that whenever she went to town, she'd have nothing to do with him. Why, only the other day he stopped off at the house, and they had a terrible row. I don't think he'll ever come back to see Juliette again, the way she treated him."

"So, you were set on having Frankie become your son-in-law when Juliette returned," I asked.

"We only wanted her to marry into a good family, and to some nice boy who'd look after her. We had hoped for grandkids, but not like this. Her and her big secret. She said she married the man, but I don't think it was a proper marriage."

"Listen, Carmen, why don't I try to talk with her. I know this must be a very emotional time for all of you."

"I'd appreciate it, honey. I really would."

I left the eggs and herbs on the counter for Carmen. I turned and left the house walking in the direction I had last seen Juliette. I climbed to the wooded knoll and looked for footprints or anything that would lead me to Juliette. Where the thick ferns grew beneath the shady canopy of trees, I heard a soft weeping sound. I stopped and listened to her rhythmic sobs, wanting to give Juliette time to cry. When I heard the sobs lessen, a large sigh filled the glade and then silence.

I called out, "Juliette, Juliette, my darling girl. It's okay. It's Auntie Angelica. I've come to talk with you. No matter what's happened, it's okay. You aren't the first young woman to face the future alone. . .at least feeling she's alone."

Juliette's head popped up among the ferns, her large brown eyes looking startled. She reached her arms out toward me, calling, "Auntie Angelica. I called for an angel to help me, and they sent me you. My dear auntie."

I walked over and I held her. We both sat down on the grass and I began massaging her shoulders. I could feel the muscles ease under my fingertips.

"Come," I said. "Let's walk beside this great river that has quenched the thirst of people of this valley, nourished the animals, trees, flowers, and vineyards. Let's go and let her nourish us."

I took Juliette's hand and pulled her up. I could see her center of gravity was becoming off balance by the developing weight in her belly.

Juliette took my arm and we walked side-by-side down the knoll, and followed the deer path to the river. It seemed like we were two sisters of the universe, she and I. Two sisters bonded by time and love.

A stray strand of hair fell into her eyes, and she pushed it behind her ear. She smiled at me, and I could see her tears had dried now.

"Auntie Angelica, I know I've disappointed my family. I never had that in mind at all. The problem is, I never wanted to marry. I see marriage as enslaving a woman. It leaves her nothing in her own right. The only creativity allowed a woman is having children. I want to experience that while I'm young, but I also want other things in my life. I have so many plans I want to fulfill. I have aspirations, dreams."

"I know you're an ambitious woman, Juliette."

"I've always feared if I married I would never be free to be an individual. I want to be an artist. I do have the talent. I know I do. Before I left France I was beginning to sell my paintings."

"That's wonderful, my dear. I didn't know."

"Here in America, I'd have to sell my paintings under a man's name. . .which I will do, if I must. I'll be known as Jule. Here, if you are a woman, they don't think you are capable of being an artist or thinking of anything but babies and raising kids."

"Juliette," I said, "would you tell me about the baby's father now? What happened to you in Paris?"

Chapter Thirty-Nine
Juliette's Love Affair

Juliette and I sat down on a large boulder alongside the river. She started to run her fingers through my long hair. She told me she was going to weave it into one long braid down my back. As she worked, she began to talk.

"When I was in the Parisian finishing school, I had an art teacher who would come once a week to teach art to the students. Most of our school subjects were silly, like sewing, cooking, and decorating a house, or how to be a good hostess. We would learn French literature, but that was about as deep as our subjects went. When the art teacher came, I was very excited to be learning something creative."

"Ah, so that's where you learned to paint," I said.

"Yes. Chesan DuPont was the teacher's name. He was a very attractive young man with thick dark hair, which reached his shoulders. His eyebrows were dark and wide, and his eyes, almost black. He had a thick beard, rosy lips, and large well-formed teeth. When he smiled, the world lit up. . .and he smiled often when he spoke of art, his true love."

"It must have been nice to meet someone with such a passion for art."

"Yes, Angelica. It was because of our shared passion that Chesan seemed to single me out as his favorite student. Often he would observe my canvas and comment on my painting and compliment me. He said I had talent, and I should continue working on my art."

When Juliette finished my braid, she told me she wanted me to braid her hair as she talked. I pulled the pins out of her chignon, and then I started running my hands through her hair to straighten it.

Juliette said, "Chesan told me he had a studio not far from the school, and needed a model on the weekends. He said I would be perfect, and he would pay me, plus give me free lessons on the side. I was ecstatic thinking I could pose for a famous artist, and also learn from him."

"Yes, Juliette, that was a wonderful opportunity for you."

"I started going to his apartment every weekend. Many of the girls at the school had family nearby, and so when they would leave, I pretended I was going with them. I had grown very homesick, and became especially lonely on those long weekends."

"Juliette, I hope you were concerned about your reputation and were discreet. I'm sure any information about being alone with a man would spread through the school."

"Of course, Auntie Angelica. Anyway, Chesan had me pose with Grecian type clothes, and he'd drape me with silk and chiffon. He placed fresh flowers around me, and in my hair. He would laugh and call me his princess. I loved the attention."

"Oh, boy. I know where this is going, my dear sweet, naive Juliette."

"Yes, you're right, Auntie Angelica. After some months, when I became used to him, he asked me to begin posing in the nude. At first I was very reluctant, but I decided I was being prudish and gave in. I became accustomed to sitting draped in a chair with a silk scarf about me, exposing my pink, chilled skin to the light and Chesan's all-seeing eyes."

"I must say, you're one of the most daring young women I know."

"Chesan made me feel desirous and beautiful." As Juliette said this, she wrapped her arms about herself and her eyes sparkled.

She told me Chesan would spend a long time draping her just so, sometimes running his fingers along her thigh or bare arm. Whenever he did this, his cheeks would redden, and she knew he was desirous of her.

I finished braiding Juliette's hair, sat back, and admired what I had done. Then I said, "Of course, he desired you Juliette. You're a beautiful woman."

"Thank you, Auntie Angelica. After sitting for him like that, the suspense was getting to me. I felt this burning desire for him that I had never experienced before. I wanted him, even if it meant I was to die."

"So, let me guess. You made the first move."

"When my desire was too much, I grabbed his hair and pulled him toward my lips. He started to turn away, saying that I was too young and vulnerable, and that he couldn't take advantage of a young innocent."

"Good for Chesan. I hope you took no for an answer," I said.

"I became angry, and pulled on my clothes, and stomped out of his studio. All week my desire did nothing but increase. It became my obsession to love him."

"You sure are headstrong."

"When he came to school that week to teach, I acted as if nothing had happened between us. I told him I needed the air of the country, and would he accompany me that weekend on a hike through the farmland to paint. He looked at me and winked. I knew I would prevail over him, if I persisted."

"You are a wild woman, Juliette."

She put her hand to her mouth and giggled. She then continued her story.

"Early that Saturday morning, I put on my blue cotton jumper over my blue and yellow spotted blouse, and then a straw hat. I walked out of the cloistered school, taking my basket, as if I were going shopping. I ambled into the open-air market, which was filled with colorful umbrellas, shading the wares. I bought red wine, glasses, cloth napkins, oranges, fresh cheeses, both yellow and orange, and freshly baked bread. I even bought some chocolates with their centers soaked in vermouth."

"Oh, yes. I love those, too."

I kneaded my hands as I worried where this story was taking my innocent Juliette.

She continued, telling me about how Chesan was waiting for her at an outdoor cafe smoking a cigarette, and drinking a cup of coffee.

"I'll always remember him sitting there with a blue scarf around his neck and wearing his dark brown corduroy jacket."

"Your memories are so vivid, Juliette."

She told me that when he saw her, he jumped up and took her basket. He flung his backpack over his shoulder, which he told her was filled with paint supplies. Then they left, arm-in-arm.

"Where did you go on your picnic," I asked.

"First we boarded the train at the stone bridge near the school. We rode into the countryside, and then I insisted we get off when I saw the mustard flowers and poppies along the tracks. Chesan wanted to paint the flowering apple orchards nearby which were filled with wild parsley and thyme."

"Oh, it sounds just gorgeous," I said.

"As Chesan and I walked hand-in-hand, I felt happier than I had ever been. Life was rich and full. I was so in love."

"I'm happy you were able to find such a deep love."

"Yes, me, too. When Chesan and I found the perfect spot that thrilled us, he put the basket of food and backpack on the grass, and we proceeded to set up our easels. I organized the paints, and put out the water and brushes. It was then that he told me his secret."

Chapter Forty

Juliette Reveals Chesan's Secret

As Juliette and I sat there, she told me what she'd never told anyone before.

"Juliette, you know the thing that fascinates me the most about you," Chesan said. "It's that you're half American Indian. I love your high cheekbones, your light brown skin, and dark shiny hair. I adore the wildness you carry inside you. You have the mystique of the primitive, the unknowable. You also have a natural artistic genius with colors and form. I'm so happy you chose me to be your mentor. It's a great responsibility, this mentoring."

"I'm honored that you have chosen me," I said.

"I, who will have such a short life," Chesan said. "I want to savor it, and spend my last days with such a wild youth. Would you like to spend your summer break with me going to the Swiss Alps where the air will be cooler and the flower colors crisper, and the sky translucent?"

Chesan was scaring me with this talk of last days. What was he thinking? I responded, "I'd love to go with you. But, Chesan, life is not always so short. I think it's only our desiring which makes time seem that way. Perhaps if we lived more in the moment, our lives would seem an eternity."

"Yes, my dear. Ah, if only it was so. My doctors tell me I have maybe a few months, at most, if I take it easy.

At this news, I ran crying to Chesan and fell at his knees sobbing, saying, "Chesan, Chesan. My darling man. I didn't know. I'm so sorry."

"My heart is poorly," he said, "and always has been. I was born this way. That's why my family encouraged me in art, so I would have a sedentary life."

When my tears stopped, I said, "From now on we should play the game of eternity. If one of us forgets, and speaks of a memory or a future wish, the other should raise an eyebrow, or make some other kind of sign."

"Sure, my dear," Chesan said. "I would love to play this game with you."

That summer was filled with such love. Knowing Chesan's life would last but such a short time, gave our tryst a greater intensity. The two of us stayed in a small rustic cabin in a Swiss resort, which was a short distance from the main hotel where we took our meals.

Every cabin along our winding road had blue shutters painted with mountain flowers. In the evenings, a fireplace and a good supply of wood was all we needed.

We spent our days walking the hills about the countryside. Chesan would huff and puff. He always pushed to go higher in the mountains, because he loved to see the views. I scolded him and told him we shouldn't climb too high because the air was thin.

One day, Chesan told me, "Being in the mountains is like being God on high, looking at his magnificent creation. Besides, I need to practice being an angel, so I can fly about and find you wherever you are."

In the evening, we'd start a large fire in our rustic, stone fireplace. Chesan would have me lie on the sheep skin carpet, bare except for my dark blue shawl, which he draped over my breasts and woman's parts. He said he loved to paint me, but couldn't match my beauty on the canvas.

Chesan would never do more than give me tender kisses on the lips and face. In the evening he would tuck me into our bed, the headboard and bed posts made of pine. Then he would sleep on the sheepskin carpet.

One day, when he was not feeling well, he insisted I perform an Indian ceremony for him. For a rattle, I found a gourd and filled it with beans. I bought some goat hide and sinew in town, made it into a drum, and dried it in the sun. I then searched about the meadows for herbs to make into a potion.

Chesan said, "I have a very selfish wish, my Juliette, my princess. I'd like you to become my bride, even if it's for a little while. After my death, my parents will look after you. They're very dear people. You can live with them on their small estate, with their large gardens and many pets. They too love art, and would appreciate your paintings as I do."

"I'd love to be your wife, my darling Chesan. Your parents do sound charming."

"I want to speak the word, wife, to you. You're so dear to me. And if, by chance, you have a little Juliette or Chesan, you will give me this immortality of passing on our artistic genes to that little one."

"Chesan, I've never desired to marry. I was always afraid I would become enslaved to the business of being a wife, and not become fulfilled in any other worthwhile pursuits. Most of the women I've known have empty heads, and spend their days chasing after children and doing needlepoint."

"I'd give you all the freedom you desire. I feel you are destined to be a great artist."

"You're so understanding," I said as I took his hand. "In my hometown, a boy named Frankie wanted to marry me when I returned from France. I told him not to wait. . .that I wasn't the marrying type because I had other things I wanted to do with my life."

"Ah, poor Frankie," Chesan said.

"Here, with you, in our own heaven, I'm not afraid. I could marry you and be happy."

"Yes, I feel that angels surround us when we're together."

I was overwhelmed by his statement, and a tear rolled down my cheek.

"I will do a shamanic Indian ceremony and ask the spirits to tell us what to do," I said.

Chapter Forty-One
Juliette Tells of the Visions and Wedding

I burned some logs of pine in the great rock fireplace with the massive wooden mantel. The light from the fire filled our room with its essence. As I sang a rhythmic shamanic song my father had taught me, I shook the rattle around Chesan's body. I picked up a sprig of sage and put the tip by the burning logs. When it caught fire, I blew on it, making the flame go out. The smoke trailed over my head. I then moved my arm, so the wisps went over Chesan's head, around his heart, and then his entire body. I put the glowing sage in a glass of water. I shook the rattle toward the sky to call down the spirits. Then I had Chesan shake the rattle over me.

I said, "We're going to take a symbolic journey to either a cave or into the sky. I want you to watch for your power animal, who will keep you safe and guide you on a journey. Listen to the wisdom spoken or shown to you." I found the drum I'd made sitting near me on the floor. "When I beat the drum faster, you need to return from the place your journey took you, and sit up."

Chesan and I leaned against the bed. For an hour I used a thick stick to drum a steady beat. Right away, I saw a vision of a bald eagle. She came for me and I climbed on her back as she flew into my future. I saw myself standing next to Chesan on a mountain meadow. Villagers stood on the narrow pathway, dancing to the music played by a small wedding band. I saw our faces painted turquoise, and heard the sound of thunder.

After I told Chesan of my vision, he told me of his.

"I saw an owl. I was totally absorbed into the bird's large amber eyes which were warm and inviting. I allowed myself to go with the owl into the unknown and unknowable. I had no fear. The vision I was shown was filled with warm embraces, gentle kisses, and a sharing of love. . .but nothing else after that."

I said, "You have done very well for a first journey. You're a real natural. I think we know what we're to do, now."

The next morning, Chesan went into the village and found a minister to marry us. He invited the villagers we had become friends with, and even asked our landlord and his family to come. Chesan hired some pipers, fiddlers, and horn players. On the narrow pathway to the meadow, villagers danced and threw flowers on the trail.

When we stood and affirmed our vows, the villagers whooped and hollered. Some of the men grabbed us and put us into a very large blanket and threw us up and down into the blue sky. When we soared together, we could see the valley below, as if we were birds flying over the meadows and wild flowers.

When the villagers left, the two of us retreated into our mountain cabin, which had enough wood to keep us supplied for an entire season. The kitchen was filled with all the foods and homemade village pastries we could desire. Vases of wild flowers, and even some braided purple mountain asters had been placed upon our pillows. When I saw the flowers, I began to weep.

Chesan said, "No. No tears. Only joy do I want to see in your eyes. Please always try to see the beauty in life."

Then, Chesan removed his shirt. With great gentleness he removed my dress. He found my cosmetic cream, and laughed as he rubbed it on our faces and bare chests.

Chesan said, "I know your favorite color is turquoise, my dear. Look, I shall paint turquoise on one side of your face, and lavender upon the other. Lovely flowers I shall paint upon your chest. Afterwards, you may paint anything you like on me. I'm your subject, my princess."

When Chesan finished painting my face and chest, we ran to the nearby pond, hand-in-hand, so I could see my reflection in the water.

"Ah, you have created a masterpiece," I said. "I shall never remove the paint."

I then painted Chesan with his favorite colors of purple on the one side of his face, and blue on the other. I painted roses around his breasts, and ivy ambling down to his belly button.

As the sun went down, we howled at the moon, along with the coyotes. The two of us ran through the tall grasses and wild mustards. We laid in the grass and rolled down the hill, laughing.

I was the first to become chilled, and ran for the cabin for warmth. We each put on a blanket and started a blazing fire in the fireplace.

The wind whipped at the windows as the darkness overtook our cabin home. Soon, the stars blinked out, one-by-one, as the black clouds blew in. A soft rumbling in the mountains sounded in the distance, and then grew closer and louder.

Chesan said, "Come with me, my love. Be not afraid of either life or of death. We'll intertwine each other and become as one spirit this night."

Chesan led me outside to the ladder placed against the cabin wall. We climbed onto the roof, and leaned our backs against the stone chimney. The thunder was close, and very loud in our ears as we hugged each other under our blankets.

I wondered at times if we might be consumed in the storm. Lightning could strike the roof at any time. I didn't care, because we were in each other's arms. The rest of the world didn't matter — only the storm, wind, and thunder had any meaning. We were two souls meeting, swirling in and out of life, and death.

I could see our essences as a mist — a light lavender-gray light leaving our bodies. I saw that, despite our corporeal bodies being a temporary abode, our spirits were eternal and would continue on.

As the meadow began to light up with the dawn, the winds died down, the thunder clouds moved on, and the rains came. The two of us climbed down the ladder and into the warm bed to sleep in marital bliss and total contentment.

The days went by, as we were wrapped in the mist of our happiness and love — learning the joys of each other's body.

One day, Chesan said, "Let's make this our last time. This last embrace. I'm ready to go and leave this body. . .this weakened heart will beat no more. Tonight, I'll do my best to make little Chesans or little Juliettes. . .a child of love in this one last burst of my dying energy. I give to you, my princess, our love child. I'll carry a part of you in my soul, as you carry our child. I will wait to dance and play with you in the wind again one day, my love."

I hesitated and put my finger upon his lips, and said, "I cannot. I cannot let you leave me. I want to go with you. Together, we shall join hands, and jump from our mountain into the abyss of sky. I want to join you in your eternity. This time together has been my bliss, which I don't want to end."

"No, you weren't meant to die young. This has been my destiny since birth. It's what is meant to be and I accept it, my darling. Please, let me end it this way, knowing you shall carry our child in your womb, bless it, love it, cradle it, and nourish it with your love."

"If your wish is for me to live on and raise our child, I will do it for you," I said.

"I shall be there watching each time you sing our baby a lullaby," Chesan said. "I shall be there whenever you catch him when he falls, or when you burst with pride at his wonderful abilities, and feel wonder at his innocence. I shall be there when you stroke his soft hair, and kiss his face and hands in remembrance of our love."

"Yes, Chesan. I will do that for our child," I said.

"I want you to carry on. You truly are a great artist and you need to bring your light and love to the world in this way. You'll do this through your artwork, and by the art of your motherhood and raising of our child. Our child will carry this great joy within him. He'll know from the beginning how to love in eternity. He can then go on to teach others what we have learned."

"Yes, my darling. I shall teach our child. Come and touch my womb, our child's home, and say hello. I shall never forget you, and your kind and tender ways, and what you have taught me about life, love, and art. I accept this mission you have offered me."

Chesan kissed my tears, which I could no longer hold back. He then kissed my belly and breasts, eyelids and lips. With great gentleness, he climbed onto me and we became like the sweet in-and-out breath of the waves on a sandy beach. Chesan let out a joyful sound, and that was the last breath of life he ever took. He died in my arms.

I held him until dawn. I put him on a blanket and dragged his body into the meadow, and piled flowers upon him. I sat and waited for the shepherd who came each day to bring us fresh bread.

I asked the shepherd to help me bury Chesan in his favorite meadow, in the midst of the spring wild flowers. The sheep milled about watching us, as if they truly understood this death, and how it wasn't really an ending at all but only a beginning.

After Chesan's death, I went to the school where Reynard's children lived, and said goodbye to them. I told them I'd see them back home. I stayed only long enough to meet Chesan's parents, and tell them of the marriage. They encouraged me to return soon after the baby's birth. They said they would be happy for us to live with them. Afterwards, I caught the next ship home.

Chapter Forty-Two

Permission

When Juliette finished her story, she and I sat without speaking for a few minutes. Then I said, "That's a powerful love story. But why, Juliette, didn't you want to tell your parents?"

"I wanted to hold my love inside and treasure it. I didn't want to ruin it by talking, especially to my parents who I knew wouldn't approve of the fact that I didn't marry with their permission, or in their church. I guess it's time now to discuss it. Would you help me bring it up to them?"

"Of course, Juliette, I'll be happy to speak to your parents for you. Why don't you stay here at the river another hour, and I'll come back for you after I discuss it with them."

I held Juliette's hand and said, "You know I'm so happy for you. . .that you could experience such love, and that you had the privilege of knowing a beautiful human being like Chesan."

Chapter Forty-Three
Sisi Gives Birth

Geraldine came to stay at Rancho de los Zorros Grises to tend to Sisi and Juliette's pregnancies. Sisi lived at the women's Indian lodge situated near the vineyards. She didn't like to be fussed over and would cut any physical examinations as short as possible. She was always pale and often said she felt nauseous throughout her pregnancy, having little appetite. I noticed crusty scales appearing about her face, hands, and arms.

I took Geraldine aside and asked her opinion on how Sisi was progressing. Geraldine sat with me in the tall grass under the oak near the vineyard. She said, "Sisi will start labor any day. It's not likely that she'll live through her labor, nor will her baby survive. It looks to me like she has syphilis. The cures are tough, and I wouldn't even try the medicine while she's pregnant. If she survives, maybe we can try to dose her, but not now."

When we were walking back to the house, I saw Sisi who was lying on her side in the sun near some bushes behind the oak tree where Geraldine and I had talked. Her reclining body was hidden from view until we neared the house. I commented to Geraldine that I thought Sisi had overheard our conversation.

The next day, Watu told me she woke early and noticed her sister was missing from their bunk. She said, at first, she thought perhaps her sister had gone to the river to daydream and to wash. Sisi had been very spacey and quiet as of late, and she often wandered away by herself to be alone. When Watu didn't find Sisi at any of her favorite spots, she grew concerned and ran to the house to find Geraldine and me.

"I can't find Sisi," she said. "I afraid she go off alone to give birth. She talk about dying and how she love me. She say I no need be afraid as she gone to heaven. I safe. She say people here take good care of me."

"Is there anything else she said," Geraldine asked.

"She didn't want anyone bother her when she give birth. She want make no trouble."

We asked workers from the rancho to help in the search, and Geraldine, Carmen, and Juliette joined us.

Geraldine looked concerned and said, "With these cold nights and brisk days, she doesn't stand a chance of making it without some help. We've got to find her soon before it's too late."

I called for Jack. When he came, I put a collar on his neck and attached the leash. After he smelled Sisi's bedclothes, he dashed toward the surrounding woods. When we got to a thicket of trees, Jack started barking and circling. He was off again, pulling me along. Once I fell, and the skin on my knees was torn. I called Jack to halt. I stood up and brushed the leaves from my skirt.

Jack came over, sniffed my knees and whined. I said, "It's okay, boy." I reached down and scratched his head and patted his back. "I'll be fine. Now, let's keep looking for Sisi. Go, boy."

Jack let out a loud bark, and wagged his tail. He started running again, and I had to push myself to follow his pace. The wind picked up, and I felt like it was pushing me toward where I had to go.

Jack started barking again, and circled a tree. He whined, and sat down in a small grassy meadow surrounded by some bushes, and lush, soft ferns.

There, lying on her side was Sisi, with her arms curled up, holding a little bundle of towels. She had a blanket about her body, and she looked peaceful and contented in her repose, as if she were sleeping. When I looked down at her face, she had a slight upward curl of her lips, almost like she was smiling at a beautiful dream. I opened the towels and saw a dark haired, tiny baby. It, too, looked contented, and at peace in the crook of its mother's arms, as if there was nothing left to be desired.

I touched Sisi and she was cold, as was the baby. I knew then, they were both dead. Sisi had delivered the baby alone in the night, knowing somehow she wasn't going to survive. She must have found solace in the fact she could die with the baby in her arms.

I fell upon my knees and put my hands together in prayer of thanksgiving. "Thank you God for such blessings of peace. What more could one want from life but this? People search their entire lives hoping with desperation to find this contentment. . .and here on this mountain those two creatures have been joined in birth and death, in the continuing cycle. They found rest here amongst the beauty of the vast blue sky, ever greening meadows, the colors of the mountain aster, the orange poppies, the purple lupines. Help the autumn winds cleanse their souls for their eternal rest of their bodies, to be replenished in the soil and then back into the cosmos of ongoing and unending life. I give thanks, oh God. Amen."

Tears streamed down my face, and I felt cleansed there by my hot tears and the burning wind.

Jack sat with me with his head down, and his paws crossed, as if appreciating my prayer and joining with me. He whined and licked my cheeks. He looked me in the eyes with understanding, and he barked.

"Let's go, fellow. Let's find the others, and tell them. These two innocents are no longer in their impermanent bodies, but have moved onto the next world."

Jack jumped up and wagged his tail, following me. As I walked, I realized it would be important to bury Sisi and her little one here at her favorite place amongst the ferns and grasses.

Chapter Forty-Four
A Walk in the Garden During Labor

We were sitting at the breakfast table, drinking tea when Juliette said, "Oh, I think I felt something. Angelica, please call Geraldine. She can check and see if I'm starting labor."

I ran into the kitchen where Geraldine was pouring hot water into a teapot from a kettle. In her psychic mode, she looked at me and said, "Yes, I know. It's time."

Geraldine walked to the breakfast table and took Juliette's arm and led her outside to the porch. She said, "While I talk to Aunt Lila about preparing some linens and towels, it'd be good if Aunt Angelica walks you around the garden. It'll take your mind off your discomfort."

"Shouldn't I go to bed now, Aunt Geraldine?"

"Oh, there's plenty of time for that, Juliette. First labors are usually slow, which I know yours will be. It'll pick up soon enough, but for now you've got to be patient."

Geraldine paused as if thinking. "Angelica, take Juliette to the garden. Here's my list of birthing herbs the two of you can pick while you're there."

I took Juliette's arm and we headed toward the white picket fence that surrounded the garden. At the entrance, I picked up a basket from the white wicker table sitting under the arbor. I handed Juliette the list, and asked her, "Okay, now what's the first herb we're supposed to pick?"

"Geraldine's writing is pretty scratchy, but I think I can make it out," Juliette said. "It looks like sage."

"Okay, I see some purple sage here. It's good I thought to bring this twine. I'll make bundles and tie each one separately, so Geraldine can easily find what she needs."

"Here, let me hold the basket while you pick." Juliette reached her hands out to take the basket from me. "Oh," she said, holding her stomach, as she leaned on the white picket fence. "That one was a little stronger. We better get busy."

"What's next on Geraldine's list?"

"It says comfrey."

"Let's see if I can remember what it looks like. It has large, hairy broad leaves that have small, purple, bell-shaped flowers. It feels sticky and prickly to the hand. I'll go look for a cutting tool."

"Here's one, Aunt Angelica, sitting on the wicker chair. I also see the comfrey next to the sage."

"Thanks. I have to be careful as I tie it so that I don't get pricked to death. Now, what else?"

"Cumin."

"What we're looking for has a slender, branched stem about a foot tall with a couple sub-branches and thread-like leaflets with small dried seeds on the umbels."

"I see it. Ow-w-w," Juliette said, as she leaned against the fence again. "If these pangs get any stronger, I might have to sit down."

"Have the contractions passed, yet?" I asked.

"Yes, so far they last about thirty seconds, and are starting to get a little stronger. Being out here in the garden is good, though. It does help take my mind off worrying about what's going to happen."

"That's just what Geraldine said."

"Auntie Angelica?"

"Yes, dear. What is it?"

"Will I die like the Indian woman did?"

"Oh, Juliette. Don't worry. The Indian woman was sick. She had syphilis. She didn't have much chance of survival, but you. . .you are young and healthy. I'm sure this labor will go well."

"If anything happens to me, promise me you and Geraldine will do all you can to help my baby survive."

"Yes, but of course."

"And, will you raise my baby, if I die?"

"If anything were to happen, which it won't, I'll raise your baby. And yes, I know you want me to raise him to be an artist. He carries great genes, this baby of yours."

"Thank you, Angelica. I knew you would understand."

"Okay, let's get busy. I've got the cumin. What else do we need to pick?"

"Mint. I can spot it right off. It's growing in a pot all by itself, because otherwise it might take over the entire garden. I love the smell of mint."

"Me, too."

"Let's find the. . . Wow. That was a bad one. I think I should either sit down, or go in the house and lie down."

"Here, let me help you walk. I think we've got enough herbs for now. I can always come back and pick more, later."

I entwined my arm with Juliette's, and we took our time walking back to the house.

Chapter Forty-Five
Labor

Reynard was waiting on the porch steps when Juliette and I arrived. His face looked anxious. He took Juliette's other arm. We walked through the front door of the house.

"Hey, you two," Juliette said. "I'm not an invalid."

I laughed. "Of course you aren't an invalid. It's just that we're so excited about this baby."

I asked Reynard to help Juliette to her room, which was on the first floor. I told him I wanted to take the basket of herbs into the kitchen, and would be with them soon. He nodded and winked.

Aunt Lila was in the kitchen boiling a large pot of water. She had piles of towels and linens stacked on the breakfast table. "Ah-h-h, Angelica. You're back. I was surprised when Geraldine told me Juliette had started labor, and the two of you were in the garden picking herbs. I could've done that for you. You only had to ask."

"Thank you. I know I can rely on you, Aunt Lila. It's just that Geraldine thought picking herbs for the delivery would help take Juliette's mind off her labor."

"I think it's odd," Aunt Lila said, "the moment Juliette went into labor, Geraldine ordered her to go for a walk. It just seems preposterous. But, who am I? I'm an old woman, and things have changed since my time. However, let's not forget that two of the women in this family have died in childbirth. It's nothing to be taken lightly."

"You're right. But, Aunt Lila, I feel we can trust Geraldine," I said. "She's very experienced in midwifery. She's delivered many babies. But, don't worry. I'll be in the room with Juliette when she gives birth. I'll be sure everything goes well."

"Thank you, Angelica. You've made me feel better. Here are some towels and sheets. Take them to Geraldine, and ask her if there's anything else I can do. I'll be happy to help. But wait. Before you go, let me express one more concern. You said before, that Geraldine is Joseph's sister. That means she's my niece. She looks very different from how I remember. I'm not sure about this, but is she really Geraldine?"

"Since I didn't know her when she was young, all I can tell you, Aunt Lila, is that Carmen is certain of it."

When I left and walked down the hall, I had doubts as to whether or not I had convinced Aunt Lila.

I approached Juliette's room. Reynard was waiting for me with a smile on his face. Geraldine and Juliette were busy sorting linens.

Reynard gave me a hug and then led me outside the door. He said, "I am so glad you are here to help, and so happy my Cousin Geraldine is going to help Juliette. I understand she's a wonderful midwife."

"Yes, she has a good reputation from what I've heard."

"Angelica, I must tell you, I am a little afraid. I was there when my dear sweet Suzette died giving birth to my adorable twins. I know it isn't that unusual for a woman to die in childbirth. It is so difficult for us men to stand by and wait. Would you come out of the room from time-to-time and let us know how she is doing, and if we can help with anything?"

"Certainly, Reynard. You're so sweet," I said as I stood on my toes and kissed him. "Now, go. You might check on Aunt Lila in the kitchen. She seems beside herself with worry. Maybe you can soothe her a bit. I love you."

"I'll go check on her. I love you, too." Reynard turned and walked toward the kitchen.

When I went back into Juliette's room, Geraldine was helping her undress. "I put the herbs in the kitchen, Geraldine," I said. "I can finish helping Juliette if you want to go prepare them."

"I'm sure Juliette would like it better if you help her undress, anyway," Geraldine said. "I'll be back in a few minutes."

Juliette looked frightened as she stepped out of her petticoats. She stopped and held the bedpost with one hand while she waited for another contraction to pass. I had her sit in a chair so I could remove her shoes and stockings. Then she put her arms in the air, as I helped guide her cotton nightgown over her head.

When we were through, I pulled the covers down, and fluffed up the pillows. Juliette climbed into bed and got settled.

"How about if we read for a while to help the time pass."

"Yes, Auntie. I'd like that. I brought a book from France that I haven't had a chance to read. It's all the rage in Europe. I heard that despite the fact that the author's pen name is Currer Bell, she's actually an English woman named Charlotte Bronte. You can find it on the shelf by the bed."

"Ah, yes. I've heard of that book and, indeed, it was written by a woman. That should make you feel good. . .a woman in a man's profession," I said. "When you're painting, will you print your name as a man, or declare yourself a woman?"

All of a sudden, Juliette doubled her fists and made a face.

Chapter Forty-Six
Delivery

"Oh, my dear Juliette," I said. "I'm sorry to ramble on like that. If you're interested, I'll tell you what I've heard about easing labor pains."

When Juliette's contraction passed, she wrinkled her forehead and said, "Please tell me what you know."

"Well, where I come from, my friends had learned of a technique developed by a Frenchman, Dr. Fernand Lamaze. After years of observing childbirth techniques, he came up with classes to help ease women in labor. Some of my friends who had babies told me about this Lamaze."

"Oh, Auntie Angelica. Of course, I'd love it if you'd teach me those things, if it isn't too late."

"Of course, it isn't too late. To start with, I can show you some of the doctor's breathing exercises."

"I'm so excited."

"Okay, let's get started. There're some breathing techniques that help you relax, and get more oxygen for the baby. I was told it speeds up the delivery process, plus you'll have less pain."

"Sounds great to me." Juliette threw her arms in the air.

"When each contraction starts, I want you to focus your eyes on the wall across from the bed and look at the snow covered mountain you painted. With each pain or contraction, take slow breathes through your nose, count to three, and then release it through your mouth to the same count."

Juliette focused her eyes on her painting, and when the next contraction came, she used the slow breathing technique. When she was through, she had a big smile on her face.

"Wow, I felt more relaxed that time."

Geraldine walked in, carrying a tray filled with a pot of tea, a mug, and some canning jars.

"Here's the tea I want you to sip. It's a concoction of ground cumin seed, sage, and comfrey, which will help the birth along." Geraldine set the tray on the dresser. She watched as Juliette started doing her slow breathing with the next contraction.

"Wow, she looks pretty calm for a first labor," Geraldine said. "You work miracles, Angelica."

When Juliette was finished, she said, "Angelica is teaching me some breathing techniques and they really help me relax."

Geraldine turned to me. "You're full of surprises, as I knew you would be." She poured Juliette's tea, and told her to drink as much as she could.

I explained the breathing tools to Geraldine. I then went on to teach some of the more advanced breathing techniques to both of them.

"Geraldine, part of the technique is to educate Juliette about what to expect with each phase of labor. I'll let you do that part."

"That's a good idea," Geraldine said. "Some women don't want to know a thing, but I think if they knew what was going to happen, there'd be less fear."

Geraldine went on to explain the phases of labor and delivery to the two of us, and then watched as Juliette started another breathing cycle.

"She's doing great," Geraldine said. "These breathing exercises really make sense to me. She truly looks less anxious than women I've help birth, even the ones who'd had lots of children."

"Yes, I've had friends who used this, and they told me it really helped. They felt more in control."

After a couple of hours, Geraldine said, "Juliette, I've got to put my fingers inside you to see how much your womb has opened. It'll be a little uncomfortable, but maybe you can take some deep breaths while I do it."

First, Geraldine washed her hands in the ceramic basin on the side table. She pulled the covers back, and asked Juliette to put her knees up. When she finished the exam, she said, "Your womb is fairly well open. Your labor pains are going to get harder, so follow Angelica's direction. You'll have to stay focused."

Smiling, Juliette said, "I don't know if I should be scared or happy. I'm both, I guess. This is going to be the hard part." Juliette's cheeks turned red and she said, "Oh, my God. I think I'm more scared than anything."

"Listen to me," I said. "If you keep thinking that each contraction means your baby is coming, you'll be able to stay in that happy mode, instead of the scared one. By the way, I think it's time I went out and told the family that the baby will be coming soon."

Juliette squeezed my hand and gave me a brave smile. When I walked out the door, Carmen was standing there wringing her hands. "How's she doing?"

"Great. She's getting close to the delivery. She wanted me to let everyone know."

"I'll go in and give her some moral support," Carmen said. "You go ahead and tell Reynard and the rest of the family. They're all in the kitchen, pacing."

Carmen was giving Juliette a foot massage when I returned from talking to the family. I noticed that Juliette had changed her breathing to the last stage, and was making little Hee-Hee-Hee-Hoo sounds with her breath.

Watching her with a strange expression on her face, Carmen said, "Geraldine told me about this Lamaze thing. It's pretty peculiar, but it seems to be helping her."

"Juliette," Geraldine said, "I better check you again." She washed her hands once more in the basin, and then did the exam. She had a look of concern on her face, and said, "The baby seems to be turned the wrong way. It'll make the delivery more difficult, but nothing we can't. . ."

There was a loud crash, as Carmen fainted on the floor. I rushed to help her. I splashed some water on her face, and when she came to, I said, "I think it'd be best if you leave the room. It's going to be too hard for you to be here watching your daughter. I'll call you, if I need you."

Carmen's face was pale, and she said, "I think you're right. I'll sit in a chair just outside the door. I'll come, if you call."

When Carmen left, Geraldine told Juliette, "I have something that might help the baby move into the correct position. I want you to get on the floor on your knees, and then lean over the bed. I'll put some pillows down so your knees will be padded. In between labor pains, I want you to rock your pelvis up and down and back and forth."

Juliette got out of bed, and I assisted in getting her arranged into the position. After leaning on the pillows for about half an hour, Juliette said, "Geraldine, I can't do this anymore. I'm too tired. Can I get back into bed now?"

"Sure. Angelica and I will help you. By the time you are back in bed, I think you'll be ready to push."

"Yes. My body is wanting to push, now. I can feel the pressure."

After Juliette was settled into bed, she grunted and pushed with each contraction. After about thirty minutes, Geraldine said, "The baby's coming, and he's facing the right way."

I yelled, "You did it, Geraldine. Good job."

Geraldine smiled as she said to Juliette, "One more big push."

White Owl came running into the room at that moment. He jig-jagged over to the bed, and I could smell alcohol on his breath. He slurred his words as he said, "You can't have this baby. It's too dangerous. I forbid it."

Juliette gave one big push and the baby slid out. Geraldine caught the baby, and said, "Well, Grandpa White Owl, it's too late. Your grandson was very anxious to come see you."

Carmen rushed into the room, and grabbed White Owl by the nape of his collar, and said, "Get out of here. You have no business coming into the birthing room." She looked up and saw the baby boy crying on Juliette's belly and Geraldine cutting the cord. "Oh, my God. It's a baby boy. Juliette, you gave us a grandson."

Chapter Forty-Seven
Gold Foray

Reynard seemed recovered from his injuries by early spring. He was full of energy, and even a little restless.

The workers trimmed and trained the grapevines so they would grow close to the stakes and splayed out the sides onto the wires. The hillside grasses were lush and green. New leaves had unfurled from the maple trees on the hillside.

Carrying a lunch basket, I approached Reynard who was trimming vines. "There you are, *mon amour*. Come, let me hug you to my heart." Reynard picked me up and swung me around.

I placed a wool picnic blanket on the ground, and we sat down to watch the fog rise from the river in the distance. Reynard said, "Angelica, it is almost as if I can make out my father's face in the fog. I think he is coming to remind me I have important promises to keep."

I nodded at him in agreement, and said, "We both have promises to keep."

"*Ma petite*, I have decided I need to go to the gold fields, now that most of the spring work is done around here. It is only about a three or four-day ride. I am going to take a few of my ranch hands, including White Owl. You and Carmen can manage the ranch while I am gone."

"Reynard, you're going away? And you say, you're leaving me and Carmen in charge? Perhaps she can manage things, but I have no experience with ranching."

"I know, Angelica, but I can't see any way around it. You and Carmen managing the ranch is only temporary, and you will do fine."

"By the way, Reynard, when is Father Jean returning?"

"Sometime in the late summer, so I have to return by then so he and I can formulate a plan to help Joseph's Indians escape. No matter what we come up with, I am sure we will need plenty of money for their future needs until they can become self-sufficient."

"I also have a good idea," I said. "I'll go with you to the gold fields."

"Thank you, my dear, but I can't let you do that."

With my hands on my hips, I said, "Why not? I can pan for gold as well as any man."

Laughing, Reynard squeezed my bicep. "I am sure you can, but Carmen needs you here. You would be good at convincing the workers to stay at the rancho rather than running off to mine for gold. I have even told the workers we will bring back a bag of gold for each of them. The most anxious ones I am taking with me to help."

"Good idea, my dear," I said.

Reynard took off his cap, and held it in his hand. His hair came loose from its leather tie and fell into his face. I admired the dark, rough stubble of his beard outlining his well-formed lips. Small beads of sweat ran in rivulets down his cheeks.

I reached up and kissed him. "I'll miss you, my love. I'll miss your hugs and long kisses. I'll miss our talks."

Reynard reached his arms around me. I could smell the marvelous muskiness of my man, and feel the strength in his embrace. His love surrounded me, creating an aura of warmth and safety. He pulled me onto the blanket and cuddled close to me. I could feel the soft beard of his face on my cheek, and became ignited.

"*Mon amour*, I will miss you." Reynard sighed. "I love you beyond words, beyond all worlds, beyond time and space. You give meaning to my life."

Each honeyed word spoken vibrated my soul. I kissed him, and said, "I, too, love you beyond all time and space. I want to be with you, forever."

Reynard squeezed me so hard, he made it difficult for me to breathe. He sat up and pulled me to a sitting position and said, "I'm starved. What's for lunch?"

I grabbed a sandwich out of the lunch basket and started feeding Reynard little bites. A smile curled around his mouth as he accepted my offerings.

Reynard opened the wine bottle with his teeth and spit the cork on the ground. I held one glass as he poured the dark wine. The two of us took turns drinking it. Before we finished the glass, we heard White Owl calling, "Reynard where are you? Reynard?"

Reynard stood, and said, "I am here, my brother. I am with Juliette. Come join us for a drink, if you will."

White Owl took his time getting to us. I rushed to straighten my blouse and smooth my hair, giggling as I tried to look presentable.

When I stood, I poured wine into the other glass and called out, "Here, White Owl, I have a glass ready for you, and a sandwich if you're hungry."

White Owl looked at Reynard and winked. "Lunch is often my favorite part of the day. Nothing about becoming fully nourished when one has a large appetite."

Reynard looked at him and said, "Why were you looking for me? Is there something I can help you with?"

White Owl said, "I want you to check the packing to make sure we have all the supplies we'll need for our trip. I have five men in all who seem anxious to accompany us, and they'll be ready by morning. In fact, if we weren't going, I think they would be leaving the rancho without us in order to try their hand at the gold."

"It is good the workers will get it out of their systems. They hear of how easy it is to find gold, and believe those stories. They will see what hard work panning and sluicing are."

Reynard kissed my hand, and said, "I'll see you this evening at dinner. Thank you for lunch."

I let go of Reynard's hand, only as he walked away. I held out my hand toward him as he strolled to the barn.

Pain bore through my heart as I realized how much I would miss him.

Chapter Forty-Eight
Claim Jumper

You'd never guess, Heather, what happened to Reynard and White Owl. Since I didn't accompany them on their gold panning trip, White Owl told me a few weeks later how their adventures began.

After a four-day ride, Reynard was anxious to find a good spot to settle and try his hand at gold panning. His horse's breath became labored. He knew his horse was exhausted, and it was a good bet the other horses in the pack were too, after a long, steep ride.

Reynard called the men to a halt, so he could observe Weber Creek, a tributary of the American River. Upcreek rapids were rushing over rocks and boulders. The water in the creek was higher than normal due to the heavy winter rains and spring snow melt. In front of him, the creek turned calm. Down creek he could see a "S" curve that resulted in a big sand bar.

As he held his hand over his eyes to shield them from the dying rays of the sun, he said, "This looks like as good a spot as any to stop and have a try for gold."

The men let out a synchronized whoop and galloped their horses toward the creek. Some of the men jumped off their mounts and leaped into the water, and then splashed those standing on the shore until everyone was soaking wet.

Reynard and White Owl watched the men cavorting, looked at each other, and grinned. They both jumped off their horses and ran full speed for the creek. Reynard leaped from a boulder into the creek. He let out a loud yelp as the cold water hit his skin. White Owl made a shallow dive into the water, swam beneath Reynard, grabbed his leg, and pulled him under. Reynard came up, sputtering. He reached for White Owl's head and pushed it under the water. White Owl swam to the surface.

Reynard noticed that the men had stopped their whooping to watch his antics. Feeling self conscious, Reynard swam to shore, got out, and started gathering wood for a fire. He yelled, "Hey men, let's get a big bonfire going in case some of you sissies get cold."

The men joined in the search for wood, while White Owl pulled the pots off the wagon. Reynard went to the creek and filled the coffee pot with water. Then he scooped water in a pot for the beans. When he got back, the men had the fire started. He set the pots over the fire on sticks he fashioned into a cross bar.

The men took off their wet clothes and tossed them on the manzanita and ceanothus bushes closest to the fire to dry. The rest of the evening, they sat by the fire in their long underwear and played cards.

In the morning, Reynard showed the men how to use a gold pan, sloshing it along the creek bottom, picking up gravel and dirt as well as water. He swished all the water out through the screened bottom. Black sand, and small gravel rocks were left in the pan. After a good swirl, he saw small, shiny gold chunks in the bottom of the dark gray, gritty dirt.

The men gathered around and stared at Reynard's pan. He was as surprised as they were. "Why, maybe this is a good spot after all," he said.

A burst of gunshot broke their reverie. The men, startled, looked up. All of a sudden a man yelled, "Hey, don't you damned buzzards know a marked claim? Isn't it obvious, even to a retarded moron, that you're trespassing?"

A grizzled man with gray hair poking out from under his straw hat moved from behind a bush pointing a rifle at them.

Reynard held his hands in the air, and said, "No, we didn't know this was your claim. Today was our first time at what we hoped would be our bonanza.

We're newcomers here, so you will have to explain to me how I can tell when I have come across someone's claim."

The man lowered his gun and spoke to Reynard, saying, "Go look for yourself. I've got all this area down to the bend marked out. I even filed a claim at the assayer's office at Sutter's Fort." He pointed with one hand, while holding the rifle with the other. "Have a look see. I've tied my long underwear onto the tree branches as a claim marker. By my cold ass, I had to use somethin'."

Reynard looked up and noticed the piece of red material swinging from the tree branch above his head.

"Yeah, old man. I am real sorry. We had no idea. Can you tell us where we might go where there are no claims?"

"Just a dang minute here, boy. Let's talk business first. Virgil's my name, and I've a mighty thirst. Got any good liquor in those saddle bags?"

"Sure we do," Reynard said. Turning to his ranch hand, he said, "Bring this poor man something good to drink. He looks parched."

Reynard motioned to Virgil. "Here have a seat, sir, and we will get to be friends. How many people are working this field of yours?"

Virgil motioned away the tin cup that was offered to him, and took a big swig right from the whiskey bottle. "It's just me and Randolph, my donkey. Randolph's been with me for twelve years going from place to place, but this here gold run is the best we've chanced on."

Reynard got a cup, filled it part way, and took a drink. He said, "Would you and Randolph be interested in selling this claim of yours, or is it for sale?"

Virgil stared at Reynard, then took a long drink of whiskey. "You seem like a nice sort, unlike so many around here. You've got manners and make a man feel at home. I appreciate that."

"Thanks." Reynard sat down next to Virgil.

"Randolph's not always the best company, although he never sasses me. Tell ya' what. I'd be interested in becoming partners with you, if you buy in half way. Say a case of whiskey would do. You got a lot of whiskey, do yah?" He looked toward the wagon.

Reynard realized he was getting a bargain, but to give Virgil the feeling he was also getting a deal, he decided to haggle a bit.

"Say, not a whole case. I've heard what a bottle can bring in this country. I would consider nine bottles of whiskey a bargain."

Virgil screwed up his face real tight, and said, "Nine's not enough. Nope. Not enough. I'd take ten bottles, and the one I'm holding. That would do it just fine."

Reynard held out his hand, grabbed Virgil's and shook it hard. "It's a deal then. We're partners."

Chapter Forty-Nine
Gold in All Its Glory

After a month of working the claim, Reynard's feet became swollen and blisters formed on his toes from walking around all day with wet feet. Dry lips and a sunburn were an everyday occurrence for him.

Reynard's stomach grumbled as he finished hauling more rocks out of the freezing creek. He said to no one in particular, "God, the food we have to put up with in this place. It is the worst I have ever had to endure."

White Owl stopped panning for gold, and said, "Boy, what I'd give to have a good meal."

"Me, too," Reynard said. "Another thing that's darn disappointing, is this claim. Seemed pretty good in the beginning, but the cost of supplies are eating us alive."

"What did they cost you this last time, White Owl," Reynard asked his brother-in-law.

"Let's see if I can recall. At the hotel I stopped for lunch, and a slice of bread was a dollar. Buttered, it cost me two dollars. When I was at the store, the cheese cost six dollars per pound, a plug of tobacco forty cents, pick axes seven dollars and fifty cents, a blanket, fifty to one hundred dollars depending on how worn it was, shirts sixteen dollars, and wine and whiskey eight to sixteen dollars a bottle. Why, I even saw one guy with a barrel of brandy selling it by the glass." White Owl smiled. "He told me he made nearly fourteen thousand dollars."

Reynard laughed. "Smart guy that man."

"A lot smarter than us. We're lucky if we make upwards of thirty dollars a day and with darn hard work, too," White Owl said.

"We sure are not making the money I thought we would. Let's stop for now. The sun will be going down soon, and I want to eat dinner before it gets dark."

"Come sit by the fire," White Owl said, "and we'll watch the sun go down. Carmen loves to do that at the end of a hard day. She says, no amount of money can buy the sunset. Every pauper and rich man can enjoy it."

Reynard climbed out of the creek, and pulled off his boots, turning them upside down to let the water drain. He took off his socks and hung them on a branch. He sat next to White Owl and looked at the dinner spread out on a blanket — hot coffee, moldy bacon, soggy hard tack, and the last of the tough beef jerky.

White Owl smiled. "The specialty tonight is a little smoked salmon I bought off the Indians a mile or so east of the creek."

"What I would give to have some fresh fruit and vegetables," Reynard said.

"Come with me tomorrow," White Owl said. "I'll introduce you to the local Indians. Perhaps we can find something fresh for you to eat."

While the two men talked, Reynard's partner, Virgil, came into camp and brought a stranger. "This here's Mr. Tom Rangel," Virgil said. "He's an old hunting friend of mine from way back. He could shoot the eyes out of a bobcat at twenty yards. I found him working up-creek a bit from our claim. I invited him to dinner."

The side of Mr. Rangel's face was all swollen and he had a wet rag tied around his head so it covered his puffy cheek. "Glad to meet you," he said in a muffled voice. He held out his hand. Reynard and White Owl shook it.

"Excuse my appearance, but I've got this gawl durn toothache. Haven't met anyone yet with pliers so I can pull it out. This cold rag is supposed to help bring the swelling down. A little whiskey rinse helps, but it's so durned expensive in these here parts. I've heard if you stand on your head it keeps the pains from getting worse."

After his speech, Mr. Rangle sat on his knees, put his head to the ground, and groaned. Reynard and the other ranch hands sitting nearby put their hands to their mouths to stifle their laughter.

Early the next morning, Reynard yawned and said to his friends, "Since today is Sunday, and the miners' day of rest from work, why don't we set out across the creek to visit the local Indians. White Owl said he'd lead us there and interpret for us. Perhaps they will have some fresh food to help our stomachs."

Mr. Rangle, Virgil, and White Owl nodded. Reynard and the three men set off on their mounts to follow White Owl to the Indian camp. The animals splashed through the polluted creek, white from the washings in the cradles and constant scraping of sand and soil. They rode through the woodlands of live oak, buckeye, and ponderosa pine. A rolling grassland, dotted with gray pine opened up before them.

Reynard and his friends didn't have to go far to find a group of natives. They were sitting in silence around the front of their thatched huts throwing occasional dark looks toward the strangers who were riding into their village, into their lives, and into their once virginal forests.

Most of the squaws wore blankets around their shoulders and a skirt made of reeds or rushes. They sat in the shade of the tall pines surrounded by piles of roasted acorns spread on blankets. They crushed the acorn's hard shells with their teeth and dropped the contents onto a piece of cloth on their laps.

Some of the men were naked. A few sat wrapped in blankets, still others wore European-type clothes, minus shoes. Many of them had tattoos on their chins with fine lines running down from the corners of their mouths. Several of them had their ears pierced with a piece of painted wood or quill for earrings.

Some of the Indians sat in the warm sunshine. Others sat back-to-back with their arms crossed, not looking at the strangers passing through their village.

Many of the women got up and went into their huts as the white men passed. The children stared wide-eyed at them in apparent curiosity.

All of a sudden, Mr. Rangel appeared to be overcome by severe pain and jumped down from his mule. He put both hands on the ground, and put his cheek upon his outstretched hands, his right leg pushing, as if attempting to get the angle right. His hat dropped from his head, and the pack he carried fell onto the ground upside down next to him. He moaned as his left leg flailed in the air.

Several of the Indians observing this strange behavior, ran into their huts and hid. A woman, who had been cleaning a rabbit, dropped everything on the ground and ran into the nearby bushes.

Mr. Rangel's red, distorted face was enough to scare anyone. His strange behavior affected Reynard and his fellow travelers. They held back as long as they could, then roared with laughter at the sight of the poor, moaning Mr. Rangel.

The village people, seeing the stranger's hilarity, burst into screams of laughter. The timid men and women came out of their huts and from behind trees and bushes. When Mr. Rangle was able to right himself, he was in no mood to join in the merriment. He grabbed his hat, swung his backpack over his shoulders and jumped on his mule. He rode on, leaving Reynard and his friends still laughing.

With sign language, White Owl indicated they needed fresh food for which they would trade beads. In response, one of the Indians put some hot stones from the fire into baskets to warm the acorn mush.

Reynard watched an old man with but a few teeth reach into the mixture with his four fingers made into the semblance of a spoon. The old man appeared quite satisfied with his mouthful and made motions for Reynard to try it, which he did. Reynard could tell it would take time to acquire a taste for the nutty, yet bitter flavor.

Next, some young Indian girls approached the strangers with a flat basket which they had filled with small seeds and live coals. They swung the basket back and forth until the seeds appeared to be toasted. The girls pushed the coals out with a stick. Reynard reached out his hand and they poured a handful for him to taste. Reynard smiled and rubbed his stomach.

One squaw offered roasted roots of various flavors to Reynard's group. Reynard, who was craving any food that was green, reached his hand into the basket that had sweet, fresh Miners lettuce mixed with peppery water cress. This satisfied him more than the other food.

Reynard was the only one who refused the roasted grasshoppers and baked wasps. The Indians guffawed when Reynard pinched his nose and made a face at the food.

When the Indians ran out of gourmet tidbits, Reynard paid the Indians with the beads White Owl had promised. Having satisfied their urge for fresh food, Reynard and his friends left the village camp looking for more adventures.

Chapter Fifty
Indian War

Instead of going back to their claim, Reynard and his friends decided to make their way to a nearby mining town, Donkey's Bend. They headed west and soon came to a dirt road surrounded on both sides by dense toyon bushes, manzanita, Douglas fir, and maples. As they entered the town, Reynard noticed a small steepled church with a scaffolding. A man, intent on hammering pieces of wood to the new structure, waved at them as they rode by.

From horseback, Reynard noticed a couple of saloons, a horse stable, a restaurant, a dry goods store, a hotel, and some small cottages. Most of the buildings were incomplete, with canvas on the roofs and no glass in the windows.

Main Street paralleled a bend in the adjacent creek, and made a sharp turn to the left. Reynard stopped at the makeshift shack with a sign above it that read, Town Haul, in big letters. Written in smaller print was, Donkey's Bend—Meeting Place, Bar, and Trading Post. Mr. Rangel's mule was tied to a hitching post in front of the building.

"Our old friend is here. Maybe we can make it up to him," Reynard said as he tied up his horse, alongside Rangel's mule.

"Let's have a snort," Virgil said as he rushed into the bar. He ordered whiskey all around, which the bartender served in tin cups.

When the alcohol began to warm their stomachs and dull their minds, a man with a thick accent came running into the cabin yelling, "Them gawl durn Injuns. They stole my nine hundred dollars in gold dust, they chase me, knock me down and take me money."

Many of the men in the saloon had gone past the point of drunkenness, and their addled brains knew nothing of logic or fact. As they listened to the upset man speak, many of them hopped from their chairs and formed a circle around him. The dark, thin, dirty man struggled on, despite his thick accent. "Me money. Me hard earned money. Them damn Diggers stealed me gold. They can't get away with this."

A murmuring of many voices filled the air. One man stood up so fast his chair fell down, and everyone got quiet. A loud voice rang out.

"Them damn Indians." This proclamation came from a raggedy miner with unkempt hair and a long graying beard. He continued with his tirade. "You can't trust a one of them. I say death to them all, and the sooner the better. They're nothing but heathens."

Reynard remembered seeing the raggedy man in other camps down the road. He leaned over and whispered to White Owl. "That's Texas Jack, one of my cousin Joseph's friends. He is always trying to get someone into trouble."

Virgil, who had been watching the scene unfold, stood up and yelled, "Don't jump to conclusions. Maybe we should look into this. We can't blame all them Indians for the sin of one."

"Shut up, old man. Mind your own business," Texas Jack said as he shoved Virgil.

"Virgil is right, you know," Reynard said, "and don't you accost that old man again or I will let you have it."

"Hell, I say all Indians are bad. Let's get the dirty savages," Texas Jack said. "Let's show 'em." Enraged, he ran out of the saloon followed by several excited and half-drunken men.

Reynard turned to White Owl and said, "You better stay put, or you could get mixed up with the other Indians. I am fearful this crowd is not capable of distinguishing one Indian from another. I'll leave Virgil and Mr. Rangel to make sure nothing happens to you."

Reynard leaped on his horse and rode in the direction the men had headed. After about a mile or more north of town, close to where the Indian village was, he saw a naked Indian who ran for the woods when he caught sight of the crowd of men. Texas Jack aimed his rifle at the Indian and shot him in the back. "I got the bastard. C'mon let's get the rest of them villagers," he yelled.

The angry men rode their horses behind Texas Jack. A small group of Indians had converged on the hillside to see what the shooting was about. The drunken men fired off a few shots in the direction of the Indian band. The Indians ran and hid in the thick trees on the hillside. They returned a few arrows, but kept missing their targets by a few feet.

"Leave them alone," Reynard yelled to the crowd. "They are just trying to defend themselves."

The men ignored Reynard and kept shooting.

When the Indians ran away, the motley crew of men turned their horses toward the Indian village, their voices raised in an angry swell. By the time Reynard arrived, the drunken men had set the village huts on fire and most of the Indians had fled or were hiding.

Reynard rode back to the bar and got Virgil, Mr. Rangle, and White Owl to help him put the fires out in the huts before the entire village burned down. They used large pine boughs moistened in the nearby creek to pound the flames out.

The acrid smell stung their eyes and noses as they worked. Some of the Indians came out of hiding and helped them smother the fire.

White Owl commented on the sad circumstances to Reynard by saying, "Some of the Indians are going to lose everything they own. . .the acorns and grain they stored. . .their utensils for fishing and hunting. . .their only clothes and bedding, and even the huts they built with their own hands."

"You are right," Reynard said, "and no one had stopped to ask why the Indian man ran, or bothered searching anyone for the missing gold. The assumption was made that the Indians were all to blame."

Reynard and his friends decided to ride north of town and east of the Indian village so they could make camp and sleep unperturbed by the drunken men. When they got to a grassy meadow, they decided to make camp for the night.

As they unpacked their horses, they saw a cabin near a clump of cotton wood trees. Reynard decided to check with the owner of the cabin to make sure he wouldn't mind their sleeping in the nearby meadow. When he knocked, a tall, burly man opened the door.

"What can I do you fer?" the man, who was holding a rifle, asked.

"I'm Reynard Rutherford, and I am here with my three friends. We wanted your permission to sleep in this meadow. I didn't want you to think we were squatters, just tired travelers. We have a claim a few miles from here, and we will be headed back in the morning."

"Sure. As long as you leave right after daybreak. I appreciate that you thought to ask me first. I like a considerate man. My name's Captain Wilcox."

"Good to meet you, sir," Reynard said.

"I'm the elected alcalde or mayor of this town. I was one of Captain Fremont's battalion, and was at the Bear Flag Revolt when General Vallejo was captured in Sonoma in eighteen forty-six. Ever since then, everyone calls me Captain Wilcox, even though I was never ranked so high."

"I'm impressed to be meeting a man who helped us become independent of Mexico," Reynard said.

"Well, a lot of other men in town feel the same way. You might say I'm quite popular, but I have a need to live away from the hoards of men who come through, even though my job requires I commute into Donkey's Bend at times. I'd rather be out here in the quiet of the meadow, working my claim at my leisure."

"I have a feeling you will need to make that commute again," Reynard said. "There was a problem in town earlier today. A miner claimed he was robbed by the Indians. The drunken men in the bar chased down the Indians, shot one, and burned many of their huts. We did all we could to stop the violence and put the fire out, but we were not much help."

"I appreciate a level-headed man. There isn't much one can do when the miners get overheated like that. Hopefully, the problem has run its course. I'll have to check on it in the morning. Good night, men."

Reynard and his friends tied their horses to the trees surrounding the meadow, and set up a make-shift camp a couple hundred yards to the side of the Captain's cabin, then lit a fire to keep off the night's chill.

As he unrolled his blanket, he felt disgusted at what the drunken miners had done to the blameless Indians. The world had gone insane the last few months with gold lust and Indian hatred.

Chapter Fifty-One
Captain Wilcox

In the early morning hours, Reynard was awakened by a group of Indians pounding on Captain Wilcox's cabin door. They yelled for Captain Wilcox, who came outside to speak with them. One of the Indians said, "What the reason whites make war on us, and shoot man and burn village?"

Captain Wilcox said, "I'll look into this for you, and get a jury together to see who's to blame."

Reynard followed Captain Wilcox on horseback to the Indian village, and they found the man who had been shot. The injured Indian was lying on his side, holding his belly where the blood oozed between his fingers. Reynard could see by the man's pallor, he was near death. A woman sat by his side, sobbing. When the white men approached, the wounded man looked up.

Reynard bent down and made the sign of the cross upon the wounded man's forehead, and started saying the Lord's pray aloud. Several of the men present got on their knees and joined him. When Reynard finished the prayer, the men got up and walked away. The woman attending the wounded man started wailing, as if she realized the white men could bring no healing magic. When the Indian woman's sobs rang in Reynard's ears, he felt ashamed of being a white man.

Reynard and his friends took Captain Wilcox to the burned village so he could inspect the ruined huts and blackened belongings of the villagers. Then they rode into town to round up some jurors. Captain Wilcox asked Reynard to be one of the jurors and he accepted.

Next, Captain Wilcox led a search for the tall, lanky man who said he had been robbed. The search party found him passed out behind the saloon. Reynard woke him by pouring a bucket of water over his head. He was taken inside the bar to the makeshift witness chair, so he could be questioned before a jury by Captain Wilcox.

A crowd had gathered as soon as Captain Wilcox rode into town, and it took no time to organize a jury. Reynard was sworn in as well as the other eleven jurors.

Captain Wilcox called on the first witness. "What is your name sir, and what is your claim?"

"McDougall's me name. I want the money that was stolen from me by the durn Indians," he said to Captain Wilcox.

A couple of miners who had come to town from the mining claim upcreek, said they could describe McDougall's character. A short bald man came forward and said, "This McDougall, he didn't have any money to pay for drinks, so we had to kick him out of our tent yesterday afternoon."

The bald man's hefty friend said, "Next, McDougall went to the Indian village and took to molesting some of the Indian women, and was thrown out. This ain't the first time he done that, neither. When he tried to return to the Indian village, he was chased by some Indians and told to stay away from their women. That's when he made up the story about being robbed."

Two witnesses came forward and they both testified that they saw Texas Jack shoot the Indian in the back when he was running away.

After listening to all the witnesses, the jury was unanimous in its verdict. The decision was that Captain Wilcox would administer five lashes to McDougall for false testimony, and twelve to Texas Jack as punishment for shooting the Indian. In addition, the Indian chief would flog Texas Jack an additional twelve times.

The Indian elders were present when the punishment of Texas Jack was announced. One of them yelled out, "This not enough. We think man who shoot Indian should die." At that announcement, several other Indians started yelping in reply.

Captain Wilcox said, "The punishment stands. The jury has decided. Since it is almost dark, we'll whip the two men in the morning. In the meantime, I'll keep them in my cabin with me. I'll shoot the first one who tries to injure these men."

The Indians left, but came to Captain Wilcox's cabin a little past dark and grumbled about the punishment again. They left after Captain Wilcox told them to go back to their village.

When they were gone, Captain Wilcox whistled for Reynard who walked over to the cabin door. "Reynard, would you and your men stand watch as guards for me tonight? I doubt the Indians will return, but you never know. I'd sure appreciate it."

"Sure thing, Captain," Reynard said.

Reynard's group moved their camp a few feet outside Captain Wilcox's cabin door. Everyone settled into their blankets to sleep. Reynard took first watch.

A few minutes later, Mr. Rangel started moaning about his tooth. Captain Wilcox came out of the cabin, and said he had pliers in his wagon to pull the tooth, if anyone dared go fetch them. Mr. Rangel stood up, and said, "I'd chance being shot, rather than have this tooth festering another night." He then set off at a fast pace for Mr. Wilcox's wagon.

With a lit torch in his hand, White Owl yelled out, "I'll help you, Mr. Rangel. You'll need a hand to hold the torch while you search for the proper tool for this surgery."

As White Owl started off after Mr. Rangel, he stumbled on a tree root in the dark. A yell resounded through the woods as White Owl's ankle bent under him. Reynard ran over to White Owl who was sprawled on the ground. Mr. Rangel picked up the torch White Owl had dropped. By its light, everyone present could see that White Owl's ankle had started to swell.

"We better get you back to our campfire so you can rest your ankle," Reynard said as he helped White Owl stand.

"First things first," White Owl said. "Let's help Mr. Rangel, then we'll tend to my ankle."

When the three of them reached the wagon, White Owl went through the cabinets on the side of the wagon as Mr. Rangle held the torch. When White Owl found the pliers, he held onto Reynard's arm as he hobbled back to Captain Wilcox's cabin.

A great gush of blood poured out when Captain Wilcox pulled Rangle's tooth, who then ran for the creek bed to wash. When he returned he had a great smile, shy one tooth.

"Doc Wilcox," Mr. Rangle said. "You've got yourself a new career with these here pliers. You'll go far in this country. Here's a bag of gold dust for your troubles. It was well worth it."

Mr. Rangel turned to White Owl and said, "Here, let me help you with that swelling. I'll get you a pail of nice, icy creek water to soak your foot in."

Chapter Fifty-Two
Hangtown

White Owl realized he wouldn't be of much help in the gold fields with a sprained ankle, so he volunteered to go to town for supplies. Captain Wilcox warned him not to go to Donkey's Bend since some of the town's people might still have hard feelings against any Indian who might pass by. White Owl asked Captain Wilcox for advice as to where he should go to get supplies.

"Hangtown. It's got to be the best in these here hills," Captain Wilcox said. "Crazy name for a town, but a lot of towns, round about here, have strange names. Take the towns of Dead Mule Canyon, Nutcake Camp, Barefoot Diggins. There's a reason for all them names. I'd personally like to visit the town of Gomorrah. Hear it's a might lively."

"Why," White Owl asked him, "did they give a place the name Hangtown?"

"It's because there were so many hangings there. Why, one time there were five men hanged after a vigilante committee found them guilty."

"Swift justice around here," Reynard said.

Virgil let out a long whistle, "Shore is."

"Yeah," Captain Wilcox said, "and that wasn't the last hanging in what used to be known as Dry Diggins. I'd say it's a good place for criminals to stay away from."

The next day, White Owl drove Reynard's wagon twenty miles to Hangtown. He wore his hair tied back, and his usual brown, broad brimmed, felt hat with a feather in the band. His brown wool suit looked a little worse for wear with miles of road dust on it.

On the trail to town, he got off his horse to pick up a five foot "U" shaped tree branch. He smiled as he tied it to his saddle. "This will make a perfect crutch for walking."

When White Owl got into town, he went to the trading post and hitched the horses to a railing in front. With his makeshift crutch under his arm, he hobbled into the store.

When he got inside, he noticed two men. One was stocking the shelves with canned goods, the other sat behind the counter reading a newspaper. He caught the eye of the owner, and said, "Good afternoon, sir. I need two, fifty pound sacks of flour, twenty pounds of bacon and dry tack, and five pounds of coffee. Got any candy? I'm dying to eat something sweet."

The owner looked him up and down, and said, "What you got to pay for all those items? I don't like Injuns mining their own claims. They ought to be working, helping the white folk out. I can give you a job sweeping and lifting heavy things into wagons and such, if that's what you're looking for. Last Injun run off after I paid him. Don't last long, these lazy critters. Paid him good, too. Gave him a pound of beans and a pound of flour for a week's work."

White Owl leaned on his crutch and said, "I'm helping my brother-in-law with his claim a couple camps over. Since I sprained my ankle and can't help out much, they sent me in for supplies. I've got gold dust to pay you with." White Owl took out a sack filled with gold from inside his leather satchel and put it on the counter top.

After opening the satchel, the store owner stood staring at it. "Why that's more money than any Injun's ever seen. Where'd you say you stole it from? Some white guy a couple camps up?"

The man stacking cans stopped work, and snuck behind White Owl. He pulled White Owl's arms behind him, and then put a gun to his temple. "Better not have any ideas of running away, or I'll shoot you. Won't be the first Indian I killed."

The man fastened White Owl's hands behind him, cinched the rope up tight and tied him to a post. "You can just stay put until we get a jury. And don't think you've got anything to say about this. Law around these here parts makes it illegal for an Indian to testify in court, so we'll figure out the facts as we see them."

Chapter Fifty-Three

Prisoners

Reynard was standing waist deep in Weber Creek when he heard Virgil yelling for him. He slogged out of the water as fast as he could, and said, "What were you saying about White Owl?"

Virgil raised his voice and said, "They've got White Owl tied up at the trading post in Hangtown for stealing a white man's gold dust. Durn fools. It's probably our money for the supplies."

"Where did you hear this?"

"Heard it on the creek. People been passing the information down, claim to claim. Don't take long for news to travel."

Reynard jumped on his horse. As he rode off, he considered how he'd help White Owl and whether his testimony would be believed.

He turned his horse around, and went back for Virgil. When he got back to camp, Reynard yelled down from his horse, "I've got to have you as a witness, Virgil, to testify that I sent White Owl for supplies with our money. They may not believe one man, but they have to believe two."

"Hold on and I'll get Randolph," Virgil said.

"There's no time for you to take your donkey. Here, jump on behind me."

Reynard leaned a hand down to help Virgil on the horse. They rode off together. As they approached the bend in the creek, they saw a couple trying to push their wagon wheel out of the mud in the creek bottom. The woman appeared to be pregnant. She struggled to drive their horses forward. A man stood knee deep in the water and pushed on the wheel.

Reynard jumped off his horse and ran to the side of the creek. He said to the couple, "May I be of service, madam and monsieur?"

"Thank you, kind sir," the lady said.

"My pleasure."

As Reynard walked back into the creek, he yelled to the woman. "On three, get the horses to move." When Reynard yelled out three, he and the man pushed the wheel with all their might. The horses struggled forward as the wagon moved out of the creek.

As they rested on the shore, the man introduced himself as Jedidiah Sloan, and his wife as Teresa. Jedidiah said, "I've been mining with my wife, but when she got pregnant, I planned on taking her to the Russian River settlement to have her baby. I heard tell there's some midwives or healers round about Rancho de los Zorros Grises."

"Why, I own that rancho," Reynard said. "My cousin is staying with us and she's a good midwife."

"Wonderful news," Jedidiah said. "And, since you helped us, is there anything we can do to return the favor?"

"Could you stop at the rancho and give my sister, Carmen, and my fiancé, Angelica, an urgent message for me?"

Reynard leaned toward the couple when he spoke, so that Virgil wouldn't hear. When Reynard was back on the horse, Virgil asked Reynard, "What's that you were saying to the couple about wine?"

"I'll tell you later," Reynard said. "I've got to focus on getting to White Owl as fast as possible."

With Virgil sitting behind him, Reynard rode Red hard, splashing through streams, up steep hills, and galloping through meadows and valleys. The ride jarred Reynard down to his bones, and he wondered how Virgil was holding up. When they reached Hangtown, Reynard tied his horse to a gigantic oak tree that arched over the street. He helped Virgil down from the horse, and said, "I really appreciate this, old man. I hope the ride wasn't too much for you."

Virgil hobbled a bit with his back bent over. "Boy, I haven't ridden that fast since I was a kid, racing with my brother. Better give your horse something special tonight after he gets his rub down."

"That will have to wait until we take care of White Owl. I am afraid he might be in great danger."

As they approached the trading post, they saw a crowd of men gathered outside. Reynard overheard one of the men say, "Damn Injun. Stealing white man's hard earned mining money. Can't trust them for an instant, or they'll rob you blind."

Reynard looked at the man who had spoken, and said, "I'm looking for my brother-in-law. You seen him? His name is White Owl."

The man's mouth flew open, and he got quiet for a minute. "Why that's what the Injun we got tied up calls himself, White Owl. You say he's your brother-in-law? You mean your sister's married to a dirty Indian? What kind of woman would do that?"

Some of the men standing around started to snicker.

Reynard said, "My sister is as good a woman, if not better, than any of your sisters. She raised me when I lost my mom. I owe her everything. She's a good, kind woman. Anyone have a problem with that?"

The crowd grew quiet. Reynard and Virgil pushed through them, and entered the trading post.

White Owl was sitting with his hands tied to a post, his hat beside him. White Owl looked up, smiled, and said, "It's about time."

The storeowner came over to Reynard and said, "Why, you ain't going to spoil our fun with the Injun are you? We're going to get a jury up and decide how many lashes he's got comin' for stealin' your gold, or maybe we'll get out the old hangin' rope. You wanna give him a few lashes yourself?"

Reynard said in a firm voice, "There is not going to be a whipping or a hanging. This is my brother-in-law, White Owl. I gave him a sack of gold dust to buy supplies. If you don't believe me, ask my mining partner here, Virgil."

Virgil had been holding his hand over his chest, since they walked through the crowd. He doubled over and fell to the floor with a thud. Reynard ran to Virgil, squatted down and held his head in his arms asking, "What's wrong old man?"

Virgil drew in a breath, and said, "Sorry partner. The old man's been called to Paradise." Virgil gasped and his head flopped forward. Reynard held Virgil to his chest and started sobbing. "No, Virgil, not this way. Virgil."

The crowd gathered in the store to look at Reynard holding the old gray-haired man. One of the miners who looked eighteen at most, said, "Wow, we hardly ever seen anyone around here with gray hair."

As Reynard held Virgil's head in his lap, he spoke to him. "I am sorry Virgil. I should not have subjected you to this."

The owner of the store observed the old man in Reynard's arms, and said, "Well, out of respect for the dead, we'll give you a day to bury him, and then we'll hold the proceedings. It appears to me you may be messed up in this gold robbery yourself. Too bad you don't have a witness."

A couple of burly men came over and grabbed Reynard. The bald one tied Reynard's hands to the same post as White Owl. "Guess we'll be roommates," White Owl said. "Make yourself comfortable."

Later in the day, after the crowd dug a grave for Virgil, they brought Reynard and White Owl to attend the funeral. With their hands tied behind their backs, the two of them were pushed to the front of the crowd. They looked down, their feet inches from Virgil's grave.

A man with long black whiskers officiated over the ceremony. He said, "Since I'm the only one for miles around that owns a Bible, I guess this qualifies me as a minister."

He read some verses from the Bible, and then added his own sermon. "Ashes to ashes, and dust to dust, after a life of lust. May the good Lord look well upon the wrinkled brow of this hard working old miner. May the Lord grant him some peace and well deserved rest, as we'd all like to have in this here life."

Reynard watched as one skinny, young miner appeared to get bored with the long sermon. He picked up some loose dirt and sifted it through his fingers and small gold flakes glistened in the sun. He picked up another handful and found more sparkles of gold.

The minister stopped the sermon to say, "This here funeral's adjourned until such time as we can find this old man a piece of ground that's not quite so valuable."

The crowd lost interest in the funeral, and ran for their shovels. Dirt flew in all directions as they began to dig. Reynard and White Owl were forgotten for the moment.

The two of them backed up until they were hidden in the thick gray pines that lined the graveyard. After they helped untie the ropes from each other's wrists, they ran as fast as they could toward the end of town where Reynard had left his horse.

After a couple of whistles, Red came running. The sweat in Red's coat had dried and his matted hair was all curled up and ruffled.

"Poor old horse. I ran you too hard, didn't I? Sorry, old boy, but I've got to call on you again."

Reynard and White Owl jumped on the horse's back and started off through the pines.

Chapter Fifty-Four
Angelica's Sole Sojourn

A wagon pulled up in front of our ranch house. We didn't get many visitors, so Carmen and I went outside to see who they were.

A thin, bearded man helped a pregnant, bedraggled woman down from the wagon. The man introduced himself as Jedidiah Sloan and his wife as Teresa. He then asked if this was Rancho de los Zorros Grises.

"Yes. Welcome," Carmen said. "Come inside and rest yourselves. I'll have the ranch hands unhitch your horses and feed them."

When the couple was settled in the living room on the couch, I brought them each a cup of steaming tea. Carmen offered them cookies from a silver tray, which they accepted.

"Now," I said, feeling very curious about our visitors, "what brings you to our rancho?"

"We'd been prospecting," Jedidiah said, "and when I realized my wife, Teresa, was in a family way, I decided it was time to head to civilization. We'd just started our journey, when our wagon became stuck in the muddy bottom of Weber Creek."

"That sounds awful," I said.

"Teresa was driving the wagon, urging the horses forward, and I was pushing the wagon."

"Yes," Teresa said, "and then a man came from out of nowhere. After asking if we needed help, he got into the water to push the wagon with my husband. Together they were able to get the wagon free. Reynard Rutherford was so charming and such a gentleman."

Jedidiah said, "We told him we were headed toward the Russian River settlement because it's getting near my wife's time to have her baby, and we'd heard there was a good midwife in the vicinity of Rancho de los Zorros Grises."

"Yes," Carmen said. "The midwife is my cousin, Geraldine, who lives here at the rancho with us. You'll be in good hands with her, and are welcome to stay. We have a spare bedroom on the second floor."

"Oh, no," Jedidiah said. "We're used to sleeping out under the stars. Just tell us where to camp, and we'll be going."

"We wouldn't hear of it," Carmen said. "We insist you stay here."

"Thank you so much. We'd love to," Teresa said. "By the way, the gentleman who helped us, Mr. Rutherford, said to tell his fiancé, Angelica, to find him, and to leave at once. He said he has need of her. He also said to bring as many barrels of wine as she could fit on a wagon, and sell it along the way."

My heart fluttered at the news. When I heard that he wanted me, I was ecstatic. I could soon be with Reynard, my beloved. I also knew the wine would be very popular with the miners, and would help defray the expense of the trip.

"Was Reynard okay," I asked. "Did he look strong and healthy?"

"He looked in fine shape. He looked tanned and strong," Teresa said. "You're a lucky woman to have such a kind man."

"Yes, you're right. He's a dear to me and a good person."

Carmen spoke up. "Did he have White Owl with him? That's my husband. When he left home, he wore a brown suit and a broad brimmed, brown felt hat."

"No," Jedidiah said, "but there was an old man with white whiskers and a straw hat. He called himself Virgil."

"It isn't anyone I know," Carmen said. "It's too bad. I wonder why White Owl wasn't with Reynard?"

"Carmen," I said, trying to cheer her up. "Let's get these good people to their room. I'm sure they'd love to rest up before dinner, and then we can introduce them to Geraldine."

When we had the Sloans situated in their room, Carmen said, "Let's get you prepared for your trip."

"I've got to dress like a man to make it safely into the gold country unescorted. You think you can help me with that?"

"Sure," she said. "Let's see what we can do."

Carmen pulled my long hair back and tied it up with a leather strip she took from her own hair. She took a brown cowboy hat off the rack in the living room, and put it on my head. She pushed my hair under the hat and then pulled up the strap to keep it snug.

I followed her to Reynard's room. She opened his closet and pulled out some of his work shirts. "You already have the pants I gave you, but you'll need these other clothes," Carmen said. She handed me a leather vest to button over Reynard's shirts, and a brown leather coat trimmed with fox fur. Carmen stuck a hawk's feather under the hat's ribbon.

"Nice touch," I said. "How did you know the fox and hawk are Reynard's and my animal totems?"

"There're a lot of things I know without your having to tell me, Angelica. . .like how much you're in love with my brother, and how good you are for him." Carmen winked.

"I'll pack a dress and a pair of tie shoes for you in the duffel bag in case you need them. You never know when there might be a call for a lady to appear unexpectedly."

Carmen warned me, "Don't be all dreamy-eyed about this adventure you're embarking on. You've got to realize there aren't many women in the gold country, and many of the men in those hills are going to be lusting after a woman. Watch yourself."

I responded, "I'll go straight to Reynard. I don't intend to get side tracked."

"You never know what life's going to hand you."

"What I'm really worried about, Carmen, is how you and Aunt Lila, Uncle Gabe and Juliette are going to manage," I said. "There are so few Indians who wanted to stay here on the rancho, and most of them are the elderly ones. There's a lot of ranch work to be done. I have no idea how so few people can manage it."

"Don't worry about us. We'll be fine."

"I feel like I'm running out on you when you need my help, but I'm afraid Reynard must really need me or he wouldn't have sent me that message."

The next morning, Aunt Lila, Uncle Gabe, and Juliette came out on the porch. Each one of them gave me a hug. Carmen whispered to me, "I'm so worried about White Owl. I've had such bad feelings lately. . .like he's in a lot of trouble. Would you look in on him, too? If he's in trouble, send for me."

I kissed Carmen on the cheek, and replied, "Now, now, I'm sure White Owl is fine. He's with Reynard."

I left Rancho de los Zorros Grises anxious to see Reynard. I'd had too much time on my hands. My whole body ached to hold Reynard — to kiss him and linger a good while over the taste of him.

As I started down the road toward the Gold Country, I experienced a combination of exhilaration and fear. Here I was going to experience one of the most exciting times in Western history, the Gold Rush of California.

Chapter Fifty-Five
Hank and Stan

A fter two days' ride, I was nearing Sacramento and Sutter's Fort where I planned on selling a little wine to buy supplies and spend the night. As I approached a thicket of alder and black oak, I saw a couple of young men walking on the road. When my wagon drew near, they yelled, "Hey, can we get a ride? We're tired."

I was anxious for company, and the two looked wholesome enough, so I decided to stop.

"Hop on up, fellas. The name's, ah, Alex. You can ride with me to the gold country. I'm looking for my partner, who left before me."

"Who's not interested in anything but gold these days," the shortest of the two said. "My name's Hank, and this here's my brother, Stan."

"We left our elderly parents in Monterey," Stan said.

"Yeah," Hank piped up, "along with three sisters and our grandpa."

Hank had peach fuzz cheeks, brown wavy hair, and big blue eyes under long eyelashes.

I reached down and shook Hank and Stan's hands with as much strength as I could muster, pretending to be a young man.

"Good meeting you both, I'm sure," I said.

Stan looked about nineteen, thin, muscular, and of average height. He had straight blond hair, and appeared to be the quieter one.

Hank took Stan's pack from him and threw it on the wagon along with his own. He got up on the seat next to me, and said, "Thanks a lot. We sure appreciate your taking us along. We'll make it up to you somehow."

Stan jumped into the back of the wagon. I watched as he laid his head on his pack, closed his eyes, and appeared to sink into a deep sleep.

I turned to the horses and coaxed them into a slow walk.

Hank proved a talker, and knew all the gossip from Monterey to Northern California.

"In Monterey, when the gold news struck, there'd be about twenty-five to fifty men who'd leave town each day. It all started when Charles Bennett stomped into the office of none other than Governor Richard B. Mason and told him about the gold strike."

"That was exciting news, wasn't it?"

"You bet."

"So, what happened then?"

"Heck, when the word got out in Monterey, first guys to leave were the soldiers and sailors who deserted their posts. Gold was all the men talked about. They'd say you could earn twenty to thirty dollars a day working the gold fields. Why, that's about ten times what a man in our town would make at a decent job."

"So that was a fortune to them," I said.

"You bet. I even saw carpenters drop their hammers in the middle of building a barn, and run off with picks and shovels and not much else. We was happy when the landlord left before he collected our rent. That's how excited he was."

"You were sure lucky."

Hank explained to me that he and his brother talked it over and decided to make their mark before all the gold was taken up. He said, "Our parents were pretty worried, but excited for us. My pa almost went with us, but our ma cried a lot, so he decided to stay. We promised we'd bring back enough gold for them to buy their ranch outright. . .maybe even hire some hands to help them farm." Hank told me his pa was getting on in years and bent over from working the plow.

"That would be great. . .you paying off the mortgage. What a good son you are," I said.

Hank stopped at my last comment, and wiped a tear from his eye. He asked that I pardon him, but he was worrying about his family he'd left behind. I reached over and slapped him on the back, and said to cheer him up, "It's good to be young and healthy, and on your way to an adventure, isn't it?" He nodded in response.

"Besides, if it's gold you want, check out the hillside ahead, rife with golden poppies."

Hank smiled real big at my comment, and showed me his dimples.

Chapter Fifty-Six
Driving the Road to Fortune

I drove the wagon with the reins in my right hand. I held onto the seat with my left as we bounced over the rutted road which was made up of dirt, roots, and rocks.

Passing through a small deserted town, I could see cows grazing in the unharvested fields. Doors were left flung open, garbage was piled against the sides of houses, and weeds grew out of the wooden sidewalks.

Day after day, along the rough road we passed men on horseback. Other times, men were walking alongside wagons packed with tools and sacks of flour and beans. We saw men of every description, wild-eyed, and motley. Accompanying us on our long march to the gold fields were Mexicans, Chinese, Caucasians, South Americans, Germans, and even Frenchmen headed for fame and fortune.

One afternoon Stan woke up all of a sudden and yelled, "Look at those men breaking down the fences, and letting the cattle out. I just saw one dirty old man take a horse from a field and he done rode off with it."

We gazed at the cattle and horses spilling onto the dirt road and watched as the animals clomped over the broken fence posts.

As we plodded along that day, I could see charred remains of fields of wheat and grassy meadows. It seemed as if there had been careless men, too busy to put out their campfires, who had left the fires to burn whatever was nearby.

We passed an abandoned cabin, and saw someone tear up the floor boards and put them in a blanket. Hank said he thought they were probably taking the wood to the gold fields to make a rocker for separating the rocks and gravel from the gold.

"Just because they need wood is no excuse to steal a person's private property," I said. "It seems like some people feel the gold rush is a good excuse to abandon all morals and principles."

We made camp farther up the road in a large open field, along with several other parties of men. We could see roaring campfires scattered about with men organizing their gear or cooking, and chatting.

Stan unhitched the horses, and then brushed them. Hank pointed at his brother and said to me, "He's great that way. Any work to be done, he's the first one at it. He's old Mr. Reliable, he is."

Stan led the horses down to the creek to drink. Afterwards, he tethered them next to some tall grass. While he did that, Hank and I gathered wood and got the campfire going. From the wagon I took out the metal stand, and hung the coffeepot on its hook.

Stan said, "Camp coffee's always the best. There's no way to duplicate it."

Hank and I exchanged surprised glances as we noticed Stan had decided to talk.

"Want me to go hunt something up, or you got any grub we can borrow for now," Stan asked.

"I've got some dried biscuits and honey, and some salt pork we can stir into the beans," I said. "Let's get this pot on the hook now, and we'll boil up some water for the beans. Hank, can you go down to the creek to get a bucket full?"

"Sure thing," he responded.

When Hank left, Stan said, "I only hope I'm doing the right thing taking my brother along. He's young for this kind of adventure, but I figured I'd need a partner, like you've got."

"I think he'll be just fine," I said. "It'll be good for him. You certainly wouldn't want him spending his elder years wondering what the gold fields had been about."

Stan replied, as though thinking out loud. "No, you're right about that. He'd resent it later, wouldn't he?"

After supper, we unrolled our blankets and laid down near the fire. I stared at the starlight in the dark sky as long as my eyes would stay open. I fought sleep, trying to absorb that moment—the wonders of the west, all its marvelous opportunities, a world in the making.

When I awoke, the smell of bitter smoke reached my nostrils. The rising sun was turning the sky to pink. I jumped up and headed for the creek. On the way back, I brought an armload of fallen branches and twigs to start a fire for the morning coffee.

When I got back, Hank had poured out the old grounds left from the night before, and was preparing to make fresh coffee. The young men's bedrolls were tucked away in the wagon, and Stan was hitching up the horses.

We fried some salt pork, and ate the remaining biscuits from the day before. Stan and Hank were big eaters, and my provisions were going faster than I'd planned. We'd have to stop at Sutter's Fort to get more food.

Chapter Fifty-Seven
Captain Sutter

As we got into Sutter's Fort, I saw Indian men carrying supplies or tending horses. They were dressed in long white shirts and pants tied with red cloth belts. Around many of their necks were strips of leather from which a copper disk hung.

I went into the fort's store to see what supplies they might have. I saw a miscellaneous assortment of blankets, furs, shovels, pick axes, guns, dried salmon, coffee and sacks of flour. I started gathering up things I thought I'd need for the rest of the trip. Then, I saw a man dressed in buckskin talking to a distinguished, gray-haired gentleman wearing a well-cut black suit, vest, and a black ribbon scarf around his neck.

The man in buckskin said, "Say, Captain Sutter, it looks like somebody done stole a couple guns from these here shelves."

"They're stealing me blind they are," Captain Sutter said. "They've stolen cattle and horses. They even pinched the bells from the Fort and the weights from the gates. They pilfered the hides and the barrels."

"Who's stealing these things," I asked.

"Why, the so-called gold miners, the ones who didn't come with enough money or brains to figure what they'd need for such an expedition. They take whatever they want without thinking who they're stealing from. . .only that they want to be millionaires overnight with very little work on their part."

"That's not right," I said as I pulled my hat down tighter to make sure my long hair didn't show.

"It most certainly isn't. I had a great working rancho here at one time, with hundreds of Indians tending the wheat and the cattle. Many of the Indians ran off to go to the gold fields. Can't keep 'em working anymore. I had to abandon some of my crops. Just gave up." Captain Sutter sighed and said, "Why do you ask, young man?"

Relieved that he didn't realize I was a woman, I put my hand out, and I said, "I understand you're a friend to the pioneers, and have helped many unfortunate people get on their feet. Your reputation precedes you, Captain Sutter."

Sutter grabbed my hand and shook it with enthusiasm. "Good to meet you, young man. Yes, indeed, I have helped many a pioneer, and look what good it's done me."

"I'm sure there are many grateful people," I said. "It's just that they aren't around anymore because they've become successful."

"You're right. By the way, what's your name?"

"Alex Hayes is the name, and these are my two traveling companions, Hank and Stan. We're on the way to the gold country to find my partner who went on ahead."

Sutter acknowledged Hank and Stan with a nod.

"I need some supplies," I said, "and wondered if you'd like to do a trade? I've got some great wine in the wagon."

Sutter's eyebrows went up. "Wine, you say? Why, I haven't had good wine in a mighty long time. Sure. Bring a couple bottles in for me to sample."

A young Indian girl followed me to the wagon to help. She was very attractive, and looked long and hard at Hank.

When the Indian girl brought the wine to Sutter, he grabbed her and gave her a big hug and kiss. She looked embarrassed and then reached for the wine glasses. I popped the cork from a bottle and began to pour a sample for Captain Sutter.

He grabbed his glass, sniffed the wine, and sipped it. "Ah, yes, indeed. This is fine wine. Why, I'd buy all the wine you've got, but I have no cash, only supplies to give you."

I stated, "I only need enough supplies to get me through the next month, so I can trade a few bottles for them."

He replied, "Sounds good. Why, I was just shutting down here for the day. Come along to my quarters and I'll fix you up with some supper."

"By the way, I'd love to sleep in a bed for a change. Do you have a place for us to stay the night?"

"Sure thing," Sutter said as Hank, Stan, and I followed him out of the Fort's store. We walked together on the dirt pathway surrounding the interior of the adobe-walled fort. We entered a large room with a fireplace at one end. The young Indian woman I saw earlier was tending the fire. She turned and smiled at Hank before going into the next room.

We sat at the long table with some other men. The Indian woman brought out plates of steaming beef, along with some crusty bread. I put the wine bottles in the middle of the table for everyone to sample.

Sutter stood and said, "I'd like to make a toast to these fine young men who brought us this great wine. Here's to your fortune in the gold country."

The other men in the room stood, and clanked glasses with us.

I turned to Sutter and said, "What are those copper disks I saw hanging around the necks of some of the Indian men?"

"Oh, those are an invention of mine. The Indians work a day and they get a hole punched in the disk. In return, I give them muslin shirts, and other supplies when they turn the disks in. It worked pretty well until this darn gold rush."

"That's very clever of you. Sounds like a great system, similar to a credit card," I said.

"I don't know what a credit card is, but I used to have up to six hundred Indians here to bring in the wheat crop each year. They also worked in the tannery and distillery. I've used their labor for many things, including the building of the adobe walls of the fort, catching deer, and making candles."

"You sound like a good business man. I noticed a little settlement outside the fort. What do you call it?"

"New Helvetia or new Switzerland. Years back I'd asked Governor Juan Bautista Alvarado if I could build a colony of settlements on the Sacramento River. Being that I was a Captain and all, he agreed wholeheartedly. He figured I'd help settle the place."

"I guess having a colony was good incentive for the Governor," I said.

"Yes, it was. Well, my party sailed up the Sacramento River in three boats. I brought a group of trappers, some Hawaiians I met from my past travels, and an Indian boy from the Rocky Mountains. We didn't see any Indians until we reached the upper part of the delta region, about twelve miles south of the American River. At that point, two hundred Miwoks confronted me. I assumed they were neophytes, or x-missionary Indians, so I waded ashore and spoke to them in my best Spanish, which wasn't all that good."

"That was very brave of you to approach them like that," I said.

"Oh, I have a way with people, being friendly and all. I explained to them I was their friend and wouldn't force them back to the mission or make war on them. I said I had presents to give them in exchange for letting me live peacefully in their territory. They liked the presents, and sent me on my way with a guide."

"How did you get the Indians to work for you?"

"I gave them beads, blankets, sugar, and shirts as an incentive to want to work, and some liquor to get them to befriend me."

I smiled as he talked, hoping he wouldn't discover my identity.

"I also made friends with the nearby ranchers who I rewarded for sending me Indian workers. But to those who didn't, I sent some of my armed soldiers to scare them up a bit, so I always got my Indian laborers that way."

"Sounds like you ruled with an iron fist."

"Damn right I did. Out here in the west, that's what you've got to do sometimes. But, I'm sure you know that, being a young man."

Sutter poured more wine for himself, and continued. "You know, it was hard to train the Indians to the white man's clock and calendar. They had no concept of time, except that of daybreak and sundown. They'd only work until they had enough food and then stop. Theirs was a schedule of gathering acorns and seeds, or catching salmon when they were in season, and picking berries. I couldn't let them be running off to do those things, or my crops wouldn't make it. Hard. . .darn hard it was."

"I'll bet."

"But nothing to what it is today. Why you could get the Indians to work for days for shirts and beads. Now, they know they can go to the creeks, and after an hour of sifting pebbles, get a cup filled with gold dust and buy whatever they want. Ruined, is what I'm becoming. Ruined. How's a man to survive, I ask you?"

The room grew quiet, except for the crackling of the fire.

"Well," Sutter continued, "you young men are the new adventurers, now. . .off to change the world and make your fortunes. I wish you well."

With that, Sutter trotted away with his arms around two of the pretty young Indian women who had been clearing the table. As they left, I heard one of the Indian women giggle.

Hank and Stan and I were shown to a bunkroom with several low cots, the wooden legs tied and crossed with rawhide. Straw was thrown over strips of rawhide that formed a mattress. I grumbled to Hank. "I suppose it's better than sleeping on the hard ground."

As I lay on the cot, a little tipsy from the evening's festivities, I felt something bite me on the arm. I leaned down and scratched. Next, something bit me on the back of my leg. I pulled up my pants and saw that fleas were crawling all over my legs.

"Darn," I yelled, as I jumped up. "Fleas. I can't sleep in a bed of fleas. I'm going outside under the stars."

Hank and Stan followed me. After shaking out our blankets, we threw them under the big oak behind the bunkhouse. A couple soldiers joined us and bedded down on their blankets behind us.

One of the soldiers whispered, "The old guy's got a wife and kids in Europe. Heard tell she's coming here soon, and he's going to have to give up his fun. Poor guy."

The other soldier whispered, "Better knock off that kind of talk, if you don't want to get into a lot of trouble."

"Ah, what do I care. I'm going to the gold fields after I finish this month. I'll have enough for supplies then, and I'll become a rich man. No more working for me. I'll retire, and marry me a young Indian girl and have me a family."

In the morning, with our supplies loaded, we now headed toward Hangtown to search the creeks and tributaries nearby for Reynard. I remembered the Sloans had told me he was camped about ten miles south of Hangtown. How was I to find Reynard with directions that vague?

Chapter Fifty-Eight
Discovered

On the way, our wagon passed by creeks filled with men standing knee deep in water panning for gold, or using wooden rockers. The waters were murky and filled with debris.

I'd yell out to the men we passed, "Have you seen a man named Reynard with an Indian named White Owl?" No one seemed to have heard of them. I felt discouraged.

Hank and Stan were getting anxious to start mining, but told me they'd wait until I'd found my partner. They probably were sorry they'd made that promise.

Whenever we'd stop near a group of men, I'd have Hank or Stan yell out, "Wine for sale. Good wine. A pinch of gold for a cup, or a sack of gold for a bottle."

Most of the men would stop whatever they were doing and come running to get the wine. They'd bring coffeepots, pans, or metal cups, whatever they'd have about. I had a few metal cups of my own lined up at the back end of the wagon. I noticed Hank's pinches of gold dust for each cup of wine he sold were getting larger and larger, but nobody seemed to mind.

On those nights we spent in miners' camps, somebody would have some kind of musical instrument, and oftentimes the men would start stomping and dancing with each other.

I wouldn't let Hank or Stan drink any of the wine for fear I'd get them started into a life of debauchery at a young age. We'd sit and drink our coffee while we watched the men dance and play cards.

Oftentimes, the miners would place a blanket on the ground and start gambling. One evening, a particular fellow thought he had a good hand and was out of betting-money. He asked everyone to wait, and put his pickaxe over his shoulder, and said, "Give me ten minutes." Off he went into the dark night, and before the time was up, he had more than enough gold to raise his hand, and then some.

One day, we pulled into a tiny mining town, and wandered into the only store there. I ordered a pound of cheese, a blanket, and asked the price. The storekeeper announced, "That'll come to fifty-six even."

My mouth flew open, and I said, "Fifty-six dollars. Are you sure?"

"Yup," he said. "You must be a newcomer to these here parts. Thems the going prices. If you don't have it, you'll have to leave without the cheese and blanket, 'cuz I can probably sell the same stuff for seventy-five dollars tomorrow."

I paid the man, and walked out in a huff. "Ridiculous prices," I mumbled.

I was walking fast when I bumped into a tall, dark-haired man. He said, "Oomph, watch out where you're going. Durn kids."

I looked up and saw Reynard's cousin Joseph. Oh, my God. I don't want him to recognize me and blow my cover. Then I noticed a strand of hair had come loose from my hat and was hanging in my eyes.

"Why, what's this," he asked. "This looks to me like my dear cousin's friend, Angelica." Joseph pulled off my hat, and my long hair flew out and covered my shoulders.

Hank and Stan stared at me in shock.

Joseph grabbed my arm and started walking with me. "My dear, dear Angelica. Fancy meeting you in these parts. Why, what's a woman doing in this wild place without a man to protect her?"

Hank and Stan followed us. Joseph continued walking fast, trying to outdistance them.

"I'm not alone, Joseph. I have my two friends here, Hank and Stan. They've accompanied me through this country. If you must know, I decided to join Reynard and encourage him to come home. He must have enough gold, by now, to supply several families for the rest of their lives." I stopped dead in my tracks and gave Hank and Stan time to catch up to us.

I realized other people were following us, besides Hank and Stan. To my dismay, it appeared as if all the men in town were walking behind us, smiling and taking off their hats, and acting excited, like men who hadn't seen a woman in weeks or months.

Joseph stopped, looked back at the men, and yelled, "What's the matter with you? Haven't you seen a woman before? Now all of you git."

Chapter Fifty-Nine

A Lone Woman Amongst the Miners

As the miners stood there staring at me, I felt very uncomfortable. I looked at Joseph and said, "I'm sorry, we can't stay around, but we've got to go onto the next town where I've heard Reynard has set up camp. I'll let him know you said hello."

As I walked away, I heard Joseph yell out, "Bugger's still alive, is he?"

I broke into a brisk walk. Hank insisted on helping me into the wagon, which he had never done before. Stan drove the horses away as fast as he could get them to move through the crowd.

I knew it would only be a matter of time, and the word would spread from camp to camp, river to river — a single woman was traveling by wagon. I could no longer keep my secret.

Before we got to Hangtown, I had Hank pull off near a massive oak tree. I found my dress, tie-up shoes, and hat in the wagon, and went behind the tree to change.

When I got back to the wagon, Hank and Stan stared at me. Even Hank, who was never at a loss for words, was quiet.

After a few moments, I said, "I'm sorry to have kept a secret from you. You see, I thought I would be safer in this part of the country if people thought I was a man. Please, no hard feelings. I'm still your friend."

Stan looked at me, and said, "No hard feelings, ma'am."

Hank kept looking straight ahead, and said, "No hard feelings, Alex. Wait, is your name really Alex?"

"No, my name's Angelica."

When we drew into Hangtown, there appeared to be a small celebration going on. As Hank tied up the horses, I could see a sign that read, "Welcome." A crowd of miners formed two lines. They held their shovels overhead forming an arch for me to walk under, and they cheered. I smiled and waved as I sauntered through.

I then headed for the handmade sign, "El Dorado Hotel, Bar and Diner," which hung from a make-shift wooden building with a canvas roof. I entered the door to the right which was the diner. The proprietor looked up and said, "Hangtown Fries. That's our specialty. Have a seat and I'll whip some up for you."

Hank and Stan and I sat on the wobbly wooden chairs at the hand-hewn table. The owner brought us our dishes. "Yes, this is the miner's favorite around here. It's eggs, bacon and oysters. It's on the house for the lady, since you're the first one that's ever stepped foot in my establishment. It's five dollars a plate for the men." He eyed Hank and Stan with curiosity.

Men lined the windows and doors and stared at me as I ate. I felt so self-conscious, I only hoped I didn't drop food all over my dress and embarrass myself.

"What's your recipe for these good edibles, my man," Hank said, who seemed to be pleased to be part of the center of attention.

"Why you dip the oysters," the cook said, "in egg and bread crumbs. You pan fry the oysters until almost cooked. Fry up some bacon until crisp and then add the oysters and pour beaten eggs over them. In a minute or two, it's ready to eat."

I took my time eating the food. Hank and Stan woofed theirs down, and excused themselves. They said they were going to find the bar so they could watch the gamblers.

After I finished my meal, the food sat like a stone in my stomach. I felt sleepy, so I walked next door to find a room at the El Dorado Hotel which was situated above the bar. The building was so new, it still had the fresh scent of cut wood. Ah, I thought. Perhaps I can sleep in a feather bed. Wouldn't that be a delight.

After I booked my room, I climbed up the stairs. I felt weary. As I reached the landing, someone was standing in the dark. He grabbed me, put one dirty hand over my mouth, the other around my breasts and dragged me through an open bedroom door. He slammed it shut.

I tried to see by the pale light from the lantern on the side table.

"No, you don't know me, Angelica, but I'm Texas Jack. Your boyfriend made an enemy of me a while back, and I'm out for revenge."

Texas Jack's heavy beard grated on my cheek, and he turned his mouth toward mine and kissed me. I tried to move my face away, but he pulled my chin toward him. "Now I know what Reynard wants you for. Mighty fine piece of woman you are, but won't be when I get through with you."

He flung me on the bed and ripped my bodice, stuffing some of it in my mouth so I couldn't scream. He tore my dress open, leaving my bosoms and back naked. I tried to cover my breasts, but he immediately turned me on my stomach. He pulled a rope he had stuffed inside his shirt and tied my arms to the bedposts. The ropes dug into my wrists.

Texas Jack tore off his own shirt. He exclaimed, "Here. Look at my back. Your sweetcakes was one of the jurors who voted I get a dozen lashes by Captain Wilcox, and a dozen by the Digger Indians. The jurors let Indians whip a white man. I'm going to show you how it feels."

He pulled out a whip and lashed it across the dresser, breaking the mirror. Pieces of glass shattered and tinkled to the floor. He lashed out at my back. As it hit my skin, it felt like fire burning me. I tried to scream, but the sound was muffled by the piece of bodice in my mouth.

I turned my head against the blanket, and pushed the cloth out of my mouth, as he lashed me a second time. I screamed from the pain. I screamed for Reynard. I screamed for all people stuck in hopelessness and agony.

In between lashes, I yelled, "Stop. Stop whipping me, you bastard. I never did anything to harm you. Why, I've never even met you before, you devil."

The window near the bed exploded in slivers of glass as a large, gray fox crashed into the room, having jumped from a branch of a tall oak tree right outside. The gray fox's eyes looked wide and wild. He leaped into the air striking Texas Jack with his full weight, his teeth sinking into my attacker's neck, drawing blood. Texas Jack took a knife out of his belt, wrestled with the fox and then stabbed at the animal's ear. I heard a loud yelp. After the fox jumped out of the window, and disappeared into the dark night, I saw blood on the floor.

I heard the sound of feet stomping up the stairs, as I continued screaming and yelling. Stan was the first one in the room, followed by Hank, a close second. Texas Jack ran toward the window. Before he could escape, Stan flung himself on Texas Jack, knocking him down.

As I lay tied up, half-naked on the bed, a group of men rushed into the room. One of the men yelled out to Texas Jack, "You bastard. You rapist. You vile, filthy man. You would dare harm this beautiful woman."

Another man yelled, "Let's string him up right now. Somebody get a rope."

Hank grabbed a blanket and threw it over my back. He untied my hands and helped me sit up.

My gentle sobs built to a raging torrent of tears.

"There, there," Hank said, rocking me back and forth. "You're safe now. Don't you fret."

The men struggled with Texas Jack who resisted as they shoved him out the door and down the stairway. I could hear his body bang against each step down to the landing.

I got to my feet, and walked to the stairway to see what had happened to Texas Jack. I looked down and saw a man in a long black raincoat and hat come riding on a horse through the swinging bar doors. Chairs and tables flew in every direction. He rode over to where Texas Jack was stumbling down the last set of stairs. The horseman yelled, "Jump."

Texas Jack leaped on the horse. Right before they bolted out the door, I got a glimpse of the rider's profile. I realized it was Joseph's.

Some of the men ran out of the bar in an attempt to catch Texas Jack and Joseph, but they were unsuccessful.

Deep frustration welled up in my belly. How could I ever feel safe, knowing Texas Jack was wandering around this great open country with Joseph as his friend?

Back in the room, I held the blanket in front of me while Hank bathed my back with salt water. I cringed but refused to cry out, to save him from seeing me in pain.

When Hank was through, he handed me a whiskey. I took the drink in one hand and gulped it down. The last thing I remember was falling asleep on the bed with Hank sitting in the chair next to me, holding my hand.

Chapter Sixty
Escape

The next morning when I awoke, Hank was slouched over in the chair, snoring. I pulled myself up from my belly to my side, and then out of bed. I moaned as the lashes on my back burned at the movement. I noticed some blood on the sheets. I was glad Hank had given me whiskey to anesthetize me enough so I could sleep through the night.

I looked around the room for some clothes to put on. In the closet, I found a man's shirt, coat, and pants, along with a hat.

As I pulled the shirt over my head, the wounds on my back stung as if they had opened. By cinching the belt, and rolling up the legs, the pants almost looked like they fit me. I wasn't worried. Fashion wasn't really an issue that day. I put the hat on, and tucked in my hair.

I sat on the edge of the bed putting the boots on. Hank's head jerked up. "What's this," he said. He ran over and grabbed me by the back of my neck. "You can't be disturbing the lady. Now get out."

Laughing, I said, "Hank, Hank, it's me. It's okay."

He sat back down on the chair and his cheeks turned red. "Sorry, I guess I'm still worried about you. That incident last night really got me going."

"It's okay. Really. I appreciate your concern for me. I might not have survived if it wasn't for your worrying about me. Let's get out of this God forsaken town. I'm ready to leave before anyone else gets a chance to make a fuss over me. Ready?"

Still looking sleepy, Hank stretched his arms over his head, and said, "Yup, Let's go."

We found Stan sleeping in a chair outside the bedroom door as a guard. Hank woke him up. He whispered, "Let's get the heck out of here. Be as quiet as you can."

By the time we found the wagon behind the stables in town, the sun was starting to rise. The pink glow filled the streets.

Hank said to me, "Wait here," and he walked into the stable.

As we waited, Stan kicked the dirt beneath his feet, and said, "I'm mighty sorry the man hurt you last night. I felt so bad I didn't watch you better, now that I know'd you're a woman. You feelin' okay this mornin'?"

"Don't worry about me, Stan. I'm tough. Nothings about to get me down. Why think about the past, and let it bother you, is my motto. I could stand here all day and feel sorry for myself, or for the next week or next month. However, I don't choose to do so. Today is a brand new day. Let's think about the adventure we're about to embark on. Now, where're the horses?"

Hank walked out of the barn holding the reins of my four horses. One of them whinnied at me as if in recognition. Hank handed me two buckets of oats to feed them.

I said, as I held the buckets, "Here, my dear darling horses. Here're some oats to give you the energy to help us with our escape from this town of crazed men."

When I was finished feeding the horses, Hank hitched them to the wagon as Stan paid the stable man. The animals seemed anxious to get moving.

"Which way you want to go, ma'am," Stan said.

"Don't ever call me ma'am. Call me Angelica. That's my real name, Angelica. I have a feeling Reynard would head south, so south it is," I said.

Stan and Hank didn't question me. I appeared to be the leader of the group and I felt my new found confidence was wearing off onto them.

The last star in the morning sky faded as we began our trek. The wagon rolled out of the small town before the first man walked onto the wooden sidewalk.

"You know," Hank said, "the men of that town will sure miss you. I bet you're the most excitement they've known since starting their gold mining, unless, of course, they'd struck it rich."

Stan looked up at Hank, who was holding the reins, and nodded his head. Stan smiled and said, "Yep. She's a barrel of excitement, she is."

"I'm going to climb into the back of the wagon and rest my sore back," I said as I looked for a comfortable place to lie down.

The last thing I remember hearing was Hank saying, "She looks so innocent sleeping nestled on her side, snoring, doesn't she?" Both of the young men laughed.

Later in the day, after my back felt better, I asked to take the reins.

"I can feel this tingling in my body," I said. "It's like I have a magnet in my head. Did you notice those red-tailed hawks flying ahead of us? It's like they're guiding us for some reason. Perhaps they know something we don't. What do you think, Hank?"

"Birds don't follow people," Hank said. "If they do, it's because they think they're going to get fed or something. Right, Stan?"

Stan replied, "Yup. Remember when we found a baby hawk squawking in a tree? Looked like it'd been abandoned or its mother killed. We decided to bring it down, so we could feed it. We ended up raisin' the hawk 'til he was big enough to fly. Even then, he'd come back and hang out near our house sometimes."

Hank smiled and said, "That's right. We called him Pete, and he'd come when we whistled. We'd give him a piece of meat if we had a fresh kill."

"Perhaps that's why you like me so much," I said. "I've been a hawk, flown the skies and arched my wings into the wind. I've soared over mountain tops, and gazed down at the valleys while the wind rustled my feathers."

"You sure that Texas Jack didn't bop you in the head, too?" Hank said, looking concerned.

"I had an experience some time back when I was with my partner, Reynard," I said. "We were doing these Indian ceremonies and next thing I knew, I was flying. It felt pretty darn real at the time. I know it sounds funny, but my body changed its shape, and I grew feathers and a tail and had a beak."

"Oh," Hank said. "I've heard of the strange things the Indian Medicine Men conjure up. I was always curious about their ceremonies and such."

"When I first got to Rancho de los Zorros Grises," I said, "the people there told me I was part of a legend and they'd been awaiting my arrival to help change a family curse."

"Wow," Hank said, "That puts a lot of pressure on you, don't it?"

"It sure does. You see, that's another reason I've got to find Reynard, besides the fact that I love him. I want to help him and his family. They've all been so good to me."

Chapter Sixty-One
Indian Women and Children

While riding in the wagon, we passed several tall oak trees whose spreading mantles created dappled sunlight along our path. A few Indian women were filling baskets with acorns which were scattered on the ground under the trees.

All of a sudden, an Indian child ran in front of the horses. I put the brake on, and tried to change the horses' path. The child fell. I couldn't see if we hit him or not.

As soon as I was able to get the horses to stop, I jumped off the wagon and ran toward the child lying on the roadside.

An Indian woman came running. She was screaming, "Tashito, Tashito."

We both got to the child at the same time. His black shiny hair covered his face as he laid on his side. When he looked up at his mother, I saw his sweet face. With his short pudgy arms outstretched, he reached for her. She laughed and said, "Tashito, okay. He okay."

I laughed and hugged them both. "I'm happy he didn't get hit. I was so frightened. I barely missed him."

The woman motioned for us to follow, and then sit down by her campfire. She gave us some acorn mush she had heating in a basket, and pine tea.

Hank pulled the wagon near the trees for shelter and unhitched the horses. From the back of the wagon he carried out some meat he had bought in the last town. He gave it to the woman. She cut the meat and threaded the pieces onto sticks, then leaned them over the fire. Hank went back to the wagon for a sack of corn meal which he placed at the Indian woman's feet. She went to work adding water and making patties which she cooked on a flat rock near the fire.

We put our bed rolls out, and sat leaning on logs. A couple other Indian women with children wandered over to our fire, and joined in the feast of fresh meat and cornmeal patties.

The Indian children chased each other. The little boy who almost got hit by our wagon wrestled with some of the other children. What a relief to see him healthy and unhurt.

One of the Indian women spoke English quite well, and sat and talked with us after we had eaten.

"Our men all gone. Many killed by white men. Some gone away to work on white man's gold fields and never come back. It hard to find enough to eat. Sometimes children cry when bellies empty."

I stood and looked at Stan. "Stan, didn't you say you were the best fisherman in Monterey? Why don't you teach these women how to fish these streams and then leave them some fishing gear? Seems like they shouldn't starve if you could show them how to make a couple of snares for small animals, too. These two little boys look to me like they'd love to learn."

Stan, who wasn't used to being paid much attention to, turned a bright shade of red.

"Why, sure I've got some extra fishing line in the wagon, and hooks. I can teach these here women and kids some of my fancy techniques on how to fish and do a little huntin'. I'd be pleased to do it."

Stan took a group of the women and kids down to the river. One of the kids caught a fish so big, when he tried to pick it up, he fell into the stream. He sputtered as he waded back to shore.

Hank asked the woman who spoke English well, "What's your name, and how'd you learn to speak English?"

"I used to work on ranchero near Sutter's Fort. I cleaned, cooked. I liked work, but my tribe moved into hills to hunt, to gather. I go to help. My name Brave Feather. Your name?"

"I'm Hank and that's my brother Stan down at the river. This here's Angelica, who's our friend. She's looking for her partner, Reynard."

"What Reynard look like?" Brave Feather said.

"Reynard has dark brown hair, blue eyes, and he usually has his hair pulled back with a leather thong," I said. "He was traveling with his brother-in-law, White Owl, who wears a brown felt hat with a hawk feather in the headband."

"I saw some men like you say, one day ago. They go south. They rode by field where we dig roots and pick plants. They look tired, like ride long time. When they get off red horse to rest, Indian man had limp."

My heart raced and I said, "See, Hank, I told you we were going in the right direction. I'm sure we can catch up to them soon."

Hank studied me for a moment, and then looked at the horses. I followed his gaze and realized for the first time how worn and thin the horses had begun to look.

"Seems to me, Angelica, we've got to take it a bit slower than we did today if we don't want to wear the horses out. This wagon you've been pulling all over hell and back is darn heavy. Besides, you've got the added weight of three people."

"What do you suggest we do?"

"It might help if we sell more wine at the next town. We sold most of the barrels, but we need to sell out if you want the horses to make it back home."

I'd noticed what good care Hank took of the horses, brushing them every night, and finding good stands of grass for them to munch on.

"You've got a good heart, Hank, and you take good care of the horses. I must admit I've been in such a rush to find Reynard, I've forgotten the horses' welfare. We'll take it slower tomorrow, I promise."

I walked over to the wagon and looked in. "Looks like we've only got two barrels of wine left. We've done pretty well and made a nice profit."

Chapter Sixty-Two
New Gold Claims

In the morning, I started frying up the potatoes and an onion I'd bought in the last town. Then I cooked some pancakes on the griddle. As the coffee simmered in the pot, I thought of how happy I would be to find Reynard. I poured the coffee into the tin cups, and wondered — shall I throw my arms around his neck and smother him with kisses, or yell at him for being so hard to find?

Before I had a chance to call Hank and Stan for breakfast, they were dishing the food onto their plates.

"Let's get started as soon as we get these dishes washed up," I said. "I'm anxious to get an early start."

Stan and Hank nodded in agreement, as they scarfed down their food.

While I poured river water on the fire, Hank finished washing and drying the dishes with a towel. He then put the dishes into the wooden box stored in the back of the wagon. When Stan had the team harnessed, I went over and patted the horses, and said to them, "Come on boys, give it a good try today. I'll find you a great meadow to munch in when we stop tonight."

I put my foot up on the wheel and climbed into the wagon. I sat next to Stan, and he took the reins. Hank lounged in the back. We waved goodbye to the Indians we'd met, who were already at work gathering more acorns for their winter storage.

After we had gone a few hours, Stan said, "Angelica, this part of the trip looks like it might be gettin' steeper, so it'll be more of a strain on the horses. It might be a good idea if you and Hank get out and walk. I think we ought to make it a short day for the horses, too, or we may over-tax them."

Hank and I jumped down from the wagon and walked behind. My back still hurt whenever I moved. The trail steepened. I could feel the strain on my own body, after being used to riding. My breath came quicker as the hill grew steeper. I looked over at Hank who was huffing, too, and said, "Can you imagine what it would be like if we pulled the wagon up this hill?"

Looking back at me, Hank replied, "Yep. You know Stan has always been one to worry about the animals. Why, on the ranch he wouldn't let our dad use the mules to plow more than eight hours at a stretch, even with the long days of summer. Of course, it always seemed our animals out-lived our neighbors' animals, so maybe he was right."

The three of us took turns driving the wagon and walking, so everyone could get some rest, except, of course, the horses.

A couple hours after noon, Stan led the wagon into a lupine and poppy filled meadow shaded by a few cottonwood trees at the edge of a small stream. Stan and I brushed the horses who had become lathered up from their ascent to the top of the hill.

After dinner, I took one of the gold pans out of the wagon, rolled my pant legs up, and then waded into the stream. I picked up some dirt and gravel, and rocked the pan back and forth, letting most of the large rocks fall out while watching the bottom of the pan.

"Yahoo, look at this," I yelled. "Why, I think I found myself some gold. There's some small stones that sparkle in here."

Stan ran over and looked in my pan. With a big grin, he said, "Why, I think you ought to mark your claim right now. It's yours."

Hank joined us and said, "Stan, I heard there's a rumor that a woman can't have a claim, only men. If she were married to a miner, she'd put it in his name."

Stan looked at me, and said, "Sorry. I guess you can't claim it."

I looked at them both with a frown. "Why that's ridiculous. Why can't a woman own a claim like anyone else? I'm equal to a man, aren't I? Haven't I proven myself?"

Stan and Hank both nodded.

Hank said, "Guess since you're dressed like a man, you may as well mark your claim same as any man. Here, we'll help you."

Hank and Stan started gathering some of the large volcanic rocks that surrounded the meadow.

"This shouldn't be too hard," Hank said. "As far as I know, we've only got to mark the four corners by this stream, leave a tool such as a pick or trowel. Then put your name and date, and the claim is yours. Of course, you've got to fill out some papers when you get to a town."

I went to the wagon for a pencil and paper, and started writing my claim. I signed it, "A.A. Hayes." I helped Stan put the last rocks on one of the corners, then put my paper underneath one of them and set a hand trowel down in one of the other corners.

"There. Now I've got a gold claim. Feels pretty exciting, whether or not I make my way back here. Life is pretty unpredictable these days."

I walked back into the stream and started panning some more. By nightfall, my feet and legs were frozen from standing in the creek bed, but I had a small leather pouch full of gold dust and a few small nuggets.

Hank had been gone a little while when we heard a hoot and a holler. Hank came running into the camp holding a lump of sparkling gold wrapped around a large quartz stone. "This ought to bring a nice bunch of money. Now I can ask Anabelle to marry me."

Once the truth escaped Hank's lips, he blushed a deep crimson. Stan looked at Hank in surprise. "Why Hank, I didn't know you were that serious about her, you old dog, you."

Chapter Sixty-Three
Delirious

I woke up before the sun rose to find I was soaking wet. It had rained during the night and my blanket was now drenched. I was freezing. As I rekindled the fire and got the coffee started, I watched the stars fade out. I could see the sun's first pink rays of sun spread in the east. I stood before the fire shivering. I wrapped my hands around my coffee cup, feeling the heat of the metal. The day was still. Everyone was asleep. As the sky became brighter, the foxes started yipping and the birds began to chirp.

Excited, I spoke to the rising sun. "Reynard's nearby. I can feel his presence. He's so close. I can almost touch him. I'll be with him today. I know I will." My heart pounded harder in my chest and a gentle warmth filled my body.

I stood up and opened my arms. I spoke louder. "Time hasn't stopped our love. I can't feel whole unless I'm with you."

After breakfast, Hank hitched up the horses and we got underway. I felt very distant, spacey. In a trance-like state, I held the reins and stared at the road in front of me. As we neared a hill, I noticed a small wooden cabin in the distance, which sat on a knoll. I looked up and saw hawks swoop so close to our wagon, I could hear their wings beating the air. Then I saw them circling over the cabin we had just passed.

The wind whistled through the pines. The big puffy cumulus clouds darkened into threatening thunderclouds.

A loose strand of hair whipped into my eyes as I drove the wagon along a narrow rocky ridge. I looked back at the cabin and noticed the hawks were still circling. All of a sudden, I realized that Reynard was there. I felt sure of it.

"Reynard. Reynard. He's in the cabin," I yelled to Stan, as I attempted to turn the horses.

Stan tried to grab the reins from me, but I fought him off. One of the wheels went over the cliff, and I was flung onto the rocks below.

I was aware of a sharp pain to my head, and everything went black. When I came to, I saw Stan jump off the wagon. Hank quieted the horses and brought them to a standstill.

Raindrops began to fall in an increasing frenzy. The wind picked up and pieces of rough tree branches and loose dirt swirled about.

As I went in and out of consciousness, I noticed Stan making his way down the cliff. He picked me up and several rocks and boulders became dislodged and fell hundreds of feet to the bottom. He inched his way back up the cliff, pulling and tugging my body. The heavy rain turned the dirt to mud, and my feet and legs became covered with muck.

Hank helped Stan lift me into the back of the wagon and they pulled the canvas over the bed to keep the rain off.

I heard Hank say, "She looks like she's half conscious, but alive. This is going to be a good storm. We'll need to get a water-tight shelter tonight to keep her dry, so let's head for the cabin."

As I became more aware, I noticed the black clouds roll and boil around the hills. Lightening came in flashes. Thunder sounded in the distance. The horses reared back, and Hank tried soothing them. "It's okay, boys. It's just a little thunder."

Stan yelled, "I think the cabin is behind those tall trees. Let's head over there."

The cabin was nestled between two large pines. Black smoke came out of the chimney. When we reached the cabin, Hank handed my limp, wet body to

Stan, then jumped down and threw a blanket over me. Hank pounded on the door and then pushed it open. He walked in and yelled, "We need help."

A middle-aged Indian limped toward Hank to assist him. As I became more conscious, Stan laid me on a bed beside a man who was asleep, lying on his side.

"Sorry," the Indian said, "but this is the only real bed we have. My partner here has a fever, and has been out of it for a few days. I think your friend will be better off here by the fire than in the drafty loft."

After pulling off my boots, Hank dabbed at the blood on my face with a wet cloth, and tied a cotton scarf around the wound.

Hank and Stan went over by the fire to warm themselves, their wet clothes steaming. The Indian man, who I now realized looked a lot like White Owl, handed them cups of coffee to warm their insides. They appeared exhausted. The three of them climbed the ladder to the loft to go to sleep.

The firelight danced on the wooden walls of the room as the man on the bed stirred. I saw him rise up on one elbow and look at me. The scarf covering my head hid half my face. The man pulled off my scarf, and I felt my long wet hair come straggling down.

My sleepy eyes opened at the command of Reynard's eyes on mine. My conscious mind tried to comprehend what I was seeing. I could remember a fall. I wondered if I'd died, and found Reynard in heaven. Maybe we were two souls without bodies, together in eternity.

"My Angelica, my darling," Reynard whispered. "We are in heaven together. I want for nothing more, but to kiss you."

Reynard climbed atop my splayed body, and kissed me.

"I will be your blanket, my dear. Let me warm your cold body with my feverish one."

I now felt awake and covered Reynard in kisses and tears, whispering, "Reynard, my heavenly one, my love."

Reynard answered with, "*Ma chérie* , I missed you so. Marry me, my dear. Marry me, and stay with me forever. We will entwine our souls here and now, and never be lost from each other again."

Chapter Sixty-Four
A Plan is Brewed

In the morning, I slept late, waking to find White Owl had fried pancakes, and left some on the table for me and Reynard. A dull throb drummed at my temples. I touched my head and felt dried blood. I turned and looked at Reynard, who still lay sleeping on the bed, his face red and damp with sweat.

He woke and put his hands on my back. I winced, and he asked what was wrong. I turned around so he could see the welts on my back, which were partially healed.

"What the hell happened to you," he said. "I'm going to kill the son-of-a-bitch who did this to you."

"It was Texas Jack back at the hotel in Hangtown. A fox jumped through the window and fought with him. Was it you Reynard?"

"I thought that was a dream I had. It's kind of foggy, but I remember my ear getting nicked." Reynard touched his ear and said, "Ow. Well, darn. I guess it was real after all."

"Texas Jack said he was going to teach you a lesson by whipping me because you voted to have him whipped by the Indians for some reason."

Reynard groaned, held his head and laid back down on the bed.

White Owl climbed down the ladder from the loft and handed me a cup of coffee. "Hi, Angelica. Glad to see you."

I jumped out of bed when a searing pain shot through my head and I remembered my fall. I staggered over to White Owl and hugged him. "I'm so glad to have found you."

"You know, Reynard's had this fever for three days. It just won't break. He gets delirious at times, and calls out your name. I don't have any medicine to give him. All I've done is put cold cloths on his forehead and try to get him to drink water."

"White Owl, I'm sure you've been doing the best you could with Reynard, under the circumstances. Perhaps I can help," I said, smiling at my old friend. "I'll be right back. I've got some medicinal herbs in the wagon."

I took two sips of coffee, and walked out of the cabin looking for the wagon. One of the wheels looked eschew. A sudden pang of guilt filled my chest as I remembered my insistence on turning around on the narrow mountain trail.

Before I climbed into the wagon, in the distance I could see Hank and Stan brushing the horses, and I waved at them. I searched under the canvas and found my leather satchel in the back and carried it into the cabin.

I pulled out the dried herbs I had brought from the garden of Rancho de los Zorros Grises. "Look, White Owl. Perhaps we can fix him up a bit. I brought Carmen's favorite cures. I've got echinacea, angelica, willow bark, rose hips, and lemon balm. I'll brew up a tea for Reynard, and we'll see if we can get him to drink it."

White Owl handed me a pail of water, which I poured into a pot on the stove. I put another couple of logs on the fire and stoked it. When the water boiled, I pulled it off the fire and put the herbs in it, then covered it with a lid.

I woke Reynard by kissing his forehead. "Come on my darling man. It's time to awaken and drink your tea. It's your Angelica, your personal nurse."

Reynard opened his eyes and smiled at me. His grin widened, and he replied, "My sweet *amour. Ma petite.* Anything for you. I will drink of your essence."

After I had gotten two cups of tea into Reynard, I was able to get him to eat a few bites of pancake.

I looked at White Owl who was watching. "Hey, nurse. Can you look at my ankle? It appears to be turning different colors. Is that normal?"

White Owl pulled his pant leg up, and took off his sock. One whole side of his foot and ankle had turned many shades of purple, blue, and green. I felt his ankle.

"White Owl, you look to me like you're healing okay. I saw you walking about with barely a limp. The skin color on your ankle looks to me like a resolution of a bad sprain. My prescription is for you to soak your foot in cold water three times a day. It will help take the swelling down. Stay off your feet as much as you can, and keep your foot elevated. You'll be right as rain in about three to four days."

Reynard's loud snores filled the room. White Owl and I looked at each other and chuckled, trying to stifle our laughter, afraid we might wake him.

We watched as Reynard tossed, turned, and moaned. He mumbled in his sleep and then growled. White Owl said, "Sounds like a fox, doesn't it? He's been doing that off and on all week. He told me he had a dream where you were in big trouble, so he shape-shifted into a fox's body, and saved you from some guy who was attacking you in a hotel. In the process of the tussle the fox got his ear cut by the attacker's knife. The fox escaped out the window after he saved you."

I put my hands to my cheeks in surprise as I listened to White Owl.

He continued. "I told him it was just a dream and to forget it, but he's had the same dream several nights in a row. When I told him, again, it was just a dream, he lifted his hair back and said, "Just a dream, huh?" He had a knick out of one of his ears. Beats me what happened."

"I think I understand, but you'll never believe me," I said.

White Owl winked and said, "With Reynard, I'll believe just about anything."

Hank walked in the door, wiping his muddy boots on the doorstep. "The horses made it through the storm just fine. Last night Stan found them shelter under some big pine trees, which kept most of the rain off. However, it doesn't look like we can repair the broken wheel."

White Owl gave Hank a cup of coffee, and said, "I've got to get word back to our crew from Rancho de los Zorros Grises. They're still at our gold claim on Weber Creek. They're going to wonder where we went. I'm thinking Reynard and I better not head back to our old claim, or those miners near Hangtown might remember they missed out on hanging us."

"You almost got hung?" I said.

"Yes," White Owl said. "I sprained my ankle, so I volunteered to go to town to get supplies. The store owner thought I'd stolen the money I brought to pay. When Reynard arrived later, they assumed we had stolen the money, and were ready to hang us. We were lucky to be able to sneak away and make it to this cabin."

"What do you think we should do now," I asked.

White Owl continued. "Before you arrived, Reynard and I had agreed that it's time to head home. The three of us would be better off going south and then veering west to get home. We can head on down to the City of Angels and east to Stockton. The farther away from Hangtown I am, the better I'd like it."

Reynard let out a loud snore, and Hank jumped about a foot. Everyone laughed so hard they woke Reynard. He started coughing, so I went over and encouraged him to drink more of the tea. I gave him some horehound candy to suck on for his cough. I dipped a handkerchief in cold water to place on his head.

When Reynard settled back on the bed, Hank said, "Stan and I don't mind going back the way we came to tell your men. However, before we do that, we'll ride off tomorrow to the City of Angels to see if we can find anything to fix the wheel, and see if there're any horses in town we can buy. We'll need to buy two horses to ride to Monterey."

"There's only a couple barrels of wine left in the wagon," I said. "Why don't you see if someone in the closest town would trade us a horse for the two barrels? If you can get the wheel fixed, maybe you can sell the wagon, too, and get another horse. It'll be nice not having to haul the wagon out. Going on horseback will be quicker." I smiled at the thought of being without the cumbersome wagon going over rocky roads and down steep ravines.

"Besides the two horses, I want to give you a spare horse, plus a bag of gold for any supplies you'll need traveling back to find Reynard's men."

Hank took the bag of gold and put it in his pocket.

"Listen," I said, "if you or your family are ever near our rancho, you're very welcome. We'd love to see you."

I went over and gave Hank and Stan a warm hug before seeing them off.

Chapter Sixty-Five
The Irishman and the Swede

About where Angels Creek and Six Mile Creek meet before flowing into the Stanislaus River, a settlement of tents was starting up and a few buildings were being built. That was the City of Angels.

It had been a week since Reynard was well enough to travel after his fever. White Owl was anxious to get home as were the rest of us.

Reynard led the pack horse as White Owl and I followed behind. When we rode into a town, we looked around for a place to quench our thirst and get a bite to eat.

"Look over there.," said Reynard. "It appears to be a makeshift restaurant. Who knows what they'll have to eat in a small town like this, though."

After Reynard helped me down off the horse, I said to him, "You're looking awfully spry these days, my dear. You'd never know you just got over the influenza."

I still wore the britches, the coarse shirt and hat I had found back at Hangtown. They were the only clothes I owned. A sudden gust of wind took my hat away, and I chased it down the street. My hair fell out and down my shoulders. When I picked my hat up, I realized some of the miners walking by me had began to stare.

Reynard, White Owl, and I ventured into a wooden building with a canvas roof that touted the sign, "Froggys Tavern, Best Fresh Fish West of the Mississippi." The proprietor was wiping off a table when we walked in. I could see him staring as I tucked my hair back under my hat.

He said, "Hey, there's no women allowed in here with pants. Why, that's durn uncivilized of you. Who ever heard of women wearing pants? By God, get the heck out of here. I run a clean establishment."

Reynard grabbed the proprietor by the front of his shirt. "Look, Mister, if you value your life, you'll treat this lady with respect and serve her. She's been through a lot. These are the only clothes she's got after all her mishaps."

The man stuttered. "Yes, yes, si-si-sir. I understand. I'll be glad to se-se-serve the lady."

A red-headed man sauntered in. He wore a green wool suit, and a hat with a bill. "Top of the mornin' to you all. Now, yush serve me up a beer, waiter, and be quick about it."

"Rusty, why Rusty O'Day. To what do we owe the pleasure of your company?" the proprietor said, walking over to his table. "Why aren't you working in the gold fields like all the other young men hereabouts. I just see you walking about town most of the time, talking to your friends. How're you going to get rich, and send your ol' maw in Ireland some of that gold stuff?"

"Eh, now. What's this? Givin' me a bad time again, are ye?" Rusty said. "How many times I got to tell you. My little Leprechaun friend said there's no sense wasting your energy when you could be chatting with your friends. All I have to do is wait for a good cloudburst on a sunny spring day, and presto, here comes the rainbow. And what, might you guess would be under the rainbow?"

I walked over to Rusty and sat down beside him. "What's this you say about Leprechauns and rainbows? Are you for real?"

"I'm real as ribbon, and serious as a heart attack. Why you ask, uh, little lady?"

"Just thought it was a fascinating theory. Have you gotten any gold this way before?"

"Well, I don't know whether I should be givin' away any of my family secrets," Rusty said. "Let's say, I know from the source and leave it at that."

A loud yell came from the street. Out of the tavern's window, I could see men running by. We jumped from our seats and rushed out the door to see what was happening. A big, burly man held a wiry blonde man by the hair and was pulling him toward a large maple tree in the middle of town.

"Let me go. I didn't do nothin'," the blonde man yelled, attempting to wiggle away from the strong hold.

"You won't pull this again in our town," a dark haired man in a suit said, who was walking alongside the two men. "I'm the alcalde of this town, and I declare we're marking you for all to see. A thief deserves a big T across his forehead, and that's what you're going to get, along with twelve lashes."

Another man, this one sporting long sideburns and a scruffy mustache, strode over to the alcalde, and said, "Stole my gold right off the donkey in front of the store. I had gone in for some supplies. When I come out, this here Swede's got his hand in my saddle bag, helping himself."

"Go on," the alcalde said.

"My name's Alberto Jordan. I've been working my new mine for some time. I was in dire need of some coffee and flour, so I come into town. I've always felt a man could leave his mule for a minute and trust his property would be safe. I guess I was wrong," Alberto said, his eyes squinting with anger.

Another man in the crowd stepped forward. "The Swede looks a lot like the man in Jamestown who was stealing gold from the miners. Seems to me they knicked his ear, as a warning. Let's take a look to see if he's the same guy."

The Swede's hair was long, and hung over his ears. He struggled against Alberto's grasp and shook his head back and forth to keep Alberto from pulling his hair aside.

Alberto wrestled the man to the ground, and another one sat on the Swede's chest. Alberto pulled the Swede's blond hair back to expose both his ears. One of them had a deep knick at the top of the earlobe, which was still quite red.

"Just as I thought," Alberto said. "This here's the guy who has been stealing. I vote for the branding T, and twelve lashes. What about it, Alcalde Martin?"

The alcalde walked over to study the situation. He examined the ear, as did all the other miners on the street who had come to observe the excitement.

The Swede, who was sweating by now, yelled, "I just knicked my ear on a wire fence, a way down the road. I didn't steal no gold, and I didn't steal this here miner's gold, neither."

A teenager, no older than thirteen, came forward, and said, "The Swede was looking around like he was into mischief. I saw him take some gold dust sacks from the miner's saddle bags and stick them under his coat."

The crowd started murmuring amongst themselves. The alcalde reached over and searched the Swede's coat. He found two bags of gold dust. "What's this we have here, Mr. Olaf?"

"That thar's my own gold dust. I have a little claim down on the river aways." It appeared the Swede was doing his best to try to smile.

"I'd say the evidence is overwhelming," the alcalde said. "I say we whip him the full twelve times, and brand him. He not only lied about stealing the gold, and seems unrepentant, but he's done it before. We've got to teach him a lesson so he won't be doing it again."

The crowd roared their approval.

The alcalde handed the blacksmith the branding iron and ordered him to heat it up.

The crowd grabbed the Swede and one of the men pulled the Swede's hands and tied them around a thick maple tree. They tore his shirt open so his back was bare. The bartender brought a whip from behind the saloon and handed it to the alcalde who applied the whip with relish.

Each time the Swede was hit, he let out a yell. At first the crowd was noisy, but after the third hit, they grew quiet. The teenager started counting, "Four. Five. Six. . ."

The crowd joined with the teenager. "Seven. Eight. Nine. Ten."

The numbers seemed like an eternity as the hits came one after another in slow succession. When the last blow came, "Twelve," the alcalde handed the whip to the bartender, and said, "Go and get the branding iron from the blacksmith. It's got to be hot by now. And bring the whiskey and all the glasses you can round up for when we're done. I also want you to bring me some salt and water in a bucket.

The Swede had fallen to the ground, his arms still around the tree. One of the men untied his hands, and the crowd walked him over to a fence. A piece was missing from the top of one of the boards. They stuck the Swede's head in the hole.

The blacksmith came back carrying the branding iron that glowed red. The alcalde yelled, "Let's get a move on. We don't need to have this last all day."

Alcalde Martin took the branding iron from the blacksmith and marched over to where some men were holding the Swede's head between the boards. He put the hot iron on Mr. Olaf's forehead and held it there a second. Steam rose up, and I could smell the terrible stench of burning flesh. Mr. Olaf's mouth opened wide as he yelled, and I could see his tonsils and bad teeth.

After the branding, the bartender came up behind the Swede and threw the bucket of salt water on his back. The Swede hadn't expected it, and started yelling and swearing.

Someone brought the Swede a clean towel and patted his back, and helped him put on a clean shirt. The bartender handed the Swede half a bottle of whiskey and a loaf of bread. He said, "Now, skedaddle out of town before we vote to do it all over again. You ain't never welcome here. If we see you in town again, you'll get it worse next time."

Mr. Olaf wobbled over to his horse, and the bartender helped him up. When he was seated, the bartender hit the horse's rump, and off it went, the Swede moaning at every bounce. Some of the men in the crowd laughed. Others looked disgusted.

Chapter Sixty-Six
Indian Boys Rescued

Reynard and I rode side-by-side on the way to Stockton with White Owl behind us. The blue sky seemed to open in front of us as we ambled along the road, not feeling in a hurry to get anywhere. Where was there to go, other than that moment in time?

As we passed within several hundred feet of a stream, we noticed some Indians working the streambed with their gold pans. They looked very thin, and their clothes were torn. I noticed a man who looked like Texas Jack yelling at the Indians while they sifted the mud and sand.

"Keep those pans moving," the man yelled. "You better come up with some better gold tonight than you did yesterday, or you'll not get any dinner again. No sense feeding loafers."

I jumped off my horse and motioned for Reynard and White Owl to do the same before the men saw us. The two of them walked into the bushes with me, and we tied our horses out of sight.

I whispered to Reynard. "That's Texas Jack, the guy who whipped me because he said he was angry with you. That's one evil man."

Reynard pounded his fists against a tree trunk. "I'll beat him to a pulp for whipping you."

White Owl restrained Reynard and grabbed his hands, and said, "Don't be too hasty. You don't need to have a murder warrant on your head. Maybe we can mess his life up a bit and not get into trouble."

Reynard relaxed his arms and replied, "You are right, White Owl. It would almost be worth going to jail over, but I won't miss our chance to get home and finish our plan to rescue the Indians."

"Oh, Reynard," I said. "I'm so glad you aren't going to take a chance getting yourself killed. Maybe we should get out of here, pronto."

Reynard put his finger to his lips, and said, "Quiet. Let's spy for a minute to see what they're up to."

Cousin Joseph came out of a tent near the stream and walked over to Texas Jack. "Get anything today? Yesterday's haul wasn't so good. Those Indians seem to be slacking off. We'll cut their rations in half and see how they like it. When they go to sleep, tie them up to a tree again. I don't want any of them trying to run off like they did last week."

Texas Jack grunted in reply, and banged a spoon against a pan. "Okay, you grunts. It's time to bring me your gold. One ounce gets a bit of food. Let's take a look."

Some of the Indians were young men, others just boys. One of the boys had black and blue marks about his face and eyes. He shook as he approached Texas Jack. "I no find gold today, but hungry. Can I have bread?"

Texas Jack approached the boy and slapped him across the face. The boy fell backwards, and Texas Jack kicked him in the ribs. "Damn, I hate a greedy kid. Always begging for food. You cost us enough to keep you in grub. Think you'd act grateful and bring me some gold today? Nah. So that's what you get, kid. A nice kick from Uncle Jack."

The young Indian rolled into a ball holding his side, and cried.

The Indian men and boys had stopped working and were staring at Texas Jack. He looked at them, and yelled, "Back to work, you red bastards. I'll give you all a lot worse if you don't start working."

I whispered in Reynard's ear. "Let's stay here tonight and wait until everyone's asleep. We've got to take the Indian kids away from here. We can each carry a boy on our horse. After that, we'll get a bit off the beaten path, so we can't be found in the morning. The adult men can fend for themselves. It's the kids I'm the most concerned about."

"Good plan," Reynard said. "I know, according to the local laws, anyone can kidnap an Indian man under twenty-five years old. If he is found to be a vagrant, they can force him to work, and do the same to an Indian girl until she's maybe eighteen, but this is crazy. They shouldn't make them into slaves and beat them and starve them. The idea behind the law is to be a caretaker for these people and teach them white man's ways, and hopefully they can take care of themselves. But this is downright slavery. I'm all for taking the Indian children somewhere safe. Maybe even my rancho."

"I'm with you," White Owl said. "Let's do it."

The three of us laid down and slept a little. I kept waking up every half hour or so, to look at Reynard's pocket watch.

Finally, everything seemed quiet, and I shook Reynard awake around 2:30. "Reynard, I think we should do it, now."

Reynard sat up, and rubbed his eyes. "Angelica, are you sure you want to do this? If we get caught, we might be accused of stealing someone's property. Who knows what they would do to us?"

"Okay, Reynard, if you aren't going to help me, then I'll do it myself."

"I'll help, but I only wanted to warn you first."

White Owl woke up and said to me, "You wake the boys and Reynard and I'll cut their ropes. Let's go."

Reynard popped open his buck knife, and White Owl pulled a knife from his belt. Reynard motioned to the pine tree where the Indian children were tied. Texas Jack and Cousin Joseph were in the tent sleeping a couple hundred feet away.

We tip-toed, trying not to trip on the tree roots, or make noises stepping on twigs or dry leaves.

When we got to the tree I awakened one of the boys. He looked startled. I put my fingers to my lips, and the boy shook his head and smiled. I woke up the other two boys and motioned for them to be quiet. Then, Reynard and White Owl cut their ropes.

I led the boys past the white tent to our waiting horses. Reynard handed me a child and I situated him on my horse in front of me. I put my arms around him, and we started off. Reynard pushed his child up on the horse, and jumped behind him, following me. White Owl took the last child and edged him onto his saddle before jumping onto his horse.

We rode several miles along the moonlit trail. As the sun began to rise, we heard the cries of coyotes. Pinkness filled the sky, tinting everything with pastel light. The boy riding with me had fallen asleep, his head resting on the horse's neck.

The bright sun started to cheer me as the brisk morning air hit my cheeks. The warmth of the little body in front of me made me feel maternal. Those young boys were entrusting their lives to us. We had to watch after the boys now, and care for them so they could grow into self-sufficient, independent young men.

Reynard pulled his horse alongside mine, and said, "Let's stop in about an hour and make some lunch. I'm sure these kids are hungry. By the way, Angelica, I was watching you as you gazed at those kids with so much love. I envied them for a minute."

We pulled off when the sun was straight overhead. I gave the boys salted potatoes I had boiled at the cabin a couple days before. When they finished eating, Reynard reached in his pocket and took out some sugar candy that he'd been keeping awhile. Their faces lit up as they ate.

Reynard asked the boy who had the black eye, "What's your name, son?"

"My name is Joe. And this here's Sammy and Johnny. Our parents die of fever. We sold to miners looking for workers. Many Indians forced to work. Die 'cuz don't feed much."

"We want to take you back to our rancho, Joe," Reynard said. "We have other Indians there who will look after you. We'll teach you ranching skills and I'll pay you a wage."

"We feed our Indians very well," I said, "and buy them clothes. You're welcome to stay with us as long as you like."

Joe smiled real big, and said, "I like you, lady. I like you a lot. I go with you. I want live with nice lady like you, and nice man who give candy."

Reynard patted the boys on the back. Then he turned to me and said, "Let's get back on the trail. I want to make good time, and be sure no one tries to get these boys away from us."

Little Joe moaned, holding his ribs as Reynard helped him back on the horse.

"Sorry, Joe," Reynard said, "I know you must be hurting, but we don't want those bad guys to get you again, so we've got to keep moving."

Chapter Sixty-Seven

Ears

When we arrived at a makeshift town, we pulled up in front of the local store that consisted of a wooden frame with canvas for walls. We dismounted and tied our horses to a skinny pine tree. The boys and I sat on the wooden sidewalk to play clapping games while we waited for Reynard and White Owl who were shopping for food.

Some men came by and looked at the boy with the black eyes and swollen face. They looked at me like I was evil, and then walked away.

Reynard came out of the store carrying some supplies, which he put in the saddlebags. He told me White Owl was finishing up his purchases.

A couple of men came over and watched while Reynard put the items away. "Damn bastard is what I'd call you, hitting a little Indian kid like that," the man in the shiny black suit and dirty clerical collar, yelled. "Now, if that was a white kid, we'd string you up from a tree."

Reynard looked the man square in the eyes and said, "My name's Reynard, and I didn't do that to the kid. I agree with you, it's a damn shame. I just freed these boys from some men who were mistreating them. I asked the kids if they would like to live on my rancho and learn a few skills. I pay my laborers and take good care of them."

The Reverend spoke to his buddy who wore a top hat, and said, "Yeah, we really believe you, don't we, Frank?"

The kids gathered about me and hung close. The smallest boy, Joe, quivered as he clutched my leg for security.

"What'd you say about stealing the kids? You not only beat the kid, but you stole him, too?" Frank yelled. He grabbed Reynard by the shoulder and pulled his hair back from his ears. Everyone could see the knick on his ear. Frank laughed. "Just as I thought, a criminal. Everyone who knows anything about criminals, says they can't be believed."

"Okay, then," I said, trying to stay calm. "I'm not a criminal. You can check my ears." I pulled my hair back and the men came over to look.

"I wish to make my declaration here and now in front of all who will hear. My name is Angelica Hayes, and I come from Rancho de los Zorros Grises about seventy-five miles north of San Francisco. I'm the fiancée of this man, and I swear he's honest, and kind, and would never beat a boy. His only offense is to listen to me. I insisted he help these dear young boys who were forced into slavery, starved, and beaten by some miners. Reynard received the nick on his ear when he was saving my life. So help me, God," I said.

"I'm Reverend Fitch, and I want you to swear on the Bible to what you just said."

"I'd be glad to." I stood up as straight as I could, while my knees trembled.

"What kind of lady are you who rides about in pants, and not in a proper skirt?" Frank said.

White Owl strolled out of the store and stood in the doorway, listening.

Joe walked over to Frank and Reverend Fitch, and spoke to them. "Hi. I'm Joe. These my brothers. It true. We kept by miners and worked hard. We get little food and if I complain, miner hit me. These good people come help me and my brothers. I want live with nice lady and man."

"Little Joe makes a great witness. Everything he says is true," White Owl said.

Reverend Fitch looked at Joe, and White Owl and said, "Don't you know? Indians can't testify. Nobody can believe an Indian, anyway. Also, children shouldn't speak unless spoken to."

Frank looked at Reverend Fitch, and motioned for him to come close. The two men huddled together for a moment and spoke in quiet voices. When they were finished, Frank said to us, "I'm going to find the alcalde to decide this. In the meantime, you and your Indians can hole up in this here log house. The alcalde should be back in a day or two."

Frank tied Reynard's hands behind his back, and pushed Reynard down the road in front of him. White Owl, and I walked right behind them. I held two of the boys' hands. One held onto my pant leg.

Reynard was shoved into the log house, and we followed him. They shut the door behind us. I looked up and saw the roof was made of canvas. One man camped outside the door to make sure we didn't escape.

I whispered to Reynard. "Did you notice the roof is made of canvas?"

He nodded.

I asked White Owl, "Do you still have your knife?" He smiled at me and removed his knife out of the leather sheath hanging from his belt. He went over and cut the ropes holding Reynard's hands.

All of us were exhausted. We made ourselves as comfortable as we could on the dirt floor and fell asleep. I bolted awake around midnight and felt somewhat refreshed.

I woke up Reynard and White Owl, and put my forefinger on my lips to indicate they should be silent. I pointed toward the canvas roof, and then White Owl and I clasped our hands together. Reynard put his foot in our hands and was able to reach the top boards. He pulled himself up and slit open the canvas ceiling. He climbed out and disappeared for a while. I began to worry he had been caught, and started to fear they'd really think he was guilty.

After some time had elapsed, the front door opened. I enfolded the boys in my arms and waited, not knowing if Reynard had been successful or not. "Don't worry," Reynard said, smiling as he walked through the doorway of our makeshift jail. "I convinced the guard to go deeper into sleep. He won't wake up when we stroll out the door."

We snuck outside the building, and then looked for the horses. Behind the store was a little grove of live oak trees and a field of grass. The horses had been tied there to feed. We lifted the sleepy children onto the horses' backs. I climbed on behind Little Joe who whimpered, holding his ribs. I patted his head to console him. To be as noiseless as possible, Reynard and White Owl took the reins and led the horses to the trail. When we were a distance from town, they jumped on their horses and we escaped, riding into the starlit night.

Chapter Sixty-Eight
Wedding Bliss

Upon our return to Rancho de los Zorros Grises, we took our new wards to meet the resident Indians. Two of the Indian women, who had lost children to illness, rushed out to take the boys in tow, embracing them. Then laughing and chattering, they walked hand-in-hand to the river to wash.

When we got to the house, we were greeted by the family with hugs and good news. We learned that Father Jean would be returning any day to Rancho de los Zorros Grises. We were feeling excited to see him again. He'd been gone for months on his various missions to outlying ranchos. We not only looked forward to Father Jean's help on formulating a plan to free the Indians on Joseph's rancho, but Reynard and I wanted him to perform a marriage ceremony for us.

The following week, after recuperating from our trip, we began making plans for the wedding. Juliette and Aunt Lila planned the banquet, and Carmen started fitting me for a wedding dress.

One morning, Carmen, was on her hands and knees in the sewing room, marking my wedding dress. She held the pins in her mouth as she marked the hem line with them. Reynard stole into the room to have a look at me. "Oh, my God, Reynard," Carmen screamed, pins spewing out of her mouth. "Don't you know it's bad luck to see the bride in her bridal gown before the wedding?"

I laughed, as Reynard ran out of the room like a little boy caught stealing a cookie.

Carmen grinned. "That Reynard," she said. "I've not seen him so excited since his last wed. . .oh, pardon me, Angelica. Never mind. Here, slip out of the wedding gown. I've got it pinned now, and you can go and chide the groom-to-be."

Carmen helped me pull the gown over my head. I then put on my white lacey blouse and long gray skirt. I went downstairs to the front room and found Reynard sitting before the fire pretending to read a book he held in his lap.

"My darling Angelica, you looked so beautiful in that gown. You are my heavenly angel put here on earth. . .you, who have saved my life, and I yours. There are no two people more bound to each other than we are."

I walked over to Reynard and took both his hands in mine and said, "It's you who has given me the will to live my life fully. You've given me passion and joy."

Carmen came into the room and announced, "I just looked out the window and saw Father Jean at the door. Reynard, would you do the honors of being the first to greet your friend?"

Reynard sprang from the leather chair and ran for the door. Upon opening it, he found Father Jean patting Jack on the head, saying, "Where's your master, big boy?" Father Jean stood up as soon as he saw Reynard open the door.

Reynard gave him a bear hug, and then lifted his friend into the air. When he landed back on his feet, Father Jean shook Reynard's hand, laughing. "My, such a greeting from my old friend. I see you are well?"

"Never been better in my life, now that Angelica and I are getting married. But come in and sit by the fire, and let us get to planning. We would like you to marry us in the morning, first thing. When we return from our honeymoon, you and I can finalize our plans to rescue Joseph's Indians."

The morning started very early at the rancho with all the preparations that needed to be made for the wedding. The horses tails were braided with intertwining colorful ribbons and they wore their best leather saddles etched with silver.

I sat sidesaddle on Red, Reynard's horse. I wore my creamy white lace dress with a matching shawl over my head. Carmen had fixed my hair into a thick French braid that hung down my back.

Sitting on Red, I was led by White Owl from the barn to the porch. All the relatives, friends, and workers of the rancho were gathered in front of the house to watch. Reynard strode up to the horse and I slid down into his waiting arms. He carried me up the porch steps to the wooden altar.

Father Jean wore a clerical collar under his black coat. Around his neck he wore a silk shawl embroidered with green, blue, and red designs. His face beamed as we approached. Reynard set me down, and we stood hand-in-hand.

Father Jean took our hands in his, and said, "This day brings me great joy. I'm so happy to be performing a wedding ceremony for my college friend, Reynard Rutherford, and his beloved, Angelica Hayes. These two deserve much love and happiness in this life. May their union be blessed with many children, and may their days be long and fruitful."

Father Jean then let go of our hands and went over to the altar, opened the Bible and recited some words in Latin. He performed a mass, including wafers and fine Rancho de los Zorros Grises wine.

As Father Jean began the wedding vows, I looked at Reynard and saw the face of a man who had waited for me through years of sorrow and pain. . .whose need was so great and love so strong that he pulled me from my century back to his.

After I finished my vows, Father Jean had Reynard repeat his vows, "To have and to hold from this day forward."

When Father Jean said, "I now pronounce you man and wife," Reynard leaned me back with his strong arms and gave me a passionate kiss.

Everyone clapped and cheered.

Reynard and I strolled through the crowd of people. He picked me up, lifted me onto Red's saddle and then climbed on behind me. I was surprised, since I thought we would go into the house for the reception. He kicked the horse and we went into a full gallop through the cheering crowd of friends and family. At the edge of the drive, Red reared back on his hind legs, opened his mouth, and whinnied.

Reynard kicked Red and we sprinted away with Reynard holding me tight. After a few minutes, he turned Red to the left and we went up an embankment and back down again.

Reynard jumped down from Red, lifted me off, twirled me around and around, then set me down. He unbuttoned my wedding dress, and lifted it over my head.

Then he started running toward a pond about fifty feet away, yelling, "Last one in is a mud hen."

As he ran, he threw off his coat and shirt, having already removed his shoes, socks, and pants. I could see where his tight buttocks met with his powerful legs as he raced toward the pond.

I took my shoes and stockings off, then followed him as fast as I could. As I ran, I removed my petticoat. Reynard was too fast for me and he jumped into the air, his legs tucked under his body as he cannon-balled into the pond.

I could see steam rising as I got closer. . .another volcanic pond filled with hot water.

When Reynard bobbed up, he turned around to watch me as I sprinted nude toward him, then flung myself into the water.

Reynard dove, and when he came up, he grabbed my feet and pulled me down. I opened my eyes under the water and could see his feet kicking. Out of the corner of my eye, I saw what looked like a water nymph, hiding below in the vegetation. She looked at me and winked. I winked back.

As we climbed out of the pond and onto the grass, Reynard fetched a blanket and some wine from his horse and laid them down on the leaf-covered ground. Our bodies were steaming in the cool air. Reynard put a blanket of fox pelts over us. He reached for the bottle of rancho Port, which he opened. We took turns drinking straight from the bottle. Soon we were giggling like truant school children.

Reynard said, "Angelica, I wish to drink of you."

I held some of the Port in my mouth and as Reynard kissed me, I let it release across his lips.

I likewise said to him, "My darling Reynard, I wish to drink of you, also."

He smiled with a mischievous look in his eyes. Sitting on the blanket, he took a big swig of the wine and held it in his mouth. I kissed him and drank not only of the wine, but also the sweetness of his lips.

He laid me down and looked into my eyes. His soft gentle kiss seemed to last an eternity. Next, he laid down and pulled me on top of him and we stared into each other's eyes. Nothing else existed for us, not his past love nor mine, not our future or where our love would go, not the century I came from or my friends and family I left behind. Not even his family curse.

Only that moment was real. As he kissed me again, I felt myself disappear into his body. I became Reynard and his body was my body, his form mine. For a moment, I experienced a strong fear of losing myself, as though I was dissolving. The passion of the moment overtook me, and I let go.

I began to dream that Reynard had turned into a gray fox and I, in turn, became a red hawk. Our two bodies blended, until I was uncertain what kind of animal the amalgam had become. Our one body had red wings, a sharp nose, furry ears, and claw feet. What a strange brew that mixture was. What unusual textures and grains of that blend of man, woman, spirit, timelessness — a melting into the universe.

Chapter Sixty-Nine

Mr. Sloan's Argument with Father Jean

Reynard told me later that evening about how his friend, Father Jean, had changed Mr. Sloan's attitude about childbirth. Heather, since you are a nurse, I knew you'd be thrilled to hear about it.

Reynard had been glad to learn the Sloans made it to the rancho. When Reynard got together with them, they reminisced about how Reynard had rescued them when their wagon was stuck in the river so many months before. Reynard was pleased Mr. Sloan had brought his wife to the rancho so that Mrs. Sloan could have a good midwife. Reynard reassured them that his cousin, Geraldine, had a fabulous reputation for delivering babies.

Mr. Sloan insisted on helping Reynard about the rancho to repay him for their lodging. In return, Reynard taught him all he could about raising sheep, and growing apples, walnuts, and wine grapes.

One evening after dinner, the family and the Sloans sat by the fire enjoying their tea. Mrs. Sloan asked Reynard where Angelina and Carmen were. He said, "They told me they're weaving a carpet for your new house, so excused themselves to prepare the loom."

Mrs. Sloan smiled and said, "Why, that'll be mighty fine, having a carpet."

Reynard got up to stoke the fire. Mr. Sloan handed him more wood to keep the fire from going out. When the fire was blazing, the two of them stood side-by-side smoking pipes.

Mr. Sloan said, "After observing your rancho, I realized that ranching can often be more rewarding than mining for gold. This land is rich and fertile, unlike the plains where we came from. I'm thinking Mrs. Sloan and I should find a place to settle down, now that our baby is about to be born."

"Great idea," Reynard said. "After trying my hand at gold mining, I heartily agree with you."

Geraldine walked into the room and sat on the couch next to Mrs. Sloan. "Well," Geraldine said, "it's about time I started to work with you to prepare for the birth. I'll teach you some breathing exercises I learned from Angelica during Juliette's birthing. They ease the pains and help with relaxation. That quickens the labor."

Mr. Sloan tapped his pipe into the fire to knock out the tobacco, and then turned and glared at Geraldine. "Don't be ridiculous, my dear. Taking lessons on birthing is not natural."

Mrs. Sloan looked up from stirring her tea, and said to Geraldine, "My husband always says it's the will of God that women be made to suffer during childbirth. . .that it helps cleanse us from original sin we carry from Eve. I'm prepared to suffer for this and for the well-being of my child. I don't need your breathing exercises."

"Why, that's ridiculous," Geraldine said. "If you have tools like herbs and breathing, you should use them to help with the labor."

"Don't you know the scriptures," Mr. Sloan asked. "For women it's decreed that in sorrow thou shalt bring forth children. Also, how can a woman love her child without the pain, for it's also written in scriptures in the book of John that a woman when she is in travail hath sorrow, because her hour is come?"

"Why, that doesn't sound right," Reynard said, "that a woman should suffer any more than is necessary to be delivered of a baby. It only makes sense that she be comforted as much as possible, so she will have the energy she needs to nurse and care for the baby."

Father Jean, who had put his tea cup down on the table, jumped up from his chair and stood in front of Mr. Sloan. "Yes, yes. I know that old line, and I don't believe it for one minute. Some people are so close-minded. Why, I heard some years back, a woman in Scotland was tried for hearsay from making an effort to relieve the pains of labor and was adjudged a witch and burned at the stake."

Geraldine said, "Hopefully, we've come a long way since then. Those scripture interpretations are hog wash. I've seen plenty of women give birth. The love given those babies was equal no matter how easy or difficult the suffering."

"Well, I must admit," Mr. Sloan said, "burning someone as a witch for relieving the pains of childbirth is extreme. However, you can't go against Scripture. It's a sacrilege."

"Why does man think it wrong to use human means to contravene in childbirth," Father Jean asked. "Mankind changes nature to suit himself all the time. He works daily to find ways to make his fields more fertile and increase productivity of his crops. Many in the clergy were against vaccination for smallpox in the beginning. I've even heard some denounce the winnowing machine for separating the wheat from the chaff on the grounds that if God had ordained it, how can man change it."

Mr. Sloan's face softened as he stared into the fire. Mrs. Sloan cupped her two hands upon her widening belly, possibly thinking of an easy birth.

Father Jean continued. "If one objects to the relief of pain as a sin, does that say one shouldn't improve that which the Creator in His Almighty will and providence has ordained from the creation of the world? Then why is it okay to build a bridge or a tall building? This is an improvement upon the Creator's original work, yet this seems okay with the religious man."

"You have a very good point there, I must admit," Mr. Sloan said.

Mrs. Sloan smiled and went over to her husband and held his hand.

"Can you give me any further Biblical proof," Mr. Sloan asked.

Father Jean said, "Did not God use anesthesia during the operation of removing Adam's rib to give to Eve in Genesis, second chapter, twenty-first verse, where it says, 'And the Lord God caused a deep sleep to fall upon Adam and he slept: and He took one of his ribs and closed up the flesh thereof.' As you can clearly see, here the Creator himself used means to elevate poor human nature from unnecessary endurance of physical pain."

Mr. Sloan looked thoughtful for a moment, and then said, "By golly, I never thought of it that way. . .God, himself, giving anesthesia to relieve pain. Why, when you put it that way, it sure makes sense. Yes, sir, it sure makes sense."

Mrs. Sloan's face lit up at her husband's remarks. "Then, my dear, you don't mind if I work on the exercises with Geraldine?"

"No, my dear, go ahead and practice. Anything that will make this birthing thing easier for you. Why, I'm sure if you can get the little one out quicker, you'll recover sooner. You're certainly going to need your energy for a young'n."

Geraldine and Mrs. Sloan disappeared into the next room to practice.

Chapter Seventy
Gathering Herbs

The next morning, Geraldine accompanied me into the herb garden. "Angelica, let's see if you've got everything here on my list. Have you got any sage and comfrey to help move Mrs. Sloan's birth along?"

I led Geraldine to the plants, and pointed to the sage with the blue flowers, and the big-leafed comfrey.

"Okay, how about some pennyroyal for easy passage of the fetus and to ease the mother-to-be's pain?" I pointed to the plant which grew in great profusion against the fence.

"Yes, and I see the peppermint right next to it. We will use it in case she has an upset stomach. Now, how about basal to help expel a tardy afterbirth? Yes, I see some growing little blue heads."

I made myself busy picking the peppermint and then the basal.

"Alright, now anise. Angelica, do you have. . . of course I see an anise plant that is at least seven feet tall. It must like this climate. I guess I've seen you put it in our tea and mix it with your flower bouquets."

"Is there anything else you need," I asked.

"Nothing from the garden. In the house I have some ground cumin seed to help the birth along, and sassafras tea, which is a good tonic after the birthing to help recovery."

"I guess we're as prepared as we're going to be," I said.

"Yes, and Mrs. Sloan told me she's feeling confident now that she has a midwife to help her. She told me when she was in the goldfields, she'd been afraid she'd be stuck out there with no women around to help her. Since it's her first birth, she wasn't sure what to expect or what to do. I doubt if Mr. Sloan would have been much help, being a man and all."

"Well," I said. "you have to give men a little credit, now, don't you? They're the ones that help create the little ones in the first place."

After we both had a good chuckle, I said, "You never know. I might be needing your services one of these days. Reynard and I are anxious to start a family."

"Of course, you are, my dear," Geraldine said. "I doubt that the time will be too far away."

As we strolled back toward the house, I said to Geraldine, "Please call me when Mrs. Sloan's pains start, even if it's in the middle of the night. I want to be there to help."

Chapter Seventy-One
Another Birth

Mrs. Sloan and Watu followed me into the orchard to pick apples. Watu seemed to need companionship to alleviate her loneliness now that her sister had passed away. We began picking apples while Watu carried the baskets for us.

She told Mrs. Sloan, "When Indian woman give birth, she go away from village to shelter. Some relative go help. Mother kneel, pull on strap hang from roof of shelter or tree when pain strong."

"Yes," Mrs. Sloan said. "Geraldine told me it's easier to sit up holding your knees when you're pushing. She says she'll put pillows behind my back. Geraldine knows so much. I really have confidence in her."

"Yes, she good woman," Watu said.

Mrs. Sloan reached high in the tree to pick an apple to put in the basket. As she did, she made a moaning sound, and grabbed her belly. "I think my time has come. Help me back to the house."

Watu held one elbow and I held the other. Geraldine came running down the pathway to meet us. "The vibrations from the baby told me this is the time for it to come into the world, and I ran to meet you. I can tell you now, that yours will be an easy first birth. You have nothing to worry about."

Mrs. Sloan looked at Geraldine with trust in her eyes.

We walked Mrs. Sloan into the rear bedroom. Watu pulled back the big down comforter, and I put blankets and towels over the bottom sheet. Watu put extra pillows on the bed to support Mrs. Sloan's back.

Geraldine sent me to the kitchen to boil some water for tea, using the birthing herbs we had picked the day before. When I returned with the teapot and cups, Mr. Sloan and Reynard peeked in the doorway. Geraldine motioned for Mr. Sloan to come in.

"My dear, is there anything I can do for you?"

"Yes, I want you to pick me some apples for a pie. That's what I had on my mind when my labor started. I'll have a pie to look forward to when I'm done, besides the baby."

Before the two men left, I overheard Mr. Sloan ask Reynard if he knew much about childbirth. Reynard said, "Very little, but I know it can take as little as an hour or as long as two days. It depends on how the woman's built and how the baby's head comes out."

"Let's hope it's a short one. I don't want her to have to bear this for long. She's all I've got in this world."

After Reynard and Mr. Sloan left, Geraldine asked Mrs. Sloan, "My dear, may I now call you by your first name."

"Teresa. Yes, you can call me Teresa."

"Now, Teresa, don't forget how we practiced. You've got to remember to relax as much as you can. Your womb is working very hard right now, and you don't want to be taking any energy away from it."

Teresa exclaimed, "Here comes one. It's getting really tight."

Geraldine replied, "Okay, here we go. Imitate my breathing. Breathe in slowly. Now breathe out slowly. Watch me. Very good. Breathe in. Now breathe out."

When Mrs. Sloan's contraction ended, I spoke to Geraldine. "I have the tea ready for Teresa. I added a little mint to it to keep her stomach settled."

I went over to the bedside and lifted Teresa's head and held the tea cup for her. She drank all the tea in a few gulps.

"This breathing has got me thirsty, that's for sure. Oh, oh, this one's coming on real strong. Geraldine, would you breathe with me?"

I watched as Geraldine and Teresa breathed together. Geraldine guided, persuaded, and kept Teresa centered and relaxed. Then she directed me. "After you give her more tea, I want you to put some powder on her stomach. Start by gently rubbing her belly when she gets the next one. That'll help ease the labor, too."

"Because you taught her the breathing techniques, I can really tell it's helping her relax. Another positive thing is the fact the contractions are good and strong, which probably means this will be a quick birth."

"Ugh, Ugh. The pains. They're so strong. Geraldine," Teresa yelled.

"Look into my eyes," Geraldine said. "Follow me. You're going to be fine. Don't forget to breath."

After some time had elapsed, Teresa started grunting. Geraldine looked at me and said, "She's in the pushing phase already. She's coming along great."

I shook my head, smiling.

"That's a girl, Teresa," Geraldine said. "Go on ahead and push all you want. Push with all your might."

Watu piled more pillows behind Teresa, and gently eased her into a sitting position. Teresa opened her legs and grabbed her knees and pulled herself up as she pushed.

Geraldine yelled, "Keep going girl. I can see the baby's hair. Keep pushing. That baby wants to come out."

Teresa's grunts sounded like an animal. She seemed to be grunting with all her might — pushing the baby's head through the birth canal — pushing life into existence.

Geraldine put her hands into the pan of hot water next to the bedside and washed them with soap and dried them on the clean towel. She put one hand upon the baby's head and the other one underneath. Once the head cleared, the rest of the baby slid out.

Geraldine held the baby up and said, "Look, Teresa, you have a little girl."

Tears rolled down Teresa's face as she shouted, "A girl. I have a girl."

Geraldine laid the crying baby upon Teresa's belly, and pulled the scissors out of the bowl of hot water. She snipped the cord and tied it.

The baby continued crying on Teresa's belly as she patted her, saying, "It's okay, baby. It's okay. You have a Mommy and Daddy who love you dearly."

"You'll have another pain soon, and this time push hard to get all the afterbirth out. That'll be your last push and you're done. You've earned your apple pie."

Teresa sat up again, grabbed her knees, and started pushing. The after birth slid out with ease.

While Geraldine and Watu were busy cleaning Teresa, I took the baby and washed her. I dressed her in clean white cotton clothes and wrapped her with a baby blanket. Afterwards, while the women were finishing up, I carried the baby out of the room. I took her to the porch where the men were sitting smoking. Mr. Sloan jumped up, smiling.

I shouted. "A baby girl, and she's healthy."

He put his arm around my shoulder in a hug, took the baby and rushed back into the house to see his wife.

Reynard came over and hugged me long and hard, and gave me a loving kiss. He had a big grin on his face and said, "I understood it all, standing here waiting. It's like there's two kinds of births and two kinds of deaths. One kind of birth is through your parents, your mother and father. That is the birth through the body. Then there's the birth of the spirit, the soul awakening to God. It came to me that if my ego dies, then I can become one with God. Then I can never die. Despite the death of the body, I will continue on, but in a different form. That's what you were trying to tell my father."

"Yes," I said. "It's like the grapes you are so fond of. They have a very short season and can be kept only a short time in the form of a grape. Our bodies are like the grapes. We can discard the skin to find a new form. We can ferment into the spirit of the wine, which can become more potent with age."

I grabbed Reynard's hand and led him up the stairs to our bedroom, saying, "Let's you and me ferment together into the bubbling effervescence of the Spirit."

Chapter Seventy-Two
Discovery

"It's a lovely day for a ride, isn't it," I asked Reynard as we led the horses outside the barn."

"It sure is." Reynard helped me onto Honey and then mounted Red.

"You know," I said. "I love how your horse has that thick, black mane against the rust color. If I were a horse, that's the color I would be."

"Now, don't tell me, Angelica. You aren't going to change forms into a horse, now."

"Of course not, silly," I said acting insulted. "I was only admiring Red, that's all."

"I feel like riding toward Joseph's rancho," Reynard said. "It'll help me think better about the decision I'm trying to make. I haven't ridden that way in a long time."

"Sounds good to me. Let's go."

"You know, when I was growing up, I played with Cousin Joseph from time to time. I know he's no angel, but he couldn't possibly treat his Indians as the town's people say. He just couldn't."

"Are we going to have this argument, again, Reynard? Remember, when I wore my invisible cape and spied on Joseph's rancho several months ago? I saw how cruel he and his men were to the Indians."

We were distracted from our discussion by a large wagon in the distance, pulled by a team of four horses. The horses were all lathered up, and breathing hard as they tugged their heavy load up the hill. The driver whipped them over and over again, yelling, "Git up, you beasts. We ain't got all damn day."

"Look Angelica, there's one of Joseph's wagons turning off his land onto the main road. Let's hide in the trees and see what they're up to."

Several dozen large bundles were tied with red and green striped material in the back of the wagon. I could see wool sticking out of the stuffed bags.

When the horses went over the last bump to get from the plowed field onto the main road, one of the bundles fell off and landed on the ground. The driver appeared not to notice and kept going on the road to town.

We waited until the wagon was out of sight, then walked to where we saw the bundle fall. Reynard untied the knots and inside he found a dead Indian. I gasped when I saw the bruises on the Indian's face, and fresh whip marks on his thin back.

Reynard grimaced. "Let's take him back to our rancho so I can give him a decent burial."

I felt for a pulse in the Indian's wrist, and discovered a faint beat. When I rubbed his arms, the Indian opened his eyes and sat up. I gave him a canteen of water. He said, "Thank you. I thought I dead. You awaken me to life."

"Please, don't talk just yet," Reynard said. "We will take you to our rancho. I am going to put you on my horse. I'll try not to jostle you too much, young man."

Reynard struggled to get the Indian to his feet and pushed him onto Red.

"Why do you think they put him in the sack," I asked.

"They were probably going to dump him in a ravine at the edge of our property. They will be surprised when they discover he has vanished."

"I doubt it. They'll probably figure his sack fell off the wagon."

When we got back to the rancho, Watu came running out to help us. She put one of the young man's arms around her shoulder, and the two of them walked to the bunkhouse.

Later that evening, Reynard insisted on accompanying me to check on our young Indian friend. He tried to sit up in bed when we entered the room.

Reynard said, "That's okay, young man. Just lie back down. You've been through a lot. It looks like you got badly beaten, and left for dead. Why would they want to beat you like that?"

"My name Go Slow. I fit my name. Texas Jack, he hate me 'cuz I no hurry. He mean one."

"Yes, I know about Texas Jack. He is mean," Reynard said.

"My mother always say best way in life is not hurry. That way one choose right path. Not stumble. She right."

"Your mother is wise, Go Slow. What else did Texas Jack do?"

"He mad ever since back from gold fields. Maybe he not do so good."

Reynard and I looked at each other and smiled.

"Here, Go Slow," I said. "I brought you some broth to drink. It should warm your stomach. Watu baked you some fresh bread to eat with it. I think she's taken a liking to you."

Go Slow smiled at the mention of Watu. He grabbed the bowl with both hands and sucked the soup down. He sopped up the remaining soup with the bread.

"Tell her she make good bread," Go Slow said.

"You can tell her yourself, tomorrow. That is, if you're able to get up by then and walk about a bit."

"You bet. I feel better tomorrow," he said and smiled.

I brought out a bucket and a wash cloth to bathe his face. "Here, now hold still a minute and I'll dab at that cut over your eye. I've brought a bandage to dress it for you, too."

While I worked on Go Slow's wounds, Reynard told him, "I can't believe they would beat such a nice young man. What are they like with the other Indians on their land?"

"Get beat if not work fast or if not obey. Get beat if talk back, or laugh too much."

"Yes, go on," Reynard said.

"Children get little food. Foreman say don't get much 'cuz don't work much."

"That's horrible."

"My people live this land many moons. Many years go by. Joseph's father ask us to work for trinkets, flour, sugar. Then, his men come with guns. Force us stop hunting, and the women from gathering. They say we lazy, and should work on rancho. We made to stay in shacks and not leave."

"I never would have believed Joseph was capable of this. It's downright slavery," Reynard said.

Go slow continued. "Sometimes put shackles on legs."

"Do you have any relatives that are still alive?"

"My mother at Joseph's rancho. She getting old and gray. Can't work fast. They whip her last week. She not pick fruit fast enough. She good woman, my mother. I want go back and get her, but they kill me."

Reynard jumped up and started pacing. Go Slow furrowed his brow and said, "Sometimes my people made to work in hot fields from sunrise to sundown. Can you help my family?"

Reynard made his hand into a fist and started beating it in the palm of his other hand. "The bastards. How could they be so cruel to these gentle people?" He turned and walked out.

Chapter Seventy-Three
Planning in Earnest

Since bringing Go Slow to our rancho, I noticed Father Jean, White Owl, and Reynard having frequent, heated discussions. Most of the time they talked out of my earshot.

Reynard would fill me in from time to time. He explained that the plan so far was for Father Jean to give mass to the Indians and workers at Cousin Joseph's rancho. Father Jean would spend the night there and sneak out with the intention of unlocking the gates and buildings at Joseph's, so it would be easier for Reynard's men to rescue the Indians.

I asked him what they would do with the Indians once they were freed. Reynard said, "I've made arrangements to buy a farm near Monterey so I can take the Indians there and set up a new rancho.

"Wow, that'll be a big adjustment. By the way, when did you have a chance to go to Monterey last?"

"Remember when you first arrived at the rancho? I took some barrels of wine to be sold. After I received the money, I rode to Monterey and made a down payment on a nice piece of land."

"Oh, yes. You made a good sum of money then, as I remember."

Reynard went on to say, "However, it wasn't enough to buy the land outright. Now, with the money you made selling wine in the gold country, we'll have enough to pay off two farms. The property owners were selling their land for next to nothing so they could get a stake in the gold fields."

"It seems a very wise move on your part, getting away from Joseph." I said. "Also, I've heard that holding onto land grants like your rancho, after the

Mexican War, is becoming almost impossible. If you can buy some land at a great price, it seems the best solution."

"Yes. I'll be able to get enough land to allow the Indians to support themselves, and for us to prosper. They will need shelter and food for at least a year to get started. I'll oversee their land and train them to farm. When the Indians are ready to manage themselves, I'll deed one of the farms to them."

"I like your plan about starting a new rancho. Shouldn't you get the land set up with some kind of shelter before you take the Indians there?"

"Of course. I thought of that already. I've hired Mr. and Mrs. Sloan to build shelters for us before we arrive. They're leaving in a few days to get things set up. They plan on buying some land near ours, so we'll be neighbors."

"I'm so glad. The Sloans are good people."

"Yes, Carmen was excited when I told her earlier today."

"You have a great plan, Reynard, as far as where to take the Indians once they're free. However, the part of your plan about Father Jean unlocking the gates and buildings is rather iffy. What if it doesn't work?"

"That part of the plan is weak, I must admit," Reynard said.

"I don't think it's formed enough. You have more thinking to do."

Chapter Seventy-Four
University Friends United

One rainy evening, I sat with Reynard and Father Jean on the dark leather couch before the roaring fire where my wedding bouquet was still drying on the heavy wooden mantel. A loud knock at the door jolted us.

Reynard jumped up and went to the foyer. When he opened the door, the wind whistled into the house stirring up the lace doilies on the arms of the couch. The fire blazed higher.

"Reynard, you old rascal, I've found you," a curly haired, heavy-set man with a drooping moustache said. His broad-brimmed hat dripped water on the carpet.

Reynard grabbed the man's hand, and yelled. "Henri, you old Gypsy, you. What a marvelous surprise."

A thin, shorter man stood waiting at the door. He wore a heavy, black wool coat and a red striped ascot at his throat. His glowing, joyous smile contrasted with his intense eyes. This clean shaven, rosy-cheeked man said, "Reynard, it's David. I've come to share my dance with you, again."

David threw his shoes and wet coat off, and then burst through the doorway with his arms out. He began dancing in large circles, making marvelous leaps into the air. Henri pulled a violin out of the case he was cradling under one arm, and started playing a very fast-paced, passionate melody. David didn't skip a beat in his dance, and continued around the room, jumping over couches. When he bounded over Jack, the dog stood up and started barking and then broke into a howl. David fell down laughing.

Reynard shook the hands of his friends. He then turned to me and said, "Angelica, these are two of my friends from the French university I attended. We were a very strange crew, the four of us. . .Father Jean, David, Henri, and me. We hung out in taverns and coffee houses where we preached our own philosophy and wisdom."

"Sounds to me like you were a bunch of renegade students, probably cutting classes and teaching each other," I said.

"Yes. Well, Jean Jacque, I mean, Father Jean, preached Rousseau's pureness of man in his primitive form. He had the idea he could change the Catholic Church from the inside by becoming a priest, didn't you, Father Jean?"

Father Jean made a low bow, and said, "I was interested in stopping the debasement of society by the institutions of government as well as by religion."

"Interesting concept," I said, "changing the church from the inside."

Reynard continued. "Our friend, Henri, had a fascination with the way of the Gypsies. Earlier in his life he traveled with a Gypsy band and they adopted him. He played music with the Gypsies and learned their dances. His passion is the way of spontaneity and of the heart."

"So glad to meet you, Henri," I said and bowed.

Henri clicked his heels together, saluted me, and then said, "It's a pleasure to meet you. I'm at yours and Reynard's service. He is my heartfelt friend and I would die for him."

"Then," Reynard said, "there's David the Dervish, as we nicknamed him. He went for the passion and freedom through dance of all kinds. He traveled from land to land in search of dances that transform the soul."

David took my hand and gave it a moist kiss. "My dear Angelica, it's a pleasure to meet you. We have come to help your husband in his dangerous enterprise. Father Jean wrote us he needed our help."

"I'm so very pleased to meet you," I said. "You're quite the fascinating group. I'm eager to get to know you all."

I took everyone's coat, and said, "Please bring your luggage in, and Reynard and I will show you to your rooms."

That night, I fell asleep to the sound of our company's laughter echoing through the house.

The next morning, Reynard woke me by kissing my eyelids. "My dear, we've more or less formulated a new plan, and wondered if you wanted to take part in it?"

"Of course, I would do anything to help. What's the plan?"

Reynard said, "Father Jean tells us there is to be a wedding of Joseph's ranch manager, and Joseph is inviting everyone in the area to attend. Joseph even sent an invitation to our rancho. Therefore, we're going to take along our ranch hands and my friends, David and Henri, and the family. It'll be a semblance of kin getting together. There may be a chance we'll be able to free the Indians that night."

"I hate having to face Cousin Joseph again, but I guess it's the only way," I said.

Chapter Seventy-Five
David Meets Carmen

When Reynard and I walked into the dining room for breakfast, Carmen sauntered in, her skirt and petticoats rustling. The night before, I had visited her room prior to retiring and found her in bed reading. I told her to expect company from two of Reynard's old school friends, David and Henri.

Today, she surprised me by wearing a beautiful cobalt blue cotton dress with a boned and pleated front bodice, deep V waist, and lace collar. Her hair, which she often wore down, was in a high bun with isolated long, curls dangling down the side of her face. I had never seen Carmen dressed up, and was amazed at how wearing a fashionable dress that accentuated her figure could transform her from a rancho owner to a gentile lady.

David looked taken with Carmen and said, "Ah, such a lovely sister, Reynard. You have kept this secret from me too long. I'm enamored by her great beauty."

Reynard patted David on the back, and said, "Sorry, dear boy, she is not for you. She has been married over nineteen years to White Owl who helps me run the rancho. Juliette is their daughter. Hands off, David."

David looked back at Carmen and said, "My dear, if there's anything I can do for you, I'm your servant and your champion."

Carmen turned crimson at the flattery and attention. She said, "Thank you, dear David. It's a real joy to finally be meeting this wonderful friend Reynard has talked about. I look forward to getting to know you better."

White Owl said, "I guess I'll have to introduce myself." He stood close to David and looked him in the eye as he said, "I'm White Owl and I'm Carmen's husband."

"You're a very lucky man."

Henri interrupted them by bowing before White Owl and Carmen. "I'm Henri, Reynard's friend. Glad to meet you."

Before they could respond, Reynard said, "White Owl and Carmen have a new grandbaby, Simon. Perhaps you'll see him at dinner tonight."

Reynard looked at his sister funny, and put his hand on David's back, then led him to a seat at the breakfast table, away from White Owl and Carmen. He said, "Have a seat, David. Breakfast will be served shortly."

Chapter Seventy-Six
The Wind Storm

A couple evenings later, Reynard's family and friends sat in the formal dining room drinking tea after dinner. Juliette took a sip of tea, and then bounced her baby boy on her knee.

"Simon is such a happy baby," Carmen said. "I love his little belly laugh when you tickle him."

"Yes," Juliette said. "He's such a little love, and he looks more like his father every day."

"Ah," Henri said. "Where is your husband, my dear?"

Juliette turned to Henri and said, "He died before Simon was born. My husband had a bad heart."

"Oh, I see," he said. "I'm so sorry to have brought it up. I hope I didn't sadden you."

"Oh, no. Chesan always knew he would have a short life because of his heart condition. He turned his misfortune into a blessing by living his life with great intensity and joy. My husband taught me a lot about how to live that I didn't understand before."

"What do you mean," Henri asked.

"Well, for example, he didn't want to think about the future, or dwell on the past, so we made up this wonderful game. We called it, Living this Moment."

"What did you do to live in the moment," Henri asked.

"When we were on our honeymoon, we did things like paint each other's bodies, run through mountain meadows, pick flowers, and weave them into each other's hair. We even rode out a thunderstorm sitting on the roof of our cabin."

"Ah, that's lovely," David said, who had been listening to the conversation.

"Oh, Juliette," I said, "when you told me about that game earlier, I thought it would be marvelous to play. Maybe we can do that tonight."

"The actual practice is difficult," Juliette said, "although I'm sure, David, you'd fall right into the game from all I've heard about you. I'll challenge you to be the leader."

"I accept the challenge," David said. "So, everyone follow my example if you want to play. Let's all retire to the living room, while I think of something exciting to do."

Aunt Lila said, "Gabe and I are going to finish cleaning up the dishes and go to bed early. You'll have to excuse us."

White Owl spoke to Carmen. "I'm not sure if I want to do this game. I have chores to do tomorrow. Maybe I'll turn in early."

Frowning at White Owl, Carmen said, "Do as you please. Go to bed early. We don't get guests often, so I think I'll stay up and play."

White Owl grumbled under his breath, and then said, "I'll stay up and play if that's what you want."

"I, too, have to get up early," Reynard said, "but I think it may be worth my while to experience this game. Maybe I will learn something."

As the group of players entered the living room, a fire was burning in the stone fireplace.

Before anyone could sit down, David said, "I want everyone's glasses full because I want to offer a toast to you all. When I toast you, I want you to do as I do."

Reynard stoked the fire, and ashes flew from the logs and then died down. He said, "David, what's this business about following you? Can we trust you?"

"Reynard, you've known me for years. Have I ever led you astray? Of course you can trust me. We'll just have a little adventure, that's all."

Juliette sat the baby in the bassinette and then poured Rancho de los Zorros Grises wine into the glasses that sat on the oak coffee table. The fire reflected off the glasses as if setting them aflame. Juliette proceeded to hand a glass to each person.

David raised his glass and said, "A toast to this marvelous family for inviting us to share in their adventures and intimacies. I love this family dearly, especially Reynard, my old university friend."

At the end of the toast, David downed his full glass of wine. He got a mischievous grin on his face and then tossed the empty glass into the fireplace. Reynard looked at Carmen and smiled. She glowered back at him. After downing the wine, Reynard threw his glass into the fire.

Carmen exclaimed, "Is that really necessary? You know how difficult it is to get glasses shipped to us?" She then watched as the rest of us threw our glasses into the fire.

"Oh, hell," she said, and her glass joined the others.

Henri, who was slouched in the easy chair, began to snore, and appeared unaware of our shenanigans.

David looked out the window and said, "It feels like we're getting a southern storm. They're usually warmer and windier than most. Okay. I know. To start the game, I want everyone to sit facing the windows and look outside at the wind.

Carmen sat squeezed between White Owl and David on the couch. Reynard and I sat on the floor.

Juliette picked up Simon and said, "Before you get started with this game, I need to leave you. I plan on playing by helping Mrs. Sloan bathe her baby tonight and then my own sweet baby. You can tell me in the morning how it turned out. Good night, all."

When she'd left, David said, "I guess it's just us five."

He began to sing a song to the wind. He stood and swayed as if being pushed by the blustery weather.

"I've got it," David said. "Come. Let's get the horses and ride bare back. I have a surprise for you all."

He jumped to his feet and ran out the front door in the direction of the barn.

White Owl leaned toward Carmen and said, "I'm only going because you want to play. You're not going to change your mind are you?"

"No," Carmen said. "I told you, you don't have to do this, but I'm following David."

I grabbed my cape on the way out, and Reynard pulled on a sweater. Carmen followed close behind David. White Owl went out the door wearing a scowl on his face. When he got to the barn, he led the horses from their stalls. We each took a horse and walked it outside.

David pushed Carmen onto her horse, and then whapped the horse's butt. It galloped into the stormy night. He watched her for a moment and then jumped on his horse and followed. White Owl, Reynard, and I had to goad our horses in an attempt to catch up. Carmen and David's horses were galloping in a frenzy.

The winds howled overhead. The branches of the pine tree bent down, almost touching my head as I rode by. I was cool but comfortable in my red wool cape.

My horse was galloping so fast, I was fearful I might fall off. We had been in such a hurry no one had saddled the horses, and riding bareback was difficult. In an attempt to keep from sliding off, I squeezed my legs and held onto Honey's mane. Reynard came up behind my horse and slapped it on the rump to get it going faster.

Finally, I could see David and Carmen's horses grazing at the top of the hillside. David ran toward a grove of pines. He turned back to us, and said, "Now find a tall tree and climb as high as you can. We'll ride out the wind storm and learn how the birds feel nesting in the trees."

David gave Carmen a push up her tree, and she climbed hand-over-hand, as if she had done that every day. Reynard came up behind me and lifted me onto a branch. The men climbed trees near ours.

The pitch stained my hands and the bark chaffed my skin, but I kept climbing higher into the tree's arms. I found a nice niche to settle into, and made myself as comfortable as I could.

The sound of the wind had increased. I watched the sun fade to pink and disappear.

I could hear David yelling and whooping with joy whenever the wind increased. I heard Carmen's voice singing to the wind. White Owl chanted, "Ha ya, ha ya, ha ya haw."

Sometimes my tree felt like it would bend all the way to the ground. I wondered how on earth David had convinced us to do this crazy thing. And then I felt like a child — young and innocent. That was when I really grasped the game — this being in the moment — yes, this moment and no other.

After awhile, I became sleepy and climbed down. I found Reynard had anticipated my move and was at the bottom of the tree ready to catch me as I jumped the last few feet. I fell into his arms and we tumbled onto the ground, laughing.

Reynard took my hand and we dashed off into the deep woods away from the others. I followed my love. He grabbed me and we fell to the ground together, kissing. He wrapped my red wool cape over us, and slipped his hands under my blouse. His strong calloused hands were cold, but inflamed my heart.

I felt safe there in the dark night, merging into one with Reynard. I yelled my joy which blended with the wind. I became the wind.

Chapter Seventy-Seven
Carmen and David

I was amazed to learn, Heather, that White Owl had a change of heart. A few days later Carmen confided in me what caused his transformation.

The next morning after the Sloans left for Monterey, Carmen approached David and said, "Come with me to the river. I need to talk to you about something important."

David followed, keeping up with her brisk pace. "What is it you wanted to talk to me about?"

"Did you ever notice that White Owl is always off working at some project or other?"

"Yes. He does seem to be a pretty busy man."

Carmen went on. "Did you know that we don't sleep in the same bedroom?"

"Well, no, but I think it's none of my business," David said.

"Ever since the birth of Juliette, White Owl has stayed away from me. It's been eighteen years, now. He keeps himself busy, often until late at night."

"He must be crazy not to want to sleep with his beautiful wife."

"When I ask him why he doesn't make love to me, or even hug and kiss me anymore, he says it's because he loves me so much. He's afraid I'll die in childbirth, as all the women in the family have done with their second child."

"Yes," David said. "Reynard explained the curse to me. What a terrible thing that is."

"White Owl says he yearns for me," Carmen said, "but he can't even touch me for fear he won't keep his promise to himself. He says he feels it would be murder on his part if he were to get me pregnant."

"Of course," David said. "What man could sleep with you and not burn with desire."

"I'm nearing the end of my childbearing years, but I still want to have one more baby, especially after holding Mrs. Sloan's and Juliette's babies. I'm a healthy woman with desires. I get very lonely at times."

"Did you tell your husband these things," David asked.

"I told White Owl, but he only pushes me away, and won't even hug me when I'm hurting. I told White Owl that it might be good if I became pregnant because he would be forced to help Reynard free Joseph's Indians. I don't think he really wants to participate in Reynard's plan. I tell him he's afraid and has no courage, that I have lost respect for him."

"What does he say to that?"

"He only walks away and won't discuss it. David, I love your adventuresome ways. I think I'm falling in love with you. I could see having your child, maybe even our running away together, if you desire."

David leaned over and kissed Carmen with great tenderness. Then he kissed her again and put his arms around her, and dipped her to the ground.

"I, too, am falling in love with you, my enchantress. I feel as if I've always been a part of this family."

Carmen squeezed David's hand.

It's too soon to act," David said. "We need time to make a decision, but I'll think about it to see if it's the right thing."

"Yes. It's something we need to consider seriously."

"Tomorrow night," David said, "Henri and I are putting together a festival for your family and the rancho workers. I want to dance for you and your family. Henri has created a small band from some of the musical rancho workers who will play for us. I want you to dance with me."

"Yes, I would love to dance with you. I look forward to tomorrow."

David was such an exotic and enchanting man to Carmen—so passionate and full of life. A fire had started to burn in her heart that would not be easy to quench.

The next day, White Owl built a large bonfire in an open field in preparation for the festival. When everyone was gathered, Henri played his fiddle, going from slow and sweet, to a hurried frenzy of deep tones. He started a quiet melody which brought tears to Carmen's eyes when she heard the sweet notes. Henri then proceeded to a full fortissimo with great vibrato, then back down to a quiet lullaby.

When David appeared in front of the musicians, he wore his hair tied back with a red silk scarf. He was bare chested, bare footed and wore tight white pants. Carmen noticed his physique was slender and his chest was well formed and muscular.

David danced in circles, turning and twisting. He flung himself into the air in an ecstatic flight. His arms reached to the sky, and his eyes focused with such intensity. His face shone with joy, as if in prayer to his God. It was apparent that, to him, nothing existed but the dance and the music. When the dance ended, he bowed.

David approached Carmen, kissed her hand, and then removed the pins from her hair. Her dark hair flowed down her back, reaching her waist. Carmen glanced over and saw White Owl watching. His face turned scarlet and his hands made tight fists at his side.

David took a flower from a bouquet sitting on a table, and placed it in her hair. Looking at her, he said, "Ah-h-h. You're ready to dance, now."

Henri started up another tune on his fiddle, and David started clapping. Carmen rushed onto the plank floor and danced with her arms in the air. She swirled her skirts, twisting her body from one side to the other. She motioned for the rest of them to join her, and soon everyone danced to Henri's fiddle.

When the music stopped, David stood beside Carmen and took her hand. She noticed his skin glowing in the firelight and his eyes sparkling. He led her to a table filled with pitchers of sangria, and offered her a drink. After she gulped one down, he asked her to follow him away from the dancing crowd.

Chapter Seventy-Eight
Carmen's Desire

When David and Carmen reached the river, they sat down. David clutched her hand. "Perhaps this is the right time, Carmen. Let's see if the two of us can make music with our bodies. I'm willing if you are."

David kissed her neck. Carmen felt goose bumps on her arms and shivered. He put his lips on hers and the two of them fell onto the grass.

Carmen jumped up and began pulling off her clothes. She said, "I'm so hot after dancing, I want to swim. Can you beat me to the water?" Then she started to run.

David removed his pants and threw them into the air. He sprinted toward the river and dove into the water ahead of Carmen, making a large splash.

Carmen jumped in right after David and pushed him under. He grabbed her and kissed her, their hair tangling together.

David took Carmen's hand and they walked out of the river to the grassy bank. He looked at her body in the moonlight, and smiled. "Ah, you are so beautiful, my Carmen."

She, feeling shy, laid on her belly in the grass. David massaged her back and neck. Desire rose in Carmen. She sat up and grabbed David, pulling him on top of her. He pushed her away, and put his arm over his eyes.

"What's wrong, David. What is it?"

"I'm sorry Carmen. I just can't do it. I thought I could, but something in me won't allow it. It's a combination of things. I'm nervous and overawed at your allowing me this intimacy, but I also feel guilty betraying your husband and his friendship."

Carmen sat up, put her hand on his damp head. "It's okay. I understand. Don't feel bad. Perhaps this is the right thing. Let's go back before they notice we've been gone. We can talk about this later." She put on her clothes as fast as she could and walked back to the party.

Chapter Seventy-Nine
White Owl's Passion

White Owl came up to Carmen and asked, "Where have you been, Carmen. Your hair is wet. Were you swimming this time of night?"

"Hello, White Owl. Well, I got very hot from dancing and went to the river to cool down. I'm feeling much better, now."

"Come," he said, "dance with me."

White Owl held Carmen close and put his cheek next to hers. When David tried to cut in, White Owl said, "I want my wife to myself, tonight."

Carmen felt pulled by her attraction to David, but enjoyed the attention White Owl lavished on her.

After a couple dances, White Owl said, "This will be our last dance for the night. I have plans for us." Then he whispered, "I can see how I've been wrong all these years. I've yearned and pined for you, and tried to avoid you. I even slept in a different bed, but would dream of your sweet arms all night."

"Oh, White Owl, I've missed your love for too long."

"I've decided," White Owl said, as he stopped in the middle of a waltz, "if you really want a baby, you can have one. Tonight I talked to Reynard and have agreed to accompany him when he goes to Joseph's. Now, you and I have nothing to fear because the curse will be ended."

White Owl picked Carmen up and held her in his arms, looking into her eyes. He carried her away from the party, back to the house. When they got to Carmen's bedroom, candles were burning and rose petals were scattered on the bed.

"You can't change your mind. I'll see to that," White Owl said. "We're committed now, one hundred percent. You're having my baby, even if I have to keep you locked in this bedroom with me all week."

"White Owl," Carmen said. "This is ridiculous. You can sleep with me later tonight. For now, take me back to the party. We'll be missed by our family and guests."

White Owl laid Carmen on the bed, and took her dress off with great tenderness. He took her arm and pulled it back and tied it to the bedpost with a leather strap.

"What are you doing, White Owl," Carmen asked. "Why, what's got into you. Let me go this minute."

White Owl took Carmen's other arm and tied it back with another leather strap. He grabbed one of her kicking legs and tied it to a bedpost. "White Owl, you can't do this. You can't. Let me go. I don't know if I still. . ."

White Owl's lips fell onto Carmen's. He kissed her with more passion than on their wedding night. He kissed her with the love built up by many years of unfulfilled desires.

He undid his headband, and ran his shiny hair up and down Carmen's naked body. He started with her face and then moved down her breasts and belly, down to her legs and feet. He took a rose from a vase on the bedside table, and rubbed it over her lips.

He climbed upon her body and pushed himself full into her. She gasped at the passion which filled her, and let her unfilled desire of the past years be released.

White Owl kissed her forehead, her eyelids, her nose, her lips. "My darling, I have given you my seed, my progeny and my undying love," he said. He untied her and threw the straps on the table.

They laid together in a fetal position and fell asleep. When they awoke, Carmen picked up the leather straps. She pulled White Owl's muscular arm back, and kissed it with great tenderness. She then tied his right wrist to the bedpost. When White Owl tried to sit up, she pushed him back, and said, "It's my turn," as she grabbed his other arm and put the leather strap on his left wrist.

Chapter Eighty
Preparation

A couple weeks after the festival, Reynard took me for a walk after dinner. He said, "I can't understand it. For years White Owl has resisted doing anything against Joseph, despite the fact some of those captured Indians could be distant relatives of his. I could never understand why he didn't have the courage, but he always said it would do him no good trying to change a system. Being Indian and all, he didn't want to get in trouble with the law. Now, all of a sudden, he's pushing me to form a plan to free the Indians on Joseph's property. He says he has no choice now, whatever that means."

"Well," I joked, "If you ask me, the way Carmen and White Owl are always smooching lately, Carmen might end up pregnant. Now wouldn't that be something. Juliette's baby would be the niece or nephew to Carmen's baby."

We both had a good laugh at the thought of the two babies being born to the family in such a short span of time.

"On a more serious note," Reynard said, "I want you to prepare yourself. As you know, everyone at our rancho will be going to Joseph's rancho for the wedding in two days. I have decided we will all go to the family cave for a ceremony tomorrow. I thought it would help gather our courage before going to Joseph's rancho. I was hoping to solidify our rescue plans while we were at the cave."

"That's a great idea. I've overheard some of the workers talking and many of them are nervous about the rescue plans. Having a ceremony should help buoy their spirits."

He said, "I don't know if you were aware of the natural cave in the bottom of Black Mountain, which leads under the family house. We store our wine and apples there because of the coolness. I figured it would be a good and safe place to have our ceremony."

"Yes, Carmen took me down there a few times to bring back some wine supplies."

"There is a secret passage in the back of that cave which leads to an inner sanctum. In that place there is a beam of light that fills the cave in the middle of the day. The walls of the cave turn a reddish hue. That is the room where the family and the Indians sometimes hold their ceremonies."

"Oh. I thought Indian ceremonies were outlawed."

"Well, they are. A lot of people think Indian ceremonies are sacrilegious and only Christian practices should be used. If someone is caught rattling or drumming, they can be thrown into jail."

"I know Father Jean doesn't feel that way," I said. "He's pretty open-minded about the Indians."

"Yes, you are right about that."

"I don't suppose you'd mind if I bring my special deer hoof rattle to the ceremony? I received it when I worked at the museum where I was an intern. I always knew it was special, and now I know how I'll use it. I'll be right back." I ran into the house.

Reynard caught up to me as I was returning with the rattle in my hand. He grabbed it from me and held it up, turning it around and around. "I can tell this rattle has a lot of magic. I've only seen rattles like this from powerful medicine men."

"Oh, yes," I said.

Reynard held the rattle to his heart for a moment and he closed his eyes. "Much magic it has brought you, dear shape-shifter. . .shifting in and out of centuries, space and time. . .shifting from a feathered one to a lovely human form. Perhaps this is why you were meant to come into my century, to my people, to my land."

Reynard opened his eyes and had a far away look as if he had gone into a trancelike state.

"My dear, you may be right," I said. "There're people waiting for you to fulfill your plan. You'll be their guide, their leader. Your power comes from your courage and determination."

Reynard tied the rattle with some leather strips and hung it around my neck. "For safe keeping, my dear."

Chapter Eighty-One
The Cave

T he next day, we prepared to leave for the cave. Reynard loaded my arms with blankets. He carried out baskets of food, which we had prepared that week. Some men were putting wine and various musical instruments into a wagon. The presents for the wedding couple were tucked away under a blanket.

Six wagons were lined up for the various people attending that evening's festivities, some loaded down with gear.

Reynard and White Owl sat in the front wagon. I climbed into the wagon bed with the other women who were already tucked under their blankets. Juliette held her baby with Carmen at her side. We cuddled up to keep warm on that chilly afternoon.

The excitement ran high as we talked and laughed and told jokes in the back of the wagon. We started singing some songs, and found our voices blended well together.

Henri, who was in the wagon behind us, stood up, leaned his back onto the wagon seat, and played his violin. We sang the French songs he had taught us.

We didn't have far to go. The rancho ancestral home was on the top of Black Mountain, high above the river. We rode the wagons to the bottom of Black Mountain near the base of some craggy rocks. The men stopped the wagons and jumped down, unhooking the horses to graze. The women loaded their arms with party supplies, and I followed them into what looked like a bushy area. Carmen pushed some brush out of the way exposing the opening of a large cave in the hillside.

Reynard lit a torch and we started our procession into the cave. As Reynard walked beside me, he said, "We store our best wine in here until it has matured and is ready to sell. Part of the cave was drilled and dug out, but most of it is natural."

"It's so well hidden," I said. "I never would have seen it. I'll bet there's some interesting family history that you haven't told me about."

"There are stories about some of my ancestors who hid here to escape marauding Indian war parties from a neighboring tribe. One of the adjoining caves has a tunnel walkway, which leads back to the house. That's the one Carmen showed you, where we store the wine."

The exterior entrance was narrow and opened into several passageways. We turned right and then left and entered a large cave with a flat, dirt floor. The sides were lined with racks of wine. The men placed lanterns on hooks set into the rock walls.

The men carried in tables and the women proceeded to load them with food. Straw was put on the floor to one side. Blankets and pillows were stacked along another wall. Reynard led Jack over to the straw to lie down. Some men came in with sacks of sawdust and sprinkled it on the dirt floor.

Father Jean held up his arms and the crowd of people got quiet and bowed their heads. "Friends, and relatives, we welcome you all. What we're about to embark upon may be dangerous to your bodies, but liberating to your souls. God bless this enterprise and help bring us success in freeing those poor, wretched Indian men and women. God keep us safe from harm. God grant that we may be able to accomplish this feat without violence or blood shed. Help us keep in mind when there is love, anything is possible. Amen."

"Amen" reverberated throughout the cave as the crowd of people made the sign of the cross.

I looked around the room at the grim faces. Some looked frightened, others determined. Father Jean looked resolute.

Chapter Eighty-Two
The Family Celebration

Reynard stood beside Father Jean and announced, "As you all know, we are gathered here on this night to prepare ourselves for a dangerous undertaking. If anyone wishes to change their minds, there will be no questions asked. When the wagons leave tomorrow, it's your choice whether or not you wish to come along. Remember, I can't promise that you'll come out unharmed. Only God knows what the outcome will be. I want to thank you for all your support, and if you desire to come tomorrow, I thank you for your help. God be with us. Let us all say a silent prayer."

The crowd of people became hushed as if each person was considering their possible fate the next day. The enormity and seriousness of the undertaking seemed to settle on the room.

After a few moments, he looked up at everyone and exclaimed, "What unites us is our love and friendship. We, at Rancho de los Zorros Grises, respect each other's backgrounds and religions. In keeping with this, tonight, I will introduce French wine, Indian drumming and dancing, Gypsy music, Whirling Dervish dancing, and whatever else you want to throw into the mix. No matter what music is played, we dance to the sound of unity and love."

A cheer went up. When the crowd had quieted, Reynard continued. "I now want to introduce the first performers. White Owl and some of our Indian hands from the rancho will do a special dance to bring in fog to serve as our shroud. This dance requires the assistance of everyone here, so after you watch their steps, go ahead and join in."

White Owl walked up to the front of the room, and announced, "Tonight we have the honor of playing the Mother Drum, which has been in our family for several generations. She has a fine tone as you will see. Yes, please join us in this dance, and put your heart into it. Spirit will hear you then. If any of you want to join in the song, stand next to Carmen and she'll lead you."

Some of the Indians sat at the very large Mother Drum and started to beat. Carmen began the high plaintiff Indian call, over and over, reverberating through the walls of the cave.

White Owl began doing an Indian dance. I was amazed at how graceful he was, despite his size. Several Indian men and women joined him.

The Mother Drum vibrated in my chest like my own heart beat. As I heard the emotion in the singers' voices, my eyes filled with tears as I became moved by the song, despite not knowing what the words meant.

Many of the people went over to join in the drumming, picking up the drumsticks that lay in a barrel. Some people took rattles and others gourds. I brought out my deer hoof rattle and joined the drummers as they beat and sang. The rhythmic sounds of the rattle and drum echoed off the walls. The shadows in the cave reflected the dancers' silhouettes. Father Jean picked up a drumstick and beat the Mother Drum with the others. The various Indian workers smiled at him as they moved to make room. The deep bass throbbed in my chest and the room became the flutter of our hearts, the pulsation of our lives, the rhythm of our fates. When the music stopped, silence filled the room.

After a moment, the Indians started beating out a new rhythm on the Mother Drum. This one was faster and more exuberant. White Owl motioned to the crowd of people to join in the dancing. When Watu and Go Slow saw their friends dancing, they also joined in.

After about fifteen minutes, the drumming got faster, louder and more impassioned. I stood right behind Carmen and sang in unison with the singers. I could feel the electricity in the room. Sweat dripped from the drummer's faces and their arm muscles tensed and bulged as they hit the drum. Their faces turned into grimaces of concentration. They closed their eyes or turned them upward toward the flickering light on the ceiling.

Children danced near the drummers. Men and women swayed and gyrated with the rhythm, their bodies becoming the beat. The drumming resounded in my chest as I shook my deer hoof rattle. A sound emanated from the drum that was like a humming, a wavering of spirits soaring and weaving in and out. It seemed to be levitating above our heads, in and out of children, and mothers and fathers, old women and young men.

The rhythm appeared to surge through us like the Earth revolving around the sun, the flow of dawn to dusk, movement from autumn to winter and spring to summer — from youth to old age — the ebb and flow of tides. The sound was like the breathing of frothy ocean waves on the endless shores — all rhythms of life melding together.

Excitement swelled up in my chest, and I couldn't contain my energy. A high-pitched keening sounded from my lips. It turned into an exotic chant, welcoming spirits freed from their human form into the soft ether stopped only by those cave walls. Like soft clouds, we mingled our spirit bodies, making waves of light.

Chapter Eighty-Three
Gypsy Music and the Whirling Dervish

Henri picked up his violin, held the bow up and said, "One and two and three," and then led the musicians in a Gypsy melody. Reynard walked to my side and bowed. Smiling he said, "My dear, would you accompany me to the dance floor?"

I curtsied back, and said, "Yes, of course."

He put his arm around my back, took my hand, and we waltzed. Other couples walked to the center of the room and also began to dance.

After about an hour, David whispered in Reynard's ear. Reynard looked at him and nodded his head. David walked over to the band, hummed a melody, and clapped his hands in time.

David wore a tall, black turban, a white billowy tunic blouse fastened at the waist with a thick black belt. He had tucked the legs of his full black pants into his boots. He wore brown prayer beads around his neck.

David spoke to the group. "As you know, I am David. Some call me David, the Whirling Dervish. I have gone all over Europe and the Middle East in search of dances of the soul. One of my favorites is Dervish music. I lived in Egypt with the Dervishes for a time. Their dance is a ritual and an act of love and faith, as your mass is to you. The dance and music bring on a state of trance. If some of you wish to join me, you'll find it's mesmerizing. Be careful though. You may feel you are soaring from the ecstasy of this mystical flight."

In my excitement, I walked to the center of the room to follow David's instructions.

David continued. "I'll start with my arms crossed, standing ready to begin. Turning, or revolving is the fundamental condition of our existence, as it is for planets and stars. The ones who whirl, participate in the shared revolution of all existence. I stand very erect, testifying to God's unity. As I whirl, I become a channel for divine grace. I will bow to you when I start, honoring the spirit within each of you. As my arms unfold, my right hand opens to the skies in prayer, ready to receive God's beneficence. My left hand, upon which my gaze rests, is turned toward the Earth in the gesture of bestowal. Turning from right to left, I chant the name of God within my heart. May you find peace in this dance and music."

As the band began to play an exotic melody, David started revolving to the music and then in a deep resonating voice, he chanted. As the music picked up, some other people joined in and soon they fell over laughing from being so dizzy. I was one of the first to fall. The younger people kept it up for a good ten minutes before falling. The music got faster and faster and louder, and David kept on twirling. I felt as if David was bringing God and ecstasy into the room. We all watched his face transform into solid tranquility. The music stopped and David fell to his knees, his hands clasped as he looked upward.

After a short break, Henri, the Gypsy, appeared wearing a flowered sash about his waist and a crimson red shirt. He tied a scarf behind his head, which covered his hair. With his violin, he played a deep soulful lullaby. He walked around the room looking at everyone as he played. Juliette followed him, singing French words to the lullaby. After the tranquil song, Henri played a spirited tune.

I got up to do some modern rock and roll steps. No one had ever seen anyone dance like that before, and they copied me. Juliette and the younger people were the most enthusiastic about the dance.

I felt tired from my exuberance. Reynard came over and took my hand. "Let's walk outside for some fresh air. I have some things I need to talk to you about before tomorrow. There's something I need to know."

Chapter Eighty-Four

Commitment and Communion with Reynard

Reynard took my hand and led me outside toward the river. We walked down one of the plowed dirt rows, between yellowing leafy vines. Reynard stopped and put his hand on my shoulder and said, "My dear, I…"

I put my hand over his lips before he could finish, and said, "I know what you're going to say. I want you to know that I have no hesitation about tomorrow. I now understand I was brought here from another time for a reason. . .and the reason was to love and be loved by you, and by that love to assist you in freeing your family from this curse."

Reynard looked at me with a twinkle in his eye, and said, "Whatever happens, remember I love you. Follow me one last time before I depart, so that we can be alone together."

When we arrived at the river, we ambled onto a gravel bar surrounded by cottonwood trees. "Here," Reynard said, "lie beside me and close your eyes. One last time we will shape-shift together to be intimate in a way only you and I can."

I laid down and Reynard cradled my head in his lap. He rubbed my cheeks and brushed my lips with his fingers. He leaned over and kissed me. Then he, too, laid back and closed his eyes.

The sun was beginning to go down and the sky was changing to a dark blue. Without effort, my soul emerged from my prone body. I felt Reynard's energy close by. As I looked toward the sky, two yellow hawk eyes appeared. Reynard spread his wings and took off into the night air. I leaped up to follow him, feeling the ecstasy of flight. We soared on the dark currents, wings touching, feeling the lift of the air as we rose higher into the endless night winds.

The humid air billowed through our wings, whistling in our ears. The feathers on our faces were trussed by the ethers. We were in the place of the winged ones.

In and out we soared. We lowered our wings to feel the exhilaration of the speed and the increase of the wind's sound and pressure. We flew around the moon and through the stars. Higher and higher our love took us upon that night wind.

A faint glow of light came upon us, and I followed Reynard into the pre-dawn sky. As my body floated from that great height, I felt Reynard's claws settle on my back and his beak bite my neck with great gentleness. Oh, so soft and yet so tight we arched, pressing into one another on the wildness of the morning air.

As the stars faded, the rays of the sun filled our bodies, making our feathers transparent. Our two bodies became one in the changing sky.

We moved with increasing speed toward the ground, as an explosion of orange light overtook the vast valley, filled each meadow, and topped each tree. The blood throbbed in my temples, and the wind forced my eyes to tear.

Our bodies hit the lush meadow with a thud. We were tangled together, arms, legs, and hair, as we rolled down the incline. I looked at Reynard who was back to his man form.

Reynard and I laughed from the thrill of our adventure. He took my face in his hands and kissed me. His embrace was so intense it was hard to breath.

"Remember this night, my angel, my shape-shifter," Reynard said. "We have been so close, you and I. Few people fly to the moon and into the sun."

I reached over and plucked a feather out of Reynard's hair. "I shall keep this as a momento," I said. "I will forever remember this night and my darling man."

We both laid in the meadow grass until the sun shone higher in the sky.

Chapter Eighty-Five
Wedding Preparations

Reynard roused me by rubbing my cheeks. "Ah, so soft, my dear. Awake, it is time to go to our destiny."

I sat up and kissed him.

"Walk with me to the cave and help me pack up the wagon."

As we entered, I could see the lanterns were turned on. People were waking up and picking straw out of their hair.

I went over to Juliette and started brushing her hair. "Why," she asked, "do people dislike Uncle Joseph so much? I think he's very charming. He's always been nice to me."

"You know the stories about him enslaving his Indian laborers, don't you?

"Of course, I do. But I think they exaggerate. He can't be all that cruel, can he?"

"I guess we'll find out for ourselves. Hurry and get your things and I'll meet you at the wagon."

When I walked outside I could see a heavy vapor of fog had rolled in and blanketed everything in its web of gray. Our ceremony had worked. Fog would encompass the wedding and hide our intentions.

Our caravan of people left in high spirits. Everyone seemed to feel happy to be sharing in this adventure.

The earthbound clouds swirled along the banks of the river, and then rose like spirits floating upward toward the misty sky. The orange of the new sun's rays filtered here and there into the gray mist. The morning light and the gray shroud fought each other for domination.

As we neared Joseph's rancho, the caravan stopped. Reynard and three men got out of one of the wagons. I could see their guns bulge under their coats. The men unhooked the horses from their wagons and tied them to nearby bushes to graze.

Reynard took me to his side, and held me close for a long time. "Be careful my love. Stay away from Joseph and watch Juliette. She is young and naive, and doesn't understand the ways of wicked men. She has always been protected."

"I'll be careful, Reynard. Now tell me the plan again, so that I can keep it straight in my head."

"We attempt to act like a normal wedding party. You are there to enjoy the wedding and to act as if the family wishes to unite again. Tell Joseph I was unable to come because I am still recovering from my arduous adventures seeking gold."

"Yes. Yes. And then what happens?"

"Our men will attempt to sneak the Indians out during the night when Joseph and his men are asleep. We hope to get them drunk and overconfident. I will stay here under the cover of trees with David and a couple of workers. My men will come into Joseph's compound to free the Indians when it is dark. It appears that it will be foggy tonight, which will also help.

"Oh, so Father Jean, White Owl, and Henri and the rancho workers will be going with our family?"

"Yes. That's right."

"And then what will happen after we have freed the Indians?"

"We will split up then. I will take the Indians to the new rancho in Monterey. You and Carmen, and the rest of the family will go back to the rancho to watch over everything. I'll have a half dozen men or so stay with you. I was hesitant to leave you, until you told me that you and Carmen are with child. Riding in a wagon at high speed over bumpy roads would be dangerous in your condition."

"Don't worry about us. We'll stick close to the rancho and Carmen and I will oversee the workers. Just hurry back, darling."

Reynard kissed me and said, "You are my warrioress. I am proud of you and all you have accomplished. Just don't put yourself in danger, please."

"I'll try my best. You be careful, too, my love."

My stomach hurt as I watched Reynard mount Red and ride into the thick pines with his companions.

When we approached Joseph's house, I could see a bent-over oak tree, many of its branches broken off. The caravan proceeded up the dirt road toward the rancho. A lookout at the gate yelled, "Who are you and why have you come?"

White Owl yelled, "We're invited guests for the wedding party. We are from Rancho de los Zorros Grises."

With a great deal of effort, the heavy wooden gate was pushed open. As we entered, we approached a grove of oak trees that dripped with long gray lichen. The air was heavy with a feeling of gloom.

Black buzzards flew in circles around the large oak in front of Joseph's dark gray house. I could see men throwing bits of garbage and chicken bones into the yard. The buzzards fought over the scraps. I turned my head away, not wanting to see them fight.

Our caravan of wagons parked behind the main house. A wooden platform sat on the front lawn, and there were chairs placed nearby.

Joseph walked out of the house in a black tuxedo with long tails. He had on a black top hat that he removed as he bowed. "My honored guests, I'm so happy you could come to join in this celebration."

An older man walked out of the house, also wearing a tuxedo. He escorted a young woman who looked half Indian, half white. She looked very frightened and uncomfortable.

Father Jean strolled over to the couple, and asked, "Is this the couple I'm to marry here today?"

The man smiled. I noticed some of his teeth were missing and the rest were yellowed. His shirt parted a bit at the waist and his bulging hairy belly showed through. "Mah names Bernard Bones. This here's my bride to be. She's a sweet one, too. Young and healthy and perty."

Chapter Eighty-Six

Escape

Father Jean asked if the couple wanted to have confession heard first. The groom said, "Now, why in tarnation would I want that fer? Just marry us, and be quick 'bout it. I ain't got all day."

Carmen handed a bouquet of roses and lavender to the bride who bowed her head. The groom started to push the bride toward the wooden platform where the ceremony was to take place. Father Jean intervened and asked Bernard Bones if he could speak to the bride alone. The groom, with some reluctance, let her go. Father Jean led her to where Carmen, Juliette, and I stood on the porch of the house.

"Do you speak English, my dear," Father Jean asked.

"I speak French, English, and some Indian dialects. My father is French and my mother is a full-blooded Indian."

"What's your name, my dear?"

"My name is Naomi."

"Why would a beautiful young woman like you want to marry such an ill spoken, rough-looking man?"

"Oh, please. I'm not supposed to talk about it with anyone."

"I'm a priest. You can tell me anything in confidence and I won't tell a soul. I'm here to protect you."

"Be sure you tell no one, Priest, or they may beat me.

"I swear to you, I will keep the information you tell me secret. Go on, my child."

Carmen and I had our backs turned to Father Jean and Naomi, and pretended not to listen. We busied ourselves with organizing flowers in some vases.

"I came to the rancho to work in the kitchen," Naomi said. "It wasn't my idea to marry. I have a man in the village I am promised to. He's young and starting up a small farm. I was going to stay here, and work as a cook for a short time while he built a house and prepared his farm. My family thought I was too young to marry just yet, and figured a year of work would be good for me."

"Oh, so you are engaged already," Father Jean said.

"Yes. Can you help me? I don't wish to marry this vile old man. He disgusts me. I think Joseph has sold me to him, like I was his property. I overheard him say it was his right because I'm an Indian."

Father Jean turned crimson at this news. He spoke in whispers. "My dear, I won't use my powers as a priest to do a true ceremony. Anyway, if you feel married after this, you can get the marriage annulled."

Naomi made a little smile and said, "I'll speak some Indian words saying I refuse to marry this man. You don't have to worry. I won't feel married. If you hadn't come along, I was thinking of ways to kill myself before the honeymoon. I would rather die than lie with that man."

"You don't need to do anything so rash. We've come to free you and the Indians who Joseph has been keeping here against their will. Promise you won't tell anyone."

Naomi shook her head as tears ran down her cheeks.

Father Jean continued. "Don't drink anything we pour out of the big jugs. If you must drink, we'll have small bottles of wine that are safe for you. Watch closely for the right time to flee. We're taking anyone who wants to go with us to Monterey, so they can have a new start. Or, when it's safe, we'll assist you with getting back to your village, if that's what you want."

"Thank you, Father," Naomi said. "I'll never forget you."

Father Jean blessed her, and said, "Remember, be watchful."

Naomi put her white lace shawl over her face which hid whatever emotions were written there, and then walked to the platform. The groom rushed over and held Naomi's hand.

Father Jean gave the shortest wedding ceremony I'd ever heard, never really pronouncing them man and wife, but saying something like, "I pronounce you repentant bride and groom."

The groom yelped and threw his hat into the air.

I looked around at Joseph's friends and workers who were cheering. Some of them looked scraggly with long dirty beards and greasy hair. Others had attempted to wash up, cut their hair and wear clean clothes.

Leaning against a post, with his arms crossed on his chest, was a man who looked like Texas Jack. I looked again to make sure. He wore a striped suit coat and black pants. With his hair trimmed and slicked behind his ears, he looked tidier than when I saw him last. A broad-brimmed black cowboy hat framed his evil face. He looked at me and grinned. Terror surged in my heart. I hoped to God I wouldn't have to talk to him. It would be impossible to act polite.

Henri, the Gypsy, and some other men were lined up with their instruments. They started playing a lively tune. Henri's violin filled the air with bittersweet melodies.

The groom grabbed Naomi and started dancing with her. Soon the wooden platform was filled with stomping dancers. The platform became so crowded, some of the people moved to the dirt alongside, and the air became thick with the dust kicked up by their feet.

Texas Jack approached and asked me to dance. Then he said, "Why, aren't you Reynard's girl? You still owe me a date, my pretty one."

"Don't even think about it, you bastard. I can never forgive what you did to me. I'd make a scene here, but I don't want to ruin the wedding. Just stay away from me. I'm Reynard's wife, now."

I grabbed Father Jean and started to dance with him, and whispered in his ear, letting him know about Texas Jack. Father Jean turned and glared at him, and led me farther away.

As the night came on and the sun descended into the heavy mist, the purple dusky light was swallowed by the velvety dark night.

Henri allowed someone else to play his violin while he walked around the yard to cool off. He offered me a drink out of his ceramic vase. "Here, Angelica. This is okay for you to drink. It's the Rancho de los Zorros Grises wine which is watered down. We've got to keep our heads clear. Sip, my darling girl, only sip. Bring a glass to the bride in case there's a toast. She must stay clear-headed, too."

"Okay, I'll take some to Naomi, but what's in the wine that Joseph's men are drinking?"

"Ah, well," Henri said. "The Gypsies I lived with in France taught me many brews and concoctions, some of which I used tonight. Things should get very interesting, soon."

I walked over to Naomi who was sitting on a chair next to the groom. I poured Naomi some wine from the ceramic vase. Henri told the groom he was pouring him a special brew from his jug. When the groom finished off his first glass with gusto, Henri poured him some more.

Joseph raised his glass for a toast and then everyone drank to the bride and groom. I saw the groom sitting in his chair with his head slumped over. I could hear him snore.

I noticed some men from the Rancho de los Zorros Grises motion for the Indians to follow them. As they walked away from the platform, they disappeared into the thick miasma of smoky haze.

I walked into the house and looked through it to make sure we didn't miss any Indian servants hidden away. I found two older men locked in the attic. I unlocked the door, and led them down the stairs and out the back door. One of our rancho men was waiting, and led the men away.

I heard Joseph yelling, "The women. I want to dance with the women. Angelica, Carmen, Juliette."

We came running to the platform and started to kick up our heels and swirl our petticoats. Joseph grabbed Juliette by one elbow and Carmen by the other and went in dizzying circles. He started stumbling and steadied himself against a chair.

I noticed many of Joseph's men were lounging in chairs, or sleeping. Some had passed out on the floor.

All of a sudden, Joseph stopped in his tracks, and said, "You've poisoned my men. Look at my men. Why, I'll have to. . ."

Joseph then fell head first onto the planks and passed out.

Reynard opened the gate and brought his empty wagon inside, ready to load with people. Reynard's men moved fast, rounding up the last of Joseph's Indian slaves and servants, and led them to the wagons.

When Reynard saw me, he ran over and said, "You're safe, and all Joseph's Indians are with us. We're ready to travel. We did it, *ma chérie.*"

With the Indians in the wagons, two of the rancho men closed the gate. A cheer went up among Reynard's men. I threw my arms in the air and then turned in a circle. Happiness welled up in my chest and I put my hands over my mouth and laughed.

I watched as Reynard threw his head back and laughed, too. He put his hands on my cheeks, looking into my eyes. "We've done it," he said. When he let go of my face, he doubled up his fists and pumped them up and down in the air.

I ran over to Carmen and Juliette, and hugged them. Juliette couldn't contain herself from laughing.

"Okay," Reynard said. "We better leave right away before Joseph's men wake up."

He gave me a tight squeeze, a quick kiss and then climbed into his wagon and yelled down to me, "Remember, stay at the rancho. If there is any danger, hide in the caves. We'll return in less than a month. God be with you, my love." He threw me a kiss.

The wagons, loaded with Indians and crew, went one way, and the rest of us left in a couple wagons going toward Rancho de los Zorros Grises, accompanied by some of Reynard's men on horseback.

Chapter Eighty-Seven
Captured

After Reynard and his men left, Carmen and I stayed close to the rancho with Juliette and her baby. When I became aware I was pregnant, I had decided it was best not to expose myself to a month of travel to Monterey by wagon. The roads were very bad this time of year with all the runoff from the rains. I had kept my pregnancy from Reynard until the last minute, for fear he wouldn't carry out his plans.

Carmen had announced her pregnancy before she was even showing. She and White Owl were very excited to be having that baby after all those years. I wanted to stay behind to look after Carmen. Geraldine also decided to stay at the rancho because she said she had work to do with all us pregnant gals.

Early one morning, Juliette and I decided, since it was the first sunny day in over a week, we'd take a picnic lunch down by the river. We approached Carmen who was sitting on the porch in a rocking chair, knitting.

"Come on Carmen. We're going on a picnic. Won't you come along?" Juliette said.

Carmen looked up from her knitting and said, "Say, aren't you concerned about Joseph's men? Joseph might do something crazy. He's probably very upset about having his Indians stolen from him by his cousin."

"No, I'm sure we'll be fine," I said. "We're staying on rancho land. In fact, we're going to picnic right below the house, so we should be safe."

"I still want you to be careful," Carmen said. "I'm staying here. I'm too busy knitting a wardrobe for my wee one. You three go on. I'm fine here, really. I'll look after Juliette's baby."

As we walked by the garden, we saw Geraldine weeding the herbs. She pulled her gloves off, and put her trowel into her basket. "I've pulled every weed there is in the garden, and I could use an outing. You can count me in," she said.

She got a strange, far-away look in her eyes, and said, "Besides, I have some unfinished business with my relations."

I had no idea what she meant, but Geraldine often spoke in strange phrases that only she understood.

Juliette was in a happy mood, skipping with the lunch basket as we wandered down the path to the river. Geraldine and I followed Juliette. When we got there we put our baskets on the boards of the small river dock, which had a railing and seats built on one side. Juliette leaned over the rail.

"So, this is the nasty river that almost took your life," Juliette said. "What was it like, almost drowning?"

I explained, "Drowning is actually an easy way to die. You take in water and then everything goes blank, or if your throat closes off, you pass out from lack of oxygen. It's very, very quick. Although when I was drowning, I did have some unusual dreams, if you want to call them that."

"Auntie Angelica, tell me. What did you see? When I was young, I heard people talk about water nymphs. Did you see any?"

"I'm surprised you knew about them. Yes, I did see water nymphs, and I think they helped Reynard save my life. They pulled me from the tree snag I was caught under and kept me alive until I could get air. They even put a crystal in my..."

Juliette cried out as someone grabbed her arm and twirled her around. I looked up and saw Joseph. He had a lascivious look in his eyes as he tied her with a rope.

"My dear, don't be frightened. I've come to take you away from this rancho. I have a neighboring friend who wants to buy you from me for his household. He needs a servant, and his three growing teenage boys need a playmate to keep them company. They were very happy when I told them you are young and nubile and of mixed breed. You will do very well, indeed."

Juliette let out a scream and Joseph put his large hand over her mouth. Tears streamed down her face.

I ran at Joseph with the knife I'd brought to cut the cheese for our sandwiches. One of Joseph's thugs hit the knife out of my hand, and then put a rope around my arms. I screamed with all my might, hoping Carmen or someone at the house might hear us, but the river drowned me out.

Joseph threw a sack over Geraldine's head, and tied her arms. One of the men picked her up and threw her into the wagon.

With my arms tied behind me, Texas Jack came over and fondled my breasts. I yanked away from him as he said, "She's mine. This one's mine. I have a scrap to settle with her and Reynard from our goldfield days."

Juliette and I were gagged, and thrown into the back of a wagon. I kicked at the tall man who sat in the wagon next to me. He said, "Save your energy, my dear. We have things in store for you where you'll need it." He and the other men laughed.

When Geraldine was pushed onto the wagon she yanked the sack off her head, and said, "I'll remember who you are. You'll be sorry."

Juliette cried all the way to Joseph's rancho. I couldn't console her because I had a gag in my mouth. All I could do was try to formulate a plan in my mind.

Chapter Eighty-Eight
Geraldine Speaks

When we got to Joseph's rancho, we passed through the open gate. The horses pulled the wagon alongside the main house. We were lifted out of the wagon and carried down some steps to the basement. A cold draft assaulted my shoulders and I began to shiver. A heavy door was opened, and we were dropped onto a dirt floor.

Before the door was closed, Joseph said to us, "Now Reynard will know what it's like to have his property taken from him." Then he laughed.

Geraldine stood up and put her hands on the bars of the door. She spoke to Joseph in a loud voice. "Joseph, my baby brother. Josito. Little Josito, it's your sister, Gerry."

Joseph stopped in his tracks and stood still for a moment. He turned and looked at Geraldine. "You're crazy, just like they say about you in town. Why, you can't be my sister. She ran off and left me years ago. They say she went to be married."

"Little Josito. Remember your mama, Flying Blackbird."

Joseph's face turned red, and he yelled. "Shut up, old woman. You don't know anything. Flying Blackbird was my father's squaw servant. My mother died while I was young. She. . ." He turned and walked out.

Chapter Eighty-Nine
Joseph's Vision

Heather, I know you're wondering what happened to Joseph. When he left, Geraldine went into a trance. When she came back to her normal self, she told me what became of her brother.

Joseph ran up the stairs and through the house. He kept running until he was in the yard.

All of a sudden, Joseph heard the sound of thunder, and a flash of light. He threw his arms up to guard his eyes. When he put his arms down he saw his long-dead father.

Maximillian's hair was dark brown and he looked youthful. He walked over to Joseph, and said, "Watch and you shall learn."

Then his father turned, laughed, and chased Flying Blackbird, his father's squaw servant. He caught her in his arms and kissed her.

Joseph studied Flying Blackbird's beautiful features — long, black, shiny hair, high cheekbones, dark brown, vibrant eyes, tiny waist and voluptuous breasts.

Joseph saw a toddler run up to her waving his arms, yelling "Mama."

Flying Blackbird picked him up and said, "My little boy. Josito, how I love you." She held him to her firm breasts and opened her blouse to him. He grabbed one of her breasts and started to nurse.

Joseph noticed the little boy wore a gold necklace with a crucifix. Joseph realized it was his crucifix, the one he always wore. He reached his hand up to his throat and touched the necklace. He felt an electric shock go through his heart when he realized he was the little boy, and his true mother was Flying Blackbird, like Geraldine had told him.

There was a second flash of light. When Joseph looked up, he stood in the yard by himself, sweat covering his face and his breath coming in gulps. He put his hands over his eyes, and yelled, "No, no. It can't be."

Just then, one of the Indian girls from Joseph's rancho ran out of the house and went to the barn to take out a horse. The girl stumbled as she led the horse, pulling it down with her. Texas Jack, who was watching, walked over and slapped the girl in the face.

Joseph ran to Texas Jack and grabbed his arm, and yelled, "Stop it, I say. Stop it now. It was an accident. Can't you see?"

Texas Jack looked at Joseph and then backed away. "Sorry, old man. I thought that was one of your favorite horses that dirty Indian squaw was taking down with her."

"Just leave her the hell alone." Then Joseph turned and stomped off toward the river.

Chapter Ninety
Imprisoned

Juliette, Geraldine and I worked at untying each other's ropes for about half an hour before we could free ourselves. When Juliette and Geraldine rubbed their arms and ankles, I saw the red welts from their rope burns. I looked at my arms and ankles, and saw the same angry marks.

Juliette began to shiver, so I suggested we pile hay on ourselves to keep warm. While I worked on covering Juliette, I noticed some chains for tying prisoners anchored to the wall.

I looked at the stone walls surrounding us. A little light shone through the bars of a high window.

Juliette said, "I miss my baby. I've got to get back to my baby."

"Don't worry, my dear," I said. "Perhaps I'll be able to come up with a plan. I only need a little more time."

We heard the sound of heavy boots on a wooden floor and the basement door opened. One of the men grabbed Juliette, and pulled her to her feet. Trying to save her, I fought with him. He kicked me across the room.

Juliette screamed as he pulled and dragged her up the stairs. After what seemed like an eternity, it became very dark and I could hear footsteps again. The same man brought Juliette back and pushed her unconscious body through the door. The man said, "We'll leave her down here to think it over. Warn her she'll have to warm up more than that or she'll be in worse trouble."

Geraldine and I ran over to Juliette, who had been knocked unconscious. She had a black eye and a bleeding lip. Her blouse was torn and her hair was disheveled. I tore a piece of my petticoat off and dabbed at her lip which startled her awake. Sobs began to shake her body. I held her in my arms and rocked her over and over as she cried. "It's okay, my dear. Just cry to your heart's content. I'm here. Just cry."

After a few minutes, her sobs lessened. She tried to speak, but no words came at first. Then she said, "They wanted me to. . .," and she started to cry again.

"I know, I know. They are monsters. They don't even have the consciousness of a human being."

"They're inhuman leaches," Juliette said. "I hate them."

"I have come up with a plan," I said. "I want you to listen to me. It'll be very difficult, but I think we can do it. You'll have to trust me. I know you think the Indian shape-shifting is all hocus pocus. I've heard you make fun of it before, but that's the only way we can be freed. You'll have to believe in order to help me achieve what I'm going to do."

Juliette said, "Yes, anything Auntie Angelica, anything. I want to go home to my baby. I want to leave this terrible place and never see it again."

"Let's try to get some rest," I said. "When the sun comes up, I'll have my plan ready."

I sat up against the wall. Juliette laid her head in my lap. I stroked her hair and she fell asleep.

When the first weak rays of the sun peeked through the bars of the window, I woke up Geraldine and Juliette by saying, "I have good news. I've figured a way to escape."

Geraldine rubbed her eyes and smiled. Juliette touched her bruised head and gave me a faint smile.

"You and Geraldine," I said, "will have to help by singing with me for a few minutes, so I can get my courage up. Then you must sit quietly. Try not to be frightened by what you see. Do you understand?"

Juliette and Geraldine nodded their heads. Geraldine sat holding Juliette in her arms, and said, "Listen to her, honey. She knows how to save us."

I held my hands over my heart and spoke. "I've come to realize that we shape-shift throughout our lives, changing from babies to children to adults. Some of us become mothers and fathers. . .others take on careers and professions. Those who are gifted allow creativity to flow through them, and they become musicians, artists, and writers. The medicine man, Mountain Screamer, taught me to shape-shift into different animal forms."

I could see a glimmer of understanding in Juliette's eyes as Geraldine stroked her hair.

"I'm going to take another shape and get through those bars. I'll be back for you, and you must make yourselves ready to run faster than you've ever run in your life. We'll go for the river. Since there's no barrier there, we'll jump in and swim for the other side. Then we'll run home. If for any reason I'm not keeping up with you, you must promise me that you'll keep running, and go to Carmen for help. Do you promise?"

"But Auntie Angelica, I. . ."

"No, you must promise me or this plan won't work. Do you promise?"

Juliette sighed and shook her head.

Geraldine had a faraway look in her eyes, and said, "Woman of great courage. You will succeed."

Chapter Ninety-One
Shape-Shifting to Escape

We sat together cross-legged, with our arms around each other's shoulders and sang the Indian women's song of courage. The sound of each other's voices strengthened us.

I told Juliette, "Okay, I'm ready. You must be very quiet now and don't be alarmed, remember?"

I removed the leather necklace with the tiny buckskin purse from around my neck. I took out some of the sage and a match. I held the sage in one hand and lit the match with the other. As an ember caught, I blew on it and it enlarged. I placed my hands over the smoke and brushed it toward myself and then into the four directions.

"Smoke of the spirits," I said.

I leaned back on the stone wall and sat cross-legged. I closed my eyes and tried to get comfortable. I pushed all panic from my heart and mind. As I concentrated on my breathing and the pulsing of my heart and blood, I soon began to lose all fear.

I visualized a red light at the base of my spine rising upwards. The more focused I became the brighter the light burned. It rose upwards and changed colors —from red through the colors of the rainbow to violet. As it got toward my head it seemed like my essence was rising out of my third eye. I swirled through a tunnel and rose out of it.

My face felt itchy as tiny puffy feathers popped out of my skin. My nose burned and tightened and hardened into a beak. My toes turned sideways, glowed and turned into claws. My shoulders and arms stretched and became widened and I sprouted wings.

When I opened my eyes, I saw Juliette staring at me. Her mouth had dropped open and she had an incredulous look on her face. "Auntie," she exclaimed, clapping her hands together, "You've become a blackbird."

She walked over to me and put her hand out and I hopped onto her outstretched finger. She stood on her tiptoes and placed me on the window ledge. I moved through the bars and then flew off, circled and then landed back on the window ledge. I looked at Juliette and Geraldine who were now smiling.

"Go meet your new sisters of feather," Geraldine said.

I flew to an oak tree near the house and sat in its highest branch. I sang and chirped my heart's song to the joy of my love, the joy of being pregnant, the joy of being alive and free. As I sang, I called in the winged ones to sit with me and rejoice, to sit in the tree and sing to the world.

From far away I could hear a lone bird chirping in return. Then I heard more and more. I could see a large, black shadow looming in the sky. It swerved and turned toward me. The swarm appeared to be made up of blackbirds. Their chirping was almost deafening.

Next, I observed a long horizontal line of crows and ravens angling toward Joseph's house which they circled four times. Next, they swooped over my head. I could hear the sound and fury of their wings.

I saw Vasco, Reynard's pet bird, leading the crows and ravens. His feathers looked shinier than usual and he appeared larger than the other crows. The crows and ravens followed him. He landed near me in the oak tree. As we sat together, I felt a sense of community with the black-winged clan.

In my bird form, I flew off the branch and toward the house. The windows in the front room and upper bedrooms were open. I flew into the front room window. The blackbirds, ravens, and crows joined me in my flight.

The men inside the house started yelling, taken by surprise. Joseph and the other men slapped and hit at the birds. One of the men opened the front door and ran out, with a raven clinging to his hair, biting him on his head. The rest of the men dashed out the door.

I flew into the basement and sat down. I focused and took deep breaths and I returned to myself, my human form. Exhaustion overcame me after all my changes. I used my will to push myself up off the floor. I found the key hanging from a hook on the basement wall and opened the iron cell door.

Juliette and Geraldine were standing, ready to escape with me. I grabbed Juliette's hand, and we ran up the basement steps to the back bedroom. The three of us climbed through the opened window and jumped down to the ground. Off we raced, running as fast as we could go. My exhaustion from my transformations prevented me from running full speed.

"Go, Juliette and Geraldine. Run as the wind. Make it to the river and swim to the other side. Have Carmen take you to the underground cave. You'll be safe there. There's plenty of food and drink to keep you until Reynard returns in a few weeks. Whatever you do, don't turn around for me. I'll be safe, I assure you. Run."

Chapter Ninety-Two
Confrontation with Joseph

When we got out of the house, Juliette ran back to kiss me on my cheek and give me a quick hug. "I love you, Auntie. Take care and thank you." Juliette turned and dashed to the river.

I looked behind me and saw Joseph running toward us. I could tell he had caught sight of us and was starting to break into a sprint. I ran as fast as I could but knew he would overtake me.

I must run faster, for my life, for Reynard, for the baby.

I made it to the rocks by the river. As Joseph chased me, I held the rattlesnake necklace tied around my neck and visualized a rattlesnake in the rocks Joseph was running toward. When Joseph put his leg down next to a boulder, I could hear a snake's rattlers. I saw Joseph pull his leg back, curse, and fall down.

Good. This will give me more time to get to the river, and on to safety.

I saw Juliette reach the river and I yelled, "Swim as fast as you can. I'll be right behind you."

Joseph jumped up, cursing. He saw me looking back at him.

I watched as Juliette kicked off her shoes, jumped in the water and swam. Joseph saw Juliette and yelled, "I'll get you, yet. You're mine."

When Geraldine approached the river, she slugged one of Joseph's guards who got too close to her. The guard slumped down on the ground. Geraldine ran into the river right behind Juliette.

As I ran, I could hear the sound of the river. I also heard another sound besides the movement of water. I realized it was the sound of the river nymphs singing, which I had heard a year before when my canoe overturned. A flash came from my forehead, between my eyes. I had received a message that if I went into the river, the river nymphs would help me.

I was almost out of breath when I reached the water and dove in. When I came up, I thought I caught the sight of a flipper. As Joseph splashed in the river in his exuberance to catch me, something that looked like a woman's hand reached out of the water and grabbed his leg and pulled him under.

In my attempt to hide from Joseph, I dove again and swam under water. I held my breath for as long as I could, not knowing if Joseph would be there to grab me. While I was still under water, a hand yanked on my blouse. I wasn't sure if it was Joseph or. . .

Chapter Ninety-Three
Twentieth Century

I felt as if I was being pulled upward. I broke the surface and gasped for air. Sounds of cars and trucks greeted my ears. I looked up and I saw a bridge filled with traffic.

I realized I was back in the twentieth century. Maybe I could find my car, go home, and tell you, Heather, about my adventure. But you weren't home and so that's why I began to write this long letter to you.

As I walked out of the river and to the street where I'd left my car, I started getting doubts about whether what I had lived through was real or had I dreamed it? I found my spare set of keys in a metallic box under the car well, and started the engine. All the way home, Heather, I missed Reynard, Carmen, Juliette, and the family.

I began to think perhaps I was crazy to even believe that lovely dream. I parked the car behind our flat and rushed up the stairs, hoping you'd be back.

The first thing I noticed, when I opened the door to our flat, was the blinking light on the answering machine. I pushed the button, and heard my own voice that said, "Heather, it's me, Alexis. Don't worry about me, I'm fine. Just want you to know I've found a wonderful place and a fabulous man, and I don't think I'll ever be back to see you. But you don't need to worry about me because. . ."

That's where my cell phone had gone dead when I called you from Rancho de los Zorros Grises.

I now have no doubts, Heather. I know my "dream" is real. I must go back. I can feel the small bulge in my belly that has started to grow there. I now belong to the crazy land where Reynard and my new family live. I have fulfilled a prophecy, and now is my chance to start a new life with my husband.

With my hands on my round belly, I feel the baby kick for the first time. This is Reynard's baby. I must go back.

Heather, I'm sorry I can't tell you in person, but this letter will have to serve as my communication to you. I can't wait one minute more. I know Reynard will be looking for me and will be worried when I don't show up.

If you really want to find me, go to the Russian River and swim under the Memorial Bridge. The water nymphs will show you the way.

I love you forever.

Your sister,

Angelica

Rancho de Los Zorros Grises,
Reynard's house, 1848

About the Author

On a warm spring day, while canoeing on the Russian River, the author, Carolyn Radmanovich, almost drowned. The strange dreams that followed propelled her into a life of writing. She has delved into the mysteries of shamanism, vision quests, and practices TM and a variety of Osho meditations. Carolyn has a Bachelor's degree in History from San Jose State University, which she has followed with years of research about the Northern California Gold Rush of the 1840s. Carolyn and her husband live in Northern California.

CPSIA information can be obtained
at www.ICGtesting.com
Printed in the USA
FFOW03n2359080917
39747FF